KU-467-490

the further adventures of SHERLOCK HOLMES

THE GRIMSWELL CURSE

SAM SICILIANO

TITAN BOOKS

Caerphilly Libraries	
BBfS	21.03.2019
	£7.99
	LIB2693

THE FURTHER ADVENTURES OF SHERLOCK HOLMES:
THE GRIMSWELL CURSE
Print edition ISBN: 9781781166819
E-book edition ISBN: 9781781166826

Published by Titan Books
A division of Titan Publishing Group Ltd
144 Southwark Street, London SE1 0UP

First edition: November 2013
10 9 8 7 6 5 4 3 2 1

Names, places and incidents are either products of the author's imagination or used
fictitiously. Any resemblance to actual persons, living or dead (except for satirical
purposes), is entirely coincidental.

© 2013 Sam Siciliano

No part of this publication may be reproduced, stored in a retrieval system, or
transmitted, in any form or by any means without the prior written permission of
the publisher, nor be otherwise circulated in any form of binding or cover other
than that in which it is published and without a similar condition being imposed on
the subsequent purchaser.

A CIP catalogue record for this title is available from the British Library.

Printed in the USA.

What did you think of this book? We love to hear from our readers.
Please email us at: readerfeedback@titanemail.com,
or write to Reader Feedback at the above address.

To receive advance information, news, competitions, and exclusive offers online,
please sign up for the Titan newsletter on our website:
www.titanbooks.com

My life has been graced by an arc of remarkable women, all of them strong, beautiful, intelligent and creative: my mother Peggy, my wife Mary, and my daughters Mara and Gina. Traits from my wife and mother, especially, always seem to creep into my heroines. This book is dedicated to the four of them.

One

Sherlock Holmes drummed with the long fingers of his right hand upon the dark sill of the bow window overlooking Baker Street. He wore the ubiquitous male garment of the times, a black frock coat, its woolen lengths falling almost to his knees, his thin silhouette framed in gray, dreary light. His shoulders had a weary slump.

"When one is bored, time crawls by as slowly as a slug or snail."

I said nothing but reflected (even as my cousin probably did) that a year had passed since the tragic case involving Donald and Violet Wheelwright had commenced, the latter being a person I knew was much on his mind.

"The empty bank vault in Geneva furnished only a trivial diversion, and since then…"

"The weather does not help matters." I extended my legs so my boots were nearer the coal fire. "Autumn can be pleasant enough, but no sooner does the first rain of November come, than the stench of coal is everywhere. During the summer one completely forgets the wretched soot and noxious yellow fog. Of course, during the summer one is treated to the fine, dried and powdered manure from several thousand horses, but even that is preferable."

Holmes turned with a sharp laugh. "I see you are in equally fine spirits. I have been contemplating some travel, perhaps a voyage to a faraway and exotic locale—the Khyber Pass, a remote Japanese village, or an island in the South Seas."

I sighed. "I envy you."

"Why not accompany me?"

"You know how wretched I grow if I am apart from Michelle for more than a few days, and even if you were willing to put up with us both, she would never leave London now. Her practice thrives more than ever, and she has become both well known and fashionable. It would be impossible to bear were she not so genuinely excellent a doctor and so loving a wife."

Holmes went to the mantel, raised the humidor lid and withdrew a cigar. A faint smile pulled at his thin lips, but his gray eyes stared briefly into space. "I envy you your chains, Henry." He held ready a cigar cutter even as a rap sounded at the door. "Yes?"

Mrs. Hudson appeared in the opening, her face pink, her hair white, and her eyes blue. "A gentleman to see you, Mr. Holmes."

"Ah, excellent! Send him in at once. Let us pray, Henry, that at last an interesting case has come knocking at my door—that ennui will be briefly banished." He put the cigar back with its brethren untouched.

I stood up as the tall stranger entered. His dress marked him as a gentleman, an extravagant one of considerable means, but with peculiar taste. His frock coat was superbly tailored, the woolen fabric with a soft luster glistening faintly from the rain, but the dark green shade was quite unusual. His silk top hat was of the same color, and his tie was a green and navy stripe with a glistening pearl midway between the knot and his black silk waistcoat. His wool trousers were of a very fine black and green stripe, his shoes and gloves a peculiar yellow-orange leather. Upon his silken lapel was a green carnation.

"Mr. Holmes? Frederick Digby, younger son of James Digby, the Marquess of Hampsford. Quite a pleasure meeting so esteemed a person as yourself."

Digby's face was pale, thin, with washed-out blue eyes and an insubstantial, reddish-brown mustache, the ends so neatly trimmed it was exactly even with the upper edge of his lip. He removed his top hat and a glove. His hands had obviously never seen a day's work, and but for the reddish hair above the knuckles, the long delicate fingers and white skin would have made a maiden envious.

Holmes shook his hand, then turned to me. "Lord Frederick, this is my cousin, Doctor—"

"Ah!" exclaimed Digby, his languid eyes opening wide. "So this is the famous Doctor Watson—your Boswell, Mr. Holmes!" His hand was faintly clammy, but he shook mine eagerly. "I have read every word of yours, Doctor Watson."

I could see from the wicked gleam in Sherlock's eyes that he would be of no help; he found it terribly amusing when I was mistaken for Watson.

"I hate to disappoint you, Lord Frederick, but I am Doctor Henry Vernier, Mr. Holmes's cousin."

Digby resembled a glass of champagne gone flat. "Not Doctor Watson?"

"Alas, no."

"Henry and I are on the best of terms, Lord Frederick, and I value him every bit as much as Doctor Watson. Perhaps a trifle more," he added dryly. "Sit down before the fire and warm yourself."

"Don't mind if I do. Beastly weather out there." He sat in the wicker chair, which was the place of honor. "You'll pardon me, gentlemen, if I'm a bit flustered. I hardly know where to begin."

Holmes leaned forward in his chair, elbows on his knees, a playful smile on his lips. "Your discomposure is understandable. Perhaps it has something to do with the rather tall young lady who embraced you so passionately."

Digby's hat tumbled out of his lap. "Oh, I say—that's very good, Mr. Holmes! Very good indeed, just the thing. Old Watson wasn't making it up after all. Tell me how you guessed. I'm all ears."

Holmes frowned. "*Guessed?*"

"I am sorry—deduced—I meant deduced."

"Your green carnation is in a sad condition, no doubt as a result of having been nearly crushed by the force of the lady's embrace. Her… chest must be at the same level as yours, for she would not knowingly press her face into the blossom."

Digby glanced down at the carnation and fingered a petal. "Yes, it is in a rather sorry state, isn't it? But how do you know it was a young lady and not my dear old mother, for instance?"

"Mothers, although ardent, are cautious. They would not willingly spoil a delicate flower."

Digby nodded. "Yes, Mr. Holmes, that is very good indeed." He hesitated, then his nostrils flared slightly, his eyes widening, as he toyed with the end of his mustache. "How do you know, though, that it wasn't a tall young man?" A smile twitched his lips.

Holmes's gray eyes glanced briefly at mine, even as his dark brows rose. My own jaw dropped slightly. "What is that supposed to mean?" I asked truculently.

Digby laughed in earnest. "Oh, I am sorry—you must forgive me, old thing. I will have my little joke. Wanted to see if I could ruffle Sherlock Holmes's feathers—couldn't resist it. A beastly habit, I know—ought to be ashamed and all that. You were absolutely right, Mr. Holmes. A young lady did embrace me passionately. I feared briefly she might crush me. And she's the problem—the reason I came to see you."

Holmes continued smiling, but I could see dismay in his eyes. He had hoped for a spectacular case, something bizarre and sensational, but so far he had only this young dandy and his affair with some young lady who was probably equally offensive.

"You see, Mr. Holmes, I have been engaged to Miss Rose Grimswell, a charming girl and an old chum. Rose and I have known each other for years. I knew her when she was still in short frocks. Anyway, dear old Rose and I decided to hitch our wagons or however they put it about six weeks ago. Some consider her a bit on the odd side, what with her unusual looks and all that poetry and music, but I want a wife with some gray matter under the skull. Anyway, the wedding was on for next June, and everything was rosy—no pun intended—until recently, and now she's gone and called the whole thing off!"

Holmes's disappointment must have been obvious even to Digby, but he tried to mask it. "Surely… the lady must have given you some reason."

Digby was silent, his lips pursing. "She… She let something slip, blurted it out. Said her father won't allow it."

Holmes gave a weary laugh. "Lord Frederick, I am not a matchmaker or broker between families. Surely you must know that fathers often disapprove of their daughters' matrimonial choices."

"Ah, but that's the peculiar part. He's been dead for over four months."

"What?" I exclaimed.

A wary hope suddenly dawned in Holmes's gray eyes. "Has he indeed? And when did the young lady blurt this out?"

"Today, Mr. Holmes, after she told me it was all over. Wouldn't say why really, and I kept pressing her for an explanation."

Holmes put the tips of his long fingers together—another hopeful gesture. "Think carefully, Lord Frederick, and tell me exactly what she said—how her father's name came up."

"Well, she kept saying, 'I can't, I can't,' and I kept saying, 'But why?' At last she said, 'Because of my father.' 'Your father?' I said. 'Whatever do you mean?' 'I mean he forbids it,' she said. 'But he's dead!' I said. 'Whatever are you talking about?' She looked frustrated and frightened. 'I can't say anything more.' And she wouldn't."

Holmes nodded. "Promising. Are you familiar with the circumstances of her father's death?"

"Of course. You may be, too, Mr. Holmes. Her father was a writer, Victor, Viscount Grimswell of Dartmoor. The poor devil fell off one of those rocky piles on the moor, tors they call them. It was in all the papers."

For the first time in several weeks I saw color return to my cousin's cheeks, and his eyes had a familiar glow. "Yes, I do recall the incident. I have read one of Grimswell's novels, *The Dark Grange.*"

I frowned. "I also recall *The Dark Grange.* I started it, but I do not much care for ghost stories."

"It is more than a ghost story," Holmes said. "Grimswell was not a Hardy, a Poe or a Dickens, but his works are not without literary merit. They are comparable to the writings of Wilkie Collins or Sheridan Le Fanu. His death caused a stir because of its sinister and sensational nature. There was… Was there not some speculation that his fall might have been suicide rather than an accident?"

Digby gave a reluctant nod. "Yes, although the family doctor apparently thinks it was an accident. Lord Grimswell had a bad heart, angina pains and all that. The doctor says he must have made it to the top, and then his heart gave way."

"And does Miss Grimswell concur with this opinion?"

Digby frowned, his left hand clutching at his garish glove. "She does not exactly… She has not said. I think she fears it may have been deliberate."

"Has she told you this?"

"No. It's just a feeling I have."

Holmes leaned back in his chair. "Your case begins to interest me, Lord Frederick. Tell me more about yourself and Miss Grimswell. You are, of course, an Oxford man. Balliol College, I believe."

Digby nodded and raised his right hand. "I'm on to you this time! The old school ring is a bit conspicuous."

"One might say the same of your dress. Are you acquainted with Mr. Oscar Wilde? His influence upon his fellow Oxford students is well known."

Digby nodded. "I have had the pleasure of his acquaintance. Oscar and a Cambridge chum of mine are friends—Robbie Ross. Oscar takes a genuine interest in the artistic and aesthetic development of the young."

Holmes's smile was faintly contemptuous. "So I have heard."

Digby raised a single reddish-brown eyebrow, hesitated, then continued. "I finished two years ago. Since then I have been seeking some profitable and fulfilling occupation. The pater urges the military, the cavalry in particular, the mater the church, but neither would suit my artistic temperament. Being a younger son is rather frustrating. My brother Tom only has eighteen months on me, but he gets the title, the land, and most of the income, while I... And the moneylenders are only too happy to give him whatever line of credit he requires. You may think a marquess must be rolling in money, but I'm afraid that's not the case, what with taxes and poor investments. Father says I can count on precious little. He actually seems to enjoy saying this—as if... But I'm wanderin' somewhat astray."

Holmes gave a slight nod. "And Miss Grimswell?"

Digby nodded eagerly. "Yes, yes—well, Rose and I have known each other practically forever. Father is an outdoorsy sort, fond of hunting, horses, angling, hiking, and all that, and the family spent a good deal of time at our Dartmoor home. He and Victor Grimswell were friends, and I remember Rose as a rather sad, dark, sullen little girl. I'm afraid I used to pull her hair. Anyway, I ran into her last July at Hyde Park. She was staying with Susan Rupert, Lord Rupert's daughter. The two had gone to the same girls' boarding school near Oxford."

Holmes tapped his fingertips together. "So this was after her father's death—after the fall from Demon Tor?"

"Yes, Mr. Holmes, and she was—and is—rather glum about it. Misses him frightfully, her father, that is. She's staying indefinitely with Susan; nothing for her at Grimswell Hall."

"What of her mother?"

"Rose never really knew her mother. She died when Rose was little."

"Does Miss Grimswell have any brothers or sisters?"

"No, Mr. Holmes. She is an only child."

"Any male cousins?"

Digby gave a laughing snort. "Ah, I see where you're headed! No, she has only a couple of maiden cousins or aunts. I'm afraid there's no male heir to pass the title on to. Victor Grimswell was the last Viscount Grimswell."

"Ah, how regrettable for the young lady. The title will therefore go extinct, and the land and the hall will revert back to the crown. I doubt Lord Grimswell would have had much money of his own."

Digby had a certain lunatic grin. "Wrong on both counts, Mr. Holmes! There was the usual entail requiring that the property go to the eldest son or another qualified male heir, but when Rose was about two, her father and grandfather agreed to cut off the entail. Her mother had died. Victor was desolate and never wanted to marry again. There were no other potential male heirs, and although the title might go extinct, he wanted to ensure that his daughter, his only child, could inherit Grimswell Hall. He managed to persuade his father, the viscount. Their solicitor drew up all the necessary papers."

Holmes nodded. "That is certainly unusual, but possible. Entailment law is quite complex, but the two living heirs in direct lineage would have that power. With the entail broken, both men could do as they chose. The grandfather could still leave everything to Victor, the next viscount, but Victor, in turn, might leave everything to his daughter. And what of the other count to which you referred?"

"Oh, yes, well, both Victor and his father were deuced clever when it came to money. For example, Victor lent a friend a sum to start an export business, and he was repaid a hundredfold. My father would call that dirtyin' one's hands in trade, but I wish he were half so sharp! Oh, and Lord Grimswell's writings were also quite profitable."

Holmes lowered his hands and set them on his knees. "I see. Lord Grimswell must have left his daughter a considerable fortune."

Digby nodded cheerfully. "Over four hundred thousand pounds."

"Good Lord!" I exclaimed. "That's an extraordinary sum."

"It is indeed," Digby said. "To have both land and money…"

Holmes hesitated, an ironic smile pulling at his lips. "Most of which must go to her husband should she marry."

Digby frowned, a red flush appearing at each cheek. "I hope… I trust you gentlemen do not think Rose's fortune has anything to do with my feelings for her. I'd marry her even if she hadn't a farthing."

Holmes gave his head a shake. "It is not for me to question your motives, Lord Frederick. I am sure they are worthy of a gentleman of your stature. Nevertheless, such an enormous sum may have some bearing on the case."

"I don't see how."

"Exactly how long had you been engaged, Lord Frederick?"

"Since the middle of September."

"And was the lady difficult to persuade?"

"Damned difficult! She kept saying she wasn't sure she wanted to marry or that she was ready even if she wanted to, but I kept at it. Told her..." For the first time he hesitated. "Well, I told her I loved her, and by God it was the truth! I said I loved her and that she needed someone to look out for her now that she's alone in the world. I know I'm not perfect, and I can be a silly ass at times, but all the same, I swear I'd care for her."

Holmes and I exchanged a glance. Digby had begun to grate upon me, but this declaration of love did seem genuine.

"And you seem to have convinced Miss Grimswell of your sincerity. That was some six weeks ago. When did she first mention any doubts?"

Digby sighed. "When her fool of an aunt Constance sent her this abominable balderdash about the family curse. Said if she were going to marry, she and her future husband should know about this dark episode in the family past. If she'd had any sense at all, she'd never have shown anything like that to a sensitive girl like Rose. Of course, it's all complete and utter rubbish, but Rose is high-strung and—"

"How long ago did her aunt send this information?"

"Two weeks ago, and I can tell you it shook Rose. I told her it was all foolishness and meant absolutely nothing to me. By the time she left she was laughing at it too, and I thought we were past it, but then this morning I received a letter saying we must never see each other again, that she must never marry, and of course, I went to her at once. I confronted her shortly before I came to you, Mr. Holmes, and she behaved very strangely. Something had badly frightened her, and I'm most worried about her. I..."

Holmes tapped lightly at the chair arm with his long fingers. "Pardon me, Lord Frederick, but I wish to proceed more methodically. Do you know exactly what her aunt wrote to her?"

Digby nodded, then withdrew a rolled-up parchment from his coat. "I have brought the very document she sent Rose."

Holmes smiled. "Excellent, Lord Frederick—excellent! And how does it come to be in your possession?"

"I took it from Rose when she showed it to me two weeks ago—with her permission, of course. I wanted to burn it, but she would not hear of it. I promised I would care for it, but I did not want to leave it with her. I knew she would re-read it and brood upon it in an unhealthy way. That is why I took it."

Holmes stood and eagerly extended a hand. "May I have a look? Thank you." He sniffed twice at the paper, then unrolled it upon a small table. "Late seventeenth century. Care to have a look, Henry?"

I stood, then put one hand on the table and leaned forward to read. The black-inked script had an archaic look, but I soon grew accustomed to it.

THE GRIMSWELL CURSE

My children, you have no doubt heard rumors of the Grimswell Curse. Some of our kin have wished to deny this affliction and its origin, a black episode in our family history, but I have no doubt as to its truth. I have, therefore, resolved to set the story down, once and for all, that it may instruct our descendants as to the power of Evil once it gains entrance to a man's soul.

Before the reign of Elizabeth, over two hundred years ago, the Viscount Reginald Grimswell built the first Grimswell Hall. He was a very learned man, interested in all the arts and sciences, but despite his cleverness and wealth, he had a melancholy disposition. He was always prey to dark and desperate thoughts. Perhaps that is why he abandoned himself to drink and lechery. His wife, Lady Catherine, was wondrously beautiful and possessed a kind and pious disposition, but Lord Reginald preferred the company of harlots and drunken gamesters. The hall became notorious for its wanton debauchery, much to the dismay of its mistress.

His lady bore Reginald four sons, then died of a wasting illness before her fortieth year. Rather than reflecting upon her demise as a warning from the Almighty, Lord Reginald plunged himself into vice with unrestrained fury. In disgust, his father-in-law claimed his grandsons to raise them apart from such iniquity.

Before long, no maiden or matron of virtue would venture near Grimswell Hall. The daughters of local farmers began to disappear. Rumor had it they were victims of foul abominations at the hall. Those who would not submit, perished, vanishing without a trace, while others gave themselves over to the wicked corruption. One yeoman discovered his daughter all bejeweled and bedecked in finery at the hall, but she laughed and pretended not to know him. A week later, the man was found dead on the moor, his throat cut.

Common folks and the gentry shared a disgust toward the hall and its lawless occupants, but naught might have happened had not the Viscount finally outreached himself. He was visited by an emissary of the crown, the Earl of Chadwick, who, knowing nothing of Grimswell's reputation, brought with him his daughter Rose. At the sight of the fair girl, Lord Reginald's evil soul was inflamed anew with lust. He determined to take the girl by force that very night, and he did so, despite her desperate pleas. Foolishly he thought she would keep silent of her disgrace or that none would dare touch him should she accuse him.

The pathetic girl wrote a brief note to her father revealing her betrayal, then thrust a dagger into her heart. Imagine

Chadwick's grief and rage the next morning when he discovered his daughter's corpse and this dreadful testament! It took several men to restrain him from strangling the Viscount, who then mocked him and had him ejected from the hall.

This fell upon a Sunday morning in October, and the Earl went straight away to the church at the Hamlet of Grimpen. Interrupting the service, he strode to the pulpit, told of his daughter's sad fate, and begged the congregation to help him bring down the wrath of God upon the miscreant. The people of Grimpen listened in horror, and when he raised his fist to Heaven, a low murmur of approbation echoed through the church. The other lords there present asked only for time to gather their forces and arm themselves. Thus, by late afternoon, every able-bodied man advanced toward Grimswell Hall, some carrying scythes or pitchforks, others bearing swords or lances.

Word of what had passed at the church had reached the hall earlier, and all the Viscount's servants and cohorts had fled, leaving him to face the angry crowd alone. Even then, Lord Reginald might have been saved, had he but prayed for forgiveness. Instead, he turned to the dark powers and begged the Devil for assistance. He found the answer he sought in an ancient tome in his library.

The sun had sunk, and a ghastly orange moon rose over the desolate moor and the dark tower of Grimswell Hall as the avengers reached the portal. Before them was a figure in a black cloak and hood seated upon an enormous black charger. Although they were many, a hush fell over the crowd, and they halted.

The Viscount threw back his cowl, and a peal of Hellish laughter slipped from his lips. He cursed the men and mocked them, but none seemed able to move until Lord Reginald began to ridicule poor dead Rose. At that, Chadwick drew his sword and charged forward with a great cry.

The Viscount headed across the moor on his black stallion, and those who had mounts gave chase. His unnatural steed could have outraced any mortal horse, but Lord Reginald kept only slightly ahead of his pursuers. He halted before the jagged pile of rocks known as Demon Tor, and even as the riders watched, he scrambled up its face like some huge black spider. Hardly had he attained the summit, than the riders drew up about the base. Soon those on foot also reached the tor and surrounded it.

The Earl cried out for the Viscount to descend and face his punishment. For all his crimes, he must surely die, but as Christians, they would let him confess and be shriven first.

After the Earl had spoken, the crowd stood silently, watching the white face of the man standing atop the tor. The moan of the wind, suddenly icy cold, was the only sound, then came again Hellish laughter. The Viscount cursed them with blasphemous and foul oaths, promising that terror would henceforth be their companion each night. He bared his teeth in a final, hideous grin, then hurled himself forward. Some say he briefly flew like some dark bird or bat, but soon enough he fell and dashed his brains out on the rocks below.

The Earl advanced and turned over his fallen foe. The full moon had risen higher by then, and its blue-white light revealed the shattered skull and leering face of the Viscount, his teeth locked in a fierce grin. All present felt the horror, and then in the distance rose the desolate cry of a wolf. They fled, leaving the shattered corpse lying there bathed in the moonlight.

Would that were the end of my tale, a sinner punished for his evil deeds!

The next day, some men returned to Demon Tor. They found the blood-stains on the granite, but the body was gone. That night, a herdsman returning late noticed a single light burning in a window at the abandoned hall. Many also again heard the terrible cry of a wolf.

The Earl of Chadwick heard it and went pale. He retired late, but no sooner had he closed his door, than a terrible scream came from his chamber. The oaken door held briefly, but when it was burst asunder, the men had a brief glance of a black figure with a dead white face, its mouth smeared with blood. The creature fled to the window and escaped, even though the window was high above the rocky ground. The men saw the Earl's murderer crawl head first down the stone wall, then run across the moor. None dared follow.

Thus began the reign of terror. No man or woman dared go out after dark. Windows and doors were barred at dusk, but still the people were slaughtered—men, women and children—throats torn open and the blood drunk from their veins.

Many saw the light burning in the high tower of Grimswell Hall, and others spoke of a man in black wandering alone on the moor or accompanied only by an enormous wolf. Others claimed to have seen the man transform into a wolf.

A poor herdsman was caught in a snowstorm, and when he came home, half frozen, he found his wife dead and their babe gone. At this, a great fury came over him. The next day, he rose up at the church and begged the people to help him, lest they all perish one by one.

Accompanied by the priest, they went again to the hall. In

the courtyard they found the herdsman's child, a mere babe, frozen and drained of blood. Outrage seized the good people. They searched the dwelling, but a great oaken door reinforced with iron blocked the way to the tower. They tried long and hard to break in the door, but to no avail. Soon the sun began to sink, and their fury changed to dread.

The stricken herdsman gnashed his teeth and beat at the door until his fists bled. At last he seized a torch and set the door on fire. Soon the entire hall was ablaze.

The people surrounded the edifice and waited. They had armed themselves as best they could. As the sky darkened, the orange flames rose higher and higher, the great conflagration lighting the moor for miles around.

Finally, even as the flames reached the tower, a face appeared at the window. A cry of dismay went up. There could be no doubt: it was the Viscount Reginald Grimswell. He bared his long teeth, and then his fearful laughter rose over the crackling of the flames. He seemed about to hurl himself from the window, when the herdsman loosed an arrow from his bow. The priest had blessed the arrow.

It struck the Viscount square in the throat. With a terrible howl, he clutched at the shaft and fell back into the waiting flames. His cries were dreadful. They were the cries of the damned, this conflagration only a prelude to eternal perdition.

The people watched until the flames had consumed the hall. The priest and the herdsman walked about the smoldering ruins until the first warm yellow glimmer of sunlight flooded the moors. The herdsman fell to his knees and wept while the priest prayed to the Almighty, thanking Him for their deliverance.

The moors have been at peace since that terrible time,

and we can only hope, my children, that we of the tainted Grimswell blood have learned our lesson. We can only hope that none of our descendants will lose their reason, bargain with Satan, and become wild beasts preying upon their fellow men. Curb, therefore, those melancholy thoughts and dark passion which may be in our nature. Remember that God in His mercy has given us the strength to rise above our baser selves.

The broken walls and granite stones are all that remain of the old hall, and the lonely site is known as an accursed place. Because the sons were raised apart from their father's evil influence, they grew to be honorable and worthy men. The eldest built a new Grimswell Hall which we still inhabit today.

Our inheritance is a dark and bloody one, but if it causes us to know ourselves better, to shun Satan and avoid his snares, then some good may yet come of what has befallen, and in times to come, Grimswells may be known for their good works rather than their evil natures.

Holmes finished reading before I did, but he waited until I had turned away before rolling up the parchment. "A singular tale," he said. He handed it to Lord Frederick. "This document is at least authentic. Miss Grimswell's ancestor shows a literary flare, which must be a family trait. So you made light of this tale? Marrying into a family descended from werewolves or vampires does not intimidate you?"

Lord Frederick's laugh was high-pitched. "Not in the least! We Digbys also have some scoundrels in our past, but no one has ever written down their exploits."

Holmes's fingers stroked his narrow chin. "I wonder which was meant. The narrative is ambiguous. One could argue either for vampirism or lycanthropy."

I frowned. "I can see how it might disturb a young woman of a sensitive nature. It is a chilling story. And even if the supernatural element is preposterous, there may be something in the notion of an inherited disposition toward melancholy." I opened my mouth, then quickly closed it.

Lord Frederick stared hard at me. "What were you about to say, Doctor Vernier? You need not spare my feelings—say it, man!"

"Insanity does seem to run in families. However, one need not presume so far. I am sure it is merely... An impressionable young lady with no brothers or sisters, no mother—she must have had many a sad and lonely hour. One could hardly blame her for being melancholy, and then to read such a thing... Then, too, she is the last of her lineage—its fate, its continuance, rests with her alone."

Digby nodded eagerly. "Very perceptive, Doctor Vernier—and to think you have never met Rose. It did shake her. She is somewhat prey to those black thoughts mentioned in the story. Sometimes in the midst of a splendid evening—a fine meal and champagne—I can see the dark clouds gather about her brow. I try to tease her out of it."

Holmes's upper lip rose briefly as he stared into the fire. "There are those who consider melancholy less an affliction than a rational response to the world in which we live." A certain bleakness showed about his mouth, and I knew he was thinking again of Violet Wheelwright's tormented mind. He turned to Digby. "While I would not go that far, I would say that the young lady may have had more than her share of sadness in her brief life. Some unhappy children never outgrow a sense of desolation."

Digby shrugged, then smiled. "Surely marriage—a husband and children, a family of her own—would alleviate that sense of desolation. I'm certain I could make her happy! Life is great fun, after all, and that's the way it's meant to be, isn't it?"

Holmes and I exchanged a significant glance. I could tell that he too did not see this self-absorbed young man in a green frock coat as the answer to a sad young lady's prayers.

Holmes gave a faint shrug of his own. "Perhaps, Lord Frederick. I am not an alienist. We must reserve discussions of a philosophical nature for another time. You said Miss Grimswell seemed to have recovered from the shock of this document?"

"She had."

"And had you any warning before the letter you received today that anything was amiss?"

"None. I thought she had forgotten the wretched thing. I thought she was learning to be happy. But today... she was almost hysterical, scared half to death, but she wouldn't say why. She did mumble something about the terrible curse... said I was better off without her. I tried to reason with her, but she hardly seemed to hear me. I... I finally got angry and said I would leave. That was when..." His voice trailed away.

Holmes's gray eyes watched him closely. "What happened?"

Digby's right forefinger toyed with the green carnation. "That was when my carnation was injured." He laughed softly and pulled free a loose petal. "Before I could leave, she embraced me, and... she kissed me. She sobbed goodbye and pushed me out the door. I was in a kind of daze." A faint blush appeared on his cheek. "She is quite strong for a woman. I had kissed her once or twice before, but it was never... I always wondered if she really cared for me, but after that..." He raised his head and stared at Holmes. "I cannot bear to lose her—not to some ghost or vampire or foolish curse. She needs me—I know she does. Someone or something has scared her half to death, and I am terribly worried about her. I wonder... Her health has never been good. I almost wonder if she is ill. Certainly she will make herself ill if—"

"Does she have a regular physician?" I asked.

Digby thought for a moment, then gave an idiotic grin. "Damned if I know!"

So much for the brief sense I had that he might have some redeeming qualities. "My wife is a physician," I said. "In fact, she is Lady Rupert's doctor. Perhaps she could examine Miss Grimswell and determine if there are any physical problems. Michelle is a good judge of character and a person in whom women of all ages want to confide. She may be able to discover what is worrying her. It may be something completely unexpected."

Digby gave me a puzzled look, then turned to Holmes.

Holmes nodded. "You see why my cousin is invaluable to me, Lord Frederick. Feminine psychology is not my strong point. The fair sex remains the great mystery. I shall wish to question Miss Grimswell, but I would like Henry's wife, Doctor Doudet Vernier, to see her first. She may well uncover something which escapes our masculine natures."

Digby slapped at his knees with his gloves. "I suppose that makes sense. Worth a try and all that. Well, I shall see if I can convince her to come. It won't be easy. However, I shall insist. If she will not let me in, I'll wait on her doorstep till—"

I shook my head. "No, no—you must not make it a matter of your will against hers. Do you know Lady Rupert yourself? You must, if you have been courting Miss Grimswell while she has been staying with them."

Digby slapped at his knees again with his yellow gloves. "Course I do! And she's always been willing to put in a good word with Rose for me. Sometimes I think it's only because she wants to save Susan for some elder son of a duke or earl, but whatever, she has been a partisan on my behalf."

"You must write to her," I said, "and tell her you are concerned about Miss Grimswell's health. You can say someone recommended she see

Doctor Doudet Vernier. Ask her to try to arrange for Miss Grimswell to come to our house near Paddington tomorrow at three. On Saturday afternoon we usually do not see patients, and I will have Michelle reserve that time."

Digby turned to Holmes, who gave a brusque nod. "Very good, Henry. You are indeed lucky, Lord Frederick, that he was present. Watson is nearly as helpless when it comes to women as I am, despite his various wives, who are a source of confusion to me. Let us follow this strategy of Henry's. I will then talk to Doctor Doudet Vernier and later to Miss Grimswell."

Digby smiled and pulled on his gloves. "I'm hoping you can get to the bottom of this business, Mr. Holmes. I'd better run if I'm to try to set things up with Lady Rupert for tomorrow." We all rose to our feet. "Yes, I'm certainly glad I came. And Rose and I shall be at your house tomorrow, Doctor Vernier." He started for the door.

I gave Holmes a puzzled look. He raised his right hand. "One moment, Lord Frederick. Miss Grimswell is to go alone."

"But she's going to be my wife—I want to be with her. She won't know I'm coming too until it's too late for her to flee."

Holmes shook his head. "She will not be likely to share any confidences with Doctor Doudet Vernier should you be nearby."

Digby smiled, but seemed only partly convinced. "Well, perhaps you are right after all. Anyway, I'd best be getting to that letter to Lady Rupert." He turned to go.

I reached into my coat pocket. "Wait, Lord Frederick—take this." I rose and handed him my card. "This has our address on it. That is where Miss Grimswell must present herself at three tomorrow."

"Of course." He nodded his head, then put on his green top hat. "Thanks ever so much. Oh, I say, there is one other matter we haven't discussed—your fee, Mr. Holmes. As you may have gathered, I'm currently a bit short on funds, but once I am married…"

Holmes shook his head and made a gesture of dismissal with his hand. "No matter. We can discuss that later. For now, the case itself will suffice."

Digby's relief was obvious. "Very good. Farewell, then." He nodded and closed the door behind him.

I shook my head. "What an insufferable imbecile."

Holmes gave a sharp laugh, then walked over to the bow window. "Lord Frederick is a man with a purpose. He walks very quickly. Dark green is actually not an unpleasant color."

"Perhaps on someone else it might be agreeable." I sat back down and leaned forward toward the fire.

Holmes turned and sat back against the window ledge. "Life is indeed hard for the younger son of a peer." His voice was faintly ironic.

"What rubbish!" I exclaimed. "He was born into a life of privilege. Nothing is denied him. He lives better than ninety-nine percent of the population, and he has had the best education money can buy. The result is that he wears a green top hat and frock coat and talks like an absolute scatterbrain."

"You are very hard on him, Henry. So near to the title of marquess, yet so far. I seem to recall something about Hampsford falling on hard times. Lord Frederick may have to fend for himself. And he is at most twenty-five. Perhaps when you are nearer forty than thirty you will grow more charitable. I recall a young man living in London who grew a goatee, a Van Dyke, and was very proud of it."

I shuddered. "He, too, was an imbecile."

"But he became a respectable physician."

"After he had renounced the goatee."

Holmes walked back to the mantel and raised the humidor lid. "He does seem fond of the girl, in spite of everything. Did you notice how unaffected his speech became when he told us how she had embraced him?" He lopped off the end of the cigar, then lit it, his gray eyes showing a muted pain which vanished almost at once.

"I grant you he does seem to care for her. Perhaps he is redeemable."

"But would he care quite so much for her were she not worth four hundred thousand pounds?"

"It is a great deal of money."

Holmes exhaled a cloud of pungent smoke. "Men—and women—have been murdered for far less. And she is the last of the Grimswells. That is a very interesting fact. But the money…" His lips formed a brief, sardonic smile. "Money has claimed the lives of far more people than have the fangs of werewolves or vampires. I have high hopes for this case, Henry—high hopes."

Two

The next day, right at three o'clock, the buzzer from downstairs sounded. I was dozing, but I sat up. My wife Michelle stood and touched her reddish-brown bound-up hair, making sure all was in place. "That must be her." She started for the door.

"I should like to have a look at her," I said, although just then I preferred looking at Michelle, an agreeable sight from behind. She was tall with broad shoulders, a slender waist and womanly hips. Since she did not believe in corsets and layers of petticoats, one could discern her true shape under the blue silk of her dress. I thought with regret of how we often spent lazy Saturday afternoons and wished I had chosen a different time for Miss Grimswell. I took my jacket from a nearby chair, put it on and went downstairs.

Michelle was reading a piece of paper, her brow furrowed. "A telegram from Lady Rupert. Miss Grimswell refuses to come."

"Well, that's that." Perhaps there was hope for the afternoon after all.

"That is most assuredly *not* that," Michelle said sternly. "I'm going to Lady Rupert's. This girl may well need our help."

"But if Lady Rupert could not persuade her..." I helped Michelle into her coat.

"Then I *will.*" Michelle selected a hat with a large brim and took an umbrella from the stand next to the door.

"You are not going to walk all that way? It has been raining much of the day."

"I shall hail a cab, although I could use the air. It is not terribly far." She put her hand on the brass knob, glanced at me, looked closer, then touched my cheek and kissed me on the lips. "Your eyes always give you away, Henry. I may be occupied this afternoon, but an entire evening remains. That is the customary time, after all, for respectable married people. I shall be back as soon as I can. Harriet should be home soon, but perhaps we should go out for supper."

The door was briefly open, gray-white light and cool wet air flooding in. I sighed, then yawned. A mournful yowl broke the silence, and I felt the massive form of our black and white cat glide along my leg. "Well, Victoria, we are left to ourselves." (Michelle had most irreverently named the cat, who did somehow resemble her celebrated namesake.) "Since I have been sleeping, perhaps I can manage to stay awake while I have a look at Donaldson's book on the vascular system."

Nevertheless, I was beginning to nod when the buzzer sounded half an hour later. It could not be Michelle, since she had a key. I went downstairs and opened the door. Lord Frederick stood before me, his frock coat and top hat transformed today to a navy hue, but with a freshly resplendent blue carnation and the same ugly yellow gloves. He smiled warily but proudly.

"Whatever are you doing here?" I asked.

"I have come to see Rose."

"Well, you have not only ignored Sherlock's prohibition, you have wasted your time. She is not here."

Digby stared at me. "Come, come, old man—you can do better than that."

I felt my face grow hot. "Of all the insolent—" I glanced about, then snatched up the telegram Michelle had set down. "Look at this, and then be off with you."

Digby's ebullience drained away as he read. "Damn," he murmured. "I say, I wasn't really calling you a liar. I only—"

"Please leave now, Lord Frederick."

Holmes materialized out of the gray rainy afternoon, a tall figure all in black with a pale face, appearing so abruptly that I gave a start. "Henry's advice is quite sound, Lord Frederick."

Digby appeared equally surprised. "Mr. Holmes! I only—"

"Lord Frederick, there must be no further misunderstandings." Beneath the narrow black brim of his top hat his gray eyes were cold, yet intense. "If you wish me to represent you in this case, you must do what we have agreed upon. I cannot have you improvising at your every whim. Do you understand me?"

"But I only—"

"*Do you understand me?*" Holmes did not really raise his voice, but something in its tone was suddenly like iron.

Digby's face reddened. "I do."

"Then go home. As soon as I have any news, I will contact you."

Digby opened his mouth, closed it, gave a weak nod, turned and walked away.

I eased out my breath. "Where on earth did you come from? You startled me."

"I was waiting nearby. I expected Lord Frederick to do something foolish. May I see the telegram?" Holmes raised the sheet of paper. "'Can do nothing with Rose. She refuses absolutely to see you. She is most obstinate and infuriating. My apologies. Jane Rupert.' I suspect

Miss Grimswell will find it hard to refuse Michelle."

I set his top hat and stick beside my own. "Harriet has the afternoon off, but perhaps I could stir up some tea. There is a warm fire going."

"There is a damp chill in the air. A fire will suffice." We started for the stairs when we heard someone at the front door.

I strode forward. "If that imbecile has returned, I swear..."

The door swung open, and Michelle said, "Come in, my dear. The house is nearly empty, but–" She stopped speaking when she saw me.

Michelle is five feet ten inches tall and of robust build for a woman. She has nothing in common with frail and petite damsels of delicate constitutions, nor is she fat–her figure is very feminine. I had never seen a woman who could actually make her appear small, but Miss Rose Grimswell did the trick. She was probably an inch above six feet, almost my height, with broad shoulders and a formidable bosom–one understood at once what had happened to Lord Frederick's carnation. She wore a black mourning dress and hat which emphasized the pallor of her face. Her hair was also black, her eyebrows thick, but she had eyes which would appear blue or gray depending on the light. Her nose and jaw were long. Her face might not be conventionally beautiful, but she was quite striking. She stared at me, then at Holmes, a flush appearing at her cheeks.

"That is my husband, Doctor Henry Vernier," Michelle said. "Pay no attention to him. He is quite harmless."

Miss Grimswell hesitated, as if contemplating bolting. She reminded me of a large deer caught by surprise. "And that other person?" Her voice sounded slightly husky.

Michelle raised her head and saw Holmes standing by the stairs. "That is Mr. Sherlock Holmes, Henry's cousin. I am surprised to see him here." She ended on a disapproving note.

"Michelle," I began, "he has just chased off–someone you would most definitely not want to meet. We did not know you were returning with Miss Grimswell."

The girl's lips parted slightly, her flush deepening. "You are Mr. Sherlock Holmes—truly?"

Holmes's gray eyes regarded her intently. With a shrug he stepped forward. "Yes. You have heard of me?"

Miss Grimswell gave a nod. "Oh, yes. I have read all of your adventures. Father read them all, too. I... I always thought you would be most interesting to meet, but father said one should avoid meeting famous people or other writers. They always disappoint."

Holmes gave a sharp laugh. "That was quite perceptive of your father, madam! I hope you are not too disappointed."

Miss Grimswell shook her head. "Oh, no." Her blush deepened. "I only mean—you do not look like your pictures, but..."

Michelle put her hand on her arm. "We can talk with the men later. The examination will not take long."

Miss Grimswell drew in her breath slowly, and again I thought of large deer contemplating flight. "Are you certain it is really necessary?"

"Yes, as I told you, I am certain. You have never had a proper examination, and you may have some questions I can answer." For some reason Miss Grimswell went even more scarlet. "Please, my dear, trust me—I am not that ancient, after all."

Miss Grimswell smiled and pulled off her glove. "Very well." She had one of the largest hands I have ever seen, but the long white fingers were graceful, delicate, despite their great size. I wondered if she played the piano; she would have an incredible reach. She glanced at Holmes, then attempted a smile. "Rickie has been to see you, hasn't he?—Lord Frederick, I mean."

Holmes nodded. "He has. But I am only interested in your well-being, Miss Grimswell, not your future relations with Lord Frederick."

She swallowed, her throat rippling, and her eyes glistened from sudden tears gathering. "I could use some help." She turned away quickly. "But it is impossible."

"Nonsense," Michelle said. "It cannot be." She gently took her by the arm and led her to the door; she turned to me before closing it. "We shan't be too long."

I glanced at Holmes. "Lord Frederick hardly prepared us," I said. "She is quite striking—and so very tall."

We went upstairs, and Holmes sat in the purple armchair, which was his favorite. I prodded the smoldering coal with a poker. "She seems an unlikely match for Digby. I suppose her height and those bushy black eyebrows scare off the suitors. Imbeciles! Delicate flowers are pretty to look at, but not to hold. One good embrace, and they resemble Lord Frederick's crushed carnation. A big strong woman can give every bit as good as she gets, and..." I realized where my words were leading. "Pardon my babblings."

Holmes smiled. "Not at all. I found your reflections most interesting. All the same, four hundred thousand pounds makes any woman attractive. Men will gather like flies about a pot of honey."

"Your metaphor is apt." I set down the poker. "Perhaps I shall make some tea. That much I can manage in the kitchen." I returned a few minutes later with our best china teapot and cups on a tray. Holmes was staring into the fireplace, his mind obviously far away. A gust of wind drove the rain against the two large windows overlooking the street. His gray eyes shifted, then came into focus.

"Thank you, Henry." He took a sip. "Ah yes, you always could make an excellent cup of tea."

I sat down. We both sipped our tea quietly. Victoria leaped into my lap and curled about, making herself comfortable. The only sounds were her dull purr, the murmur of the wind, and the tick of our grandfather clock in the corner. At last I said, "I suppose you have made inquiries about the Digbys and Grimswells."

Holmes nodded. "Yes, although I have discovered little beyond the obvious. The Marquess of Hampsford has fallen on hard times. His younger son has borrowed heavily all about town, but his credit is again quite good. His marriage to Miss Grimswell may save him from some unpleasantness with his debts."

I frowned, then gave my head a shake. "I suppose green frock coats and top hats do not come cheaply."

Holmes laughed. "I fear not. Dressing outlandishly can be an expensive proposition."

We both grew silent again, and I felt the soporific effects of a lazy cloudy Saturday afternoon before a warm fire weigh upon my eyelids. I was half asleep again when I heard the creak of footsteps on the stairs. Michelle and Miss Grimswell soon appeared. At the sight of a stranger, Victoria silently ran out of the room. Holmes and I stood.

"Please sit down. You both looked so comfortable. Miss Grimswell wanted to flee, but I told her Sherlock would never forgive me if I let her escape." Michelle went to the tea tray.

Miss Grimswell smiled but still appeared uncomfortable. She looked none the worse for her examination, although a strand of black hair had escaped over her white ear. She was so fair that even a slight flush was obvious upon her cheeks.

"Would you care for some tea?" Michelle asked her.

She nodded. "Please."

"Sugar?"

"One lump. Thank you very much."

Michelle gestured at the settee, then joined her a minute later. Miss Grimswell gave Holmes a brief, furtive glance, then stared silently at the fire. Her cheeks still had a rosy flush.

Michelle nodded. "Henry, we really should put you in charge of tea. You do a better job than Harriet or I."

I turned to Miss Grimswell. "I hope the examination was not too unpleasant?"

Her eyes opened wide, white showing about the blue-gray irises. "Oh, no—not at all. I do so dread visiting physicians, but your wife is not like them at all." She abruptly seemed to realize my profession. "Not that all doctors are that way, but it is only that…" Her face grew redder still.

Michelle laughed. "I know what you are saying, my dear. If most of our male colleagues had to be poked and prodded by female doctors, they might be more understanding and more willing to open up the profession. However, I mustn't get up on my soap box." She looked at me. "Miss Grimswell is in good health. Her heart sounds vigorous; her lungs are absolutely clear; her ears, nose and throat show no signs of infection. However, I fear she suffers from a common malady of young ladies."

Miss Grimswell looked alarmed. "But you said—"

"The malady is ennui."

"*Ah*," Holmes exclaimed.

"It is a bad companion for sadness and grieving. As I said, a vigorous walk in the park every day would do you good. You must also keep your mind occupied." She set her hand on the girl's wrist. Michelle's big hand appeared almost white against the black silk of the dress sleeve. Her hand was large, but Miss Grimswell's larger still, the fingers much longer, so that their length rather than the thickness was striking. "You will not forget your father, even if you are busy. You will remember him all the time, but it is not good to have nothing to think about, nothing to do." Michelle's eyes grew sad, and I knew she was thinking of her own father, who had died a few years ago.

Miss Grimswell gave her an anguished glance. "It is not ennui... not now. Nor sadness exactly. Oh, how I wish..." Her mouth stiffened, and abruptly it became obvious that she was afraid.

Michelle frowned, her hand tightening. "Will you not tell me what troubles you? It is true we hardly know you, but we would like to help you."

Miss Grimswell's lips parted, but she would not look away from the fire. "No one can help me. No one. Not now."

Michelle frowned again. "That cannot be true. I hope it does not have to do with that foolish curse Henry told me about. It is not... madness or...?"

Miss Grimswell drew in her breath and raised her large blue-gray eyes. Her jaw dropped, her mouth twisted. I think if Michelle had not had hold of her, she might truly have fled. Instead she swallowed and stared again at the fire.

"Tainted blood and hereditary doom are overrated, my dear. Much of their power comes about only because we give it them. Families change with each generation. The Grimswells are not the same family they were four hundred years ago. You yourself are only half a Grimswell. Your mother had her own ancestors, and we are all of us new and different. We are all greater than the sum of our inheritance. Besides, I can see that you are quite sane."

Miss Grimswell stared at her warily. "How can you be so sure?"

Michelle laughed. "Because I have seen the real thing. Madness is not so splendid as in literature and drama. Few resemble Lear in the storm. And people are not such frail creatures in the end. They are not easily driven mad."

"No?"

"No. They do not suddenly hear voices or see imaginary creatures, not unless there is an organic disorder like a brain tumor. You are far too young to have such a disorder, and it is accompanied by other obvious physical symptoms. No, other than in plays, novels and operas, people do not suddenly go mad."

Miss Grimswell stared intently at Michelle, her face still very pale. "You say that, but the alternative is hardly…" She glanced at me and Holmes, suddenly becoming aware of our presence. Her smile was forced and hollow. "I shall be fine, doctor. I only… It is late and I must be going."

"First you must at least drink your tea."

"Oh. Yes." She took a sip, glad to have something to do. "It is very good," she said to me. "All the same, I must leave soon."

Holmes had been silent, but I knew he had been watching closely, taking in their every word, every gesture. He leaned forward. "Before you go, might I ask you a few questions, Miss Grimswell? I shall try not to detain you too long."

A certain awe showed in her eyes. It won out over her desire to flee. "Very well, Mr. Holmes."

"First, you must know that your well-being is my main concern. Lord Frederick's interests are…" He smiled ironically and flicked his right hand. "They are not necessarily my interests."

An unexpected smile briefly appeared, transforming her long, sorrowful face. "I understand."

"Good. Let us begin with a subject which may yet be painful. I would like to ask about the circumstances of your father's death, Miss Grimswell, but if you would prefer, we could defer this to another time."

Miss Grimswell drew in her breath slowly. She did have remarkable lung capacity. "No. What do you wish to know?"

"Were you at Grimswell Hall when the accident happened?"

"No, I was with Susan at Lady Rupert's."

"It must have been a dreadful shock."

Her mouth formed a wistful smile. "Yes. I suppose."

Holmes's gray eyes watched her carefully. "But not a total surprise, you seem to suggest."

"My father was always… melancholy, Mr. Holmes. And his health was not good. He had a bad heart. All the same, he was such a big man. It is hard to believe someone so… so much larger than life could have been struck down."

"He was melancholy, you say?"

"Yes."

"How melancholy?"

She raised her head and stared directly into my cousin's eyes. "I am not sure, Mr. Holmes. There has been speculation that… that he jumped, I know." Michelle touched her wrist again, but she hardly seemed to notice. "He was never what you could call a happy man. I always remember him being sad, but then I never knew him before my mother's death. Mrs. Fitzwilliams, our old housekeeper, has told me he was much different then. That was nearly twenty years ago. My mother died when I was only about two years old. She never quite recovered from childbirth. My aunt… I think she thinks father's death was an accident, but I don't know. I saw him two weeks before he died, and he seemed somehow happier. When I was growing up I always felt… I think he blamed me for my mother's death, and he loved her very much. But we had finally become friends of a sort. I showed him some of my writings. I was terrified of what he might say, but he was really very sweet." She laughed, then abruptly the tears began. She reached for her handbag, but Michelle offered her a handkerchief.

"Thank you," she said, wiping her eyes. "I had almost forgotten—but I must not forget that—I must remember that—*I must.*" Her voice rose in volume, her face twisting with emotion.

Holmes was surprised and dismayed. "I should have spared you so painful a subject."

She shook her head. "No, I... I had not remembered how kind he could be, and..." Her mouth pulled back again, and you could see her struggle to master herself. She gave her head a violent shake. "I do not think he jumped."

Michelle gave Holmes a reproachful look, then stood and poured more tea for Miss Grimswell. "Some tea might make you feel better."

"Thank you, Miss Grimswell," Holmes said. "We need not discuss your father any further just now. Tell me about this aunt of yours."

Miss Grimswell sipped at the tea, her red-rimmed eyes showing above the cup rim. "I have only two living relations. I call them aunts because of their age, but actually we are distant cousins. They are the daughters of my great-uncle Phillip Grimswell, my grandfather's brother. Phillip had three daughters, one of whom died young. Jane and Constance never married. Jane is..." She hesitated, paling slightly. "Jane is not well, but Constance has always been like an aunt. She was the only relation I ever knew well, except for my grandmother who died when I was a little girl. My father had an older sister, but she died at the age of seven or eight. Anyway, Constance was father's first cousin, but I always called her aunt. She has been most... considerate since my father's death." Her upper lip curled briefly.

Holmes smiled. "Perhaps a trifle too considerate."

"She is always worrying about my health or well-being. She means well, I know."

Holmes tapped his fingertips together. "I shall reserve judgment on all matters. I would like to verify what Lord Frederick told me about your relations. You and he were engaged to be married?"

Miss Grimswell's lips twitched. "Yes."

"Since approximately the fifteenth of September?"

She nodded.

"But you broke off the engagement yesterday?"

"Yes," she said. He stared at her but said nothing. "I have been cruel to him." Her voice dropped to a whisper. "I must not marry."

"I felt that way for the longest time," Michelle said. "It is perfectly normal."

"Can you tell me why?" Holmes asked.

Her jaw stiffened, and she shook her head. Something in her eyes changed, and I was afraid she was going to become upset all over again.

Holmes raised one hand. "No matter. It can wait. I take it that Miss Susan Rupert is your best friend?"

Miss Grimswell was clearly relieved. She smiled and nodded. "Yes. She has always been such a friend, and ever since father died… She and her mother told me I could stay with them as long as I wished. Susan and I first met at boarding school, Miss Lampert's near Oxford."

Michelle sat up abruptly. "Miss Cecily Lampert?"

"Why, yes."

"I know Miss Lampert. Her school is outstanding. She does not turn out vapid dilettantes. She believes young women should be educated like young men–Latin, the classics, English literature, French or German, natural sciences and mathematics. She also believes in the value of physical exercise and has her girls involved in games and sport. If I had a daughter and could bear to send her away, Miss Lampert's is the school I would choose."

Holmes shook his head. "I confess I have not heard of this school, Michelle. You have done me a service. And did you enjoy your time there, Miss Grimswell?"

"Oh, yes." Her words were spoken with utter sincerity.

"And you must be a young lady of talent. You mentioned your writing. I suspect you have a literary bent."

The flush reappeared on Miss Grimswell's cheek. "Yes." Her face was radiant for the first time. "I was very happy at the school. It was hard at first." Her smile wavered. "Miss Lampert was always so kind. Some of the girls could be cruel, but Miss Lampert would not tolerate it. And once I met Susan…" She smiled again. "Susan was my defender."

"From what did she defend you?" Holmes asked.

Miss Grimswell shrugged. "The usual thing. Taunts and jibes."

Holmes frowned. "Why would they taunt you?"

"Because of… my size. I have always been… large. And because I am… dark and plain."

"Plain?" Holmes's surprise was genuine.

"That is nonsense!" Michelle's eyes were full of righteous fury. "I suppose they were small and blond and vicious—like some tiny poodles! What a shame we were not born men so we could strike them down with a blow of our fist!"

Miss Grimswell was surprised at this outburst, but then she laughed. "I never wanted to hit them. But they did make me cry. My mother was light-haired, but I take after my father."

I smiled. "Believe me, Miss Grimswell, there are men who prefer women of stature. And you are hardly plain now, as you must know."

If Michelle had surprised her, I had completely astonished her. She stared at me as if I were mad, her face going scarlet. She glanced at Michelle.

"He is not joking," she said. "And he has admirable taste in women." Michelle gave her a curious look. "Has Lord Frederick never told you how beautiful you are?"

Her mouth opened, but nothing came out. She managed to shake her head.

"The lout—I advise you to find another fiancé."

"We have wandered somewhat far afield," Holmes said, "but perhaps this talk has helped to convince you that you are among friends."

Miss Grimswell smiled at him. "You are very kind." She encompassed

Michelle and me in her gaze. "All of you."

"I shall let you go now, Miss Grimswell. However, before you go, is there anything more you wish to tell me?"

Her eyes grew suddenly weary, the color draining from her face. "I…" She stared at Holmes. He did not move, nor did Michelle or I. "If only… I cannot."

"A fear is never so bad when you share it with someone else," Michelle said. "Saying it out loud weakens its power."

Miss Grimswell said nothing, but I could see strong conflicting feelings gathering like dark clouds.

Holmes stood. "Another time perhaps, Miss Grimswell. This is, after all, our first meeting, and an unexpected one for you. However, you must learn to trust me if I am to help you. Again, I shall defer further questions until our next meeting, but at that time you must tell me the truth. I hope to see you soon—this next week, as a matter of fact. Is there a particular day which would be opportune?"

She would not meet his gaze. "I… I… shall have to check my schedule."

"Please do so."

She swallowed once, resolutely, then raised her eyes. "Perhaps Wednesday. Wednesday morning."

He nodded. "Very good."

She gave a great sigh. "Oh, thank you again." She stood, as did Michelle and I.

Holmes stepped toward Miss Grimswell. She was of exactly his height, both of them tall figures in black. "I must make one final request, Miss Grimswell. I am not a superstitious man. I do not believe in ghosts, werewolves or vampires." Her mouth formed a weak, ghastly smile. "However, I do believe in evil—human evil, and believe me, that is sufficiently black and wicked. You are heir to a large fortune, madam, and that may make you a prey to evil. I fear that you may be in danger.

I hope I am wrong, but if I am not, then the danger may be very grave. Will you promise me one thing?"

Their eyes were locked upon each other. "What?" she whispered.

"If you are afraid—if you are at your wits' end and do not know where to turn—will you send for me immediately? It does not matter what the hour, whether night or day."

"I…"

"I beg of you, Miss Grimswell. It is for your own protection. It does not matter whether it is a ghost that threatens you or some inner torments—please send for me. Let me be the judge of the danger. Promise only that you will send for me."

She swayed slightly, and Michelle stepped near her and took her arm. "I promise," she whispered. "I promise."

Holmes gave a great sigh. "Thank you. And I promise you will not regret it."

Miss Grimswell bit at her lip. "You are all so kind, but I really must go."

She turned and started for the door, stumbling slightly, but Michelle had her arm. "Let me fetch you a cab, my dear. I have a piercing silver whistle." Holmes and I followed the two women down the stairs. Michelle gave Miss Grimswell her umbrella and her black hat. "Sherlock has already had a promise from you," Michelle said, "but I hope you will visit me again even if you are not in dire straits."

"Oh, I shall!" She pulled her black leather glove over her huge hand. I knew they must be made to order; Michelle also had trouble finding ladies' gloves which would fit her.

On an impulse, I said, "Do you play the piano, Miss Grimswell?"

She was surprised. "Why, yes."

"Ah." Holmes gave an appreciative nod. "One gifted with hands like yours should most definitely play the piano."

Miss Grimswell frowned, but as she stared at Holmes and realized he was not mocking her, her brow smoothed out. "And do you truly play the violin, Mr. Holmes?"

He laughed. "Watson has got that right."

"A Stradivarius?"

"Yes."

"But…" She hesitated.

"Ask it, Miss Grimswell."

"Do you really fire your revolver at the wall? And have you spelled out the Queen's initials with bullet holes?"

"Although Her Majesty has no more loyal subject, I do not believe in discharging revolvers indoors without cause. The police also frown on such behavior. I am eccentric enough that Watson need not have invented that particular detail. Good afternoon, miss."

"Good day, Mr. Holmes."

He withdrew a card from his inner coat pocket. "Do not forget your promise. Here is my card."

Michelle smiled at Holmes and me. "I shall just make certain she gets a cab." She closed the front door behind them.

I smiled and shook my head. "Poor girl. What can be bothering her? She is charming. Digby had made me expect the worst. And you think she may be in danger?"

Holmes's smile was grim. "Most certainly." He opened the door and stepped outside.

I joined him, stretching my arms overhead and yawning. "A bit of air feels good, damp though it may be."

Holmes said nothing. He was peering about. Considering how near we were to Paddington Station, ours was a fairly quiet street. Another physician had the house next to ours, and a retired colonel lived across the way. The rain had abated, but it was cool and windy. The leaves of an oak rustled softly, and the signboard with our names on it creaked.

Michelle and Miss Grimswell stood before the house. Michelle's blue silk dress was brilliant and cheerful under the gray autumnal light. Alongside Miss Grimswell, she resembled a bright blue kingfisher next to a crow. Michelle took out her whistle and blew. The piercing sound made me cover my ears.

"Cursed thing." I glanced at Holmes, but he did not seem to hear me. His eyebrows sank ominously, his mouth a tight line. He was staring at a man across the street. He gripped my arm tightly.

"Do you know that man?"

He was wearing a black mackintosh and a bowler hat, but I only caught a glimpse—a long thin face, black mustache and goatee, dark eyes—before he strolled casually away. He had broad shoulders and was unusually tall. The steel tip of his stick clacked upon the walkway.

"No, I do not believe so. We get many passersby with Paddington so near."

Holmes said nothing, only stared at the man, his brow still furrowed. A hansom up the street came our way, the groan of the wheels and the clatter of the horse's iron shoes growing ever louder. Michelle raised her hand and waved. Miss Grimswell hesitated before getting into the coach, then raised her large hand in farewell, an all-too-brief smile lighting up her pale face under the black hat.

Michelle watched the hansom depart, then folded her arms across her bosom and came back to the porch. "Goodness, Sherlock, what are you frowning at?"

He turned and smiled briefly. "Nothing, I hope."

"She is certainly a sweet girl. However, if she is not deeply in love with Lord Frederick, she is certainly smitten now."

Holmes was puzzled. "What do you mean?"

"I mean," Michelle said, "that you made quite an impression on the young lady."

Holmes drew himself up to his full height, his mouth taut with disapproval. "You exaggerate," he said.

"I think not," I said. "She has obviously read all of Watson's narratives."

"Blast it." Holmes shook his head angrily. "Half of London think they know me intimately, but all they know is Watson's shallow creation." We turned to go inside. Behind us we heard Holmes mutter, "I am nearly old enough to be the lady's father."

Michelle laughed softly. "Men can be so obtuse." One hand already held my arm, but she slipped her other about Holmes's arm.

Three

The following Tuesday, shortly before noon, I received a telegram from Holmes asking me to visit him around two in the afternoon. He knew that my practice was somewhat meager and that I encouraged my patients to visit in the morning so that my afternoons were often free.

That day being no exception, I arrived at Baker Street at almost exactly two. The day being a fine one, I had walked there. Everyone on the streets had seemed relieved at this reprieve from the onset of winter. The sellers of baked potatoes or meat pies, the hawkers of newspapers, the strolling men wearing signboards advertising soap or tobacco, all savored the warmth of the sun and the pleasant breeze. The street urchins ran about with renewed vigor, and the open upper deck of the omnibus was the place of preference rather than a soggy exile.

I nodded at Mrs. Hudson, went up the few steps and rapped at Holmes's door. "Come in," I heard him say.

Not immune to the superb weather, he had raised a window and pulled an armchair closer to the opening. He sat where the fresh air and the afternoon sun might touch his face, the stem of a favorite pipe held between two of his long, slender fingers. His frock coat lay across the nearby table. He was in his shirtsleeves, the gold chain of his watch hanging between the pockets of his black waistcoat, his long legs in the gray-and-black striped trousers stretched before him, his glossy black boots up on an ottoman.

"Contemplating your South Sea island?" I asked.

"No, indolent reveries are banished. The Grimswell case has provided an interesting problem. There has been a development."

"Yes?"

He stared out the window, then exhaled a cloud of pipe smoke. "Miss Grimswell has fled."

"What?—Fled where?"

"To Dartmoor. To Grimswell Hall."

"And Lord Frederick?"

"What of him?"

"Did he accompany her?"

"No. I have not spoken to Lord Frederick today. He is certain to show up soon and likely to be unpleasant."

I set my top hat on the table, then pulled a chair about. "How did you discover this if not from Digby?"

"From Lady Jane Rupert. Lord Frederick mentioned me in his letter to her, and the young lady spoke of seeing me at your house on Sunday. Anyway, Lady Rupert's footman appeared at my door this morning and asked if I would please accompany him to his mistress's. Lady Rupert was most upset, and even her daughter, who seems cut from a different cloth to her mother, appeared somber. Miss Grimswell was waiting for them this morning when they came down. She was pale, agitated, and very upset. Lady Rupert doubts the girl had slept at all last night. She told them she was leaving for Dartmoor at once, but would give no explanation. They pleaded with her, both of them, in vain. Lady Rupert then attempted to be stern, but that was no more successful. Miss Grimswell said she would take a hansom to the railway station wearing only the clothes on her back if necessary, but she would leave. They tried to convince her to wait a day or two, but she would not hear of that either. When I arrived at Lady Rupert's at ten in the morning, Miss Grimswell and her pet, a small dog apparently, were gone. She caught the ten-fifteen train. She took little with her. Most of her clothes and belongings are to be sent after her."

I shook my head. "What can be the matter with her?"

"Lady Rupert says she has always been… reserved, in contrast to her own daughter, but both Ruperts have noticed a change in her in the past two weeks. She seemed preoccupied and fearful, but they could not say why, other than the parchment relating to the curse. They noticed a change for the worse last Friday, the day Lord Frederick came to see us."

"And they could give you no reason why?"

"None. The only thing of interest they could tell me was that on Friday she asked to sleep in a different room. Her visit with us on Saturday seemed to improve her spirits. She was much better on Sunday and Monday. She even spoke last night of seeing Lord Frederick again, but today she was more desperate than ever before."

I pounded softly at the table with my fist. "Blast it—what can be the matter? Michelle was perhaps being overly reassuring, but Miss Grimswell really does not seem a likely candidate for insanity. Well, there is little that can be done if she has gone to Dartmoor."

Holmes gazed at me. "There is little that can be done in London."

I stared at him. The ends of his mouth curved upward, but the expression could not be called a smile. His black, oily hair was combed almost straight back and glistened under the light from the window.

"You are not..." I began. "You are. You are going to Dartmoor."

"There is currently little of interest in London. I was also not exaggerating when I said Miss Grimswell might be in danger–very grave danger. Besides..." He stood up and leaned upon the window sill with one hand, pipe still in the other, staring down at the street. "Dartmoor is beautiful this time of year. I had an interesting case there once before. Watson has that one mostly right."

"I wish I could come with you."

He turned about. "Do so–at least for a few days. Call it a holiday if you will. Surely you could bear to be away from Michelle for a week or two?"

Not wishing to appear unmanly, I nodded and murmured something in affirmation. Especially among the upper classes, men were always going off alone on big-game hunting expeditions to Africa or India, treks in the Alps, long sea voyages to distant islands, their wives and children left behind without a thought. I could not understand this. I had not been apart from Michelle for more than a week since our marriage; in fact, it was my extended absence in Paris with Holmes that precipitated my proposal of marriage. It had made me realize how much she had come to mean to me.

"All the same, I am of two minds about going to Dartmoor. I would prefer to be sent for by the lady. That would signify that she was ready to reveal what has disturbed her. Were we just to appear at her doorstep, we might not be welcome, and her silence might be further reinforced. And then there is the problem of Lord Frederick."

"What is the problem with Lord Frederick?"

"You will shortly find out, for he is here at last. Lady Rupert also sent for him this morning, but a second footman had no luck rousting him." He turned away from the window, set down his pipe, slipped into his frock coat, then went to the door and opened it. Both Mrs. Hudson and Lord Frederick gave a start of surprise. "Come in, Lord Frederick."

Today the young man was wearing a conventional black frock coat and top hat, but his waistcoat and cravat were an ostentatious plum color. His face was very pale, and he appeared rather ghastly. When Mrs. Hudson shut the door, the slight sound made him wince; he stripped off his yellow gloves and put a hand upon his forehead.

"I have been to Lady Rupert's," he said, "and she has told me everything. Whatever are we to do?"

Holmes gestured at a chair. "Please, Lord Frederick, sit down. You do not look well."

"Thank you. I do have something of a beastly headache."

"How many bottles did you have to drink last night?"

He gazed at Holmes, then broke into a weary grin. "I fear I lost count some time after midnight. How did you know?"

"It required little deduction. The symptoms of a hangover are obvious. No doubt this explains your delay in visiting Lady Rupert."

"Yes. I believe it was after three when... when I fell asleep. Here now, you two needn't look at me like that. I don't make a habit of this sort of thing, after all. I've been down in the dumps about Rose, and my friends decided to try to cheer me up. It worked, but I'm not sure it was worth it. Anyway, what does it matter? Rose left before you or I could stop her. The question is what's to be done now." He raised his reddish-brown eyebrow in an inquisitive look.

Holmes had his hands behind his back, his right hand grasping the wrist of his left arm. "I have been considering whether to go to Dartmoor. If I do, I would prefer to go alone." He stared down at Digby, who smiled.

"Sorry, but I really must come along. I've done as you said and left Rose alone for a few days, and look what's happened—she's run off! Actually, I'd about decided to go to Dartmoor, anyway, and I'd be glad for your company. Maybe we can get to the bottom of this business once and for all."

He said this earnestly enough, but I could not restrain an angry sigh. "What's the matter?" he asked innocently.

"Nothing," I said. "Nothing at all. We may as well all arrive at Miss Grimswell's doorstep."

"Oh, you're coming too? Splendid!" His pleasure was so genuine, it was hard—briefly—to stay annoyed at him. "I've been meaning to stop by before, Mr. Holmes. How did the exam business go with Mrs. Doctor Vernier? Did she find out anything?"

Holmes stared down at the street, then walked back to us. "No. Only that she seems an intelligent, compassionate and sensitive young woman. I hope you realize how fortunate you are, Lord Frederick."

Digby's eyes widened, his lips parting slightly. I think for a brief instant he thought he was the butt of some joke, but then the utter sincerity in Holmes's gray eyes must have reached him. "Uh, yes. I do, Mr. Holmes." He did not sound convinced.

"And of course there is her fortune, as well."

"And she is a fine-looking woman," I said. Digby gave me a similar look, his surprise more evident. "She is not conventionally beautiful, but all the same..." Both he and Holmes were staring at me. I thought of those enormous yet graceful hands and that formidable bosom, and then I actually grew embarrassed. "I admire tall women. England has too many tiny, blond, insipid females."

Holmes was amused, but Digby still appeared confused. "Rather," he said, putting the accent on the second syllable.

"Tell me, Lord Frederick, do you know the name of Miss Grimswell's solicitor?" Holmes asked.

"Yes, he is James Rigby of Rigby, Featherstone and Godfrey. Why do you wish to know?"

"I have several questions about her father's will and the estate. I wish she had not left so suddenly. Mr. Rigby will probably tell me nothing without the lady's permission."

"No, he won't. Rigby's a very strict, severe man of the old school."

Holmes seemed lost in thought. "Tell me, Lord Frederick, have you or Miss Grimswell ever felt as if anyone was following you?"

Digby frowned and rubbed at the corner of his neatly trimmed mustache. "No, can't say that I have, nor Rose neither."

"You do not recall a tall man with a black mustache, a bowler hat and mackintosh?"

Digby's frown deepened. "No, but…"

"But?"

Digby sat up and smiled. "Oh, I was recalling some tall surly fellow in the park, but he was only a groom, a filthy sort of fellow, dirty and unshaven. I was speaking–rather intimately–with Rose, and I noticed this fellow briefly leering at us, the most insolent look in his eyes. I had half a mind to go thrash him, but Rose tried to talk me out of it, and when I looked again, he was gone."

Holmes's fingers drummed at the table. "I should have followed him–I should have at least tried."

"Are you speaking of the person you saw at my house on Saturday?"

"Yes, Henry."

"As I told you, because we are so near Paddington, there are many strangers on the street."

"I saw him earlier while I was waiting."

"He might have been having a stroll before catching his train."

Holmes shrugged. "Perhaps." He glanced up at Lord Frederick. "I have a few loose ends to wrap up, but I shall be on the ten-fifteen train to Devon tomorrow morning. Be here at eight forty-five sharp should you wish to accompany me."

Digby rose, a broad smile on his face. "Wonderful, Mr. Holmes! I shall be here—count on it. I had better get home and start packing. If the weather holds, we should have some splendid days. Dartmoor can be spectacular in early November. Nothing like a good hike on the moors. And of course, we'll get to the bottom of this business in no time! Good afternoon, Mr. Holmes, doctor." He started eagerly for the door, then winced and put his hand on his forehead. He pulled on his gloves, then took his top hat and stick. "Until tomorrow, then." He closed the door behind himself.

Holmes looked at me and smiled. "Besides your reluctance to leave Michelle, there is the prospect of days with Lord Frederick. I fear I will be on my own in Dartmoor."

I shook my head grimly. "No, I shall not abandon you to a train ride alone in his company. I shall come, for a while at least. He does seem such a dolt."

Holmes went to the window and stared down at the street. "He is not, you know. Much of his behavior is merely a role, another costume he puts on and takes off. He graduated near the top of his class at Balliol."

I was truly amazed. "Are you serious?"

"Yes. I have been doing some checking on Lord Frederick. Whatever his faults, he was never one of those students who teetered on the brink of failure and disgrace. He did quite well at Oxford. He wrote essays in a student magazine. I have been reading one on the poetry of Swinburne."

"Swinburne—good Lord!"

"I am certain he could speak quite properly if he wished to." Holmes took off his frock coat and draped it over the settee. "But you really are going to come? Excellent, Henry! You are good luck for me—two of my most challenging cases could not have been solved without your assistance."

"Rubbish. You would have figured them out, anyway."

"All the same, I shall be glad for your company. Even I, who have faced many a danger, must confess to a certain fearful tremor at the thought of that solitary train ride with Lord Frederick."

I laughed. "I wish Michelle could come."

"She would be most welcome. I am certain she could gain Miss Grimswell's confidence."

"She is far too busy to leave her practice this abruptly."

"Perhaps it is just as well. I would not wish to put her in any danger."

My stomach did a somersault, and I stared at him. "You think it may come to that?"

"Yes. As I've said, men have been killed for far less than four hundred thousand pounds." A gentle rap sounded at the door. "Come in."

Mrs. Hudson appeared. "Mr. Holmes, there is a young–"

Before she could finish, a young woman marched around her, fists clenched, her upper lip curled back in a kind of snarl. Her finery augmented her beauty, the sharp, clean lines of her nose, cheek and jaw. Her blond hair was bound up and hidden under a mauve hat which matched her elegant silken dress. She was small, barely five feet tall, if that, with a remarkably tiny waist, no doubt the result of a slender figure and a tightly laced corset.

"Mr. Holmes, I must speak to you about that despicable wretch." She had stopped before Holmes and stared up at him.

"Thank you, Mrs. Hudson," Holmes said, then lowered his gaze. "Of whom are you speaking, madam?"

"Of Digby–of *Lord Frederick*." She said his title with scorn and sarcasm.

"Ah." Holmes gave a nod, then gestured at a chair. "Would you care to be seated?"

"No, I would not care to be seated. I am too angry to be seated." She began to pace, then glanced up at me. "Who is this person?"

"My cousin, Doctor Henry Vernier. He too is acquainted with Lord Frederick."

She gave me a brief, withering smile. "Then he too must know him for an insufferable ass." I said nothing, but something in my face must have given some hint of my feelings. "You do know it—I see you do!" Her laugh was sharp and bitter.

"Well, madam, you may not wish to sit, but I do. I hope you will not object?" Holmes said. She shook her head angrily. He sat down, crossed his legs and set the tips of his fingers together. "What do you wish to tell me about Lord Frederick?"

She turned about and stopped abruptly. "What do I wish to tell you?" Her breath made a sharp, sibilant sound as she drew it in through clenched teeth, her face reddening. "What do I...? I hardly know where to begin. He is a liar, a terrible liar, and a fool as well." She began to walk again. "He thinks he can just run off with that—that poor—cow and leave me after all..."

"Which cow?" Holmes asked coldly. "Miss Grimswell, I presume?"

"Yes, and I know... it is not her fault. I do not hate her, not really. He called her a cow once, a milk cow, but usually he refers to her as the giantess. She's not to blame, after all. How can she help it if she is rich? And it is not her fault she's large and plain. I pity her, really I do—I especially pity her if she is fool enough to marry Freddie. It's her money he is after—only her money."

"Are you quite certain of that, madam?"

"I have heard him say it often enough, haven't I? He is a younger son, isn't he? And his father is an even greater dolt than he. His brother will get the land, the estate and all the income. The entail has protected that from Hampsford's stupidity, but Freddie will be lucky if he gets a hundred a year. He owes ten or twenty times that much. Of course, his debts have doubled in the last month, now that his credit is good again. They are only too happy to lend him money. Oh, I will not stand for it—I will not! I told him we could run away together and start over. We could go to Australia or America and have a new life together. We could scrape up a couple of hundred pounds between the two of us. That would be enough."

"And leave his creditors in the lurch?" Holmes asked.

She smiled fiercely. "They are mostly a bunch of money-grubbing Jews."

"Perhaps, but they will no doubt collect from someone—his family or those friends ill-advised enough to back him."

"They can afford it." She laughed harshly. "They will not starve, Mr. Holmes."

Holmes gave a slight shrug. "Pardon me, madam, but you have me at a disadvantage. We have not been introduced."

"Oh, that's easily remedied. I am Alice Dobson, the *Honorable* Alice Dobson." Her voice was again heavy with sarcasm. "My father was a baron who blew his brains out over some financial scandal. He left his wife and baby daughter with almost nothing. His brother got the title and the estate. Of course, that is how I learned to take care of myself."

Holmes hesitated. "I am certain you are quite good at it."

She gave a savage laugh which bared her teeth. "Oh, I am, you can be certain of that. I have had considerable practice. I have learned exactly what price honor and virtue have. It is much easier being virtuous when you are rich—and stupid. Virtue is worth nothing without a dowry. Even a penniless lord like Digby will not marry me. I might find some barrister or banker with pretensions and live in a hovel, but money wants money—more money, Mr. Holmes, and not virtue. In spite of all the pious hypocrisies, virtue is cheap. No one will pay a penny for it."

Holmes lowered his hands. "I fear there is some truth in your observations, Miss Dobson."

She laughed again, her eyes suddenly full of tears. "I gave Digby everything he wanted, Mr. Holmes–I denied him nothing–and this is how he repays me. I did not necessarily expect him to marry me, but I did not expect him to–to run off with the first wealthy heiress he could get his hooks into. The girl would be a fool to marry him. I know what he is–I am a match for him, but some poor innocent... *cow*." She bared her teeth, clenched them. "Some poor little romantic twit who knows no better, who takes his protestations of love seriously–who thinks he really cares for her when all he wants is her fortune... I will not have it, Mr. Holmes–*I will not*." She choked off her words. Tears started out of her right eye, but she wrenched off her glove and wiped angrily at it. Her hand was small, white and delicate.

Holmes sighed. "What do you want of me, Miss Dobson?"

"I want you to stop it–I want you to stop him. Tell Miss Grimswell that her would-be fiancé is a bounder who is only after her money. Tell her that he has already been the ruin of one virtuous maid." A sharp laugh burst from her lips, then the tears began again. She pulled out a handkerchief and dabbed at her eyes.

"Please, madam, calm yourself."

"I will not calm myself–but you must not think–he has not hurt me–I am only angry–so very angry–I can hardly think straight. I am..." She put her hand on her forehead. She had grown quite pale, her face resembling the icy white marble of a statue.

Holmes stood up. "Please sit down, Miss Dobson."

"I... I shall not."

He gestured at the wicker chair with its soft cushion. "Do sit down." She did so. Holmes walked to the sideboard, then poured brandy from a decanter into a glass. He handed it to her. "Drink this."

She swallowed about half the glass, gasped, her face reddening, then lowered it. "Thank you," she mumbled. "I…"

"Take a minute to compose yourself."

She sighed, then took another swallow. "He makes me so angry," she murmured to herself. "God, how I wish… how I wish I was someone else. If I were a man, if I were only a man, none of this would ever…" She sipped the brandy, then smiled up at Holmes. She was a remarkably beautiful woman. "I should have been a man, Mr. Holmes. I have brains and will enough. I have the strength that Digby lacks. But what good is it—without money? It always comes down to money." She laughed softly, her eyes glistening, then sipped the brandy.

Holmes said nothing, but watched her silently. The breeze from the window stirred the papers on his desk.

At last she sighed and looked up, a faint blush on her cheeks. "You both must think me a fool."

Holmes shook his head. "No."

"I can see it has been very difficult for you," I said.

She gave a dull laugh. "Difficult. Yes, it has been difficult."

Holmes hesitated. "But now you know what kind of man he is. You have learned before it is too late."

She laughed once, then sobbed, a dry, shuddering sound that made me wince. She wiped at her cheek with the handkerchief. "But I have always known what kind of man he is—since the first moment I met him. It is obvious, isn't it?" She laughed, then looked at us both. "How could I want such a vain, shallow, spineless man? I have asked myself that many times." She bowed her head. "Yet I do. And how could I ever let him wound me so?—I, who…"

Holmes hook his head. "Please, madam."

She drew in her breath, then let out a sigh. "Forgive me for this display of female hysterics. I only…" She swallowed the last of the brandy and set down the glass. "I know your reputation, Mr. Holmes. Do not let Lord Frederick marry Miss Grimswell. He does not love her—he only wants her fortune."

Holmes smiled. "Neither Lord Frederick nor the lady have asked my advice on their matrimonial intentions. Besides, the engagement at present seems to be off. Someone has been... I think someone has been threatening Miss Grimswell."

His gray eyes peered intently at her. She raised her chin and stared back calmly. "Oh, that is probably Freddie, too."

I frowned. "But she has broken off the engagement."

"That will change. It is probably all part of his plan. Digby is not stupid, even though he acts that way. He will not let her escape, not now. You must not let him get away with it, Mr. Holmes—you must not. I do not know what he is paying you—it must be her money—but..."

"He is paying me nothing. Not yet. And as I have told Miss Grimswell, I am mainly concerned with her well-being."

"Then you must save her from him." The word "save" was faintly ironic. "I do not really know anything bad of her, but of course I hate her." She smiled fiercely. "Oh God, it is all so stupid. I know I would be better off without him, but I cannot give him up. I must go. I have made enough of a fool of myself." She stood, then swayed slightly, putting her hand over her forehead.

Holmes's hand shot out and seized her arm below the shoulder. I stood up at once. She smiled weakly. "You need not worry, gentlemen. I am well." Her pallor contradicted her words. "I am a fool, but I am not... I am not an idiot. I am not suicidal. I only wish to kill Freddie." She laughed harshly, then noticed the expression on Holmes's face. "I am joking. I do not mean it. I really must be going."

Holmes still held her arm. "One thing puzzles me, madam. You heard Lord Frederick repeatedly insulting Miss Grimswell, but you have known for a long time that he wanted to marry her for her fortune. Why, then, did you remain with him? And what has changed to so infuriate you?" He lowered his hand.

"Yes, we joked about her all the time, but he had said that once they were married..." Her eyes stared out the window off into the distance. "He would have the giantess's fortune, but it would make no real difference for us. We two might still..." Her cheeks reddened.

"He is a bounder!" I exclaimed.

"Oh, yes, and a liar. He had said the marriage would not matter, but then... He told me we were finished—that it was all over."

"When did he tell you this?" Holmes asked.

"Last Friday. I could not believe him."

"What reason did he give you?"

Her mouth widened, twisting into a grin which bared her teeth. "He said... he said it wouldn't do... *wouldn't do*... for a married man to—"

"Enough, madam—you have told me enough."

She straightened her back, closed her eyes, her fists clenched. Her breath made a kind of hiss escaping through her teeth. She pulled on her gloves and started for the door. I walked over and opened it for her. She nodded.

"Miss Dobson," Holmes said. She turned to him. He had folded his arms. "Thank you for coming to see me."

Her mouth twitched, and finally formed a smile. "The pleasure was mine." Her eyes were red, her face fearfully pale.

I closed the door behind her. "Poor woman," I murmured.

"She will recover," Holmes said. "She has a strength rarely found in women—or men."

"I thought Digby was an imbecile, but now I know him for a villain. To think..."

"Come, come, Henry. We know no such thing."

"Can you doubt he has ruined the poor girl?"

"She was a willing party to it all. You heard her. And how many noble bachelors do you think go to the altar without some such sordid affair in their past? At least he had the decency to finally break things off."

"Decency—*decency*?"

Holmes laughed. "A poor choice of words, I grant you, a very poor choice."

"Miss Dobson has been gravely wronged."

Holmes smiled, but his gray eyes showed no humor. "The world is full of such wronged people. She went along with Digby. I am sure she was a match for him. Unfortunately the heart often pays little attention to the brain. Even you must admit she is probably well rid of him."

My frown slowly faded. "Yes, I suppose that is true. But there was a certain truth to her ravings. It is difficult for a woman to marry well without money."

"Miss Dobson will manage."

"How can you be so sure?" I asked.

"Because she is beautiful. Beautiful women have a way of looking after themselves."

My frown returned. "That may also be true, although I do not care for your cynical tone."

"How can one regard the behavior of men and women and avoid cynicism?" He went to the window and drew in his breath, his back to me, his fingers grasping at the sill. "What does it all mean, this pathetic mating dance? These lacerated hearts, these ridiculous longings and desires, this incessant pain—all this... nonsense." He was quiet briefly. "Why should such a simple business cause such turmoil? Man is unique among the animals in this respect. For them it is all roaring, growling or butting horns, and then they run off, or they have what they desire—for the moment. They are better off than we."

I stared at his back, astonished at his fervor. "No," I said. "They are not better off."

"No?" He still would not face me.

"No." I took a step nearer. "Once it is all settled... If you really love one another, then it is quite wonderful."

He turned, a tight smile on his lips. "I shall have to take your word for it. I fear, however, that this particular episode has not turned out so well for Miss Dobson. All the same, she is a woman—as she said—who has learned to take care of herself. She will find some lovesick puppy who will take her, money or no money, reputation or no reputation."

"That is cruel," I said. "And what of Lord Frederick? Is he blameless?"

"No one is blameless, Henry. But you are mistaken if you think I cannot see his faults. Miss Dobson told me little I did not suspect. Have I not harped upon Miss Grimswell's fortune? Are his intentions not obvious to anyone? Even Miss Grimswell must have her suspicions."

He picked up his pipe from the ashtray where he had set it. "I did learn one thing. His cruelty is something of a surprise—the 'giantess' and the 'milk cow.' He has a mean streak beneath his tiresome amiability." He relit the pipe, drew in two or three times to get it going, then eased out a breath of smoke. "I do not care for men who are cruel to women, regardless of the women's class, virtue or appearance. And if he intends in any way to harm Miss Grimswell, he will pay for it—he will pay dearly." If Digby could have seen Holmes at that moment, he might have reconsidered coming to Dartmoor with us.

Four

Late the next day Holmes and I climbed into a crude rented carriage, aptly called a dog cart, and started off for Grimswell Hall. Lord Frederick raised his hand in a grudging farewell. Stern words from Holmes and his threatening to abandon the case (something I knew he would never do) had persuaded Digby to remain behind at the Grimpen inn for one night. Holmes had also argued that it was unclear how the lady would receive us—her servants might not admit us—but two would be less overwhelming than three. Shrewdly, he also suggested he would help prepare the way for Digby's triumphal arrival the next day.

After several hours on the train enduring Digby's incessant chatter, Holmes and I were only too glad to sit in silence and enjoy the ride. A cold dreary rain had been falling in London, but shortly before we reached Grimpen, the sun had broken through the clouds. Now its golden light gleamed along the desolate length of the moor, the autumnal heath and bracken a radiant brown along the rolling earth.

I had not been to Dartmoor before, but it reminded me of the moors of northern Yorkshire. One had the same sense of the sky somehow opening up, becoming more vast, yet somehow nearer; the sky joined with the land to form a single mute presence, a great slumbering creature, brown and gray and cavernous, a dormant behemoth with a cold misty aura. The old gods of earth and sky lurked nearby, and relics of Neolithic man—a solitary monolith of jagged black granite all spotted with brilliant lichens or smaller, mossy slabs protruding from the smooth turf—were at one with the landscape, so much so that the man-raised menhir seemed a brother to the natural tors atop the hills. One set of smaller stones formed a circle, jagged teeth making the O of a giant, frozen mouth.

The air was wonderful after the stink of London, but to call something so rich, dank and heavy "fresh" would be a misnomer. Decay was predominant, the smell of all that decomposing plant matter, fallen leaves from the small patches of forest or from the brown and shriveled outer layers of ferns. The smell reminded me of wine, some vintage Burgundy or Bordeaux with a dark, smoky taste. The cold wind had a bite, the dampness making it cut through wool to touch the skin.

We had followed the worn ruts of a dirt road up the slope away from the village. Once we reached the summit and descended, all sight of the village or the modern works of man were gone. The road rose and fell, skirted a small wood of alder, their leaves yellow, the ferns thick underneath with an occasional dense growth of whortleberry bushes with shriveled blue fruit, then the road rose and fell again.

We came to a small stream, its icy rushing waters flowing over glossy brown stones. The driver brought the horses to a halt. "Best jump down, gents, and cross afoot. It'll be a rough ride o'r the bridge in the back there."

Holmes and I stepped down and saw before us one of the so-called clapper bridges, made of slabs of granite resting on supporting stone piles. Since the slabs were nearly a foot thick, the effect was like that of a step, and there were two such steps up, then two down. Holmes tapped at the granite with the steel ferrule of his stick. He wore a suit of heavy gray tweed, brown boots with thick soles, and a black hat with a narrow brim. The air had brought some color to his cheeks, and he looked better than he had in weeks. The carriage jounced and swayed as its wheels went up over the first step.

"Walking is definitely preferable," Holmes said as we strolled along the bridge behind the carriage. Beneath us the clear icy water swept loudly downstream on its long voyage to the distant sea. "Look there, Henry." A gray shimmery shape swept by and vanished under the bridge.

"Good heavens, that looked to be an enormous fish."

"Perhaps it was a pike. There are salmon in these streams, too."

"Salmon—here?"

"Yes. I have seen them swimming upstream to spawn in the torrents of early summer. A memorable sight."

The wind over the water felt very cold, and I restrained a shiver. My jacket was a thick wool, but not so heavy as Holmes's. The sun had sunk low in the sky, a muted yellow circle behind a bank of gray clouds, and the blue patches of sky seemed to be shrinking. One particularly billowy patch of clouds seemed to be swirling in from the east so fast you could see them move.

I pulled out my watch. "It will be dark in another hour. I should not like to be out here under a cloudy sky at night."

"That is when another hunter, the owl, replaces our friend up there." Holmes pointed with his stick. High above a bird soared, its immense brown wings spread straight out.

"Some sort of hawk?"

"The common buzzard, one of the largest of the aerial predators."

"Buzzard seems a humdrum name for so magnificent a bird."

"It is, especially as the Americans refer to a species of scavenging vultures as buzzards. Our buzzard up there is a cousin to the eagles, another of the lords of the air."

The buzzard suddenly circled about, dropping downward, its wings opening up as it vanished behind the stand of alders.

"No doubt he has found his supper," Holmes said. "Probably a vole or hare if he is lucky."

"Poor creature," I murmured.

"You are being maudlin, Henry. One could argue that falling prey to so magnificent a bird is a better end than most. It is quick and relatively painless. It is a vole's fate to end up in the stomach of some predator—an owl, a buzzard, a kestrel, a fox, an adder. It is a mistake to attribute human emotions to the buzzard or the vole. There must exist between them a curious sympathy, a strange bond. The vole's end is not tragic, only natural, and there is no malice in the buzzard. No, the predators of the natural world are not cruel, nor malevolent."

He stepped down off the final slab of granite onto the soft reddish earth. A weary smile pulled briefly at his lips. "That is the difference between the world of men and the world of animals." We climbed into the dog cart and sat down. The driver cracked his whip, and we were rumbling on our way again. Holmes stared back toward the trees. "Evil does not exist in their world. The buzzard does not toy with his prey. He does not enjoy suffering."

"A cat does," I said. "I have seen Victoria with a mouse."

Holmes shrugged. "That is all mere brute instinct. It is not evil. It is over in a few minutes, and the mouse is devoured. The cat does not play with the mouse for days or weeks."

"You are in a curious mood."

"I have been reflecting upon the Grimswell case and wondering what type of predator is at work."

I frowned. "You are not thinking of werewolves or vampires?"

"Certainly not. Merely someone... extraordinarily cruel. This person is toying with Miss Grimswell like your cat, but her torments are prolonged. This is not evil in the abstract."

I looked about me at the lonely expanse of the faded moor covered with the languishing heath, the splendor of summer long past, and at the gray sky overhead, all the blue gone now. I shivered, wishing I had put on my mackintosh to cut the chill. "This is truly a desolate place."

"Perhaps, although it is undeniably magnificent."

"It does seem a place..." I drew my arms about me.

Holmes stared at me, his gloved hands resting on the head of his stick. "Yes?"

"The place for a ghost, some predatory ghost."

"I think not, Henry. The moor and that sky are beyond any mere predatory ghosts. Any ghosts here I think we bring with us."

"But if a malevolent ghost did exist, this would be the place for him."

"No. London is a far better place for a ghost than Dartmoor. Such a ghost belongs amid the stench and squalor of mankind, not out there where all is clean and open and grand. Some decaying mansion would work better."

I forced a smile. "I hope Grimswell Hall is not a decaying mansion."

"It is not," Holmes said, "as you will soon see."

"But–"

Holmes raised his stick. "Ah–there it is."

I turned to look past the driver. Ahead of us rose what seemed, almost, a small mountain, though hill was probably more apt, and at the summit was a heap of jagged rocks, gigantic boulders of granite stacked in a strange shape with two protruding pieces like horns. We had passed another hill with a tor, but the granite there had been whitish, not black like this. Down the hill from the dark tor, silhouetted against the gray fading sky, was a structure of the same black stone with a single tower rising high above the moor.

"That is Demon Tor, if I am not mistaken," Holmes said, "and below it is Grimswell Hall."

"It must be quite a view from the tor," I said. "That is the highest point for miles around. Have you been here before?"

Holmes smiled. "Yes. As I told you, I know Dartmoor well."

It grew darker as the horse lumbered up the hill toward the hall, and damper as well. It seemed foolish to pull out my great coat with our destination so near, but I was soon shivering from the cold. Below us a gray cloudy mass crept out of a nearby valley and a dark patch of woods and curled like smoke toward us.

"Good Lord," I murmured after watching for a while. "Is that fog?"

"It is," Holmes said. "It can come upon you swiftly this time of year. It is not dangerous unless you are near a mire or bog. If you are, the best thing to do is to settle in for a long, uncomfortable night. If you try to go anywhere, you'll soon be wandering in circles, and then you'll land in the bog and be sucked under in a moment or two—not a pleasant fate."

I shuddered from the cold. "You have a talent for understatement. Perhaps the vole was lucky."

Holmes laughed and gave my wrist a squeeze. "We are nearly there. Surely the lady will not turn us out into the fog. At least it is not raining."

This turned out to be premature optimism, for just as we had almost reached the hall, I felt a few wet drops on my cheeks. A cold, steady rain began. My exhilaration at being away from London had completely dissipated, and I thought longingly of Michelle and our warm, comfortable feather bed. No doubt she would be seated before the fire on the settee with Victoria curled beside her, gently stroking the cat's back, a heavy volume before her.

The ground had leveled out before the hall, and trees were planted all about, a miniature park. A huge black gnarled oak looked like it must have been planted centuries ago. The carriage swayed, rumbled, then its ride evened out, the sound of the iron wheels changing. We were riding over slabs of granite, the stone forming the final way to the hall. On either side, tall yew trees reached for the gray sky, and before us rose that singular black tower, square and sharp.

"How old is that tower?" I asked.

Holmes had rested his hands on his stick again. "Victor Grimswell had it built some fifteen years ago. It is a recent addition to the hall, as is a conservatory."

"How do you know all these things?"

"The hall is a major landmark. One of the regional guide books devoted two pages to it." He smiled. "It is not to be missed."

Because of the rain I did not try to get a good look at the hall. I was only aware of a square black mass, the tower to one side, the yew trees about us swaying as a cold wind swept down the lane. An archway of the ubiquitous black granite supported an overhanging roof which sheltered the main portal. Although night was still a few minutes away, someone had lighted the lamps on either side of the door. Holmes and I got down, but the driver remained seated. His mouth was curiously stiff, his eyes restless. A black oil-skin coat covered his shoulders, and he wore a woolen hat with a ragged brim.

"I do not know how long we shall be," Holmes began, "or if we shall remain behind, but perhaps—"

"I'll wait five minutes, sir, and not a minute longer. Then I'm drivin' back with'r without you. The choice is yours."

"It's a foul night," I said. "Surely they will be willing to put us up, but it may take a few minutes to ascertain—"

"Five minutes, sirs, and then I'm gone. Best be about your business because the clock is ticking."

I shook my head. "You needn't be so surly, I only..."

Holmes shook his head. "Leave him be, Henry. Thank you for your services. Here is a sovereign for you."

The man's eyes widened with disbelief. "A sovereign? I'm not waiting no longer than five minutes—no matter what you pay me."

"Understood. And thank you all the same."

The driver ran his tongue across his lower lip, then took the coin. "Thank you, sir. Luck to you."

Holmes started for the door, and I followed. "He was surly," I whispered.

"He is only frightened."

"Frightened?"

"Yes, badly frightened. Well, if he departs, that is all the more reason they must grant us refuge."

"I cannot believe Miss Grimswell would turn us away on a night like this."

"We shall see soon enough."

Two huge oaken doors stood nearly nine feet tall, and over them, chiseled in the black granite was GRIMSWELL HALL. Holmes seized the iron ring of the knocker and slammed it twice against the metal. The clang made me wince. We waited silently. The driver had stepped down and was lighting the lamps on either side of the carriage. One of the horses snorted and stamped its feet. I began to shiver again. "We will pass our five minutes just waiting out here," I muttered.

The driver had mounted again when the door finally opened. An old man stood before us, his shoulders stooped, tendrils of white hair beginning at the edge of his bald pate. He had thin lips and pale, watery blue eyes. He wore a black suit which emphasized his thinness and diminutive stature.

"Yes, sir?"

"I am Mr. Sherlock Holmes, and I wish to see Miss Rose Grimswell."

"She is in the library, sir. I shall take you to her." He noticed Holmes and me pick up our bags. "You may leave those here. If you are staying, I'll have George take them up to your rooms."

The entryway was small and dim, but we went through it into the great hall. A fire burned in the great hearth, the orange flames leaping about the blackened logs. Our footsteps on the granite floor echoed softly overhead.

We had nearly reached the stairs when a woman's voice said, "Fitzwilliams?"

The old man stopped and turned. "Yes, madam?"

A woman in a black dress strode toward us. Behind her stood a tall young man in a black morning coat and striped trousers, a servant or footman by the look of him. The woman was tall, somewhat stout, with a pink face and gray hair. "Who are these men?" Her eyes took us in, her brow furrowing and mouth tightening.

"They wish to see the mistress." He glanced at Holmes. "Pardon me, sir, but your name escapes me."

"Sherlock Holmes."

The woman's eyes widened, her mouth opening. "You..." Some of the pink color left her face, then she thrust her jaw forward, her nostrils flaring. "What are you doing here?"

"I have come to see Miss Grimswell."

Although her hair was silver, her thick eyebrows were still black. They had come together over her nose. "You have, have you? Well, I won't allow it—I won't."

"And why not, madam? As her nearest relation, you should be most concerned with her well-being."

Something like fear showed briefly in her eyes. "How could you know who I am?"

"Your niece has told me."

"She did?" I said.

Holmes gave me a brief look. "Yes. This is Miss Constance Grimswell, her cousin."

The lady drew in her breath and squared her shoulders. Although not so tall as Rose Grimswell, she made the butler appear small and frail. She had a good six inches and some fifty pounds on him. "You can turn around and leave this instant. You know where the door is."

"But, madam," I exclaimed, "it is raining, and our carriage has left. You cannot put us out on such a night."

She smiled briefly. "No?"

Holmes said nothing. A tight, ironic smile pulled at his thin lips, and his gray eyes were fixed on hers. A heavy silence settled about the vast hall. A sudden snap came from the fireplace, an ember flying out. Miss Grimswell was the first to lower her gaze.

"I intend to speak with Miss Rose Grimswell," Holmes said. "Should she ask me to depart, I shall gladly do so. If you have her best interests at heart, you will not interfere with me."

Her nostrils again flared. Her hands were not so large as Rose's, but they were formidable all the same, the fingers much thicker. They formed fists, then opened again. She smiled, not a reassuring expression, her color returning, then laughed once. "Of course I shan't put you out on a night like this. I only... You startled me, that's all. If you wish to speak to Rose, I'll take you to her myself. Fitzwilliams, you may–"

"Madam, I would prefer to speak briefly with your niece in private."

Her jaw briefly thrust forward again, brow furrowing, then she laughed. "Whatever you wish, Mr. Holmes. I shall have George take your bags up, and the maid will prepare your rooms. You cannot possibly leave us at this late hour."

Holmes nodded, a smile still at his lips. "Thank you, madam."

"Thank you indeed!" I was immensely relieved.

Fitzwilliams had been watching us with a wary eye. He stared at Miss Grimswell, his pale eyes glowering, then turned and started for the stairs. Miss Grimswell watched us, a saccharine smile upon her lips.

The stairway was a massive thing of darkened oak. When we were halfway up, there was a sudden scuttling noise, then a ferocious but diminutive barking. By the candlelight we could see the small white hysterical dog at the top of the stairs.

"Damnation!" Fitzwilliams shook his head. "Pardon me." He called down below. "George! George! Please get the blasted dog. He'll bite or trip someone for certain."

The young servant strode past us on the stairs. "There, there." He picked up the small dog, then suddenly cursed. "Bite me once more, and I swear to God…" He went past us, the dog barking loudly and snapping at us. The sound gradually quietened as George crossed the hall.

Fitzwilliams sighed. "Not a proper dog, that, only a nuisance."

We went up to a gallery overlooking the hall, an elaborate banister along one side, paintings and doors on the other. Fitzwilliams paused before a door and rapped softly. "Miss Rose?" A voice murmured something, and he opened the door. "Two gentlemen to see you."

Miss Grimswell was seated at the end of a large table, a piece of paper before her. As before, she wore a black dress, and in the dim room the whiteness of her face and hands made them stand out, made them almost glow with a white phosphorescence. The pen slipped from her fingers onto the dark wood. She coughed once, then laughed. Her voice had a strained throaty quality, her laughter grating, and it ended in a ragged sob. She rose even as the tears slipped from her eyes and started down her cheeks.

Holmes strode across the room. "Miss Grimswell, are you…?"

Her laughter became a sobbing. She covered her mouth with her fist, then pointed at the paper on the desk.

Holmes hesitated, then seized her arm. "Please calm yourself, miss. There is no reason for–"

Her eyelids fluttered, her blue-gray eyes suddenly losing focus, her laughter abruptly ceasing. She sagged sideways, one hand clutching for the table edge. "Quick, Henry–help me." He had grabbed her arm, and she fell back against him.

I thought they would both go down, but he managed to keep her up until I reached them. I took one arm, supporting her back with my other hand. Her head lolled sideways, revealing her long white throat. Briefly she went totally limp. Now I too almost went down, but Holmes stepped sideways, propping her up momentarily.

"Good Lord, she is heavy!" I exclaimed.

Holmes stared at Fitzwilliams. "The chair–pull out the chair."

He staggered toward us as quickly as he could, then pulled the chair around. Holmes and I slowly lowered her into the chair. Her black hair brushed against my arm, and she moaned softly. Her upper arm was broad for a woman and felt strong. She slumped sideways, but the arms of the stout oaken chair kept her from falling. Holmes and I both still had a grip on her.

I shook my head. "She is a very big girl."

Holmes smiled. "She is indeed."

"I wonder what she weighs."

"One hundred and eighty pounds," Holmes said.

"So much, you think?"

"She is my height and must outweigh me by at least ten pounds."

I shook my head. "Given that, one would hope she doesn't make a habit of fainting."

"She does not." Fitzwilliams bit at the side of his lower lip, his pale eyes showing his concern. "Perhaps I should send up my missus. Miss Rose has not been well lately, not herself."

"Let us try some spirits first," Holmes said. "Brandy or whisky."

"I'll fetch some, sir." He started for the door.

"Oh, Mr. Fitzwilliams," Holmes said. "Let's not tell Miss Grimswell—Miss Constance—about this."

Fitzwilliams's upper lip rose, the smile verging on a sneer. "Very good, sir."

Miss Grimswell sat up, her head swaying to the side even as her chin rose. "Oh…"

"Miss Grimswell?" Holmes gave me a worried look. "Could she be ill?"

I touched her forehead lightly with my fingertips. The skin felt cold and clammy, not hot. "She has no fever. Perhaps she only stood up too fast. That can cause faintness, especially in tall people. And if she has not been sleeping or eating, that would make her prone to fainting. I think she is coming out of it."

She blinked her eyes, opened them, but did not seem to see anything for a second or two. "What…?" Abruptly she became alert, looked about and up at us. "What am I…?"

I felt her muscles tighten, and I squeezed her shoulder. "Do not try to stand, not yet. You must stay seated, or you may faint again."

"Faint? I do not faint."

Holmes was peering past her at the table. He gave a sharp laugh. "Henry, have a look at this paper."

Still holding her arm, I turned the paper slightly. The oil lamp on the table provided plenty of light. *Dear Mr. Holmes, I can bear it no longer. It has happened just as you said. I am indeed at my wits' end. Perhaps no one can assist me, but if you will only try. Oh please help me. If you…*

Miss Grimswell glanced down at the paper. "I don't understand.

How can you be here? I hadn't sent the note. I hadn't even finished it." She did not seem fully conscious yet.

Fitzwilliams appeared at the door carrying a silver tray with a decanter and glasses. "How does she fare?"

"Better," I said.

Holmes was staring at Rose. His face was thin and severe, but his eyes showed the warmth which I knew lay within him. He let go of Rose, then took the decanter, pulled out the cork and poured some brandy. He offered her the glass.

She stared reluctantly at the brown liquid. It smelled wonderful. "I hate brandy."

"You must drink it," Holmes said.

I nodded. "Consider it medicine."

She gazed up at me. I realized I was still holding her shoulder and let go. We three men were all watching her, and it seemed to strike her as comical. She smiled weakly, then raised the glass and drank the whole thing down, several ounces.

"No!" I exclaimed.

Her blue-gray eyes opened wide. She gasped, then began to cough loudly. Her cheeks were full of color now.

"Not the whole thing," I said. "You were supposed to sip it."

Between coughs she said, "Oh... it... burns so."

Holmes poured out more, only half an inch this time. "Sip it slowly this time."

"No, thank you." She was still coughing.

"Have a sip—go on—but slowly. It will stop your coughing, and try to breathe slowly and deeply. Yes, that's better."

Her bosom rose and fell as she took in deep breaths. She closed her eyes tightly and drank, opening them when nothing happened. She took another sip, then sighed. "I feel utterly ridiculous." She smiled at us.

"You needn't worry. I'm not going to die." She laughed, then her smile wavered and vanished. "Not from brandy. Oh God, I am so tired."

"Have you had trouble sleeping?" I asked.

"Yes—oh yes."

I looked at Holmes, who still held the decanter, his eyes watching her. "Sherlock, could you possibly... I could do with a drop myself."

He laughed. "I'll wager you could." He poured me a glass of brandy, then another. "Would you care for some, Mr. Fitzwilliams?"

The old man shook his head fiercely. "I take no spirits."

Holmes held the decanter before the light, letting it set the brandy aglow. The cut glass formed an intricate pattern. "A lovely thing, genuine crystal by the weight of it." He sipped the brandy. "Ah, this is superb, the real thing, a cognac from about seventy-five, if I am not mistaken."

Whatever the year, it had nicely warmed my insides. "It is very good," I said.

"You may leave us now, Mr. Fitzwilliams. My cousin, Doctor Vernier, is a physician, so your mistress will be in good hands."

He gave us a reluctant look, his lips puckering, his mouth shifting to the side.

Miss Grimswell smiled at him, her expression radiant in that dark, gloomy room. "Go ahead, Fitzy. I am recovered, and we can trust Mr. Holmes."

"Very well, miss." He nodded and departed.

Miss Grimswell stared at the table, a flush on her cheeks. Her black hair had come loose, and a wisp covered the white nape of her neck above the black collar of the dress. She smoothed another strand out of her face.

Holmes finished his brandy and set down the glass. He looked around the library. It was a large room, and unlike the rest of the house, there was no sign of black granite except for the fireplace. The bookshelves rose almost to the ceiling, a good ten feet high. Oak stained dark had been used extensively—the shelves, paneling near the windows, the large table and sturdy chairs, the nearby desk. The chair seats and backs were covered with burgundy-colored leather, and the room itself smelled faintly of that leather, the book bindings and tobacco. Several pipes were mounted over the fireplace. The carpet was a Persian design of many dark colors. It was a cozy room with a distinctly masculine aura, no doubt a favorite of her father's.

"Mr. Holmes, thank you so much for coming, but…" Abruptly she broke off her words and covered her eyes with her large white hand. "Oh Lord, I don't know what to do."

Holmes glanced at me, his eyes pained. I knew he was reserved about touching others, especially women. I set my hand on her shoulder. She bit at her lip, her hand still covering her eyes. "When did you last eat?" I asked.

She was silent for a few seconds. "I don't know."

I looked at Holmes. "She needs food and sleep."

"She shall have them. Miss Grimswell, we can talk after you have eaten and rested. You need not tell me anything until then. Would you care to take supper downstairs with your cousin or…?" Her hand dropped, and she shook her head wildly. "If you would care to dine alone…"

Again she shook her head, her eyes open wide. "No, no—please do not leave me alone. I can bear it no longer."

"We will be happy to keep you company while you dine here."

She smiled at us, the care and strain briefly lifting. "Oh, thank you. That would be wonderful." She lowered her gaze. "He does not bother me when others are around. Not yet."

"Who does not bother you?" Holmes asked.

She stared at him and gave her head a quick shake.

"As you wish. Henry, could you see about having some food sent up? Perhaps I shall see if I can get a fire going. Are you not cold, Miss Grimswell?"

"I am freezing."

"That is easily remedied."

I went to the door, stepped into the hallway and started slightly. Fitzwilliams was standing next to the door, arms folded. Recovering, I said, "Could you have some food brought up for Miss Rose?"

"Yes. My missus might be against it, but I cannot see letting the poor girl go hungry just because she will not come down. Why would a young girl want to sit at the table and have all our dried-up old faces staring at her?" He gave a gruff laugh, then started for the stairs.

I stepped forward, set my hands on the oaken rail and stared down at the hall below. Constance Grimswell was talking with the footman, but she looked up and saw me. My instinct was to leap back, but it was too late for that. She gave me a broad smile, then gathered up her skirts, turned, and started for the stairs. "Damn," I muttered. I considered a strategic retreat, but decided it was my duty to keep her at bay.

I walked down the gallery and met her at the top of the stairs. Her face was rosy from the climb, but she was still smiling. "How is the poor little lamb?"

Little? Having just tried to support this woman, her choice of words seemed ludicrous. "She will be perfectly well after she has eaten and slept."

"Do you think so, doctor? I do hope you are right. She has always been sickly. I have the constitution of an ox myself, but she takes after her poor mother, and of course the Grimswells have always had a... peculiar streak. Her father had a bad heart, and I'm sure Rose has inherited a similar defect."

"Rest assured, her heart is fine."

She blinked, her mouth briefly stiffening. "How can you be sure?"

"My wife, who is also a physician, examined her thoroughly."

Her dark brows came together although her smile did not waver. "Oh, really? That is… splendid news. But isn't it sometimes hard to judge the health of the heart? A friend of mine was always fit as a fiddle, but then one day she said her chest hurt and fell over dead."

"Anyone could tell from looking at your… cousin that she does not have a bad heart. She is far too robust and healthy looking." Constance had begun to annoy me. "Besides, heart problems are rare at her age."

"But she always had fevers, doctor, and coughs and sneezes, and she is so terribly highly strung. I have tried to tell her she must have rest, absolute rest. She must not trouble the brain with unsettling novels or too much study, nor must she exert herself. Doctor Herbert always thought so, too. Doctor Herbert was very good. He died just last year. Eighty-two years old. You must know a thing or two to live that long. Do you not think so?"

"Medicine has changed more in the last twenty or thirty years than all the previous centuries."

"But the old remedies are the best, don't you think? Won't you help me make Rose rest? She must have absolute peace of mind—nothing must disturb her—if she is to recover."

I stared at her in disbelief, but her smile was as bright as ever. She raised her big hand—it was hardly so shapely as Michelle's or Rose's, the fingers puffy-looking—and seized my arm. "I only want the best for her, and I am not sure we can trust that young man, that Lord Frederick. Now that she is home I can take good care of her—I know I can. We shall cure her, shall we not?" She tried to draw me down the hall toward the library, but I would not move.

"I hope you will explain all this to Mr. Holmes. I am so embarrassed at my rude behavior. It was not like me—you can ask anyone. I thought he had come to pester Rose. I did not want her agitated and disturbed.

She is the only family I have, and…" Her eyes glistened in the faint light. She withdrew her handkerchief and sniffled loudly. "You will explain to him, won't you? You'll tell him that I love Rose dearly. I never married, you know, and she has been exactly like a daughter."

"I shall tell him." I smiled and gently pried her hand loose.

"May I see her—may I see my dear Rose?"

"Not just yet. Perhaps later."

She rubbed at her eyes with a handkerchief. "I have been so worried about her. She has always been highly strung—did I tell you that? But the past day—she has not been herself—she has not. I do worry so. The Grimswells have not always been… I myself am cheerful always, but her father was a gloomy man. I loved Victor dearly, but it cannot be denied he was a gloomy man. Some of the Grimswells—my own sister, even…" She choked off a sob. "She hardly recognizes me! She had to be put away in a madhouse. Oh, promise me that will never happen to Rose!"

"I am sure it will not."

"Do you honestly mean that, doctor?"

"Yes."

A maid had started up the steps carrying a tray. The smell of the meat made my mouth water. I had not eaten since lunch.

"But can you be sure?"

"Miss Grimswell, I…"

"Will you not call me Constance? I realize we hardly know one another, and it is an outrageous breach of manners, but it will be very confusing otherwise because Rose is Miss Grimswell, too, and I think of her when someone calls me Miss Grimswell. I shall of course refer to you as 'doctor,' but please call me Constance."

"Certainly—and now I must really see how Sherlock and your cousin are doing."

"My niece, doctor—my niece. I am 'auntie' to her, and she is a niece to me—at least a niece—more a daughter, as I said."

"Very well, madam—Constance." I started quickly down the hall behind the maid, but Constance moved fast for an old woman and had no trouble keeping up. "And later perhaps you can see your niece."

She dabbed at her eyes with the handkerchief. "Oh, thank you, doctor, thank you! And you will explain to Mr. Holmes—you will tell him I was worried about Rose and was not myself—please beg him to forgive me."

"There is nothing to forgive, and if there were, he would gladly forgive you." I hesitated at the doorway, and she seized my arm.

"Are you not hungry yourself, doctor?"

I blinked my eyes, surprised at so reasonable a question. "Why, yes."

"Send Meg back down, and I shall have her bring up some food for you and your cousin—unless you would care to sup with me?"

"I… I… must attend to your niece."

"Yes, of course. Well, I shall have Meg bring you some food. There is more stew, but we also have some very good hams at Grimswell Hall. Its pigs were always the wonder of the land. In all of Dartmoor…"

"Anything, madam—anything. I leave it to your discretion. You are very kind."

She released my arm at last. Her smile revealed her teeth. "Thank you, doctor."

I let the maid leave—she was a tiny thing alongside Constance or Rose—then shut the door. "Lord deliver me," I muttered.

"What, Henry?" Holmes stood before a coal fire, warming his hands. The room was much less chill.

"Nothing. Miss Grimswell—Constance—begs your forgiveness for her rudeness."

Rose Grimswell looked up from a plate of stew. The smell again made me ravenous. "She means well, but she can be so… tiresome."

"Yes." I nodded emphatically.

Rose thrust her fork through a piece of meat, then chewed it slowly. Her eyes briefly met mine, then quickly looked away. "How is your wife?"

It took a second or two to realize the question was for me. "Oh, she is well. She wishes she could have come."

Rose sighed. "I wish she could have come, too. She was so very kind to me. She reminds me of Miss Lambert at school, but she is much younger and prettier. She seems so… sensible."

I laughed. "That she is."

I stepped nearer to the fire. Outside a sudden gale shook the windows, rattling the panes. Miss Grimswell dropped the fork and raised her head, her eyes opening wide.

"It is only the rain," Holmes said.

She took the fork. "I do not like the wind. It sounds somehow… lonely. It is eerie here in Dartmoor. It sounds like the cry of some beast, some–"

"It is air in motion," Holmes said.

I laughed. "What an unromantic thing to say."

Rose ate her stew. "Mrs. Fitzwilliams says it is the souls of the damned crying out, an echo of their misery." She picked up a piece of bread. "I do not mind the wind during the day, but at night…" She shook her head. "I do dread the night."

"There is nothing to be frightened of," I said.

A laugh slipped out, twisting her mouth, and the fear was obvious in her eyes.

"If you are having trouble sleeping, I can give you something that will help."

Holmes set one hand on the table and put the other in his pocket.

The light from the fire gave his face an orange cast. "Perhaps I shall have a maid sit with you for a while as you fall asleep."

Rose eased her breath out. "Oh, thank you. I'd give anything for a good night's sleep. When you are tired, so tired, it is difficult to think clearly."

"I think you will sleep tonight," I said. "However, the maid and I shall sit with you for a while, and if you have difficulty, I shall prepare a sleeping draft."

She swallowed the last of her bread. Already she looked better. "I can face anything after a good night's sleep."

Holmes smiled. "Even Lord Frederick?" He glanced at me. "I have prepared her for another visitor."

She laughed. "Even him." She took a drink of water, then ran her tongue across her lips. Her plate was empty. "My poor Rickie."

Five

ꙅ

Rose Grimswell fell asleep almost as soon as her head touched the pillow. I had suspected she would. The body has a way of making its needs felt, and natural sleep was better than that produced by opiates. I asked the maid to sit with her for a while, then I took a candle and stepped into the hall.

Two doors down was Holmes's room, the door ajar. He was seated before the fireplace, pipe in hand, a volume on his lap. The room was enormous and beautifully furnished, another plush carpet like that in the library, the design remarkably fine with a myriad of colors. The four-poster bed, a bookcase, the small table and chairs were all constructed of oak stained very dark. Pipes were also mounted here above the mantel. This must have been Victor Grimswell's room. It was situated at a corner of the edifice, with large windows on two adjacent walls.

"Ah, Henry, have a seat. I fear I have already claimed the most comfortable chair."

By the fireplace were two chairs covered with dark red leather. I pulled the smaller one about. Holmes's had large rounded arms and appeared big enough to hold almost anyone who was not a true giant. A chunk of coal glowed on the grate, and Holmes had his feet up on the ottoman. He still wore his heavy tweed suit and brown boots, but he had loosened his collar and cravat.

He exhaled a cloud of pungent smoke. "Victor Grimswell had excellent taste in pipes. Each one is a treasure, as is the tobacco. It puts my shag to shame." He slipped the stem between his lips. "I suppose there are some who would hesitate to smoke a dead man's pipe, but any man who owned such a collection would want them to be used. A good pipe must not be shut up in a trunk or cupboard."

"This is his room, then—or rather, *was* his room."

"Yes." Holmes smiled. "You seem to suggest by your use of verb tense that a dead man cannot possess a room."

"I think not."

"Even if he is a predatory ghost?" His smile was ironic, but I frowned. "Forgive me. It was an idle jest. I am fatigued."

I withdrew my watch and opened the cover. The hands showed five past nine, but Michelle's portrait in miniature caught my eye. She had given it to me after we were married, mostly in jest, saying it was to remind me of my matrimonial bond. She might have gone to bed by now. She wore a flannel nightgown to bed, but underneath it was none of the usual complicated paraphernalia of female undergarments, only her smooth, strong body. I eased out my breath, then snapped shut the case and slipped the watch into my waistcoat pocket.

Holmes's gray eyes watched me. "Amorous thoughts, Henry?"

I actually blushed. "I hate it when you do that."

"Forgive me. I know Michelle's picture is there, and your eyes give you away. Deduction had little to do with it. I should have allowed you the privacy of your thoughts, especially since it is I who dragged you away from her."

"I was not dragged—I wanted to come."

"Thank you all the same." The mocking smile returned. "If I had been alone this evening I fear I would have dropped Miss Grimswell. I could never have held her up without your help."

"One would hesitate before carrying her over the threshold. I tried picking up Michelle once in jest. She is probably some twenty-five pounds lighter than Rose, and I still wrenched my back in the process. Luckily, one is not often asked to haul women about." I yawned. "I cannot believe it is only nine. It feels like it should be at least midnight."

He nodded. The rain had stopped, but we could hear the low, distant cry of the wind outside on the moor. "I agree. Oh, while you were occupied, I spoke with Miss Grimswell—Constance, as she insisted I call her."

"And you have escaped to tell me about it?"

He nodded, the pipe between his lips, then withdrew it. "A charming woman. She works very hard at being disagreeably agreeable. And she begged for my forgiveness. I saw no sign of sarcasm or insincerity. To the contrary, she was so abject in her misery that I cannot believe in it."

"She is rather eccentric. The Grimswells are an odd bunch from what we have seen of them. Of course, with Miss—with Rose, there may be some explanation."

"Constance has assured me we are welcome to stay as long as we wish—until I can unravel the threads of the mystery, as she put it. She was less happy when I told her Lord Frederick is arriving tomorrow, but when I agreed he might not be a suitable husband for Rose, she grew more cheerful."

I shook my head. "A harmless old busybody. I suppose this obsessive interest in Rose is understandable, since she has no other relations or children of her own."

"Except a sister."

"Oh, yes. She said something about her being in a madhouse. She worries the same thing might happen to Rose. I tried to assure her that it would not." I put my hand over my mouth, stifling a yawn. "I am about ready to turn in myself."

"I suppose we must wait until tomorrow to question the Fitzwilliamses and the staff. Have you met the old woman, Mrs. Fitzwilliams? She is remarkable. Fitzwilliams is the house steward and has been with the Grimswells for over fifty years. He became steward some forty years ago when Victor's father, Robert, was still alive and viscount. Victor inherited the title and the hall in sixty-eight when his father died."

"I wonder what his father died of."

"I did ask Fitzwilliams that question—heart failure."

I shook my head. "Bad hearts and melancholy minds. A difficult legacy. No wonder Constance is uneasy."

Holmes drew in on the pipe, shrugging his shoulders as he did so. "Every family has its share of lunatics and drunkards. A melancholy disposition has been common in both the Verniers and the Holmeses. As for bad hearts, some 'bad' thing must kill us all in time."

I laughed, then yawned. "Are you not tired?"

"Yes, but I wish to think for a while. You do appear ready for bed."

"I am, but it would require too much effort to get there. I shall sit here enjoying the fire for a while longer."

Holmes only nodded, the pipe stem between his lips. The wind was a constant, steady murmur. Perhaps the hall was situated such that the wind always blew here. I shifted in the chair and closed my eyes.

The vistas I had seen earlier in the day passed before my eyes, the English countryside seen from the train, green fields and woods full of the brown, yellow and crimson of autumn, then the brown wastes of the moor with the desolate gray sky hanging overhead. My mind wandered, returned to Grimswell Hall and the library. Rose Grimswell stared at me, her pale face surrounded by darkness. She would fall. I started, my body jerking as I tried to catch her. I came awake briefly, taking in the dim room and Holmes smoking the pipe, and then I slept.

Later I was staring at an ancient oak tree, its limbs gnarled and black. Something was in the tree, but I could not see it. A predatory ghost? No, it was only a raven, an enormous black bird on the lowest limb. It gave the strange guttural cry so different from the caw of the rook. Its eyes were curiously alert. "Henry." Had the bird spoken? "Henry." It had!

I opened my eyes, and it took a second or two to remember where I was. Holmes's face was close to mine, reddish light bathing him, and his strong fingers gripped my wrist. The coal on the grate was smaller.

"What time is it?"

"Do not move, but look in the doorway."

I turned slowly. A figure in white stood there, the face in shadow. Rose Grimswell, I realized with a start. Gone was the usual black dress. She looked so different in the long white nightshirt, and her hair was down. She was so tall, and although her face was hidden in shadow, the black hair fell on either side, spilling out onto the white cloth. I was about to rise, but Holmes squeezed my wrist again.

"What on earth is she doing?" I whispered.

"I do not know."

"How long has she been there?"

"I am not certain. Let me handle this."

She had not moved, although she must have heard our voices. The room was absolutely silent except for the low cry of the wind and the occasional rattling sound of something up the chimney. The figure advanced a step, but her bare foot made not a sound on the carpet. The back of my neck felt oddly cold, and I resisted the temptation to jump up out of the chair.

"What does she want?" I whispered.

"Keep still."

She sighed softly, then came closer so that her face was finally in the firelight. She appeared to be staring past us at the fireplace. Her eyes were wide open, her mouth parted ever so slightly. Her black hair was all tousled and cascaded awkwardly about. Her appearance was so different with her hair down. With that wild unkempt mane, the long nose and jaw, the thick lips, broad shoulders and full bosom, she resembled some woman in a pre-Raphaelite painting, one of Rossetti or Burne-Jones's sensual damsels. The shape, the weight, of her breasts was evident under the cotton fabric. Her large white hands hung at her sides, and her bare feet were also white and big, her ankles and wrists oddly slender. I had not realized before then just how beautiful she really was. However, the expression on her face—or rather, the lack of expression—worried me. Her stare was vacant, as if she could not see or hear us.

Perhaps she is mad, I thought. "My God," I whispered. "She—"

Holmes's hand tightened, his eyes angry.

"Why do you hate me so?" Her voice was dull, yet anguished. "I love you. I have never done anything to you."

I opened my mouth, but Holmes squeezed again, his face warning me not to move.

"Please tell me why." She was silent, her eyes fixed on the same spot. "*Please.*"

I realized I was holding my breath and eased it out. This must be a hallucination—she saw someone or something standing there before the fire. She was talking to it. The sight of her staring at the empty air made the back of my neck feel colder still.

She raised her arms, her long fingers opening up, spreading out. "Please forgive me, whatever..." The pathos in her voice was heart-wrenching. "Did you never love me, not even a little? I always tried to please you, and I thought…" Her arms slowly sank, her hands forming fists as she advanced closer still. She was only a few feet away, but she did not appear to even see us.

"Oh, please, father–please… All I have ever wanted was for you to…"

She was talking to a dead man–or his ghost. Perhaps because she was his daughter, only she could see him. Now that truly was superstitious nonsense.

"Why must you torture me!" Her voice rang out. "Please stop it–please. You say such hateful things. I cannot understand. I had thought… I had thought you had come to care for me, at last. But I must have been wrong. I was a fool. Nobody could love me–not you–not Digby." She turned her head to stare at another spot about three feet away. "Is it you, Rickie? You do not love me either. Do not try to deny it–I am not so stupid. You think because I… You think you can get away with anything. You *cannot.*"

She turned away from both her imaginary beings. "I am so sick of it all. What is the point of any of it? Why should I feel so terrible? I have done nothing…" Abruptly she turned her head. "What is…? Why are you staring at me that way? You… you would not hurt me? Please stop that. You are frightening me. You are so pale. That is not your face at all–you are not my father–you are something else, something wicked, and you hate me."

Her voice had grown increasingly loud and fearful. She raised her hands again. "Please stop–before it is too late. Don't hurt me–please don't hurt me–oh, I cannot bear it when you look like that! For God's sake–do not…" Her eyes had opened wide, and she grasped the bottom of her face, covering her mouth with her big hand.

I could stand it no longer. I stood, but she still did not see me. Holmes grabbed my wrist. "Keep silent," he hissed.

"But she must be completely insane! She should be restrained before–"

"She is not insane–have you never heard of somnambulism?" he whispered.

"I…" Suddenly it all fit into place, and I felt a complete idiot. "Of course. Sleepwalking. But she is about to have a nightmare. We must wake her."

"That could be difficult and might make her worse. Leave this to me."

"Oh, dear Lord–please stop that–please…"

"Miss Grimswell, pay no attention to that thing there." Holmes's voice was loud, but oddly gentle. "It is not your father, and it cannot hurt you."

She did not move for several seconds. "It is not him?"

"Of course not. He is fond of you. He is no such monster."

She still regarded the same spot. "Are you sure it cannot hurt me?"

"Yes."

She turned to look at us. Although she appeared, finally, to see us, something was still curiously vacant in her stare. "Who are you?"

"I am Sherlock Holmes. Do you not remember me?"

She stepped closer to him. "Sherlock Holmes."

"Yes, the famous detective. You have read all of my adventures. You know how remarkably clever I am–how I am never wrong." I could hear the irony in his voice. "I am your friend, Miss Grimswell, and I have figured it all out. That is not your father. That is someone else, someone evil. Your father loves you."

"Oh, does he? Are you… are you certain of that?"

Holmes hesitated only a second. "Yes."

"Oh, thank God–thank God." Her voice shook with emotion.

I smiled sadly and murmured, "Poor girl."

"He is going away," Holmes said. "Do you see? We have frightened him away."

She turned back to where the imaginary father had been, then smiled. "Yes. He is gone."

"And now we must go back to your room," he said. "You must go to bed. You must…" She was smiling at him, her arms at her sides, but she had not moved. He stepped closer, reached out and touched her arm. They were the same height, Holmes a tall, slight figure in his dark suit, she so obviously a woman under the white nightshirt. "We must…"

She stepped nearer and grasped both his arms above the elbows with her large white hands. "I love you," she whispered fiercely.

I have never seen Holmes so completely surprised, so utterly astonished. He said nothing for a few seconds. "I–this is Sherlock Holmes."

"I know." She released him, then unfastened the top button of her nightshirt and thrust her dark hair back over her shoulders, letting her head fall back and her breasts thrust forward. Her collarbone and the long expanse of her throat were tinted orange by the firelight. Holmes glanced at me, his eyes wide, but before he could speak or move, she threw her arms about him and drew him to her.

"Miss Grimswell!" he exclaimed.

One hand touched the back of his neck, the other had him low about the waist. She pressed her cheek against the side of his face. Her eyes were closed, but she was smiling. "I am yours," she whispered. "Take me."

I stepped sideways. Holmes's eyes were desperate. "Wake her, Henry–wake her at once."

I coughed once, then said, "Miss Grimswell, this is Doctor Vernier."

"Go away," she murmured.

"This is… this is your physician speaking. You cannot… This is hardly… You must leave my examining room. Everyone is staring at you. This is hardly the place, my dear young lady. Whatever are you doing? And you have no clothes on."

"For God's sake, Henry!" Holmes said.

Abruptly she released him, then stepped back and raised her hands awkwardly. "Where are my clothes?"

"Here they are, but why are you wearing only a nightshirt?"

"I..." She stared ahead, then covered her mouth. "I don't know."

"You must have forgotten to dress this morning. It is a common mistake. Actually, you belong in bed. We must leave my examining room and get you back to bed."

"Oh, yes—thank you." Her hand reached out and seized mine. Michelle had powerful hands, but hers were stronger yet.

Holmes drew in his breath, then stepped warily back and collapsed into the chair. He was still staring at her.

"Come with me," I whispered to him. "It may take two of us to get her back to bed."

He stood without saying a word. I led her to the door, her hand still in mine. "And here is my wife, Doctor Doudet Vernier. You remember Michelle, Miss Grimswell. She likes you very much. She has brought you a robe, and she is putting it on you."

Rose Grimswell was quiet after that, but I kept up a constant stream of inane chatter. We went down the hallway to her bedroom. The maid Meg was snoring loudly on the sofa. "Your legs feel very weary, do they not? It would be very pleasant to lie down. And it is cold—so very cold."

"Yes," she murmured.

I drew aside the covers, and she lay on her side, her nightshirt rising to show her bare, slender calves and ankles. I hesitated, then touched her white foot. The skin was icy cold. "You are freezing." Quickly I drew the blankets over her. It was a relief to have her covered up. "It is good to lie still, to be warm and comfortable, and know that all is well.

No one will trouble you now, and you will sleep peacefully."

She smiled gently at me. "Thank you, Henry."

I gave a deep sigh, then turned to Holmes. He had mostly recovered, a tenuous smile pulling at his lips. "Very good, Henry—very good indeed."

We quietly left the room, then returned to his chamber and sank into the leather chairs. Neither of us looked at one another. At last I mumbled, "It is a good thing we are both honorable men."

Holmes gazed at me. A long strand of hair had come loose and curved down to touch his cheekbone. "Yes."

"She is... quite a vision."

"Yes."

"I am a married man, but I must admit..." I shook my head. "She is certainly strong for a woman."

Holmes stared at the fireplace. "She did not embrace you. Her grip..." He gave a great sigh, then shook his head. "No matter. Her words were rather illuminating."

"I thought for sure she was insane. How did you know it was somnambulism?"

"I have seen such cases before. The popular notion is that sleepwalkers go about with their eyes closed, their arms extended. They do not. Their eyes are open—hence they will not walk into walls or off cliffs—but they are, nevertheless, asleep. Everything appears to them as a dream, both reality and the fantasies of the mind."

I shook my head. "How very odd." I yawned, covering my mouth with my hand. "I felt so bad for her. Her dreams were so sad. Both her father and Digby scorned her. She wanted so much for them to care for her."

Holmes said nothing, but three lines creased his forehead. The wind was still blowing; it had never stopped. At last he stood. "I could use a nightcap."

"I, too—what a wonderful suggestion! Then I am going straight to bed." I pulled out my watch. "Twelve-fifteen—no wonder I am tired."

Holmes took a candle. "Someone may be awake downstairs, but if not, I saw a sideboard in the great hall with all the makings of a whisky and soda." He stepped into the hall, then stopped so abruptly I almost walked into him.

Before us stood George the footman. He looked as surprised to see us as we were to see him. A very tall fellow with a lean face, his blond hair combed straight back, he had a ready smile which soon reappeared. He was still wearing his black morning coat and striped trousers.

"Good evening, gentlemen. I was... Miss Grimswell wanted me to look in on you and see if you were asleep or if you required anything. I also wanted to see how Meg and the young mistress are doing." His voice was as amiable as his face, and by the sound of it, he was from London, not Dartmoor.

Holmes stared at him without speaking. At last he said, "And do you see in the dark, Mr...?"

"Just call me George—everyone does, sir." He laughed. "I could make my way about the house blindfolded, but there's a bit of light coming from the room." He pointed past us, where a dim splash of yellow light pooled out before the open door to Rose's room.

"And why have you removed your boots?"

I glanced down, and sure enough, he was in his stockinged feet. His smile wavered for only an instant. His nose had a slight curve to it, no doubt having been broken at some time. "Boots with pointed toes are a misery, sir. As it's rather late, I slipped them off."

Holmes stared silently. "Well, the maid is asleep, so you had best let her be, and we are going downstairs for a nightcap."

He nodded. "Very good, sir. Let me get the drinks for you." He turned and started down the narrow hallway.

Holmes frowned at me, his face illuminated by the flickering light of the candle, his large black shadow cast on the wall behind him.

The hallway opened up on the side above the great hall as we left one wing of the house. We walked down the stairs, then crossed that dark, empty cavern, its black granite walls hidden from us. Somehow I felt like an archaeologist inside some colossal mausoleum or ancient pyramid.

In the distance a dark, wavery figure approached–Constance Grimswell in her black dress, a white lace cap covering her gray hair. Her voice boomed out: "Still up, Mr. Holmes? It is so late. And you, doctor? I hope the beds are not amiss."

"No," Holmes said. "We were conversing and thought we would descend and have something to drink before retiring."

"A splendid idea! May I join you?" She was near enough now we could see her pink, smiling face.

Holmes shrugged. "We are your guests, madam. Of course you may join us."

"Thank you, Mr. Holmes."

We stopped before the sideboard. "What would you like?" George asked.

"A whisky and soda," Holmes said.

George opened the bottle, poured about an inch, then pressed the gasogene, filling the glass with soda. Holmes had set down the candle on the sideboard. He took the drink. George stared at me. By the candlelight his face was pale, his smile strange; Constance's smiling face also appeared bizarre, almost an echo of his–a mirage, as if I were seeing double.

"I shall have the same," I said.

Constance nodded. "And I."

I sipped the drink. It was quite strong, the whisky excellent. Holmes was staring at Constance. "You are also up late, madam."

"Ah, Mr. Holmes, it is hard being an old woman. I do not sleep well, not like I used to. I suffer from rheumatism, and it also keeps me awake. Then there was all this excitement today, your arrival, and my usual worries about Rose. How is she, poor lamb?"

I lowered my glass. "She fell asleep almost at once. She was exhausted."

Constance shook her head. "I wish I knew what ailed her! Well, it is a blessing that she is asleep at last. I suppose Meg can come down now."

Holmes turned his glass, sloshing the liquid gently. "Meg is asleep and, tiny as she is, quite comfortable on the sofa. I think she should remain there. I also find it difficult to sleep, and I will be checking on your niece throughout the night."

"How kind you are, Mr. Holmes! But don't you need your rest?"

"I require very little sleep, madam." He took a swallow of whisky.

It was quieter in the hall, the wind muted and more distant. "Well, I rarely have trouble sleeping," I said. "And I am going to bed straight away."

Constance gave her head another shake. "How good of you to stay up so late and take such an interest in Rose! I am so happy to have a competent physician under our roof. I did so like old Doctor Herbert, but this young doctor now... I wish Victor had gone to see the heart specialist on Harley Street. I begged him to, but he would not listen. He could be very stubborn–just like Rose. Anyway, now that you are here, doctor, Rose may at last be cured."

Holmes finished his drink and set down the glass. George raised the bottle. "Another, sir?"

"No, thank you. Tell me, Miss Grimswell..."

"Constance, Mr. Holmes–remember?" The corners of her mouth stayed fixed in the smile even as she spoke.

"Tell me, do you recall...? Lady Rupert mentioned something

about your niece wandering about in her sleep, a condition known as somnambulism. Has she ever…?"

Constance set down her glass (she had finished the drink very quickly) and nodded. "I do remember that. As a child she used to walk in her sleep all the time. Victor often found her before his bed in the middle of the night. He said it scared him half to death, this small pale girl in her white nightgown standing silently before his bed. I thought she had outgrown it."

"She…" I began, then noticed Holmes staring intently at me. "She probably has. It is more common among children." I finished my drink and glanced at George. "Thank you for the drink."

Holmes picked up the candle. "It was gracious of you to oblige us so late at night. Constance, how long have you been at Grimswell Hall? You did not live here before Victor's death, I believe."

"No, I did not. I have been here since Victor's tragic end. I told Rose it would not do for a young lady to be alone and unchaperoned. Of course, she has spent the whole time away from my watchful eye in London, but then, Lady Rupert is certainly to be trusted. You have met her, Mr. Holmes. Don't you think she is to be trusted with a young lady's well-being?"

"Absolutely. And now we must say goodnight. Henry will fall asleep on the spot at any moment, and I too am fatigued."

Constance raised her large puffy hand and smoothed a gray curl back over her ear. "I shall be going to bed soon, too. I hope you find the beds comfortable. There are extra blankets and pillows in the wardrobes."

"We shall be most comfortable, madam. Thank you, George."

The footman nodded, still grinning. We left them and walked into the black gloom. When we reached the stairs, I turned. The flickering candle was visible, but not their faces. Neither Holmes nor I spoke until we had reached the top of the stairs. Beneath us, we heard footsteps, mumbled words, and a burst of female laughter.

"It is cold," I said. "The great hall is an icy cave."

"Heating such a vast space would be an impossibility."

Holmes stepped into my room, and lit a candle by the bedside table. There was no fireplace or fire here, and it was even colder than in the hall.

"Are you really going to stay up most of the night?" I asked.

"I doubt it, but I shall check on Miss Grimswell frequently." His mouth formed a brief ironic smile. "And if she appears in my room again, I shall come fetch you. You certainly handled her better than I."

I laughed. "I can understand how you must have felt. I was surprised, but she did not actually embrace me. All the same, you were not so disturbed as I by her behavior. Until you spoke, I was convinced she was mad. Well, if it happens again, at least we shall be prepared."

He gave a short, soft laugh. "Yes, we shall be prepared. Goodnight, Henry. Sleep well."

I undressed as quickly as I could in the freezing room, put on my nightshirt, then slipped between the icy sheets and wrapped the blankets and quilts about me. I closed my eyes, but although I was tired out, I could not sleep. My mind would not rest.

Sleeping in a strange bed was always difficult the first night, and sleeping alone had also become difficult. I missed the warmth of Michelle. I liked to reach out with my hand or foot and touch her. I especially liked running my hand down the long curve of her back and her flank. My feet were cold and would not seem to warm up, and now I was conscious of that dull moan of the wind. It probably never did stop. Periodically the window rattled, as if some large moor creature were blowing at the panes.

I remembered suddenly the opening of Charlotte Brontë's novel, *Wuthering Heights*, where the narrator is sleeping in a musty old room on a stormy night. In a dream, a young girl's ghost appears at the window and begs him to let her in. He refuses, and then, for some reason, he viciously rubs her arm back and forth against some broken glass. It was only a novel, I told myself, only a story. Gradually I managed to relax.

Rose Grimswell's face appeared in the darkness, white with black hair billowing about her in the wind. I started, then realized I had begun to dream. The room was quiet and dim with only the flickering candle. What if she appeared in my room? What would I do?

I recalled her bare white legs as she lay in the bed before I covered her. Her foot was so large, the toes long like her fingers. I wondered what she would look like under the gown—quite beautiful, certainly—then caught myself and felt guilty at such thoughts. I knew quite well what Michelle looked like under her gown, all those hidden curves and lovely places. A wave of restless longing washed over me, and I turned onto my other side. Such thoughts will not help you get to sleep, I reflected.

The window rattled again. "I wish I had never come to Dartmoor," I muttered softly. I stretched out my legs, then curled and uncurled my toes. My feet were still cold.

Six

My dreams were troubled that night, haunted by a tall woman in a white nightgown lurking in the darkness. Sometimes the woman was Michelle, then she was Rose Grimswell; sometimes she was in deadly peril, pursued by some black creature with a white face; sometimes she smiled and beckoned to me with her long, shapely arms. Toward morning, the dreams became embarrassingly vivid. At last I opened my eyes.

The dim sound of the wind was still present, but through a gap in the curtains shone a long, thin line of dazzling yellow light. I fumbled about for my watch on the bedside table. Half-past eight—later than I usually slept. The room seemed cold and bleak, but the light at the window promised a better day.

I rose, shivered at the shock of the cold air, then clasped my arms about me and went to the window. The front of the house had many trees, but this was the rear side where one saw only the weathered brown moor stretching off for about fifty yards, until it began the rise to the jumble of black granite set against a brilliant blue sky—Demon

Tor. Even the sinister name could not mute the desolate beauty of the scene under golden autumnal light. Man could assign names to the works of nature, but they were only that, only names, mere words. The tor had existed in wild splendor before men had walked the moors, and it would probably exist after our cities and empire had collapsed and crumbled, even as those of Egypt or Rome.

I shaved, and dressed quickly, putting on a heavy tweed suit and walking boots, then descended to the hall. Fitzwilliams seemed to be waiting for me. His thin, aged face was clean and pink, the scab of a slight nick showing at the side of his jaw where he must have cut himself shaving. "Mr. Holmes is in the breakfast room—this way, sir."

The hall seemed less forbidding in the daytime. Huge windows let the bright morning light spill upon its granite floor and the dark wooden furniture. Fitzwilliams opened a door. "Here we are, sir."

I blinked my eyes in astonishment. This was a bright, cheerful room which belonged in a London townhouse. There was none of the primordial black granite or massiveness of the great hall. Above the wainscoting was a yellow wallpaper with a bronze and red pattern. The colors in the room were all yellow, gold, cream, brown or red, and delicate lace curtains hung on either side of the many windows. Outside were trees, their reddish-brown leaves moving in the breeze. The odor of an armada of food set upon the sideboard assailed my nostrils, the typical overabundance of an English country breakfast.

Holmes sat at the table, his cup and saucer on the fine linen tablecloth. Beside him was a tiny woman in a black dress, her white hair in a bun. She turned upon me a pair of piercing black eyes. They might be faintly cloudy—cataracts, no doubt—and age might have dulled their fire, but they were remarkable, all the same. In the days of Greece or Rome, she would have been an oracle or sibyl, one of those women through whom the gods spoke.

"Ah, Henry, do join us. This is Mrs. Prudence Fitzwilliams, the housekeeper and another devoted servant of the Grimswells for over fifty years. We have been discussing the family. Madam, this is my cousin and friend, Doctor Henry Vernier, a physician from London."

I nodded. "A pleasure to meet you, Mrs. Fitzwilliams."

She stared closely at me, her eyes struggling to focus upon my face. Besides cataracts, she might be near-sighted. The corners of her mouth slowly rose. "He's handsome enough, anyway."

Holmes laughed, and the old woman released a single sharp hiss of breath. I smiled. "You flatter me, madam."

"I like a man with a big mustache. William had a black mustache when I first met him."

Holmes took a sip of coffee. "There is plenty of food to fill a plate. Do so and join us."

The smells made me realize how hungry I was. All the same, enough food for ten men was set out. I raised several silver lids, took some scrambled eggs, bacon and toast, and shuddered slightly at the kippers. I cannot abide fish for breakfast. Pulling out a chair, I sat across from Mrs. Fitzwilliams.

She seized a cane, then slowly started to rise. "You'll want coffee, I suppose."

Holmes stood. "Allow me." He took a cup and saucer from the sideboard, then poured from a silver pot which had been sitting upon a flickering flame.

With a sigh, Mrs. Fitzwilliams had collapsed back into her seat. "I am the servant here, not you, sir, but thank you. I don't get around so well any longer, as you can see." She shook her head, a flash of anger showing in her eyes. "I have not been upstairs in two years now. All those steps. They are too much for an old woman."

Holmes set the cup and saucer before me. "I too thank you," I said.

He nodded, then sat down. "You should let the blond servant carry you upstairs, madam. He looks strong enough."

"I'll not let him touch me."

Holmes's gray eyes watched her. "You do not care for George?"

"Not I. He's an idle fellow, and one that cannot keep his hands off the girls. Perhaps it would serve him right to have to hoist up an old crone like me." She laughed, a dry brittle sound. "I'm happy enough down here. Nothing up there but beds to be made and rooms to be cleaned. All the same…" Her eyes shifted upward. "I'd like to see the Tower of Babel again someday."

Holmes's forehead creased. "The Tower of Babel?"

"Lord Grimswell's tower—the one he had built about fifteen years ago. You can see for miles and miles around on a sunny day like this. Of course, even ten years ago it wore a body out getting up there. All those steps! How is the bacon?"

Her black eyes were peering at me. Even her eyebrows were absolutely white. "Very good," I said.

"One of our tenant's pigs. His hams are wonderful, too. Lord Grimswell used to say he had never tasted better in any of his travels. That and the whortleberries were his favorites. He loved whortleberries even as a little boy." Another dry laugh. "Although he was never really little—six and a half feet tall he grew to be, with black hair and eyes. But he loved whortleberries, especially in a pie or tart." Her mouth slowly opened into a smile; she still had all her teeth. "I had cook make him a pie, the summer before last. When he was a boy, he'd get the juice all over his face and hands, but if he got his clothes dirty he was punished. Nasty bluish-purplish stains they make, a mess especially on white cloth."

Holmes had set one hand upon the table and leaned back in the chair. "From what you told me earlier, I take it he was a good master."

"He was…" Her voice had a tentative note. She stared down at her gnarled hands, the skin covered with kidney-colored spots. "He left every servant a generous gift. For William and me, a thousand pounds apiece. Can you imagine such a fortune? Not a servant went without something. Even George got his hundred pounds. And he said in his will William and me was always to have a home here at the hall, even should we no longer be able to work." She blinked several times, her eyes glistening, but even tears seemed an effort. "A kind man always, but a troubled man, a man that could not or would not control his thoughts. And we know where that leads."

"Where is that, madam?" Holmes asked.

"To the Devil, of course. One should not sit about all day thinking. It's true what they say about an idle mind being the Devil's workshop. All sorts of strange things will pop into your mind if you let them. That's one benefit to being one of the working folk rather than a master. We be so busy, we don't have time to worry and fret."

I swallowed a mouthful of eggs and set down my fork. "Do you truly believe the Devil can influence men for worse?"

Her eyes opened wide. "Surely. Only a fool doesn't believe in the Devil. His handiwork is everywhere."

Holmes's laugh was gruff, nearly mute. "It is indeed. One can argue that his presence is much more clearly manifest than that of the deity."

She gave him a puzzled look. "I know what I've seen. Only last week the groom Ned had a fury come upon him. He would have beat the old brown cob to death had George not pulled him away. A madness came on him. He beats his wife, too. It was the Devil—anyone could see that. I had William let him go. We all have to fight the Devil, but Ned seemed to welcome him. And Lord Grimswell, sitting up late at night in his tower, his mind melancholy and desperate to start with. Might as well hang out a signboard welcoming Old Scratch." She shook her head.

"Oh, he fought the Devil—he wrestled with him, but in the end…" Her voice faded away, but her eyes still burned.

I pushed my plate away, my appetite suddenly gone. Holmes watched her closely. "You think the Devil won?"

She hesitated, then sighed wearily. "I hope not, but it was Demon Tor, after all, a cursed place if ever there was one. Many's the time I tried to tell him 'ware of the cursed place, but he would only laugh at me. I pray he did not jump."

"In the end, I'm not sure it matters much either way," I said.

"Do you know nothing, young man? Are you some pagan heathen?"

I shook my head, reflecting that an agnostic was probably a pagan heathen in her book.

"If he jumped, he is damned for sure. Even now the eternal fires'd burn his flesh, while all about the wretches howl and writhe. Hell has a deadly stench, icy winds and fiery ones, and the understanding that you must suffer forever—that it will never end—makes the pain and fear even worse." Her voice shook slightly, and I felt something like dread coalescing about my heart. Her eyes glistened and her head sank. "I pray it is not so."

"The man who drove us here yesterday was reluctant to be caught on the moor after dark," Holmes said. Mrs. Fitzwilliams raised her head but said nothing. "I suspect there are tales about a man in black wandering…"

"There are always such tales! I heard them as a girl. Spirits… spirits have always wandered at night on the moors, ghosts and… worse. There are the damned, of course, and minor devils who wish to ensnare others, and also those poor souls trapped between Heaven and Hell. They must wander for many a year to atone for their sins, but at least they are not truly damned. They will have peace at last." Her brown eyes gazed out the window at the trees, but she seemed to see some other place. "They are not… hungry."

"*Hungry?*" I said.

"Sometimes the dead feast on the living, but though they may eat flesh or drink blood, it is souls they desire." Her eyes had not moved. "Then the victims become wanderers themselves, though good people be not truly cursed. They will be saved in the end."

A smile played about Holmes's lips—a humorless one. "Sometimes the living feast on the dead. They would steal from the dead—or from the living."

The old woman stared at him, her face grim. "That's true enough."

"Miss Grimswell—Rose Grimswell—does not seem to think her father jumped."

Mrs. Fitzwilliams's mouth twisted about. "The girl is a fool—but it's not her fault. Why should she have gone to all those schools and been encouraged to…? Her father should have found the girl a husband. He seemed to want her to end up like him. Too much thinking isn't good for a body. It's not natural. We wasn't meant to sit about all day thinking strange thoughts and writing scandalous books. Lord Grimswell could have interested himself in farming and sport, like his father, but he had to be different. Look where it got him?—dead and buried. At least he didn't end up in a madhouse. I hope…" Her eyes were glistening again, and her tiny hand fumbled at a pocket for a handkerchief.

"Calm yourself, madam," Holmes said gently.

She sniffled once, then wiped feebly at her nose. "I don't want Rose to end up that way. I told her to go back to London and marry her young man. He's a marquess's son. He must amount to something. Why did she want to come back here where there's only old half-dead folks and all those memories of her poor sad father? She should go back, Mr. Holmes—before something bad happens—before… This is not a good place for her. I know it, Mr. Holmes, I know it. Please…"

Holmes laid his long fingers on her wrist. "I shall help her."

She sniffled again. "Someone needs to look after the poor silly fool, the great ninny."

"What about her aunt?" I asked.

Mrs. Fitzwilliams's jaw stiffened, even as she sat straight up and let the handkerchief fall. "What about her? Who asked her here? Tell me that, young man, tell me that!"

"Madam, I only—"

"It wasn't me, I can tell you. And she's no aunt—she's hardly a blood relation. If poor Agnes hadn't died as a child, she would be a real aunt. Lord Grimswell didn't ask Constance—he never wanted her around. He kept her away except for a few days a year. If it was me, I'd send her packing, but William is the polite one. She's a Grimswell, he says. Well, Reginald Grimswell—that accursed one—was a Grimswell, too, and I wouldn't have him under my roof. Trying to tell cook and me what should be on the menus! Her and that George, they... I'm not dead yet, and until I am, I'll run this house, not some bossy big horse who—"

"She did not arrive until after your master's death?"

She nodded. "You have that right, and then she moves in for good. Rose could throw her out, but the old hag has her completely cowed. Blood isn't everything, Mr. Holmes—not always. And Constance is *not* an aunt, not a sister. Her father was Lord Grimswell's uncle. Maybe you can tell me what that makes her—it is *not* an aunt."

"You are correct. Lord Grimswell and Constance would have been first cousins. If Constance or Jane had had children, they would have been Rose's second cousins. I don't know what exactly the relationship between Rose and Constance would be."

The old woman's mouth was a taut, curved line of disapproval as she nodded. "Not an aunt—hardly an aunt. Hardly a blood relation at all." She sighed. "I should not let her annoy me so. It isn't Christian—but she's no Christian either. I... I do worry about Rose, Mr. Holmes. I do."

"That's natural," I said.

"I was nearly sixty when she was born. Her mother was a good woman, very sweet-tempered, but the poor girl died before she was even thirty. Rose was only two. She was a pretty child and always a big one, just like her father. She was taller than me when she was ten years old. It was hard when I was already so old, but I never had a child of my own. William and me…" Her voice died away. She had the handkerchief in her hand again.

Holmes hesitated, then set his hand on her wrist again. I knew he would have been much more reluctant to touch a younger woman. Her mouth twitched into a feeble smile. "Forgive me. I get so weary with it all. Why should some people live so long–too long–while others…? Oh, I have work to do." She put her handkerchief into a pocket, seized her cane and struggled to her feet.

Holmes and I stood. "Thank you," he said. "We must talk again soon. I have a few more questions."

She smiled, her black eyes still smoldering. "I'll be here. I'm not going anywhere. Except to the grave. I suppose the good Lord must know what he's doing." She sighed again, then started for the door. "He'd better."

I could see that she had severe arthritis. The movement we took for granted must be a torment for her. She had nearly reached the door when it swung open, and Rose Grimswell stepped into the room. Although both wore black, the contrasts were striking: besides youth and age, there was the difference in size. Rose was over a foot taller, her back unbowed, her shoulders broad and strong, her face unlined, her hair black not white.

Rose smiled. "Good morning, nanna." She looked much better. Her cheeks had some color, and her blue-gray eyes were not so haunted.

"It's time you were down, girl. It's after nine."

Rose's smile faltered. "I know, but—"

"Eat your breakfast—eat a good breakfast. You've been eating like a bird, and that won't do. You'll make yourself sick."

Rose watched her leave, then smiled at us. "Good morning."

I smiled. "You slept well."

She smiled back. "Is it that obvious?"

"Yes."

"I did have a wonderful sleep. I was restless at first... I had the most curious dreams." Her eyes shifted briefly to Holmes, then back to me. "You were in one, doctor." She frowned slightly, even as a faint flush showed at her cheekbones. She turned abruptly toward the sideboard. "Oh, I am starving."

Holmes said nothing, but a faint flush also colored his cheeks.

I took a sip of coffee. It was cold. Outside I could see the wind moving the bronze leaves of the trees. Rose sat down next to me. On her plate were a muffin, three pieces of bacon, a slice of ham, a piece of kipper, some stewed tomatoes, fried potatoes, buttered toast, and a huge mound of scrambled eggs.

She noticed me regarding the plate, and the flush began again. "I suppose it seems rather greedy, but..."

I shook my head. "Not at all. Not if you have not eaten a big meal in a while. Michelle also has a hearty appetite. After all, you are not... a tiny woman."

Her mouth drew into a smile. "No, I am not." Her eyebrows were black and thick, her eyes clear and lucid, the blue more noticeable in the bright morning light. Her black hair was parted down the middle and pulled up into a tight bun, the tops of her ears hidden. She raised the sterling fork and cut off a piece of bacon.

"I am happy to see you looking so much better," Holmes said.

She smiled briefly and continued eating. A heavy silence seemed to settle over the room. I stood up. "I shall have a bit more coffee." I poured from the silver pot. "Your Mrs. Fitzwilliams is a formidable lady."

Rose nodded. "She is. She will be eighty in another year. She and William are… sweet, in their own way, although she has become so old and bitter in the last year or two. Her rheumatism hurts her so. She can hardly move any longer. When I was little, she was all over the house, everywhere, it seemed, and now… It must be hard for her."

I wondered what Rose Grimswell would look like as an old woman–not like Mrs. Fitzwilliams. Their physiques were so different. Would she be sitting at this table with an elderly Digby? A horrible thought, that. Or would she live that long? I had seen women her age laid out cold and dead, their limbs like gray-white marble, their faces waxen and pinched. She was so young, strong and alive, such a vital presence, but she could still die. I hoped Holmes was mistaken, but I knew he was not. Someone, or something, was pursuing her–blighting her young life. I could feel it, and the morning sun suddenly seemed a feeble thing.

I sipped my coffee, then eased out my breath. Frightening myself half to death would not help matters. Grimswell Hall was a gloomy place, and being away from Michelle made me morose. Yes, Mrs. Fitzwilliams was right when she warned about letting one's thoughts run away with themselves.

"I would like to take a walk on the moor," I said.

Rose smiled. "So would I."

Holmes nodded. "A stroll would be agreeable."

"I used to like to ride on the moor," Rose said.

"You are an equestrian?" Holmes asked. "I would not have expected it."

She pushed aside a bit of tomato, then speared a potato. "I would not say I was exactly an equestrian, but I have always liked horses. I took riding lessons and had my own horse for a while. I loved galloping on the moors."

"Did your father like horses?" Holmes asked.

She thought for a moment. "Not particularly. He had a cat he liked, a big black one named Melmoth."

Holmes's laugh was akin to a snort. "A clever name. Are you familiar with *Melmoth, the Wanderer*, Miss Grimswell?"

She nodded, but I said, "Well, I am not."

"Melmoth was a fictional character similar to the Wandering Jew or the Flying Dutchman." Holmes reflexively drew out his cigarette case, realized one did not smoke before young ladies, and slipped it back into his coat. "I wish I could have met your father, Miss Grimswell."

"I think you would have liked him."

Holmes tapped lightly at the table. "Miss Grimswell, I dislike reminding you, but Lord Frederick is arriving today. Before he does, I would like to speak with you about what is troubling you."

Her muted smile faded, and something weary showed in her eyes. "Very well, Mr. Holmes. I am ready, but... might I finish my breakfast first?"

Holmes shook his head. "Forgive me, miss–I should have given you a moment's peace. I have been inconsiderate. I can only ask your pardon and plead my concern for your well-being."

She set down her fork and shook her head. "There is nothing to forgive. I only..." She stared out through the window. "If you do not speak a bad thing–if you do not say it aloud–you can pretend it does not exist. I have pretended long enough. The truth cannot be denied."

"Let it wait a little longer. Perhaps we could discuss the situation while we are walking on the moor."

She gave a relieved sigh. "That would be better." She picked up her toast and put orange marmalade on it. Her blue eyes regarded me. "Doctor, you–you are coming, are you not?"

"Certainly."

"Good. I shall want to know…" A frown had creased her brow.

"There must be only cheerful and serene thoughts at the breakfast table," I said.

The door opened and Fitzwilliams appeared. Rose was preoccupied, but I noticed he was pale. "Could I see you for a moment, gentlemen? I… It will not take long." His voice was controlled, but with a quaver beyond that of age.

Holmes stood. "Certainly. That will allow Miss Grimswell to finish her breakfast."

She smiled up at us. "I shan't be long." And indeed, little remained on her plate.

We followed Fitzwilliams into the hallway, where he pulled a handkerchief from his pocket and wiped at his face. "There has been… How shall I ever tell her?"

"What has happened?" Holmes asked.

He licked his lips, then raised his arm and gnarled hand. "See…" He let it drop. "He will tell you."

"Very well." Holmes turned, then turned again. "Oh, before I am distracted, I have a request for you, sir. Would you send someone to Grimpen and arrange for a locksmith to visit here this afternoon? It is a matter of urgency. I want the door to Miss Grimswell's room adequately secured."

Fitzwilliams licked his lips, then nodded. "I shall see to it, Mr. Holmes."

"Thank you." Holmes strode forward, and I followed. Near the entranceway was a young man, his face grim. He wore a battered tweed jacket, heavy leather breeches and muddy rubber boots. He was not over six feet tall, but he was one of the broadest men I had ever met, his shoulders, chest and neck massive. His face was reddish-brown from the sun with a smattering of freckles, his thick, light brown mustache hiding his upper lip. One brawny hand held a gray cloth cap, and under his other arm was a bundle.

"Good morning, gentlemen." His voice was soft but curt.

As Holmes surveyed him, his lips drew back in dismay, but he recovered at once. "Good day," he said. "I am Sherlock Holmes, and this is my cousin, Doctor Henry Vernier."

He stared more closely at me, then smiled faintly. "I too am a doctor. John Hartwood is my name."

My eyes again took in the worn clothes, the lack of bag and his rugged physique. "Veterinary medicine?" I asked.

His smile vanished. "No. I am a medical doctor—people, not animals."

My face grew warm. "Oh, forgive me—of course. I am used to Harley Street specialists and the like. In London we dare not be seen without our frock coats. It is the regulation uniform. Here in the country it must be quite different."

"So it is."

Holmes's mouth had curved downward in disapproval as he regarded the thing under the doctor's arm, but he did not speak. I smiled awkwardly. "We are visiting Miss Grimswell, and... Do you know Miss. Grimswell?"

He gave his head half a turn. "No."

A spark of interest flared in Holmes's eyes. "Did you know her father?"

"Yes. He was my patient. And my friend." Hartwood managed to look grimmer still.

"But you have not yet met his daughter? You have settled in the area recently, doctor, perhaps in the last year or so?"

Hartwood's blue eyes were suddenly hard. "How do you come to know that?"

"By your manner of speaking. You sound like a Dartmoor man who has spent some time abroad. Edinburgh?"

"Yes, but—"

"It could not have been London, and there is only a hint of a burr. Edinburgh is well known for its medical school. You would not have met Miss Grimswell because she has not been here at the hall much in the past year." He shook his head. "An unfortunate way to have to meet a lady."

Hartwood's eyes opened wider, and his nostrils flared. I gave Holmes a puzzled look.

Holmes pointed at the bundle. "Where did you find the dog?"

My stomach gave a lurch as I realized what was in the bundle. The white cloth had reddish stains. "Not far from the hall," Hartwood said. "Just past the trees. How did you know?"

"From the look on your face, Doctor Hartwood, from Fitzwilliams's dismay, and from the size and the blood-stains."

Hartwood shrugged. "Obvious." He opened his mouth and sighed. "I was riding by. I didn't know Miss Grimswell was here. It is a bad way to meet the lady, but then I don't seem to have luck with Grimswells."

"How did the dog die?"

"Something tore out its throat, a wild dog or fox."

"May I have a look?"

"Certainly."

Holmes set the bundle on a small table and unwrapped the cloth. The once-white fur was mostly a muddy brown, wet and matted, the tiny dog quite stiff, its eyes dull. Under the chin was a bloody mess which had stained the white fabric. "Something with quite a large jaw," Holmes said. "Much bigger than a fox. A very large dog or wolf."

Hartwood gave a gruff laugh. "No wolves on the moor, not for decades."

"I know, doctor. Idle speculation on my part."

Hartwood slapped his cap against his leather trousers. "I knew where it must have come from. Poor wee thing doesn't belong on the moor. No place for toy dogs. Thought at first it was a puppy, but a fine lady in Edinburgh had a tiny dog like that one. Might do in the town, but not here. Hardly bigger than a vole. Almost anything could kill it—owl, adder, feral dog or cat, fox."

"Fitzwilliams?" Rose Grimswell's voice echoed across the hall.

Holmes quickly wrapped the cloth about the dog, then thrust it under his arm.

Hartwood saw the looks on our faces. "Oh blast," he muttered. "We have to tell her."

Holmes gave a reluctant nod. "I shall."

"Are you sure?" I asked. "Perhaps it would be better to wait until…"

Hartwood shook his head. "No. Best have it done with. Even if…" His words trailed off as his eyes opened wide, his lips parting. He stared past me at Rose Grimswell.

"There you are!" she exclaimed. As she came closer, her pace slowed, her smile fading. "I was wondering what happened to you. Is anything the matter?" She raised her hand, hesitated, then touched her hair in back, and let her hand slip down.

Hartwood appeared to have been struck dumb, but his eyes were fixed on her. She was two or three inches taller than he, but he certainly outweighed her. His freckled hand with the reddish-blond hair on the the back was half again as broad as hers, although she had the longer fingers.

"This is Doctor Hartwood," Holmes said. "He was in the neighborhood."

"*You* are Doctor Hartwood?" He nodded but did not speak. "I thought… I thought you were much older. I did not know…" Her words trailed off, her blue-gray eyes suddenly curious, a faint flush appearing on her cheeks. "You are the Doctor Hartwood who treated my father?"

"Yes. I did want to come to his funeral, miss, but I was called away by a very serious case. I felt very bad. I wanted to come." He drew in his breath, swelling his massive chest. "I liked him, your father." He tried to smile, but then his eyes shifted to Holmes, and his face grew grim again.

Rose was still smiling at him. "I know he valued your company, doctor. He mentioned you in his letters, but he did not say... I would not have thought..." Her flush deepened.

Hartwood looked positively anguished, and he turned to Holmes, who drew himself up. "Miss Grimswell, I am afraid something has happened to your dog."

"My dog?" She was genuinely puzzled for an instant. "Oh, you mean Elaine. It has been so blessedly quiet I had almost forgotten... What has happened to her?"

Holmes looked at me, perhaps thinking a physician should have more practice at this type of thing. "There has been an accident," I said weakly.

Her lips drew back in a brief, pained smile. "She's dead, isn't she?"

Holmes nodded. "Yes."

She stared at him. "Let me see," she said softly.

"I do not think that would be wise," I said.

She thrust her jaw forward. "I want to see it. It is my right."

Holmes looked at me, then at Hartwood. "Very well." He set the bundle on the table again.

"Show me."

Holmes pulled the towel back. Rose stared silently. Her arms were stiff and straight, her big white hands forming fists. "What...?" Her chest swelled. "What did this to her?"

"Probably a dog. A wild dog." Hartwood had spoken, and she turned to him.

The tears started to fill her eyes just above the lower lids. "Poor hopelessly stupid little…"

"I'm sorry, miss, but Dartmoor is no place for such a little dog."

"I know—I know. I tried to tell him. Of all the stupid…" Her voice rose even as the tears started from her eyes. Holmes wrapped the cloth about the dog. "It was not her fault," Rose murmured, more to herself than us. "Everything I touch…"

"Did you let her out?" asked Hartwood.

She stared at him as if he were mad.

"Did you let the dog out?"

"No—of course not."

"Then you must not blame yourself, miss. It wasn't your fault."

"Have you never heard of the Grimswell Curse, Doctor Hartwood? I am the last of the Grimswells, and I… I am very bad luck. You'd best keep away." She laughed harshly.

"Bunk," Hartwood said.

"What?"

"That's bunk. I told your father the same thing. I do not believe in curses or devils. I'm not a superstitious man."

Holmes laughed. "Bravo, Doctor Hartwood. 'Bunk' is nicely put. The dog's death is regrettable, but we need not bring the Grimswell Curse into the matter."

Rose wiped at her eyes. "I… Oh, I don't know what to believe. I only… Please forgive me—I need to be alone." She turned and was about to leave when Hartwood grasped her wrist with his hand. She stopped, surprised.

"Don't go, please. I…" He let go of her arm, clearly embarrassed. "Begging your pardon, but is there anything I can do? I mean… Blast it." He swallowed. "Would you like another dog? There are no tiny ones about, but…"

Rose shook her head. "No thank you. No more dogs. Please excuse me."

"I am sorry, miss." Clearly he meant it.

"Thank you, but it was not your doing either." She looked at him, then turned and walked away.

Hartwood did not take his eyes off her until she had left the huge hall, then he lowered his gaze and slapped at his thighs with his cap. He looked up, his eyes still pained. "I must be going."

Holmes pulled out his silver case and withdrew a cigarette. "Do you smoke, doctor? No? Neither does Henry—sensible physicians, both of you. I am sure at a later date Miss Grimswell will thank you for bringing the dog here. It was kind of you to undertake so unpleasant a task."

Hartwood shrugged. "I've a patient nearby to visit."

"Could you stop by again, doctor, or might I—"

"Yes."

Holmes stared at him. "Yes?"

"Yes, I'll visit again."

"I would like to discuss Lord Grimswell with you. I have heard that you do not believe his death was suicide."

Hartwood's mouth formed a disapproving line. "I know he did not jump. He was not a man to take his own life, despite all the talk. And his heart was not good. You can never tell with angina." He scowled. "Sometimes they live for years, sometimes... I'll be happy to talk to you, Mr. Holmes, especially if it puts an end to all the nonsense."

Holmes exhaled a breath of smoke. "Which particular nonsense?"

"Men in black on the moors at night. Wolves—vampires—and all such superstitious claptrap."

Holmes was amused. "You do not fear such creatures?"

"No, sir. I'll walk the moor in the dead of night if you give me a good stout stick. I'll wager this ghost has bones that will break if you hit him hard enough."

Holmes laughed. "I may take you up on that offer someday."

Hartwood nodded, turned to go, then looked at us both. "Say goodbye to the lady for me." He soon strode out the door.

Holmes was still smiling. "A sturdy fellow there, Henry. He may be of some help to us."

I shook my head. "I still feel a very idiot—calling him an animal doctor."

Holmes laughed. "I must confess that I made the same assumption. He does remind me of horse and bovine doctors I have met on the moors, but if he attended Edinburgh he is no fool. Of course, that was obvious enough anyway."

"Mr. Holmes—Mr. Holmes!"

We turned to see Constance Grimswell advancing toward us. She wore a white lace cap and black dress that both seemed identical to those of the prior day. Her brow was furrowed, her dark eyebrows scrunched together. "What has happened? Rose just passed me in tears—she would not tell me… What can it be?" Her voice quavered.

"Her dog has been killed," Holmes said.

She covered her mouth with her fingertips. "Oh no—oh no."

Holmes nodded, then gestured at the bloody bundle. "It will have to be disposed of."

Constance's eyes widened—they were brown, not blue or gray. She raised her hand and put it against her forehead, palm out. "Merciful heavens." Her eyelids fluttered. "Merciful heavens…"

Holmes grasped her by the arm just above the elbow. "You had best sit down, madam."

"Yes—yes." She turned and staggered toward an oaken armchair, and collapsed into it. "Merciful heavens." She took a handkerchief from her dress pocket, then dabbed at her eyes. "Poor little doggie. Oh, Mr. Holmes, this is all my fault. Rose will never forgive me." She blew her nose loudly. "It was barking and yapping at the door, so I had George let her out. Then... then we forgot all about the poor dog."

I set my hand on her shoulder. "That is understandable. Little dogs can be annoying, and in the commotion... You must not blame yourself. I am sure Rose will understand."

She dabbed at her eyes. "Oh, I pray she will. But what frightful beast could have done that to the doggie?" She raised her fearful eyes. "I hope... There is so much talk about diabolical creatures on the moor."

Holmes shook his head, an angry smile on his lips. "This was no demon, only a large animal with a strong jaw."

Constance shook her head. "Rose will never forgive me, I just know it! Perhaps I should go back to London. No one wants a poor foolish old woman about!" She sobbed once, then ran her forefinger across her eye.

"I shall talk to your niece. I am sure she will understand. Perhaps Fitzwilliams might dispose of the dog."

Constance lowered her handkerchief. "Perhaps we could have a funeral. That would surely make Rose feel better."

Holmes nearly laughed. His face twisted as he fought the urge, and his eyes shifted to me. "I think not," he managed to say.

"But if we laid the poor doggie to rest properly with a few prayers... I am sure it would be a consolation to her."

Holmes bit his lip and gave me a look of appeal. I shook my head. "I think not, madam—not in this case. Better the dog be disposed of with as little fuss as possible. A funeral would be very trying."

Constance sighed and nodded. "I'm sure you know best, doctor. Do you think the dumb animals have souls?"

"I... I have not much considered the matter."

Holmes looked across the hall. "I want to talk to Miss Grimswell."

Quickly I said, "I shall go with you."

Constance wiped at her forehead. "She's probably gone to the conservatory. One of the servants can show you the way." She sighed. "Perhaps I shall just have George bury the poor creature. At least we might put a small stone before her grave."

"Yes, perfect." Holmes nodded, then started across the hall toward Fitzwilliams.

I smiled awkwardly down at her. "I had best join him. Do you feel better?"

"I do, doctor. Forgive me. I'm only an old woman, and the sight of all that blood…" She turned her head in the direction of the bundle, but would not look at it. "It shook me something dreadful, I can tell you."

"I shall tell Fitzwilliams to have George bury it, just as you suggested. You need not trouble yourself further."

She ran her forefinger across her eye. "That is very good of you, doctor, very kind indeed."

Still smiling, I took a step back, then quickly pursued Holmes and Fitzwilliams, catching them before they could leave the hall. Behind me shafts of sunlight from the mottled glass streamed down into the hall, but the table with the tiny bundle and the woman in the chair were both in shadow.

Seven

Ꝋ

Rose Grimswell sat on a teak bench before a huge pond, a crumpled handkerchief clutched in her big hand. High overhead a web of steel girders and enormous panes of glass formed the conservatory roof. Tall palms and extravagant ferns poured forth from giant, elaborately painted pots, while smaller pots held other lavish greenery. The pond was shallow, only a foot or two, almost half of it covered by some type of water lilies. The brilliant blue tiles contrasted with the fish: their torpedo shapes cruised about, some of gold or silver, others a mix of red, white, and black. One surfaced near Rose, a white leviathan nearly two feet long, his mouth forming a great O, two short whiskery appendages showing that resembled fangs.

"This is incredible," I said to Holmes. "A miniature Crystal Palace complete with a veritable jungle."

"It is considerably warmer here," he replied. "All that glass amplifies the feeble sun of Dartmoor." He stared down at Rose. "Miss Grimswell, might we speak with you, or would you prefer…?"

She extended the fingers of her left hand and let out a ragged sigh. "Oh yes. Certainly."

"It is always difficult to lose a pet," Holmes said. "Ridiculous as it might seem, I once kept a spider as a pet, and when the creature finally expired, I was surprised at the sorrow I felt."

I smiled. "And of course it is far worse with a cat or dog, animals capable of true affection."

Miss Grimswell laughed, but her eyes were all teary. "You are very kind, but that is not exactly the problem. I feel terrible, not because I miss Elaine, but because I did not care for her. She could be so annoying, always whining and whimpering and demanding attention. She got on my nerves so. I even shouted at the poor pathetic little thing. Bringing her here to Dartmoor on the train was a nightmare. I finally had them shut her up in a crate in the baggage car so I could have a moment's peace." She dabbed at her eyes. "I never wanted the wretched dog in the first place. She was a gift from Rickie, an engagement present. What could I do?"

My eyes widened. "Digby gave you the dog?"

"Yes."

"But..." Dismayed, I glanced at Holmes. I had always despised yappy little dogs, but in this case the tiny animal would have emphasized Rose's size even further. In another man it might have been an innocent mistake, but given what Digby's mistress had told us, I suspected a cruel deliberate trick.

"Odd that we could not abide one another since we were each, in our own way, freaks of nature."

I had lived too long with Michelle to let such a remark pass. "I hope that is not a reference to your stature."

Her mouth twisted into a bitter smile, her shoulders rising in a shrug. "That is... bunk, to use Doctor Hartwood's term. In the case of the dog, you may be right. Dogs were not meant to be mere toys. Such dogs are unnatural and grotesque—which you most certainly are not. You are only two or three inches taller than Michelle, and I swear I would not have her any shorter than she is. I am certain that one day some man will also love you exactly as you are—he will not wish you different in any way." I had spoken with fervor, and my face felt warm.

She stared curiously at me, her mouth rising into a questioning smile, her eyes faintly puzzled. "Oh, thank you."

Holmes nodded. "Well put, Henry. And since you found the dog annoying, perhaps you will be willing to forgive your penitent aunt, Miss Grimswell. She had George put the dog out last night. She is most contrite. She even wished to give the dog a first-class funeral."

Rose's mouth twisted, even as a laugh slipped out. "No!"

"Henry is my witness." Holmes glanced at me, and I nodded. "This might be the ideal spot. We could have a funeral in the manner of the Vikings, launching the fallen maiden upon a small barque onto the pond and then igniting her remains in a fiery pyre."

Rose actually gasped, covered her mouth with her hand, her laugh more of a groan. She looked away, laughing in earnest. Her reaction, as much as Holmes's description, started me laughing too. Holmes smiled at us. Rose's laughter had a certain antic quality, a hysterical edge. Her life would have had few amusements recently.

"Please…" she moaned.

"Forgive me. It was an ill-conceived jest."

"But a very comical one." She wiped at her eyes, then drew in her breath.

"Why was the dog named Elaine?" I asked.

"Rickie named her after Elaine the Lily Maid in Tennyson's poem."

"Ah." Holmes nodded. "Perhaps, then, we should cast her adrift on the nearest river in a barque to float on down to Camelot rather than having an immolation." Rose again groaned softly and struggled not to laugh. "I am sorry—an equally ill-conceived jest."

"Rickie meant the name as a joke. I do feel better now. It was mostly the... unexpectedness of it all that upset me." She took a long, deep breath. "Please, do sit down."

I sat in a matching teak chair. Holmes glanced briefly at me, then sat at the other end of Rose's bench. The giant white fish surfaced again, his mouth a hungry circle. His eyes were black and alert, and further back his scales formed a gray-on-white pattern.

"Oh, don't beg, Moby," Rose said. "You had plenty to eat earlier." She glanced at us. "The gardener feeds them every morning."

"What kind of fish are they?" I asked.

She was about to reply, but Holmes spoke first. "Japanese koi, members of the carp family, larger relatives of the common goldfish. These are particularly magnificent specimens."

She smiled. "Very good, Mr. Holmes. My father liked to sit here and watch them swim about. He said they would make tranquil the troubled mind."

There must have been over a dozen fish in the pond, and as they swam about slowly, their gray shadows accompanied them, gliding across the blue tiles. "There is something hypnotic about watching them," I said.

Holmes, however, was gazing closely at Rose. Her black dress and the bright sunlight from overhead emphasized the pallor of her face and hands. "And do they calm your troubled mind, miss?"

She turned her blue-gray eyes on him, the corners of her mouth slowly rising. "Somewhat."

"Good. Then this is an ideal location for our discussion. It is time for you to tell me exactly what has frightened you so."

Her mouth stiffened, her eyes troubled. "Are you certain...?"

"You need not pretend with me. I have dealt with fear and terror for many years, and I know all its manifestations. You wrote to me, even as I requested, although I arrived before you could post the letter. Therefore I am here at your summons. You must tell me everything."

She licked her lower lip, and took it between her teeth. "I would... like to tell you everything."

Holmes had begun to drum upon his knee with the long fingers of his right hand. "Then do so. At once. I believe it concerns your father."

What little color she had drained slowly from her face. "How can you know that?"

"It is my business to know. Now tell me."

She stared down at the fish, her eyes following the big one. "I suppose I must. I..." Her voice shook slightly. "Jane Grimswell, my aunt—my cousin—had to be committed to an institution, a dreadful place. I visit her when I can, although it terrifies me. Oh, I do not want to be mad—I swear I do not."

I leaned forward and seized her wrist. She started at my touch. "You are not mad, and telling us will certainly not change anything."

"It is either madness or worse."

"I do not believe you are mad, Miss Grimswell," Holmes said. "Nor do I believe in ghosts."

Her eyes were fixed on him. "Then how...?"

"Tell me all that has occurred and then I can explain the how."

She inhaled through her nostrils, clenching her fists. "I am so sick and tired of this all. It gnaws at me always. Very well. I suppose it began somehow with my father's death, but no, what interests you began after my engagement to Digby. It began with that wretched document about the Grimswell Curse. Oh, I had heard about the curse, veiled references and the like, but my father had never showed me that paper. Somehow it... it frightened me."

"It was a frightening tale," I said.

"If my father were still alive, it would be different. If he had not died under a cloud... If–if–if." She drew in her breath angrily. "Rickie was right to take it away from me. I would have read it again, but even without having it, I kept remembering. I began to have... peculiar dreams." Briefly her mouth clamped shut, and I could see the fear again in her eyes.

Holmes leaned forward. "What were these dreams?"

She shrugged. "I cannot remember specifics, only impressions. My father was in them, all in black, and my mother, whom I never really knew, and Digby. However, it was more the... voice." The pitch of her own voice suddenly went awry, becoming high and twisted.

"What did this voice say?"

"That I was cursed–that I was damned. That I was the last Grimswell–that I must not marry–that I was a freak, a monster–that I was ugly and deformed and insane–that I was mad like my father and all the damned Grimswells before me."

Again I leaned forward to seize her wrist. "Miss Grimswell, none of these things are true."

Her hand trembled slightly, and she stared desperately at me. "No?"

"*No*," Holmes said. "Tell me, were their many voices or only one?"

She stared at him before replying, struggling with her fear. "Only one."

"A man's voice?"

"Yes."

Holmes's mouth twitched, a brief grimace of a smile appearing, while his eyes remained locked on Rose. "And then you actually heard the voice, did you not? It spoke to you for real, and it was your father's voice."

Her jaw dropped, seemed to lock, and then she stood up to her full height and stared down at him in horror and surprise. A tentacle of dread seem to curl about my own heart.

"How could you know?"

"Please sit down, Miss Grimswell. Calm yourself."

"Now you understand—both of you must understand—that I must be insane."

I could not help reflecting on the logic of this assertion, but Holmes shook his head without hesitation. "No, I do not believe you are mad."

"Then—"

"Nor do I believe in ghosts of the dead speaking to the living."

"Then how—?"

"Sit down and finish relating what happened. In all my experience, mysterious voices always belong to physical personages. I have yet to encounter any genuine metaphysical manifestations, and a young lady with an inheritance of several hundred thousand pounds is tempting bait indeed."

Now she seemed more surprised than anything else. She sank down onto the bench. "Then you believe me, and you—you do not think—you do not think…?"

"You are sane, Miss Grimswell." A faint smile appeared. "As sane as the rest of us." He spoke with an assurance I did not quite share.

She reached out with her enormous hand and engulfed his slender fingers entirely, making him stiffen and sit upright. "Oh, bless you, Mr. Holmes—oh, thank you, thank you." She laughed, sobbed, then dabbed at her eyes with the handkerchief.

"Please, Miss Grimswell, calm yourself. I must hear all that happened if I am to discover the cause of…"

She stared at him, then let go of his hand. "Forgive me, I was so afraid to tell you." She laughed again—a pained sound.

"When did you first hear the voice while you were awake?"

"Around two weeks ago. I was… I had had awful dreams, but I woke up. I know I was awake. I sat up and lit a candle and waited for my heart to slow down."

"What exactly did the voice say?"

"I was sitting there, and it said, 'Did you hear me?' 'Who is it?' I cried. 'Who is there?' 'You know who I am. You must not marry Digby—you must marry no one. You are damned—like me—like all of us Grimswells.'" I could see her hands begin to tremble again. "Oh God, how he frightened me. I–I looked all over the room, but I found no one. I looked under the bed and in the closets, everywhere someone might be hiding, but…"

"That was very brave of you," Holmes said, "and a logical course of action."

She laughed. "I was terrified. I tried to convince myself maybe I had been asleep and still dreaming, but I knew I was awake."

I moistened my lips. "Sometimes in the interval between sleep and waking one may still dream."

"I was awake!"

Holmes nodded. "I believe you. And so you broke your engagement with Lord Frederick?"

She nodded. "Yes. Either I was cursed or I was mad, and either way…"

"And after that, you switched rooms."

Her eyes widened. "How could you know that?"

"A detail I learned from Lady Rupert. The rest is clear. You had a few peaceful nights, but then…"

Her face resembled some blasted flower, even her lips paling. She nodded weakly. "It was the third night. I had almost convinced myself I must have been dreaming. I had met you both in the afternoon, and your wife, Doctor Vernier, and I felt better than I had in weeks. You were so kind to me, especially Doctor Doudet Vernier." Her eyes had a liquid sheen. "I actually thought I might be better. I went to bed early, determined to sleep, but the voice woke me, I think." She drew in her breath resolutely. "It was just after one. I was afraid. I somehow knew he was there—that he was going to talk to me." One hand fluttered nervously at her hair. "Oh, I do not like to think about it—I do not..." Her breath caught in her throat.

I leaned forward and again seized her wrist. "You are safe now—you are safe."

Holmes's eyes showed a cold fury. "Your instincts to search the room and then to change rooms were wise. I am certain the voice you heard was that of a living, breathing man—a monstrous villain, perhaps—but a living one."

"Oh, I hope so."

"Go on. You have nearly finished."

"He finally spoke. 'You know I am here, don't you?' I was determined to remain silent, but he taunted me. Then he—"

"How did he taunt you?"

"He told me... how ugly I was, my features coarse, my nature grotesque. Then he told me how I had disappointed him, that I could not even write or think well." The tears slipped free and started down her cheeks. "I could not bear it. I begged him to stop—I begged him not to torture me. I asked him why he hated me, whatever I had done, but he only laughed. 'I am damned,' he said, 'and so are you. It is our blood. Our very blood is tainted.'"

"That is a monstrous lie!" I exclaimed. "There is no such thing as tainted blood."

Holmes gave his head a brief shake. "Let her finish, Henry."

"I had begun to cry. Just like now." She laughed, smiling briefly, the expression terribly at odds with her swollen eyelids and tear-streaked face. "I told him he could not be my father, that he must be some devil from hell. 'All we Grimswells are devils in hell—it is our destiny.' And he said he had always hated me. That was why he had taken Beejoo away from me." She laughed again, her face anguished.

"Beejoo?" Holmes said.

"My rabbit—my stuffed bunny. He disappeared when I was about six. I was heartbroken. My father told me that my mother had taken Beejoo to be with her in Heaven, and that was why we could not find him. The voice knew about that, Mr. Holmes. And he told me he had actually thrown Beejoo into the fire and burned him up. How could he know about Beejoo unless…?"

"Obviously your father told someone, or you did, or someone overheard your father. Someone has gone to a great deal of effort to frighten you."

Her mouth formed a quick, pained smile. "They are certainly succeeding. When he told me about Beejoo, about burning him up and then lying to me… I have never been so frightened in my life. It came in great waves—I could feel it in my chest and throat." Her hands were trembling again. "I threw aside the covers, and I think I might have run out into the street, but he shouted for me to wait, that he had one last thing to tell me. 'Leave London,' he said. 'Tomorrow—at once. Go back to Grimswell Hall where you belong.' And he said if I did not obey he would come every night and during the day as well. I asked if he would go away and leave me alone if I did. He told me he would, and I agreed to leave. He warned me I must never tell anyone about his visit. If I did, I would be sorry. And then… he was gone. Oh—I do not like remembering." She drew her breath in, a great shuddering sound, then covered her face with her large hands, so smooth and white. A muffled moan came out.

Holmes took out his cigarette case, realized one did not smoke before young ladies, and put it back. I could not recall seeing him so angry. He picked up her handkerchief, which had fallen on the bench beside her. "Miss Grimswell, please—your handkerchief."

She lowered her hands, stared at him, ground her teeth briefly, then took the handkerchief and wiped at her eyes.

Holmes's nostrils flared. "I have no doubt that you are the victim of a devilish hoax, and I mean to find the persons behind it."

"Do you honestly believe that?"

"Yes. I am absolutely certain."

My own head had begun to ache, and I felt anxious myself. "There is another possibility. The mind does play curious tricks, especially when one is weary or under a nervous strain. You said your sleep had been disturbed and the tale of the curse had troubled you. I am not saying you are mad—far from it—but desperate circumstances can cause the mind to see or hear strange phantoms. I have heard tales from soldiers who were imprisoned, half starved and mistreated. They began to have imaginary companions, but once they were rescued and returned to normal society, their illusions vanished."

"The voice was real," Rose said, but doubt clouded her words.

Holmes gave me an ironic smile. "I hardly see a parallel between the prisoners' condition and hers. The phenomenon you speak of is familiar to me, but in this case there is a much more obvious explanation. Besides, I know a simple way to test our theories. Miss Grimswell, you will not sleep alone at night until the question is resolved. We shall see if your voice manifests itself in the presence of others. We shall also have a stronger lock put on your door so no phantoms can enter your room unawares."

She eased out her breath, then smiled. "Thank you. Somehow… it seems almost childish—a foolish fear of imaginary monsters."

"There is nothing childish or foolish about your fears." He hesitated. "Have you heard the voice here at Grimswell Hall?"

"I…" She swallowed. "I don't think so."

"But you are not certain?"

"Sometimes it is hard to tell when my dreams end and when… The night before last I thought I had heard him whispering. I woke up all afraid around two in the morning, my heart beating so hard, certain he was… But there was only silence, blessed silence." She laughed nervously. "But my sleep was ruined."

"No doubt. Again, we shall not leave you alone at night henceforth. I shall get to the bottom of this."

She touched her fingers to her forehead. "It would be such a relief to know… My head hurts. I have been so confused, so torn. I had thought that my father had loved me, and to be so despised and vilified by him…"

I shook my head fiercely. "Whatever is going on, that voice was not your father's. I am certain that he must have loved you. Any father would be proud to have a daughter of your accomplishments."

Again she stared curiously at me. "You are very kind, Doctor Vernier."

Holmes stood, his hand again slipping into his pocket and withdrawing the cigarette case, even as he stared down at the koi. His rising brought them swimming toward him, no doubt hoping for another feeding. He frowned at the cigarette case.

"You may smoke if you wish," Miss Grimswell said.

"Why do we not take our stroll instead? Now that you have unburdened yourself, some fresh air might do us all good."

She stood resolutely. "That is a wonderful suggestion. It is a beautiful sunny day, and yet I feel ready to jump out of my skin. Let me change my shoes and put on something more suitable for walking. I shall meet you outside by the front entrance in about ten minutes."

Holmes nodded. "Very well." We started for the doorway. Overhead

I could hear birdsong. "Thank you for confiding in me, Miss Grimswell. I promise you will not regret it."

She smiled at him. "I already feel so much better." Her tears had been wiped away, but her eyes were still ghastly-looking.

I also needed to change, and I soon found my cousin out before the massive doors finishing his well-deserved cigarette. He appeared calmer, but a certain cold anger showed in the way he raised the cigarette to his mouth. "Tell me, Henry, did you truly believe that nonsense about the mind playing ticks?"

"I would not have mentioned it if I had not thought it possible."

He shrugged. "Do not take umbrage. I was being... No matter, this theory may prove useful. We might offer it up to Digby, Constance and the household."

The door opened and Rose stepped out. She had obviously washed her face. She looked much better. She wore a wool tailored suit, matching tweed jacket and skirt, sensible shoes, and an outlandish hat with a broad brim to shade her pale face. Michelle would have approved in that it was practical rather than fashionable.

Holmes crushed his cigarette underfoot, then pulled on his gloves and raised his stick with his right hand. "You will be our guide, Miss Grimswell, since you know the territory. What have we in marching distance?"

We started down the gravel road lined on either side with tall but bushy yews. They must have been two or three centuries old. "The nearest dwelling," she said, "is Merriweather Farm, about two miles' walk away across a level stretch of moor. An elderly couple ran it for many years, but they died a year or two ago, and there is a new tenant, a widow. Near the farm are the Wild Woods, and beyond the woods, Seldon's Mire. It's very dangerous at certain times of year. I was always warned to stay well away from it. Beyond the mire is another tor, Owl's Roost, and near it are a ruined tin mine and what's left of the first Grimswell Hall."

"It actually exists?" I asked.

Her cheeks had a healthy flush from walking, but her smile faltered. "Yes. It's nothing but a shell, a few black broken walls and part of a tower still standing. The rooks like the place, and the owls, and my father liked it, too." Her smile was sad now. "We walked there last autumn, a little over a year ago. He always said so desolate a place appealed to a melancholy soul."

Holmes strode resolutely, his stick in his right hand. "The supposedly accursed nature of the place did not worry him?"

"No, no. He said whatever curse might have hung over the place was long gone, the hall reclaimed by the ancient natural powers of Dartmoor—the wind, the water, the sky and the earth."

We walked on in silence. The pathway and the yews ended, and the moor stretched out before us, the brown of the heath and the green of the grass extending to the horizon. To our left the earth rose toward the black jumbled granite of Demon Tor. Somehow the slabs did resemble something faintly like a face, something primitive and malevolent frozen in an eyeless stare. A buzzard soared overhead, and the wind moaned in the trees behind us.

"Does the wind ever stop blowing up here?" I asked.

She shook her head. "No. This is as quiet as it ever gets. In the winter, during a blizzard, then it is truly frightful."

I felt a shiver along my spine. "I would rather not experience that first-hand."

"Is there a way up to Demon Tor?" Holmes asked.

"It is easiest if you start from behind the hall."

"That was the way your father would have gone?"

Again her eyes were pained. "Yes."

"We shall have to try it another time, after our legs are more accustomed to the terrain."

"Do you mean to stay for a while, then?" She took a deep breath, glancing about her. "This is my favorite time of year."

"I shall remain as long as necessary," Holmes said. "I too enjoy Dartmoor in autumn."

She gave him a brief, wistful glance, the blue in her eyes predominant in the bright sunlight and open air. "Stay as long as you wish. I hope you find this… person soon, but I also hope you will be here for a while." Her eyes turned to me. "Both of you. The hall often seems so lonely. It is wonderful to have such good company."

Holmes smiled ironically.

"What is it?" she asked.

"I was thinking that it is good of you to put up with elderly persons such as Henry and I."

"You are not old at all! Especially compared to Aunt Constance and the Fitzwilliamses."

Holmes laughed. "Faint praise, indeed. I only thought you might prefer company closer to your own age."

"Not at all. The girls at school seemed so tiresome and immature at times. I always preferred the company of my teachers. They were so much more interesting. I've always been… rather grown-up and serious."

Holmes smiled again.

She laughed. "Now what is it?"

"I was only thinking of what reception Lord Frederick will then receive."

She was not a woman to hide her emotions; her dismay was immediately evident. "Oh, I had forgotten." She frowned, her good humor gone. "He will be pestering me again. Should I marry him, do you think?"

Holmes shook his head. "Please, Miss Grimswell, do not ask me such questions. I am the last person you should consult."

"Why? Because he is your client, you mean?"

"No—as I have told you, your well-being is my main concern, not his wishes. I am the wrong person because the fair sex is a mystery to me and because… I have little experience in such matters."

"Oh." She looked at me. "And you, Doctor Vernier?"

I smiled. "Discretion is the better part of valor."

"But you do not like Digby, do you?"

"I…" My voice faltered. "My opinion does not much matter."

"It matters to me. And I would like to know what your wife would think. She seemed… I wish she were here too."

I sighed. "So do I. She would like Dartmoor."

We had been walking for about fifteen minutes. Flies droned softly in the air, while the bright blue sky was broken up by great banks of clouds, moving ever so slowly. The tor along the horizon had an almost preternatural sharpness. The air was so clear and clean compared to London. Behind us, slightly uphill, was the hall, its tower of black granite rising over the landscape. Only Demon Tor was taller.

We followed the dirt road through the moor, wheel tracks showing in the ribbon of red earth unraveling before us. None of us spoke, but it was a companionable silence. We listened to the gentle sounds of that warm sunny day.

Ahead appeared a black shape, a menhir, one of those great stone slabs raised by the ancient dwellers of Dartmoor millennia ago. The path passed quite near it, and only close up could we get a sense of scale. It stood a good twelve feet tall, the height of two men, the sole object rising more than a few inches above the faded brown and green of the moor. A great slab of rough black granite, its face stained by gray and green lichens, it seemed somehow a part of the desolate scene as well as an alien presence. Perhaps it was because the stone was natural, of the local earth, while its shape, position and location were the doings of men.

I felt uneasy staring at it. "I know it is ridiculous, but it looks as if it might have been there for millions of years, not mere thousands. They must have been objects of mystery and awe to the recent dwellers of the moors. One would think gods or giants must have set it there, not mere men like ourselves."

Holmes smiled faintly. "It does have an air of power, but it is only a large stone. It is all too vulnerable."

Miss Grimswell frowned. "What do you mean?"

"I mean that many of its brethren have already ended up in local houses and churches. Too many of our contemporaries have little respect for their ancestors. They topple their monuments and break them into smaller pieces to build with."

Rose gave her head a shake. "It seems a desecration. These things must have had a religious significance. I can feel it."

Holmes shrugged. "I fear men have little regard for the beliefs of their predecessors. No doubt someday our great cathedrals will be picked through by latter-day vultures the way we have picked through the tombs of the pharaohs and the temples of the Greeks."

She licked her lips, stared up at the menhir, then turned away abruptly.

"Is anything the matter?" I asked.

"No." Her smile was tenuous. "I do not like menhirs. Even as a child they somehow frightened me. They seem so old and so cold. They make one think how short life is. How many who stared at that rock are dead and gone, mere bones and dust? Even as we someday…"

Holmes eyed her closely, his lips curving upward. "A melancholy reflection for a young lady of twenty."

Her dark eyebrows came together. "I cannot help what I feel. We Grimswells are a melancholy lot. Perhaps that is the true nature of the curse."

"You misunderstand me—I meant no censure in my observation. I too frequently fall prey to such reflections. Of course, I am twice your age."

Her eyes hardened, then her mouth relaxed into a smile. "Tell me, Mr. Holmes, at the age of twenty were you a cheerful young man who never thought of death, evil or other dark matters? Was life all sweetness and light for you at that age?"

Holmes smiled, and I could not repress a laugh. "Very good, Miss Grimswell," he said. "Your instincts again serve you well. My disposition has changed very little. Perhaps the renaissance physicians were correct in their theory of humors. Perhaps you and I share an abundance of black bile, a secretion which causes melancholy."

I shook my head. "The theory of humors is nonsense. Black bile as such does not exist."

"Perhaps not," Holmes said, "but melancholy does, and it appears to run in families. Tell me, Miss Grimswell, did your studies include the ancient Egyptians, Greeks and Romans?"

They had, she told us, and if we had any doubts, it soon became even more apparent that she was a well-educated and intelligent young lady. She seemed familiar with the major discoveries in Egypt of our century. How she would be wasted on a man like Digby! But then I remembered Holmes telling me Digby was not the imbecile he pretended to be. All the same, he certainly did not seem right for this sensitive young woman. I found her quite charming, and so, I could tell, did my cousin.

After an hour's walk, we circled round and came upon Merriweather Farm. The dwelling was very old, probably a century or two, the walls formed of black granite stones, the weathered gray shale roof equally somber. Unlike Grimswell Hall it had no park, only a massive ancient oak with bronze leaves and two dark scraggly pines. Such dwellings were often home to man and beast, the cattle residing in half the house during the winter months, but the place seemed deserted, neither man nor animals present, save two rooks in the pines who cawed hoarsely with dismay at our approach.

"Did you say the farm had an occupant?" Holmes asked.

Miss Grimswell's dark brows came together. "I was told it did, yet it appears deserted."

A moment later the door opened, and a person stepped forth, a woman in a black dress, her pale yellow hair bound up, so light in the sun that I briefly thought it white, mistaking the young woman for her grandmother. She raised a hand in our direction. "Good day!"

"Good day," Holmes replied loudly. More quietly to Miss Grimswell: "That must be the tenant, a widow I believe you said. Do you know her?"

"We have never met."

The widow advanced slowly in our direction. "It is a fine day for a walk. Have you traveled far?"

A worn stone path wound toward the house; we followed it to meet her. "Not far," Holmes said. "We have been walking the moors. We came from Grimswell Hall."

"Ah, we are neighbors then. I am Mrs. Grace Neal, and you...?"

"My name is Sherlock Holmes. This is my cousin, Doctor Henry Vernier."

I was watching her and saw no sign of recognition of Holmes's name; clearly she was not one of Doctor Watson's readers. Her skin was pale with a rosy tint, her eyes blue, and she was a very attractive woman, her features and her tiny hand quite delicate. Her widow's weeds were black, but the dress was fine silk, the cut elegant and quite contemporary, sleeves puffing out at the shoulder, then tapering at the elbows. An elaborate floral pattern showed, a black-on-black design, and her impossibly small waist must be the result of a corset cinched far too tight. My physician's instinct and my marriage to Michelle made me cringe at such abuse of the internal organs by whalebone and steel.

"And this is Miss Rose Grimswell," Holmes continued.

Her smile wavered as she stared up at Rose, who was a good foot taller than she. "You are Miss Grimswell, Lord Grimswell's daughter?"

"Yes."

"It is a pleasure to meet you. I knew your father—not well, of course, not well at all, but... enough to recognize him as a gentleman. I've missed seeing him walking about the moors. He was a familiar sight. We have few visitors to this part of Dartmoor, and it was reassuring to see him and know there was a man of character and breeding close by."

Rose smiled sadly. "Thank you."

Holmes's eyes were shaded by the brim of his hat, but they peered closely at Mrs. Neal. "This seems a desolate and lonely spot for a woman such as yourself, Mrs. Neal."

"What do you mean by that, sir?"

"Only that a woman of your class is seldom found living a solitary life in the wilds of Dartmoor, and you are obviously not a native."

"How do you know that?"

"By your manner of speaking. You are from London."

A flush showed on her cheeks, but she smiled. "I am. My late husband and I lived there."

"Indeed? And how did you come to dwell at Merriweather Farm?"

"My husband and I took a walking tour shortly after we were married, and we both fell in love with Dartmoor. After he died, I... The bustle and squalor of London became too much. I fled here to be alone with my thoughts, hoping that these great vistas, the lonely majestic moors and the bleak tors, might in time comfort a heart equally desolate."

Her voice had a faint quaver at the end. Holmes raised one eyebrow and gave her a curious look. His mouth twitched, but he did not speak. Miss Grimswell's brow was furrowed, her eyes faintly uneasy.

I shook my head. "Such a course of action is unwise. Isolation and lack of activity are not likely to assuage your grief, but rather to prolong it. Solitude is not good for one accustomed to the companionship of marriage." She stared at me, and I felt embarrassed at my zeal. "Forgive me, but as a physician, I must often advise those who have lost a loved one."

"It might not suit everyone, doctor, but I am content here."

Rose stared at her, her dark brows coming together where her frown created a furrow over her nose. "What on earth do you do all day?"

Mrs. Neal laughed. "Ah, it does get tedious at times, but I have my needlework and my devotional books."

Holmes scratched at a stone before him with the end of his stick. "I assume you have a servant to do the cooking, the cleaning and assist you in dressing." His eyes swept over her figure in the elegant black dress as he spoke.

"I do, a young girl from Grimpen. However, I fear I may not count on her help for long." Her smile faded, and she stared past us at the moor.

"Why not?" I asked.

She gave a nervous laugh. "The villagers are unwilling to come here, especially at night. My Nell... Something frightened her, and her father told her he wouldn't have her spending the night here any longer. He has one of her brothers bring her in the morning and pick her up in the evening. With the days getting shorter and shorter, and winter coming... Soon I shall be alone."

I frowned. "This is not wise."

She shrugged. "I'm not afraid."

Holmes raised his eyes. "Does your servant fear a man in black?"

Mrs. Neal's tiny mouth parted. "How could you know that?"

"One need not be in the vicinity long to hear various tales. And has she spoken of wolves or dogs as well?"

"She has! The man was watching her from atop a tor, an enormous hound beside him. Probably only another solitary soul like... My dear, are you quite well?"

Miss Grimswell had gone pale, and her eyes briefly lost focus.

"Oh no," I said, seizing her arm.

She drew in her breath, nostrils flaring. "I am... It is nothing. Only some faintness."

"Would you like to come in and sit down?"

"No—no—I would rather keep walking."

"Let us do so, then." I turned her about and started down the path. Holmes was on the other side, ready to seize her arm.

"Oh, I am sorry. You must come back again for a real visit. Perhaps you could stop by for tea? Perhaps tomorrow, even?"

"Oh yes," Rose murmured.

"We shall see," Holmes said. "I would like to speak with you again. You said you knew Lord Grimswell?"

"Oh, not well, Mr. Holmes. Not well at all."

"It has been a pleasure, madam. Until we meet again."

He removed his hat, the sun shining on the pale dome of his long forehead. Miss Grimswell stared resolutely ahead, but her eyes seemed to go in and out of focus. Soon I released her arm. She took a deep breath and smiled at me. "Thank you, doctor. I... I really am not usually one of those damsels who is always fainting."

"You do not appear to be."

"I only... I have had too many... surprises of late."

"You have indeed."

Within a few minutes she had recovered, and she and Holmes began to discuss the Neolithic settlements and the early dwellers of Dartmoor. We had almost reached the hall when we heard the groan of wagon wheels. Behind us were the morose man from the village and, in the back of the dog cart, Lord Frederick. "I say–Rose!" he shouted, waving a yellow-gloved hand. He wore a gray top hat and frock coat, apparel more appropriate for Hyde Park than Dartmoor.

Rose raised her hand. Her cheeks were pink, but her smile had become a forced, feeble thing. Her blue-gray eyes briefly gazed off across the moors, as if she were seeking somewhere to escape. Digby leaped down from the cart, then gave her a proprietorial embrace. She stood stiffly, her eyes gazing briefly at Holmes and me. She appeared embarrassed.

"How I've missed you! I hope you've come to your senses." He looked at Holmes and me. "She has come to her senses, hasn't she?"

Digby kept up a steady banter while the rest of us said little. Our silence did not concern him in the least. We separated in the house, Rose giving us a brief, desperate glance before Holmes and I went upstairs.

"Poor girl," I murmured.

Holmes pulled off his gloves and stuffed them into his hat. "Henry, would you care to have a look at the tower?"

"Which tower?"

"That of Grimswell Hall, of course–Lord Grimswell's aerie."

"Oh. Do you know the way?"

"Yes. Fitzwilliams told me earlier."

I left my own hat and gloves in my room, then we went down to the gallery, through a doorway at the end, then started up a winding stone staircase. Small windows let shafts of yellow light cut through the dim interior. My cousin's breath grew labored. I felt a curious tightness in the chest, and my hands were suddenly cold. It was not from exertion.

"Sherlock, perhaps… I think I may turn back."

"But we are almost there. Do you not…?" He turned and saw my face. "Forgive me, Henry, I had forgotten. And perhaps I thought that after our adventures in Paris, you would have conquered your vertigo."

"It has not been so severe, yet I am remembering now that... Memory has little to do with it—my body will go its own way."

"The tower is enclosed, so it will not be too bad. And look—we are nearly there." An opening showed in a stone ceiling above us, and we climbed through and entered a circular room a good twenty feet across.

The wall was the usual black granite, but the room was ablaze with light from the huge windows. The walls were positively medieval, but the windows were modern, sheets of clear plate glass three feet wide and six feet tall. A circular carpet covered the floor, an exotic one of many colors with an elaborate pattern, a kaleidoscope with repeating circles which brought to mind alchemy or sorcery. The stone floor formed a black circle round the carpet. A cast-iron stove sat on one side of the room, and near it a large brass telescope. The only furniture was a massive oak table, two matching chairs and a larger leather chair and ottoman. A wooden ladder leaned against the wall, and above you could see the trap door leading to the roof or attic.

"Incredible," Holmes murmured. He strode to a window. "Henry, you must see this. Surely with the stone walls and the glass..."

I walked slowly toward the window, staying well back. A distant river formed a ribbon of light winding through the dark moor.

Holmes wiped at his forehead with his hand, then took off his heavy tweed jacket and set it on the table. "It is quite warm in here. I wonder..." Beneath the window was an iron crank; he took it, pushed one way, then turned it the other. With a slight pop the window opened, the huge expanse of glass in its iron frame swinging outward an inch or so on one side. The muted sound of the wind filled the room along with the cool air. Holmes turned the crank until the window had swung open a foot.

The air felt good, but I realized one could slip through that opening and plunge to certain death below. "I had rather you didn't open it any further."

"Very well, Henry." Holmes leaned on the casement and stared out. "These windows must be extremely heavy, yet the mechanism is very well built. I thought this tower must be idle folly, but now... What a marvelous retreat. It provides solitude, and views at every window which take one's breath away. I would I had such a tower. Most rich men build little more than monuments to their own bad taste, great dreary creations, but this is different."

"A bit Faustian," I said.

"Ah." He nodded. "I can see him sitting at his table there peering over great tomes, seeking the elixir of life, or there at his telescope exploring the mysteries of the universe. And of course Mephistopheles would have appeared in a cloud of smoke in the very center of that carpet."

Holmes went to the telescope and touched its gleaming four-foot bronze length with his fingers. The tripod of reddish cherry wood was very solid-looking. "This is a beautiful instrument, a four-inch refractor, for viewing the moon and planets. The skies of Dartmoor are frequently overcast, but on a clear night so far from the city and its ambient light, viewing would be ideal. Jupiter is in the sky now. We must have a look some evening, Henry. And yet..." He stepped back, then bent over and peered into the eyepiece at a right angle to the tube, adjusting the focusing knob with his hand.

He stood and turned to me, a weary smile pulling at his lips. "Perhaps I have misjudged Lord Grimswell."

"What do you mean?"

"The telescope is not pointed at the heavens, is it? Have a look."

"I..."

"Come, Henry, the window is closed, and you need not come too close."

I approached warily, then leaned over. The circle danced about, went black and then lighter again. The image was faint and blurry, insubstantial, but I was staring at a black wall and a window set in the wall, a square of glass, a cross of lead dividing it into four panes. "What on earth?"

I raised my head and tried to see where the scope was pointed. In the distance, across the moor and far below, was a rectangular black dwelling with a huge oak nearby. It took a second or two for me to realize what I was seeing.

"Merriweather Farm," I murmured.

"Yes," Holmes said. "Merriweather Farm."

Eight

The locksmith from Grimpen arrived late in the afternoon. He and Holmes spoke of levers and tumblers, Chubb locks, detectors, metal alloys—all of it gibberish to me, but when the man left an hour later, a shiny new circle of metal had appeared above the doorknob in the oaken door to Rose's room. Holmes gave Rose one key, kept one for himself, and sternly told her she must always lock the door whenever coming or going. He suggested she always leave the key in the same spot near the door whenever she was in her room. He also insisted that the maid again spend the night with her.

I had not slept well the prior night, and the hike on the moor, being far more activity than I was accustomed to, had left me yawning prodigiously by nine in the evening. Holmes, however, was prepared to remain awake for a long while—I knew it from a certain look in his eyes. He had removed one of the viscount's precious pipes and had just lit it when I prepared to retire. Even I could tell the tobacco was far better than his usual noxious shag.

He exhaled a cloud of the fragrant smoke. "Do you think the

viscount's vengeful ghost, this wraith or vampire, will fall upon me for borrowing his pipe?"

I shrugged. "I do not find such speculation amusing."

The ironic smile still pulled at his lips. "Do not fear, Henry. I know that a man who loved pipes and tobacco as much as the viscount must have would not begrudge another their use. He would not want them buried with him as if he were some ancient potentate."

"Are you not tired?"

"Not terribly. I have several things to consider, and I wish to periodically check on Miss Grimswell." His smile suddenly faltered. "I hope… Should there be a reoccurrence of her somnambulism, I may need to wake you."

I thought the anticipation of being dragged from my bed in the middle of the night might keep Morpheus at bay, but I slept very soundly and rose later than usual. Holmes's door was closed, which did not surprise me. As I went downstairs into the great hall, the insipid laugh of Lord Frederick rose to greet my ears. He was below with Rose, and when she saw me, her upturned face showed relief.

She insisted on escorting me to the breakfast room and keeping me company while I ate. Lord Frederick seemed faintly annoyed, a certain jealous haughtiness showing in his pale blue eyes and thin lips, but it vanished almost at once. He chatted amiably with us, as if we were all three old and dear friends. Today he wore the same green frock coat and the black and green trousers as the first time I had met him. His manners were polished, and he demonstrated that he could be agreeable when he wished.

I had just finished eating when the footman George appeared at the door. "You have a visitor, Miss Rose."

She frowned. "Who…?"

"Doctor Hartwood."

"Doctor… Oh, yes." She stood. "Whatever could he want?"

George grinned broadly. "I think he has something for you."

"Really?" She strode quickly across the room.

Digby frowned at me. "Who is this fellow?"

"The local doctor. The one who found… Elaine."

"Elaine?"

"The dog—the dead dog."

"Oh—that Elaine."

Hartwood had a resolute expression on his face, but at the sight of Digby his eyes widened slightly. He had changed his boots, the battered rubber ones being replaced with polished black leather, and his jacket appeared newer. A large black puppy struggled futilely to break free from the hold of the man's powerful arms and shoulders.

"Good morning, ma'am. Gentlemen." He nodded.

"Oh, who is this?" Rose reached out her large white hand, and the puppy licked at it eagerly. She laughed.

"Mind your manners," Hartwood said severely to the puppy.

"Oh, he's beautiful—what is he, a mastiff?"

"He is. Have a look." He thrust forward his hands, holding out the puppy, who gladly tumbled into Rose's arms.

His paws scrambled about, and his tongue sought her face. "No, no." She laughed. "He is quite a handful. Let me set him down." She did so, then knelt down (which showed she was not wearing a real corset and the usual female paraphernalia) and petted him. He calmed down some, but his tail flopped back and forth.

"I always have a patient or two with a new pup in need of a good home. This is one of Old Crimpton's, half a mile northwest of Grimpen. He's always kept mastiffs, and the mother is a fine, good-tempered dog. I thought…" His eyes had wandered all about the room as he spoke; now they settled on her. "Since you lost your wee little dog…"

Rose stared up at him (she was still kneeling by the dog). "How very kind of you."

Hartwood shrugged, but a touch of color showed about his cheekbones. "I like to see an animal in a good home."

George seemed to hesitate, then knelt at last and stroked the dog's head. "Oh, he is a beaut, ma'am, a fine pup. Look at the sheen on his coat and those paws." He held the dog's paw briefly in his hand. "Good day, master pup. He'll be a giant someday, make a good guard dog."

Hartwood smiled. "You seem to know mastiffs."

"Yes, I have… I mean, I had such a dog. There's no more loyal friend or companion. I… I miss him, but…"

Rose gazed at him, her eyes sympathetic. "What happened to him?"

"I had to give him away. Can't keep a mastiff about in a job like this. My… my old mother has him, a good companion for her."

"You must be the local animal doctor. I don't believe we've met." Digby's tone was mocking, his smile disdainful. "Digby's my name, Lord Frederick Digby. Rose is my fiancée."

Hartwood was obviously a man with firm control over his emotions, but this shook him. The signs were subtle, but mostly it was his eyes which gave him away. Rose, on the other hand, was openly horrified. Her jaw dropped in dismay, and she stood up at once, her fists clenching.

"That's not true!" she exclaimed.

"Doctor Hartwood is a *medical* doctor," I said, annoyed at Digby's behavior.

Digby said nothing, but stared at Rose. Her face went scarlet. Rarely have I seen a woman flush so. It was all the more striking because of her usual pallor. "I only mean… I… I need to think about it, Rickie. I had my reasons for…" She looked at Hartwood and me, then stoped speaking.

"I'm sure you must have had your reasons for breaking our engagement. No doubt you'll wish to share all the details with these gentlemen and the rest of the household. Your distaste for me is obvious enough, although what I've done to warrant it…"

"Please don't. I only meant… You startled me, and—"

"From now on I shall introduce myself as your possible fiancé or perhaps former fiancé or perhaps—"

Hartwood took half a step forward. "The lady asked you to stop."

Digby was surprised. "Did she? Stop what?"

Hartwood's face darkened. "I think you know, sir."

"You do? Ah, but I don't. What is it I am supposed to cease?"

"Your carrying on."

"My carryin' on? Whatever can you mean by that?—and what business is it of yours anyhows?"

Hartwood said nothing, but his look had become so threatening that Digby seemed to realize at last that he was baiting a man considerably brawnier than himself, a man who could probably knock him down with a single punch and a man who clearly would tolerate little more.

Digby had also flushed about the cheeks. "Well, whatever I'm supposed to have done, I'm sorry if I've offended you, Rose."

She stared at him without speaking, but her eyes were all liquid-looking.

"I suppose you will want to keep this enormous creature here." Digby nodded at the puppy, who was still playing with George.

Rose lowered her gaze. "No." She raised her eyes and looked at Hartwood, whose disappointment was clear. "Not that I would not like to keep him—it is only that… I have had one dog die. I do not want to be responsible for another animal's death."

"But you were not responsible for the little dog's death."

She shrugged. "Perhaps not, but I… I am bad luck of late, and I could not bear it if this dog…"

Hartwood inhaled through his nostrils. "Is this that curse nonsense again? Give this pup a few months, and he'll be a match for any ghost or spook."

Rose looked sadly at the puppy. "Thank you, but I cannot… risk it."

Hartwood's chest swelled, and he slapped at his woolen breeches with his cloth cap. "Well, I'll keep him for you, should you change your mind."

"You cannot seem to take no for an answer, Doctor Hartwood." Digby's eyes gleamed. "Perhaps the lady is not interested in either that slobbering beast or a rustic champion. A strategic retreat with your dog might be wise, if that loutish footman can tear himself away and resume his duties. Really, Rose, he's down there on the floor wigglin' about practically like a dog himself, and—"

George looked embarrassed, but it was Hartwood who stopped Digby. I truly thought he was going to hit Digby—you could see him considering it and struggling to restrain himself even as Digby's smile faltered—but then Hartwood put on his hat, scooped up the dog and strode for the door.

Rose's face was bright red again. "*Wait*," she cried, and Hartwood froze in his tracks. We were all startled by the sudden noise, Rose's voice echoing through the hall. She glanced at Digby. "If you ever behave that way again before me, I shall… I shall no longer number you among my acquaintances, let alone consider marrying you. Perhaps George… I think it would be best if George helps you pack your things so you can leave." She walked over to Hartwood. "Doctor, thank you very much for your gift. I… I would like to keep him. He is quite beautiful, but as I said…" She stroked the dog's head. "Perhaps, after all, you might keep him for me. Should my luck change…"

Hartwood smiled. "It will." He nodded at the rest of us, his jaw stiffening at the sight of Digby. "Good day, gentlemen."

"Let me get the door for you, sir." George followed him.

I was frowning, but Rose's face was still scarlet.

Digby's smile was a tenuous thing. "Rose…"

"How could you behave like that?" It came out as an angry whisper, furiously soft.

"I… Forgive me, dearest. My behavior was inexcusable. I can only… I apologize. I shan't be so churlish again."

She stared at him, confusion making lines in her forehead. I also found a chastened Digby hard to take at face value.

"When you said I was not your fiancée, I was rather taken aback, and I said the first things that popped into my head. I behaved poorly, but it was because of my feelings for you. I hope… I would like to stay here, Rose, and resolve things between us. I believe you owe me that much."

She straightened up to her full height, squaring her shoulders. Her black dress had none of the style of the widow Neal's mourning garment. "Very well."

Digby turned to me. "And I hope you will also excuse me, Doctor Vernier. Nothing is more disagreeable than being an innocent bystander caught up in a squabble."

I nodded. "It is an unpleasant position."

He laughed. "Rose, I should like to speak with you alone."

She drew in her breath, then nodded. On their way up the stairs, they passed Holmes and exchanged greetings with him. I waited for him to descend. He wore another tweed suit, a gray herringbone, and looked none the worse for wear.

"How much of that did you see?" I asked softly.

He smiled. "The entire act. I must say I enjoyed it. I wanted to applaud when Miss Grimswell turned upon Digby and told him to pack his bags. That is a side to the young lady we have not seen before."

"The stupid jackass certainly had it coming."

Holmes laughed. "I see that you are still not to be counted among Lord Frederick's admirers."

The distant clump of the great door closing sounded dimly through the hall and George soon reappeared. Blond as he was, his cheeks still had a ruddy tint.

I nodded in his direction. "There is another who is not an admirer."

George saw us, raised his hand which contained an envelope, then came toward us. "Mr. Holmes, this telegram has come for you." His manner was more subdued than usual.

Holmes nodded, thanked him, then tore open the envelope and read even as George departed. His mouth twitched once, his smile vanishing even as his brow furrowed. At last he lowered the paper and sighed, an irritated rasping sound. "Oh, damnation."

"What is it?"

"You will hear soon enough. I fear we must interrupt our lovers' tryst." He started up the stairs. "I expected better of her. This is... sheer stupidity, unadulterated stupidity. Certainly she must have known better."

"Who is the 'she' you refer to? Miss Grimswell?"

"Yes." He rapped at the library door, waited a moment, then rapped more loudly.

"Come in," said a woman's voice.

Digby was sitting on the edge of the table next to Rose, who occupied one of the large oak armchairs. "Can we not have a moment's privacy?" he asked imperiously.

"No," Holmes snapped. "Not just now. I have received a rather disturbing communication from Miss Grimswell's solicitor, Mr. James Rigby. It concerns her will."

Digby immediately lowered his gaze and licked his lips. Rose's eyes became evasive.

"I was unable to arrange a meeting with Mr. Rigby before I left

London, but I wrote him a letter inquiring about the estate and expressing my concern that Miss Grimswell might be in great danger. He was kind enough to send me this telegram. He takes his responsibilities most seriously and is worried about his old friend's daughter."

"Has he not heard of confidentiality?" Digby muttered. "I would never have thought–"

"Obviously not," Holmes said, "or you would not have given me his name."

I looked at the three of them, frowned, and said, "Sherlock, will you please tell me what is in the telegram."

"Mr. Rigby reveals that Miss Grimswell has made Lord Frederick the major beneficiary of her will."

"*What!*" I exclaimed.

"Mr. Rigby tried to persuade her this was not wise. He also appealed, unsuccessfully, to Lord Frederick."

Digby straightened up. "He was positively insolent! It was Rose's decision, after all, and who was I to contradict her wishes? I certainly did not ask to be made her beneficiary."

Holmes's eyes were fixed on him. "You did not?"

"*No.*"

Holmes turned to Rose. Her cheeks had reddened again, and her eyes appeared weary. "Is he telling the truth?"

"I say, Mr. Holmes–you needn't be quite so insulting."

Holmes kept staring at Rose. She touched her fingertips to her forehead. "Yes. I think so."

"You think so!" I said.

She bit at her lip. "I… Who else was I to leave it to? I knew Rickie needed money, and I had no one else to…" She smiled grimly. "I wasn't really planning on dying soon, anyway."

"We were engaged, Mr. Holmes," Digby said.

"But Mr. Rigby tells me he changed the will before any engagement. Moreover, he explains that a betrothal is never the time to alter a will. It is always done concurrently with the marriage."

Digby shrugged. "Well, I mightn't have popped the old question, but it was certainly on my mind. Besides, as Rose pointed out, what does it matter? She's in excellent health and'll probably outlive a wastrel like me by ten or twenty years."

Holmes stared at him, opened his mouth, then closed it. He turned again to Rose. "Had you no idea how colossally... unwise this was?"

Her eyes filled with tears. "I..." She covered her eyes with her large white hand.

"You needn't bully her," Digby said.

Holmes stared at him. His mouth twitched, then his hand crumpled up the telegram. He inhaled through his nostrils, then turned to me. "Am I being unreasonable, Henry?"

"Not at all. I too am mystified as to how an intelligent young lady like Miss Grimswell could ignore the advice of her solicitor and..."

Rose lowered her hand. "I never even wanted all the cursed money! I wish I could just give it away. And I knew Rickie needed money. He was always..."

Holmes smiled—a withering expression. "I'm sure he was. And how much money have you already given him, Miss Grimswell?"

Digby stood. "No, now this is really too much! My financial affairs do not concern you, sir."

I stared dumbly at Rose. "You gave him money?" She did not speak, but the answer was obvious.

"It was a loan!" Digby exclaimed.

Rose rubbed at her eyes. "It was not." She looked at Holmes and me. "I have so very much. What did a few hundred pounds matter? He didn't *ask* for money."

"Certainly not!"

Holmes's mouth again formed the scathing smile. "Oh no, he merely whined and whimpered until you took pity upon him in his destitution."

Digby had grown quite red. "Mr. Holmes, there are limits to the abuse I shall tolerate from you."

Holmes's nostrils flared, then he uncrumpled the telegram, folded it and thrust it into his pocket. He went to the nearest window, put his left hand in his trouser pocket and smoothed back his oily black hair with the other hand.

"Lord Frederick, I can tell it would be futile to try to convince you that your conduct has been less than exemplary. However, you have kept vital information from me. As for you, Miss Grimswell, you… you disappoint me."

Tears started down her cheeks. "I'm sorry. I–I meant well."

"I am sure you did."

Digby whirled and started for the door. "I've had enough of this." He seized the brass knob, then turned. "Rose, if you had any real pride, you would ask Mr. Holmes to pack up and leave!" He slammed the door loudly behind him.

Holmes scowled, then began to pace. Rose had covered her eyes with her hand again. I hesitated, then put my hand on her shoulder. She started, then looked up at me. "I am sure you did mean well, Miss Grimswell. It was most generous, but it put you and Lord Frederick in… a compromising position. A real gentleman would never have allowed such a thing."

Holmes was staring out the window at the distant moor. "It also gives Lord Frederick an excellent motive for murder."

Rose's lips parted, her eyes widening. "Surely not."

Holmes turned to her, and she seemed to shrink back. He eased his breath out of his nostrils. "Madam, you must understand that you are heir to a great fortune. Men have killed for far less. You must not... you must not give a man like Digby a good reason to murder you."

Her face began to go very pale. "Not Rickie," she said. "No, I won't..."

"He is a bit of a bounder," I said, "but I don't think he's really capable of..." Rose could not see my face, but Holmes could. I shook my head silently twice.

"Perhaps not, but I would like to remove..." He smiled. "'Lead us not unto temptation.' Miss Grimswell, I would like you to change the terms of your will. I am not... comfortable with the current situation. It is, of course, your inheritance to do with as you choose, but Mr. Rigby's advice was sound. Should you marry Lord Frederick, an eventuality which is somewhat in question, your fortune will largely become his, but until then... It will not do, madam, it will not."

"But what am I supposed to do with such a fortune! I really do not want it—I do not."

"Perhaps not, but does Lord Frederick deserve all your money should anything happen to you? There are those who have a genuine need." He looked at me.

"The hospitals in the poorer parts of London never have enough medicine or staff to treat the throngs of patients. You could specify that you wanted your money left to London's charity hospitals and clinics."

Miss Grimswell stared at me, then nodded.

"An excellent suggestion, Henry—excellent. Miss Grimswell, if you would write me a note expressing the desire to change your will, Henry and I could witness it, making it legally binding until Mr. Rigby can actually update the will."

Rose sat up and drew in her breath. She smiled sadly, then gave a gentle laugh. "Perhaps I too am selfish, or I might have thought of such a thing. Must I do it now?"

Holmes nodded. "It would be best, believe me."

"Very well." She leaned forward, pulled out a sheet of paper, then dipped the pen in the ink well.

I frowned slightly. No doubt Digby had weaseled his way into the will, but should we also be forcing our wishes upon her? All the same, for us, Rose's interests were paramount.

"Here." She handed Holmes the paper. "Digby will be furious." Her voice faltered.

Holmes nodded. "This is very good. Let me handle Digby." He took the pen and scrawled upon the page. "Henry, sign and date it below my signature."

The note merely said that she wished to leave the major part of her estate to the charity hospitals of London instead of to Lord Frederick Digby should she die. I signed it.

Rose stared up at Holmes. "Are you absolutely certain I am doing the right thing?"

"Yes, Miss Grimswell. I am absolutely certain."

She put her hand over her forehead. "How my head aches."

"No wonder," I said. "It has not been the most peaceful of mornings."

A knock sounded at the door. "Oh, now what?" she said.

Holmes went to the door. George stood outside. "Begging your pardon, sirs, but I wanted to speak with the mistress."

Holmes nodded. "I have some correspondence I must attend to." He left the room as George entered.

George swallowed, the Adam's apple in his thin neck bobbing. He was a handsome young man, and a black morning coat, gray cravat and wing collar suited him. One could see why he was a favorite with the maids.

"Yes?" Rose put one hand on her knee, the other hand over it.

"I only wanted to make sure... I don't really think I was being remiss, but possibly I was. I hadn't seen a pup in so long, but if I offended you, ma'am, I'm begging your pardon."

Her smile was tenuous. "Oh George, you did nothing wrong. Surely you could tell I was not angry with you?"

"I wanted to be sure that I didn't..."

"You saw me down on the floor as well, didn't you? Not very ladylike, I'm afraid. Really, George, you behaved better than any of us. I was happy to have your advice on the dog."

George smiled, something more sincere than his usual amiable grin. "Thank you, ma'am." He turned to go.

"Oh, and George, if you ever want to bring your dog here, I'm certain we could work out something. Mr. Fitz won't like it, but then today I've managed to make almost everyone angry. What is one more person?"

George's smile faded, and he stared closely at her. "You'd do that for me, ma'am?"

"Of course."

"But why?" He seemed genuinely puzzled.

She laughed. "So you could be near to your dog. If you are fond of him."

"That's... that's very decent of you, ma'am. I..." He drew in his breath, the creases in his forehead lingering. "I won't trouble you no longer." His smile was gone.

"Well, do let me know about the dog."

"So I will." He gave a slight bow, then departed, closing the door behind him.

Rose looked up at me. "He seemed so surprised."

"Many servants rarely see genuine kindness. It does surprise them."

She smiled. "It seems such a little thing." She sighed and brushed away a black strand of hair from her forehead.

I realized abruptly that I did find Rose Grimswell truly beautiful.

Being happily married did not make a man stop noticing beautiful women, even if one no longer felt compelled to pursue them. Rose also reminded me very much of Michelle.

"Doctor Vernier, sometimes I feel so... embarrassed by everything. I wish I could just go somewhere and hide! Mr. Holmes thinks... he thinks I am a foolish girl."

"He blames Lord Frederick, not you."

"But he said he was disappointed with *me*. Oh, I wish I had never heard of wills or estates or solicitors. Somehow it never felt right to me, but Rickie said I must not let Rigby bully me. I must show him and Aunt Constance who was in charge. I suspected it was wrong, but I didn't care. None of this seems quite real to me. If the money would make Rickie happy, why not let him have it? I didn't care about the money anymore than I care about living or dying."

"You mustn't speak that way."

"Why not? It's true. And if anything did happen to me, no one would care. Oh, the Fitzwilliamses would shed a tear, and Rickie might feel sad for a few minutes, but no one would really care."

"That's not true," I said gravely.

"But it is."

"No, it is not." I hesitated. "I would care."

"But you hardly know me."

"What does that matter?"

She frowned in confusion, then looked up at me. Soon we both looked away. "I believe you mean it," she said.

"And Sherlock would also care."

"Would he really?"

"Yes—why do you think he was so angry? And why do you think he is here?"

Her eyes teared up. "Oh, thank you. I must sound very selfish, but it is only that I feel so alone sometimes. I..." She resolutely stood up. "I think I shall go and sit in the conservatory for a while and meditate upon the fish. Don't... don't tell Digby where..."

"My lips are sealed." I smiled. "You will be safe for a while."

"I must talk to him soon, but I have had enough excitement for one day."

"You have earned a few tranquil moments. I shall have a look at the library here."

"You should find it interesting and quite complete. My father was fond of books." She gave me a brief, furtive look. "Thank you again, Doctor Vernier." She walked quickly to the door.

I sat quietly for a while. My face felt rather warm. How I wished Michelle were there—for a variety of reasons! I stood and turned to the bookcase. All the great English novels were present in one section—Dickens, Trollope, Thackeray, Eliot, and close by were the complete works of Wilkie Collins and Sheridan Le Fanu. In the same area were Watson's collected tales.

"Doctor Vernier?"

Peaceful solace was not to be mine. "Good day, Miss—Constance."

The other Miss Grimswell gave me a broad smile, her pink face beaming good cheer. "I hear there has been some commotion this morning."

"And who has told you this?"

"George, of course. How kind of Doctor Hartwood to bring Rose a dog! Impractical—the last thing we need is an enormous, vicious mastiff—but generous. George had some unkind things to say about Lord Frederick, but I reprimanded him. One cannot expect servants to understand their betters."

My smile grew rather wooden.

"Oh, I just don't know what to think! Is Lord Frederick really worthy of our dear Rose? It's true his family is even more illustrious than our own. After all, a marquess is two steps above a viscount–practically a duke, isn't he?"

I wanted to tell her a younger son was nothing at all–especially in Digby's case. He would inherit neither land, title, nor from what we had heard, money. From my perspective he made a dreadful prospective husband. He had no money, but had been raised to consider himself above others and above most respectable occupations. A life of idleness would be what he most desired, and Rose's money would make that possible. I struggled to think of something nice to say about him, but in vain. Instead I echoed her: "Yes, a marquess is almost a duke."

"I hope... George said he brought Mr. Holmes a telegram which seemed to cause some discord."

I gave a noncommittal shrug.

"I hope it had nothing to do with Rose's legacy."

Briefly I could not control my face.

"Oh dear, I only meant... Well, it is true I agreed with Mr. Rigby at the time, but if the girl really is to be married... Perhaps I was wrong. Has Mr. Holmes persuaded Rose otherwise?"

"Madam, you will have to ask him that question. I am not at liberty to comment upon a private conversation."

Miss Grimswell made a mass of wrinkles of her brow as she assumed a mournful face. "Oh, forgive me, doctor–I didn't mean to pry. No one likes an old busybody, and I know it's none of my business. I only want the best for our dear Rose. There's nothing wrong with that, is there?"

"No, of course not."

"Tell me, though, doctor–do you really think she should be traipsing about the moor? With her history... wouldn't rest be the best thing for her?–and not in that damp, drafty conservatory!"

"Well, fresh air can have a tonic effect if–"

"But her heart, doctor–I worry so about her heart! So many

Grimswells have been stricken by heart failure. And her nerves—she is high-strung. You cannot deny she is high-strung!"

"Even so—"

"Please tell her she must rest, doctor! I fear... I fear some dreadful breakdown, some nervous collapse. She reminds me of my poor sister. Everyone thought she was perfectly all right until she began to have her spells. And now... Oh, that place we must keep her in is so dreadful! And if Rose should..." Her eyes filled with tears. "Promise me you will tell her to rest—promise me, doctor!"

"Calm yourself, Constance. She—"

"Promise me!"

I sighed wearily. "I promise."

"Oh, thank you." Her big hand clutched at my arm; unlike Rose's slender fingers, hers recalled sausages. "Together we shall save her!"

Nine

Later that afternoon, Lord Frederick and Rose had their conference. The result seemed to please Digby. I was in the great hall reading when they came out of one of the sitting rooms. He was smiling broadly, and he gave her hand a squeeze. She was also smiling, but her eyes appeared weary and evasive. She gave me a nod, then swept out of the room, her black dress and petticoats making a slight swishing sound.

Digby gave his hair a pat, then withdrew a cigarette case. "Well, old boy, things are definitely looking up."

I stared at him, annoyed at yet another of his inane familiarities. "Indeed?"

"I'll be a married man someday, I'll wager, be fettered with the rest of 'em."

I tried to keep my voice and my face neutral. "She has agreed to marry you?"

"Well, not quite, but I may remain for the time being, and she will again consider my proposal."

I very nearly said, "Then there is still hope," but I knew I would be unable to refrain from a certain irony of tone. I mumbled something and gazed down at my book as if transfixed. Digby took the hint, pausing only to light his cigarette, then wandering away while humming a tune from Gilbert and Sullivan.

I tried to reason with myself, to admit that Digby might have some redeeming qualities, but to no avail. The thought that Rose might actually marry him dismayed me. She deserved so much better. I was absolutely certain that Digby would have no interest in her whatsoever were it not for her fortune. He may have tried (weakly) to persuade himself otherwise, but his true motives were obvious.

Dinner that night proved to be an ordeal. Constance had concocted an elaborate menu with several rich courses and sauces designed to show that Grimswell Hall was the equal of any ostentatious, profligate country estate, and the tension between her and Mrs. Fitzwilliams, who appeared briefly, was palpable.

Digby monopolized the conversation and made broad pronouncements on philosophy, art and poesy. Annoyed, I briefly sparred with him over the question of Wilde's talents. As a humorist, Wilde's appeal was indisputable, but as an aesthete I found him extremely pretentious. We skirted the topic of his morality. Holmes said little, and Rose remained subdued until after dinner when an odd transformation took place, all the more curious because of what occurred first.

Maria, the rather sour-looking maid, had set a cup and saucer before me and was pouring coffee when the most dreadful cry came from the kitchen—a woman's scream, shrill and urgent, expanding in volume. Maria's arm jerked, coffee spilling onto the saucer and then the tablecloth. Holmes and I were on our feet at once. A second cry joined briefly with the first.

We left the dining room, strode down a narrow hallway and came into the kitchen. The room was spacious, a large iron stove in one corner, pans hanging from hooks over the counters. A maid lay on her back in the doorway to the pantry; another knelt beside her, sobbing. The screaming came from within.

Holmes stepped around the recumbent figure and into the pantry, then grasped the arm of the short, stout cook and shouted, "Stop that—stop it at once."

The tiny room was dimly lit, but next to a large white cake I could see an object which turned my stomach—a large rat, obviously dead, the long pink tail drooping off the table.

Holmes shook the woman. "That is quite enough." He turned her and steered her out into the kitchen. "Hysteria will not help matters." He gazed at me. "Please get her some brandy, Henry."

I was only too happy to leave the pantry. The entire house seemed to have joined us—Fitzwilliams, Digby, Rose, and, lurking in the kitchen doorway, Constance.

"What on earth is it?" asked Digby.

"A dead rat," Holmes said. "There is no need for panic."

"Ughh!" Constance exclaimed loudly. "I cannot bear a rat!"

"Then I suggest you return to the table, madam." Holmes went back into the pantry.

I turned to Digby. "Could you fetch some brandy for the cook? I need to see to the poor girl on the floor there."

Digby nodded, and Rose took the cook's arm. "Come, Annie—you are safe now."

The elderly cook bit at her lip and struggled to swallow. The volume of her screams had been truly astounding; already it seemed calmer with her quiet. "I hate them. How could it have got in there?"

I knelt beside the girl on the floor. Her eyes opened and fluttered briefly.

"Will she die?" sobbed her companion.

"Certainly not," I said, "and if she hears you crying she will be frightened. Get me a wet cloth, please."

"Come along with me, Janie." George stood beside us, a tall figure in his black formal attire. "We'll see to it, sir."

I got the girl to a chair and managed to keep her calm. The brandy Digby returned with was a great help. Although I am squeamish myself about rats, I had determined to enter the pantry, but Holmes stepped out and resolutely closed the door.

His black brows came together in a crease over his hawk's nose, his eyes puzzled, his mouth a thin, tight line. "The dead rat in the pantry will need to be disposed of, but no one is to touch anything for now."

Fitzwilliams shook his head sadly. "I'll have to put some traps out. We've had nary a rat in the past two or three months."

"I think you should all return to the table," George said. "You've your coffee, and Janie and I'll round up some sweets. A shame to waste the cake, but no one will want it now."

I shuddered slightly. "No."

Back at the table we were all subdued. Constance wiped her brow with a large white hanky. "Merciful heavens," she muttered, "merciful heavens."

Digby grinned enthusiastically. "That's more excitement than I've had in months!" Rose gave him an incredulous stare, her fingers trembling slightly as she drank her coffee. "Not that I don't feel for the poor girls. No one likes a rat, dirty repulsive beasts that they are. They can carry plague, you know."

"God save us all!" Constance exclaimed.

"I suggest you drop such a repugnant topic," I said angrily.

Digby gave a brief laugh. "Sorry—it was a bit thick of me, wasn't it? Well, nothing coffee, chocolates and a few brandies won't fix."

Rose had a peculiar expression on her face, and her broad white forehead was creased. "Do you feel well, Miss Grimswell?" I asked.

"What? Oh, yes, my coffee tastes a little... peculiar."

Digby laughed. "How could you even tell, with all the cream and sugar you put in it? There's very little coffee there."

She smiled. "It is the only way I can abide the taste."

Constance lowered her handkerchief. "I believe the cook said something about trying a new brand of coffee. It is very dear, something served only at the best tables."

Rose shrugged. "Oh." She took a big swallow and set down the empty cup. "Well, I can't say I much care for it. My tastes must be more plebeian."

"It's certainly time for brandy, anyway," Digby said. "Never could understand why you'd want to drink coffee at suppertime, Rosie."

I stared at my cousin. He appeared grim and preoccupied, his eyes faintly uneasy. He soon rose and excused himself, saying he had further business to attend to in the kitchen.

The rest of us adjourned to a comfortable sitting room where Fitzwilliams offered us brandy or port. Constance took a large brandy, but Rose said she did not care for anything.

"Come now," Digby said, "after all that hullabaloo, a little drop would do you good. Don't you agree, doctor?"

Reluctantly I nodded, and Digby handed her a small glass of port. The brandy was quite extraordinary; Lord Grimswell had been very particular about his cognac.

The room was mostly silent for a few minutes, a melancholy time, the loudly ticking clock on the mantel dominant. It was quite warm, and I removed my jacket.

Digby gave a contented sigh and rose to pour another brandy. "Nothing like a dead rat to give a man a thirst."

I stared at him in disbelief. Rose shook her head. "Oh, Rickie, how can you say such a silly thing?"

"Well, it's true, ain't it?"

Constance looked very stern. "I do not find dead rodents amusing in the least. What a fright it gave me."

A white face with a halo of white hair appeared in the black square of the doorway, the eyes dark and angry. It hovered briefly, and then Mrs. Fitzwilliams slowly came through the doorway, supporting herself on her cane. The black dress had made her appear disembodied.

"Are you all right, child?"

Rose smiled. "Yes. Did you not hear? It was only a dead rat. It had nothing to do with me."

The old woman scowled. "Don't be stupid—it had everything to do with you."

Rose's smile vanished. "What do you mean?"

The old woman blinked. Her cataracts were worse now that it was dark; she could not quite see. "The dark one—the dark one is playing games with us."

Rose sighed, raised her head and closed her eyes. "Oh, Lord," she whispered. Perhaps it was the fire, but her cheeks seemed to have a rosy glow. "Oh, don't, nanna—please don't."

Digby smiled ironically. "So you're dragging Beelzebub into this business, are you? Surely the Devil has better things to do than leave dead rats lyin' about? I can just see the old horned fellow with a big rat in each hand, danglin' by the tail."

The old woman's smile was equally withering. "A buffoon can't help you now, Rose. This one couldn't protect you from even a mouse."

Digby's smile vanished. "I do find it wearisome that everyone seems to feel free to insult me. I—"

Rose let out a burst of air from her lips, gasped, then out came another rush of breath. I stood up, then realized she was only laughing. She tried to set down her glass, but knocked over the remnants of the port. She had only drunk a quarter of a small glass, hence her sudden amusement puzzled me. Just then I noticed Holmes standing in the doorway, another pale face hovering in the darkness.

"I say, Rose—what is it?" Digby asked.

She fought to control her breathing, her lips twitching. "I'm sorry. It only… What you said about the Devil… and rats…" That started her off again. The strain of the past few days must have been too much for her.

Mrs. Fitzwilliams shook her head angrily. "Laugh while you can, girl—laugh while you can." She turned to leave even as Holmes stepped into the room.

Constance was frowning. "I just don't see what is so amusing."

Digby smiled. "It must be the notion of old Scratch, Lucifer himself, the Prince of Darkness, the Arch-fiend, traipsin' about with a big rat in each hand."

Rose shook her head, covering her mouth with her hand, but spluttering sounds escaped. "Stop it!" she managed to say, then laughed uncontrollably, her head falling back, then lolling to the side. Her cheeks were flushed, and I had never seen her so animated. I wondered if this were a form of hysteria, but she seemed genuinely amused.

"Keep the stupid joke to yourself." Constance rose and angrily strode to the door.

"Oh, wait, auntie!" Rose struggled to appear serious, but failed even as Constance hesitated at the door. The older woman's stern expression before she left started Digby laughing, and soon both he and Rose were at it.

Nothing is more annoying than to be surrounded by laughing hyenas when you feel tired, quite sober, and thoughtful. Thus I also stood up to leave. Holmes was staring at them, his eyes confused.

"Oh, don't leave, Doctor Vernier." Rose's mouth was twisted, but the appeal in her eyes was clear enough.

"I, too, fail to see any humor in dead rats and the Devil."

Digby roared, and after a brief struggle, Rose also laughed. I shrugged and went to the doorway. Holmes followed me into the great hall. Its cold, shadowy vastness was a stark contrast to the cozy sitting room. A few lamps cast their feeble rays in that cavernous chamber.

"How much did they have to drink?" Holmes asked.

"Digby was well into his second brandy, while Rose had only a few swallows before she spilled her port. She drank nothing with dinner. She certainly cannot be inebriated, even though it may appear that way. What were you doing in the kitchen?"

"Examining the rat and talking with the servants. I have discovered something rather disturbing. The rat was poisoned, most likely some time ago because the body was no longer stiff. The blood about its mouth, the lack of wounds, left little doubt as to the cause of death."

"What is disturbing about a poisoned rat? That is often their fate."

He took out his cigarette case, withdrew a cigarette and lighted it on a wavering candle flame. "They have had no rats in recent months, and no one in the household has set out any poisons or traps."

I scratched at my chin. "Odd, but surely…"

Holmes exhaled a cloud of smoke and began to pace. "A dead rat hardly compares with a cake full of spiders, but I suspect a similar malevolent intent."

I felt an icy sensation low in my belly. He was not speaking hypothetically, but referred to an actual event we had both witnessed, along with many other people. I had never seen so many spiders in my life, and I had been terrified. Michelle had needed to reason with me to bring me to my senses.

"There can be no similarity—surely not."

"Ah, but I am certain there is. Someone placed the dead rat next to the cake knowing full well the cook would discover it. As yet, the reason eludes me."

"Perhaps it was only a prank."

"Blast it, Henry—do not speak nonsense!" I stared at him in disbelief, and his sudden fury vanished. "Forgive me, but we are dealing with a shrewd, calculating mind, not with mere pranks. Would you care to join me in my room? I am ready for a pipe of the viscount's superior tobacco, and I wish to speak with you."

"Gladly. Although…" I realized I was feeling cold because my jacket was back on the chair in the sitting room. "Let me just fetch my jacket."

He nodded, then flicked the ash from his cigarette into a large potted plant. I turned and quickly walked back to the sitting room. Rose had her head against the back of the chair, and Digby was bent over her, one hand on her large bosom. It took me a second to realize they were kissing passionately. Her large white hand clutched at his arm, and I could see the raised tendons extending to each knuckle. I froze, unsure whether I could retreat before they noticed me.

It was too late. Rose pushed Digby away, gasped for air, then saw me. She seemed to have trouble focusing her eyes, but her dismay was evident. "Oh, Lord," she whispered, turning away.

Digby still had hold of her arm. "Here now, my dear, you can't just…" Something made him turn. When he saw me, he leaped back. "You might have knocked!"

"The door was open." My voice was glacial.

"Well, even so…"

"I merely wanted to fetch my coat, and then I shall be going." I picked it up.

Rose's face was quite red. Her eyelids fluttered. She bit at her lip,

then brushed a strand of black hair from her face. "Doctor Vernier..."
It was almost a moan.

"Yes?"

"I..." She put her hand over her forehead. "Oh, I... I don't feel
well." She stood up, stumbling slightly. Her eyes would not meet
mine; they appeared wild and darker, the pupils enormous in the dim
room. "I want to go... lie down." She strode past me and out the door,
almost running.

I stared at Digby. He laughed. "Come now, old boy, it was only a kiss
after all. Did you never kiss your wife that way before your marriage?"

I drew in my breath. "So help me, if you... if you call me 'old boy'
again, I shall knock your teeth down your throat."

This amused him, but I could no longer bear his presence. I walked
into the great hall. Holmes was waiting, a stern expression on his face.
"What has happened?"

I glanced behind me, then walked across the room toward the
fireplace. I tried to tell myself there was no reason to feel quite so
indignant. After all, Digby was correct—I had kissed Michelle that
way before our marriage. All the same, I had never been so gleeful or
cavalier as that leering... "Bounder," I muttered.

"Tell me what you saw."

I stared down at a piece of smoldering coal. "Nothing."

Holmes's laughter had a grating, savage quality. "Male and female
behavior is so predictable, especially that of the female."

"That is not true!" My outrage surprised me.

"No?" He withdrew another cigarette. "Miss Grimswell swept by
me and would not meet my gaze, her hair and dress in slight disarray. I
gather she and Lord Frederick were engaged in some amorous activity.
From your expression, I take it this was not the mere virginal touching
of lips but something more extreme."

I turned and raised my head stiffly. "I will not tolerate your cynicism—not now. What you say is true, but… After all, she is only a twenty-year-old girl, a very lonely twenty-year-old with normal feelings and desires, one who has had little kindness or attention from—the male of the species, as you might say. I am disappointed in her, but I shall not assign blame. Digby is experienced and insistent. Little wonder…"

Holmes's cheeks had reddened, and he lowered his gaze. "Perhaps you are correct, but I had hoped for better from her. Perhaps neither of us is quite rational about Digby. I, too, find him quite distasteful."

"I told him if he called me 'old boy' again I would knock his teeth down his throat."

Holmes's short, sharp laugh filled the hall. "Oh, bravo, Henry—bravo!"

I smiled. Holmes's eyes swept past me, then rose. I turned. Across the hallway, up on the gallery floor, stood George. The shadow hid his formal coat, but his white shirt front and pale face were visible.

"Did he hear us?" I murmured.

"Possibly. Sound carries very well in this vast chamber. He must have seen Miss Grimswell go by."

I shook my head. "My intrusion was perfectly innocent, but I could see she was most embarrassed."

Holmes drew in on his cigarette, his forehead wrinkling. "I hardly had a good look at her, but she seemed more than embarrassed. She seemed distressed." He hesitated. "Are you sure her… activity with Lord Frederick was voluntary?"

"Yes."

He shook his head. "Forgive me, but it often does seem monotonously predictable."

"I cannot believe she will really marry Digby. She cannot. How I wish Michelle were here. She might be able to convince her of his unsuitability."

Holmes shrugged, then threw his cigarette butt into the fireplace. "Digby would not be the worst of husbands. He has a certain flare, albeit a studied one. He is also well read and witty."

"But he is a bounder!"

Holmes laughed. "There is that. Come, let us go upstairs. I am ready for that pipe, and I can tell you what I have discovered in talking with the Fitzwilliamses and the servants."

"You have not been idle like your slothful companions. What have you found out?"

We were halfway up the stairs. Holmes shrugged and smiled. "Nothing I wish to share with the rest of the household. As I said, sound carries very well."

"Ah." However, when we reached the gallery, George was gone.

We soon entered Holmes's room. A coal fire had been started earlier, and it gave off a pleasant warmth. I sat in one of the large leather chairs. Having closed the door behind us, Holmes selected a larger briar from the wall, then opened a canister and began to pack the pipe. Although I could not bear directly inhaling smoke into my lungs, I found the rich, heady odor of pipe tobacco agreeable.

"It took little probing with the maids to discover that they are very uneasy. The viscount died last June, and soon after, a man in black and a giant dog appeared on the moor. Most of the locals are certain it is the viscount. Tradition has it that the vampire originates as a suicide. No one—except possibly Doctor Hartwood—will come near Grimswell Hall after dark. While the maids may not actually believe their deceased master wanders the moors, they would certainly not venture outside. Two of them are considering employment elsewhere, even though the pay here is very good. The old gardener is the most superstitious person and believes his master's restless ghost is being punished for his wicked books. Fitzwilliams indignantly—and sincerely—denies all such supernatural talk. His wife is less sure. She thought her master a good man, but if he committed suicide, he may have earned his dreadful fate."

I shook my head. "Such foolishness. The medieval mind is alive and well on Dartmoor. I suppose the bleak landscape makes the inhabitants susceptible to superstition."

Holmes shrugged. "Perhaps."

"Surely a skeptic like you has not finally become a believer in vampires or werewolves."

"Not at all, but some mortal devil may wish people to believe a ghost wanders the moor. I also discovered that, with the exception of Constance, everyone thought the viscount was in reasonably good health before his death. Constance claims he had not been well for several years, but then she was not actually here prior to his death. I spent considerable time with Fitzwilliams. After all the years at the hall, he must know the family's history and not a few secrets. I dealt indirectly with a certain topic, then asked directly. His answer was equivocal and did little to resolve my doubts."

I stifled a yawn. "I seem to be missing something. What did you ask him?"

Pipe cradled in his right hand, Holmes exhaled a cloud of fragrant smoke. "I asked if his master had been visiting Mrs. Neal on a regular basis."

"Mrs. Neal?" I sat up. "Surely you cannot...?"

He smiled. "You have seen the lady, Henry. If you were a lonely widower with no eligible females for miles around, would you ignore her?"

"Well, perhaps not, but he would have been twenty or twenty-five years her senior."

"What has that to do with anything? Do not forget the telescope pointed at her window. I do not consider that mere coincidence. I hope to discover more when I speak to the widow."

Again I yawned. "I do not quite see the point of all these questions about Lord Grimswell. Knowing whether he killed himself or died of a heart attack may provide some insight into his daughter's temperament, but parents and children may differ considerably."

Holmes shook his head. "Henry, you are being exceptionally obtuse. Has another possibility never occurred to you? A man falls from a great height. His heart may have given out, he may have jumped, or…"

My mind may have been sluggish, but a sudden cold sensation crept up the back of my neck. "Oh Lord–I am obtuse. He was pushed."

Holmes was still smiling, but there was nothing amiable in the expression. "Very good, Henry."

"But why would anyone…?"

"Obtuse again."

"Yes, obtuse. The money–his great fortune." I swallowed. "But then Rose–she…"

"Exactly, Henry. She is in great danger. If someone has already killed once, they will not hesitate a second time. And of course, we are dealing with a fortune of half a million pounds. Many would kill without hesitation for much less."

"Half a million? Digby said four hundred thousand."

"He was mistaken. Mr. Rigby discreetly mentioned the sum in his letter."

"But Rose–she must be protected–she must be watched."

"That is exactly why we are here." He frowned and pulled out his watch. "Eight-thirty. It is early yet, but you are correct. I shall make certain her maid…" He stood up and took a step when there was a rap at the door. "Yes?"

The door opened. George smiled weakly, his eyes uneasy, his face pale. "Sir, Miss Grimswell passed me in the hall, and she seemed… distraught. I was worried that…"

Holmes set down his pipe and slammed his fist on the table. "I have been a fool—the blasted rat distracted me. Which way did she go?"

"Down the hall, toward the tower."

Holmes nodded, then grabbed a candle and strode toward the door. I followed. George stepped back. "Please, sir," he said. "Don't tell anyone I told you. I was supposed to be… otherwise occupied."

Holmes nodded without speaking. Our shadows danced about the hallway, the flame flickering off the walls. We started up the winding stairway. Holmes's breath grew labored, but he did not slow down. I tried to persuade myself that the darkness should lessen my vertigo.

As we came through the opening in the floor, the never-distant cry of the wind swelled, and I felt cold air on my face. Moonlight streamed in the great windows, flooding the elaborately patterned carpet with light. The wind came through an open window, swept round the figure in black perched in the opening. My chest constricted. The light caught her attention and made her turn.

"Stop!" she cried. "Just stop!"

Holmes obeyed, and I nearly bumped into him.

Her face, her hands and feet (she had removed her stockings) stood out against her black dress, moonlight emphasizing their pallor. Holmes had raised the candle, and her fear was obvious. Her mouth was half open, her eyes wide, her long black hair down and disheveled. The rasping sound of her rapid breathing rose over the wind.

"Come down from the window, Miss Grimswell." Holmes's voice was calm yet firm.

She said nothing, only continuing her labored breathing. Holmes stepped nearer.

"I said stop!" she cried, then turned away to stare out into the moonlit night, only one hand supporting her against the window frame.

"I have stopped, Miss Grimswell—I have stopped."

She turned again, and stared at the other edge of the casement. "I must jump. I must."

"No!" I exclaimed.

"You certainly must not," Holmes said.

"Yes—yes."

"Well, you might be so kind as to explain what is wrong before you do so."

"Sherlock," I muttered. My mouth felt dry, my hands cold yet sweaty. Falling from a great height was my worst nightmare, and here was a person about to do just that.

She turned, stumbling slightly. "Dear God," I murmured. She leaned back so her spine was against the window frame, her straight legs outstretched at an angle, bare feet on the ledge, her arms extended so her huge hands touched the opposite side of the frame. Her head hung weakly.

"Oh Lord, why does everything have to be so hard?"

She need only turn and step forward to plunge into the night. The wind rose in a great whistling sigh and blew some papers off the table and made Holmes's candle flicker and go out. The yellow-orange glow of its light was replaced by the colder blue-white light of the moon.

"Don't do that!—I don't like the dark."

"The wind has blown it out, Miss Grimswell, but the moon is quite bright. Will you explain now what you are doing in the window?"

"I must kill myself."

"And why must you kill yourself?"

"Because he told me to!" Her voice rose, the pitch quavering.

"Please calm yourself. We shall not let anyone harm you. You are safe now. Please step down from the window."

"I'm not safe—not from him—and I feel so strange—so awful. I am mad, I know it. I must be. I can... Oh, my heart wants to come out of my chest, and I can feel it in my throat and–"

"You say that you feel strange. When did this feeling of strangeness begin?"

"After dinner, when we were drinking wine. I... oh, I wish it would stop. I do not want to be mad." She let her head fall back against the window frame.

Holmes took two small steps forward. "What exactly happened?"

"I heard the fire crackling, and the sound became... It filled the room–I had never heard anything like it. The sound was familiar, but so different, so vast. And the flames themselves, the way the yellow and orange light twisted and snapped. I had never seen... The colors were so bright, and I could see nothing else around the edges."

Holmes sighed. "You were laughing at what Digby said. I heard you. Did things seem somehow more amusing than you knew they were?"

"Yes!" She lowered her head. "It seemed so silly even to me. What he had said was not that funny, but it seemed absolutely hilarious, and I could not stop laughing. I could not."

"Oh, of course," Holmes muttered.

"What is it?" I whispered.

"And then, I suppose, when Lord Frederick... touched you..."

"I felt it in my whole body. His hands were so hot, and I was hot, and I could feel my heart beating, when I closed my eyes... Oh, my lips felt hot, and..." She moaned. "Oh, I'm so ashamed. You saw me, Doctor Vernier–you saw me. And then I felt nothing but the strangeness, nothing but... I must jump now."

"No, Miss Grimswell, you are not mad. You have only been drugged."

"What?"

"Someone put something in your coffee. It has made you feel very odd, but the effect is temporary. By morning you should feel yourself again."

"Can it be so?" she said to herself.

"What could cause such peculiar symptoms?" I spoke softly.

"Probably hashish. As you know, I am familiar with the pharmacology and effects of most drugs and narcotics."

"More familiar than you should be."

"The heightening of the senses she mentions is the most striking effect. Euphoria, hilarity, increase of appetite, feelings of an erotic nature—these are all common symptoms of hashish."

"But is it not usually smoked in a pipe?"

"Yes, but it can also be ingested."

"You are only trying to fool me," Rose said. "You do not want me to know I am mad."

"Remember the peculiar taste of your coffee. That was the drug. Was it not gritty or powdery? Perhaps you noticed something like unstrained tea leaves."

"Yes—*yes*."

Holmes stepped forward slowly. "I promise by morning you will not feel so strange."

"But could the drug make me see things that are not there? Tell me that."

Holmes hesitated. "No, not generally."

"But I saw him, Mr. Holmes—this time I saw him!" Her voice had softened earlier, but now it shook with raw fear.

Holmes sighed. "Your father?"

"Yes!"

Holmes started forward again.

"Stop!—I said stop!" She straightened up, then lowered her hands and raised one foot so she was balanced on one leg. The moonlight shone on her bare white foot, her toes pointing forward out into the dark night.

"That was not your father, Miss Grimswell. I swear it was not."

"Then I am mad—it always comes back to that, doesn't it? I am mad. They'll have to lock me up just like Aunt Jane—oh, I'd rather die!"

"You are not mad!" Holmes exclaimed. "Someone is trying to convince you that you are insane, but you are not. This has gone on quite long enough—I want you to step down from the window *now*. I have explained to you that you have been drugged and that the strangeness you feel will pass. You may think you have seen your father, but that was treachery as well. Come down. Are you not cold?"

She gave a plaintive laugh. "Oh yes." She had lowered her foot. "Are you telling me the truth, Mr. Holmes, or are you only trying… to spare my feelings?"

"Miss Grimswell, you have my word of honor—I have spoken nothing but the truth."

She sighed, then slumped back again against the frame. Her jaw quavered, and made a clacking noise which was her teeth briefly chattering. "The face was his, yet it was odd, so lifeless and…" Her head fell back again, and I could see her profile in the moonlight, the whiteness of her long throat.

"You can come down now, Miss Grimswell." Holmes's voice was remarkably gentle.

"Yes," I said. "Please, Rose—you are safe now."

She sighed, then stepped down from the window ledge. Her legs buckled, and she fell to her knees. Holmes and I rushed forward. I seized her shoulder and could feel her trembling.

"I was so frightened," she murmured.

A blast of wind struck my face, the air cold and piercingly damp. Although I dared not look down, I sneaked a glance upward. A great pitted moon, well past half, hung against a blue-black sky, but a long shred of white cloud had just covered the top. Soon the light began to dim.

"Can you walk?" I asked.

"I think so."

We helped her to her feet. She swayed slightly. I shook my head. "Oh no, not again." For an instant I wished she were some wee slip of a girl so we could just pick her up and carry her, but she recovered quickly this time. I led her forward while Holmes closed the window. It groaned in the frame, and the moan of the wind was diminished as it sealed. Holmes struck a match and relit the candle.

Rose looked ghastly, her lips somehow blackish, but she tried to smile at me. "I very nearly jumped. I would have if you hadn't come."

I felt too moved to speak. My fingers pushed a long strand of black hair from her eye back across her shoulder. "Thank God you did not."

Holmes's lips formed a wary smile. "And thank George—if he had not come to the door when he did... He saw you in the hall, Miss Grimswell."

She blinked dully. "George? I did not see him."

"We need to get her to a warm room." I had grasped her arm, and Holmes took the other. We started for the stairs.

"I am very cold," she murmured.

"A fire and some brandy will take care of that."

We had started down, the candle's feeble light struggling to illuminate the black granite of the walls. "It was so dark when I came up here. My candle went out on the stairs. I couldn't see anything, and I was so frightened." She glanced at the candle, then away. "The flame..."

"Does it still appear odd?" Holmes asked.

"Yes."

"If one knows the effect is the result of the drug and is temporary, then the strangeness may actually be appreciated. Try staring at the flame. Do not be frightened of it."

She did so. "Yes." She nodded. Her teeth chattered briefly for a moment, and her arm still shook.

We went down the hallway but just before her door she suddenly stopped. "I cannot go in there. He…"

"I shall go in first to make sure it is safe," Holmes said. "Where did you see him?"

"At the window near the fire. Staring in at me. His eyes had light in them." She shuddered, something that passed through her entire body.

Holmes gave me the candle and stepped inside. She turned and sagged against the wall. "I am tired."

"You can rest now, and we shall stay with you."

Her throat rippled as she swallowed. "Thank you."

Holmes reappeared. "There is no one, and I have drawn all the curtains."

I led her into the room, then let go. We all went to the fireplace. The heat from the glowing coal was the most wonderful thing in the world. Her face was still terribly pale, and her black dress looked wrinkled. Half the buttons were unfastened in front. She touched her hair, sighed, and then her legs gave way again. Holmes and I tried to catch her, but she was too heavy and we were too late.

Holmes shook his head. "I'm glad that didn't happen on the stairway."

"Don't worry," she said. "I am perfectly well. I only want to rest here for a little while." Her legs were tucked under her, and she had risen up onto her left arm. "It feels so warm." She sighed, brushing her hair back out of her face, then glanced at the window hidden by the curtains. Her eyes widened. They were all pupils, great burning dark holes reflecting the fear within her, the gray-blue of the irises hidden.

"There is nothing there," Holmes said. "You need not be afraid."

She tried to smile, then nodded. She made a strange sound. When I realized it was her teeth still chattering erratically, I felt cold myself, despite the heat pouring from the fireplace. I turned, then yanked a fluffy quilt from the bed and cast it over her. Outside the wind continued its endless keening moan.

Ten

It was to be another long night.

Holmes asked me to watch Rose while he had a look about. She was too cold and frightened to sleep immediately. I tried to reassure her even though I was badly shaken myself. I didn't really believe in ghosts, but a palpable sense of evil lurked in the dreary hall and desolate moors. Mortal men might be responsible, but of a particularly cruel and savage nature. Equally disturbing was the possibility that the recent visions might only be the concoctions of an ailing mind. I was nowhere near so certain as Holmes about Rose's sanity.

Since she did not want to leave the fire, I also brought a pillow from the bed. She wrapped herself in the quilt, smiled wanly, then lay trembling for a long while. Our conversation did provide some semblance of normality, and soon she fell asleep. Staring grimly into the fire, I wondered what I was doing there instead of being at my home in London in my warm bed, Michelle beside me. By then, however, I was committed—I could not abandon the poor girl to whatever dark fate awaited her.

Digby appeared around ten. He was not pleased to discover me in Rose's bedroom and made some insulting assumptions. Given the hour and location, I told him he was no one to be giving lectures on morality. Rose stirred, and Digby and I went to the doorway, where I tried to explain what had happened. I was making little progress until Holmes appeared and corroborated my story. As usual, Digby was contrite and apologized profusely. He had not meant what he had said, and he offered to relieve me as Rose's guardian.

Holmes and I stared at one another, an unspoken agreement passing between us. Holmes thanked him for his concern but said Rose needed the watchful care of a physician because of the dire possibility of brain fever. I raised my eyebrows but said nothing. A penitent Digby retreated, saying he would check on his fiancée later.

Once he had left, I said, "Brain fever?"

Holmes smiled. "A suitably evil-sounding malady, is it not?"

"Yes, although it is not a clinical term."

"At this point there is no one in the house I would trust with Rose but you."

"Surely you cannot suspect everyone?"

"Surely I can, Henry—some more than others, Digby being near the top of the list. Oh, and this should go without saying, but tell absolutely no one that she was drugged. That must be our secret."

I stifled a yawn, then walked back into the room toward the fireplace. Holmes followed. I could see that he was weary, but agitated, restless. He glanced down at Rose, then gave his head a shake. I sank down into a chair with a sigh. The howling of the wind had grown worse, and I heard a smattering of raindrops hit the windows. "This is like some… some nightmare." I spoke softly, not wanting to wake her.

"If you would like to sleep, Henry, I can watch her. I am accustomed to being up all night long."

Again I yawned. "Although I feel tired, I am not certain I could sleep."

We both sat silently for a long while. I stared down at Rose Grimswell, then my eyes rose. Holmes was in a chair, one hand tapping lightly on his knee. "She is..." I said, "she is a beautiful woman, is she not?"

Holmes's face went curiously neutral, as if he were trying to erase all hints of emotion. "She is."

"If Digby were not too... obtuse to see it, things might be altogether different." The silence began to settle about us, but I was not finished. "In the tower, when she asked you if you were only trying to placate her..."

His mouth stiffened, and his eyes showed a flash of anger. "I do not give my word of honor lightly."

"Forgive me—I should have known that."

He smiled, the anger gone at once. "I can see how you might be confused, Henry, but she is not mad." He pulled out his cigarette case, then hesitated.

"Go ahead and smoke. You have earned your cigarette."

"In a lady's bedroom? No, no, it will not do." He slipped the case back into his black coat, then stared into the fire. "It is curious."

"What is curious?"

"That it should be so obvious to me and not to you. While I am an expert on crime, I know little about the fair sex, and you are a married man and have many female patients."

"Not many. Only a few."

"All the same, it was immediately apparent to me that Rose Grimswell is quite sane."

I sighed. "Well, it may compromise my ridiculous position as an expert on the feminine psyche, but I am relieved to hear you say that. It is only that... 'sanity' can be so nebulous. I have seen many people, men and women, tormented by foolish fears or thoughts. Certainly they are not mad—they do not see things or hear voices—but they are deeply unhappy. As a doctor, I would like to help them, and yet I can do almost nothing."

Holmes stared grimly at the fire. "Sooner or later, every man—or woman—has their own devils to battle, but some more so than others. Miss Grimswell may have a melancholy disposition, but some villains are doing their best to make her suffer, and I shall see that they pay for their monstrous crimes." His voice was harsh; he eased out his breath, then smiled. "But we shall not solve the woes of the world tonight. Go to bed, Henry."

I stood. "Oh, very well, but wake me in a few hours, and I shall watch for a while. You are certain the effects of the drug will be gone by tomorrow?"

"Yes, although she may feel intermittently strange. That was a particularly foul trick, giving a susceptible young woman a drug to confuse and disturb her. It was a deed akin to poisoning, equally treacherous and craven. In her case, the results were also meant to be fatal."

I frowned. "Who could have done it?"

"Almost anyone who was at dinner. In the confusion caused by the rat, anyone could have slipped something into her coffee. Most of the household would have known she used considerable cream and sugar."

"Digby remarked upon that."

"Which would tend to exonerate him. Why raise the issue if you wished to keep it secret?"

I shrugged. "Perhaps he knew you would figure it out and hoped you would make that assumption."

"Mere speculation, either way."

From the hallway we heard a loud wailing noise. Holmes and I stared at one another in dismay, then went to the doorway. Lumbering down the hall, a candle before her, Constance advanced like some black and white dreadnought. "Oh, the poor dear—the poor lamb! Oh, let me see her—let me help her!"

Holmes grimaced. "Keep her out, Henry—I do not want the young lady awakened."

"But..."

"Do not let her in." He closed the door, leaving me to face her.

"Oh doctor, is it true—is it true?" Her huge hand closed about my arm.

I winced—her grip was formidable. "Calm yourself, Constance. She is perfectly all right and sleeping well."

"Oh, let me go to her! *Please.*"

"She needs to rest now."

Constance dabbed at her eyes with the ever-present hanky. "Oh, the poor lamb! Lord Frederick told me all about it. She actually thought she saw her father. Oh, I have been so afraid of this—her mind has finally gone! It has snapped. I have been so afraid of a nervous collapse, and now—brain fever! Oh, dear God, help us!" She sobbed loudly.

"Please, Constance, she needs to rest. You will wake her. There is nothing to worry about now."

"Nothing to worry about when she is seeing her father's ghost? Oh, it is madness, pure and simple, just like my poor sister—just like poor Jane! Oh, God help us." She began to cry loudly.

"Please, you must not—"

The door behind me jerked open, and Holmes's pale face appeared, his eyes furious. "Madam," he whispered fiercely, "you will wake your niece with your caterwauling. I must insist that you keep quiet—that is the best thing you can do for her just now."

Constance gave him a stunned look. She ground her teeth once, and now that she was blessedly silent, I could see something odd in her eyes, a hint of some strange, dark emotion. She sniffled loudly, and it was gone at once.

"I only want to be with her—to help protect her."

"As I suggested, your silence would be particularly golden just now." Holmes closed the door.

Constance sniffled again. "I only wanted to help, doctor. I know I'm only a useless old woman, but I wanted to help." She began to cry—but quietly.

"And so you shall, but just now she needs her sleep. Come, I must go to my room, and..."

We walked side by side down the hall, her lamentations continuing. She seemed convinced her niece had finally gone mad. I considered telling her that Rose had been drugged, then remembered that Holmes had said that must be kept secret. I did tell her all might not yet be lost, that "brain fever" did not inevitably lead to death or madness.

"God help us, no!" We stopped before my door, and again she clutched at my arm. "She has overstrained herself. I told her she should not go out walking on the moor. She needs absolute rest, doctor—absolute rest! She must not be disturbed in any way. Probably it would be best if she remained in bed for a few days—wouldn't that be best?"

"Bed?" I was so weary I could not think clearly, and I just wanted to be rid of her. "Possibly, although—"

"I knew you would understand! You're not like that dreadful Doctor Hartwood. Really, he's nothing but a farmer's boy, not a real doctor at all—not like you. He should have been a veterinarian."

I blinked my eyes dully. "Goodnight, Constance."

"Goodnight. It is good to know there is another voice of reason in this house."

I eagerly closed the door behind me. Two candles on the desk had been lit, but the room was cold and dreary. Outside the wind murmured, and I could hear the rain buffeting the window. I looked at the empty bed, and my heart ached with longing. It had only been three nights in Dartmoor, but it seemed an eon of time. "Oh Michelle, how I miss you."

I pulled off my shoes, took off my jacket and got under the blankets. It seemed foolish to get undressed if Holmes might wake me soon. I closed my eyes, thinking I might just rest for a moment, and then I was outside walking on the moors in the dark. For some reason, I was not wet, despite the dreadful storm.

The rain ceased, and the moon slowly rose, a cool, dazzling bluish-white. Behind me I saw my shadow cast on the grassy moor. Holmes tried to speak to me, but a desolate howling began. Atop the tor was a figure in black with a strange white and black face. His eyes were yellowish, and his nose changed from human to something lupine, even as his jaw stretched outward into a muzzle. He grinned at me, and made a laughing sound. Frightened, I turned away, but he was in front of me, only ten paces, and he was human again, or his face was, but now he was down on all fours and had an enormous tail and was growling low in his throat.

I ran, trying to find Holmes, trying to find the way back to the hall, but the howling began again. The dream seemed to repeat itself, the creature alternating between man and beast. "What in God's name are you?" I cried. I could not seem to escape the dream, even though I knew it was not real. Dark clouds had risen over the moor, obscuring the moon, and at last I managed to escape into a deeper sleep.

"Henry?"

I opened my eyes and looked about. For an instant I could not recall where I was, then the cold, dark chamber was depressingly familiar. Holmes had seized my arm. Just behind him was the tall, silent figure of Rose, still in her black dress.

"What time is it?" I asked.

"Just past two."

I blinked dully and sat up. "I was finally fast asleep. What is wrong?"

"It is Rose."

I realized she was holding his arm loosely at the elbow.

"I need your assistance. She is sleepwalking again."

"Ah." I sat up. "She does not seem upset."

"She was earlier. In her dreams she saw her father and was terrified. I managed to calm her, but now... She thinks we are married."

I stared at him. "Indeed?"

"Can you help me get her to bed?"

I threw the covers aside and stood. Rose smiled, then took my arm with her free hand. "Come, Rose," I said.

"You shall have my answer on the morrow, Henry."

I glanced at Holmes, then started for the door. He picked up a candle which he had set on the table. She let go of him and grasped my arm with her other hand as well. She leaned her pale face closer to mine. "If only I were free of him, and you... It is wretched to love two men, I who thought... And there is my father. He still wants to kill us all." Reflexively, she brushed a strand of black hair from her face.

I glanced at Holmes and shook my head.

"That is the type of thing I have had to endure. I am at my wits' end."

"I can take care of your father," I said. "You need not worry about him." We were walking in the hallway.

"You do not know how dangerous he is. A vampire cannot be killed. Moonlight will reanimate his corpse. He wants me to be dead like him. And he has... I think he has killed Sherlock Holmes." Her voice had an odd quaver.

"No, you are wrong. Holmes is here beside me."

She glanced at him, then gave her head a quick shake. Her voice was almost a whisper now. "That is not him—that is another vampire. See how pale he is, and his teeth…" She drew closer to me, hiding her face from Holmes.

I led her into her bedroom, then glanced at Holmes. "I see what you mean about her behavior."

"She has been this way for some time."

Rose let go of me and stepped back even as her eyes widened. "Oh, you are like him—and you no longer love me. You—you want to kill me, too."

I took her arm. "No, Rose, that's not true. I…" She is not awake, she is only dreaming, I told myself. "I do love you. You are safe with me. You are… you are my wife, after all."

Her eyes grew wider still, but somehow she only half seemed to see me. "Am I?"

"Yes, of course, and now I want you back in bed."

She squeezed my hand tightly. "Oh, I am so glad. I thought… Never mind what I thought. I love you, too, Henry."

Holmes drew the covers aside, but she stood staring at me. "Are you sure you are not one of *them?*"

"No, of course not. You know me, don't you? Please, you must get back to bed. It is very late."

"I feel so confused and miserable. Nothing makes any sense at all." Her eyes shifted, and her mouth stiffened. "He is outside the window, you know. I can see him watching us."

The back of my neck felt cold, and I turned. The curtains were drawn, the window hidden.

"His face is so white. It is because he is dead. Oh, I hope you are not…"

"Rose, you must get into bed. I will not let him hurt you, I promise. You must trust me, and you must rest. Go on now."

She sat down on the edge of the mattress, then sighed. "My legs are weary. They ache so."

Again I recalled how I would massage Michelle's legs and feet before bed, especially on those days when she had been at the volunteer clinic. I was fully awake now, and my head had begun to ache. I also found my role in this drama both confusing and unsettling.

"Get to bed, Rose. No one will hurt you, I promise."

One large white hand rose and seized her dress below the collar. Half the buttons in front were still undone. "Shouldn't I take off my dress first?"

"Uh, not just now. First you must warm up a little."

"All right." She lay down on her side, and put one hand just before her face. "And you'll come to bed soon?"

I inhaled through my nostrils. "Yes." I drew the covers over her.

Her eyes stared past me, her forehead creasing again. "I do not like him in the window. How I wish he would go away and leave me alone." Her voice was both weary and agitated.

I drew in my breath, then sat on the bed beside her. Sometimes, especially with the very young or the very old, a touch of the hand would comfort patients who would respond to nothing else. I learned that technique from Michelle. I set my hand on her shoulder and squeezed softly.

"You must go to sleep now. There is no one at the window."

"Yes, there is."

"But he cannot get in. He dare not enter. Soon the sun will rise, and it will drive him far from here."

"Will it?"

I began to stroke her shoulder. "Certainly it will. Vampires cannot abide the sun. You are quite safe now. Sherlock and I shall not let anyone harm you."

"And you do love me?"

I hesitated only an instant. "Of course I do."

She finally closed her eyes. Briefly her lips formed a smile. "I never thought... Come to bed soon. I..."

I continued to gently massage her shoulder and mumble reassuring words. At last I sighed and looked up at Holmes.

He looked exhausted, the muscles around his eyes strained. "Your bedside manner is most impressive, Henry. Thank you. I did not know what to do. She..." He reached into his jacket and withdrew his cigarette case.

"The lady will never know if you smoke only one cigarette in her bedroom."

"Very well." He withdrew a cigarette, then took a candle to light it. His hand shook slightly. He inhaled, raising the other hand in a long stretch.

"I am awake now," I said. "I can watch her for a while if you wish to sleep."

I slowly withdrew my hand from her shoulder, and her eyes immediately opened. "What...?" she murmured. I lowered my hand, and she was asleep again at once.

I shook my head. "If Digby comes in, I shall never be able to explain this."

Holmes smiled, then drew in on the cigarette. "I turned him away around midnight. I doubt he will return. I am almost ready for a nap in the chair here." After finishing his cigarette, he sat down, closed his eyes, turned sideways, and was asleep in an instant. His head slumped against the padded arm of the wing chair, his mouth opening slightly.

I could hear the rain outside die down, but then the wind increased. My neck and arm were beginning to feel stiff from the awkward way I was twisted. I murmured comforting words as I massaged Rose's shoulder slower and slower. At last I withdrew my hand. Her breath came out in a long sigh, and she seemed to sink deeper into the pillow.

I stood up and raised both hands, trying to stretch out the stiffness. The heavy silence and preternatural stillness of early morning had settled over the room. The clock showed that it was nearly three. The world of day and light and active, working, talking people had vanished. I did not care for this time. I had watched over too many dying patients in the early morning. I was weary to the bone, but I knew a certain troubled agitation would keep me awake even if I could go back to bed. Besides, the presence of Holmes and Rose was reassuring: I was glad not to be alone.

"You do not understand." Rose's voice was troubled, and she turned restlessly.

I touched her hand. "I understand. You are safe, Rose. Sleep."

She settled again. I went to the fireplace. Holmes must have added coal earlier. I added more to the glowing remnants. The time dragged by. I thought about Michelle. I thought about how strange it was to be in Dartmoor, and I worried about what might happen to Rose, Sherlock and me. If someone had murdered Lord Grimswell, they would not hesitate to kill again and again. A stubborn fear began to settle about my heart. I paced about, soon exhausting myself.

When Holmes awoke around six, it was a relief. The gray of dawn appearing at the windows also helped ease my fears. We talked in quiet voices while the light grew. At last I rose and drew aside a curtain. The sky was shredded with dark clouds, and mists made the trees near the house look ghostly. However, the rains had stopped.

I returned at last to my room, took off my evening clothes and put on a heavy wool nightshirt. I doubted I would sleep, but I wanted to be comfortable. The conversation with Holmes had relaxed me, and I fell asleep at once. A woman was in the dreams, a woman in danger;

sometimes she was Michelle, sometimes Rose. At one point the dream took a sensual turn, and the woman continued to change shape and form, even as she slipped in and out of my grasp.

"Oh, Henry." That was Michelle's voice. Her hand caressed my cheek with a familiar intimacy that made me long for her. "Oh, my dear."

I did not want to wake up. It was like swimming to the surface from far underwater. My eyes opened at last, and a face I preferred to all others stared down at me. The past few days had brought too many surprises.

"Is it really you?"

She caressed my cheek again, her pale blue eyes staring down at me. The creases at the corners were becoming permanent. Slowly she leaned over and touched her lips to mine. The kiss was long, slow and passionate—there was no mistaking her.

My arms fumbled out of the covers, and I pulled her down and embraced her. "Oh, thank God you've come—thank God."

She rose up and stared at me, her eyes troubled. "Is anything the matter?"

A smile pulled at my lips, came and went. "Everything is the matter, but now that you are here... nothing is the matter."

"I should have let you sleep. Sherlock told me how late you were up, but I wanted so badly to see you. Marjorie had her baby, so I asked Nigel to cover for me. I took the night train."

"Oh Michelle, I don't think I've ever been so glad to see you."

She stared at me, her eyes worried, touching my cheek just below my eye. "Oh, my darling." She bent over, and we began another long kiss. Gradually she stretched out on top of me, even as my arms gripped her. "Perhaps I should lock the door," she said at last.

"Please do."

My nightshirt and her multitude of garments and undergarments were soon thrown with little care onto the floor. Afterward we both fell asleep for about an hour. We got out of bed around ten, and as we dressed, I told her all that had happened. I did omit the details of Rose's sleepwalking episodes.

"Sherlock spoke with me briefly, but all this…" She shook her head. "Voices frightening her half to death, then telling her to jump—and drugs in her coffee. Who could dream up such terrible things? I think… I think it must be Lord Frederick, after all, although he seems more insipid than dangerous."

"Ah, you have met him then?"

She made a face at me. "Yes. I do not care for affected men. He acts as if he is always playing to some unseen audience. Will you lend me your brush? My hair is certainly a mess—not that it wasn't worth it, you wretch." She took the wooden handle in her big hand and brushed vigorously at her long reddish-brown tresses.

She had on her shift, but I grasped her bare shoulders from behind. "I really have missed you terribly."

Before long, I was doing up the tiny hooks at the back of her blue dress. Regarding herself in the mirror, she coiled up her hair neatly, put in some pins, then gave the bun two pats. "That's better."

I drew down her collar and kissed her lightly on the white nape of her neck. "You are even more beautiful than I remembered. I wish we were alone on holiday together."

"Sadly, that is not the case. Let us go see Sherlock. He is probably still in his room. Miss Grimswell was awake; I have already spoken with her."

"Constance or Rose?"

"Oh, Rose—or actually, both of them. Constance must be the old dragon. What a disagreeable woman. When she heard I was a physician, she wanted to discuss Rose's health at length, but I would not."

"She is harmless enough, although tedious to endure."

"I think we should get Sherlock and Rose and go for a walk on the moors. I believe we may be lucky–Digby was going somewhere. The day has turned sunny, and I am longing to finally go outside. The country is quite splendid, Henry. While we walk, we can discuss our strategy for dealing with these villains, whoever they may be."

She was so resolute I could not help smiling. "You do not believe in ghosts or vampires, then?"

"Certainly not!"

"We shall see if your resolve lasts the night."

"You know it will."

I squeezed her hand. "I believe it. You have always been the brave one." I put on a heavy tweed jacket and took a woolen cloth cap. "Be prepared, however, for objections from Constance. She believes bed rest is the thing for Rose."

"*Bed rest.*" She spoke with such scorn that I laughed. "That is the worst thing for a healthy young woman like her. She needs fresh air and exercise to take her mind off this dreary business. I shall handle Constance."

I laughed again. "Poor woman. Little does she know what fate awaits her. However, you must promise me one thing." I took her hand, my smile fading. "You must promise to be careful. This is a dark, dark business. Even if there is no ghost or vampire, there is evil–overpowering evil. I can sense it. Whoever is behind this will not hesitate to kill. Sherlock believes Lord Grimswell was murdered."

"Oh no."

"He believes he was pushed–the fall was no accident. I half think I should put you back on the train."

She squared her shoulders and raised her chin. "You must know I would never leave now."

"I do, and I am selfish enough to want you near me. I feel… only half a man when I am away from you."

"I can help Rose—I know I can."

"Yes, you can. But promise me…" I raised her hand and kissed her knuckles. "Promise you will be careful, that you will take no foolish risks."

"I promise, and you must swear the same."

I smiled. "You know I am by nature cautious."

A frown creased her brow. "Yes, but Sherlock makes you behave foolishly. I have never been so frightened in my life as when you told me of your journey with him into the Underton rookery."

I shook my head. "I don't like to remember that either. We shall both be careful." I touched her cheek with the back of my hand. "Because we have so much to lose."

Holmes's room was near mine, and we found him sitting before the fireplace with a pipe in hand, one with a long, straight stem. Although he had had only two or three hours' sleep, he did not appear weary. Michelle's suggestion of a walk made him nod.

"Yes, that would do us all some good." He rose and took a heavy pair of boots from the wardrobe, then sat and slipped off his thin leather shoes.

"In all the excitement last night," I said, "I forgot to ask if you discovered anything when you looked about the hall."

"I have some idea how Rose was deceived, but let us wait and discuss it with her."

I shook my head. "Thank God she did not jump. She gave me such a fright."

Michelle gave my arm a sympathetic squeeze. "Knowing you, merely being up in a tower that high would be frightening. That was very brave of you."

Holmes finished lacing up his boots, took a last draw on the pipe, then regretfully emptied its contents into the fireplace. He took his hat, gloves and stick.

Rose was also in her room. She looked somewhat pale and tired, but remarkably well, considering. The suggestion of a walk made her smile. "What a splendid idea! I shall just change my clothes and join you."

"You look more yourself today," I said. "I take it the feeling of strangeness is gone?"

Her smile wavered. "Yes, for the most part. It really is such a relief. I felt so very odd. And my dreams were unsettled all last night, although I did sleep." She stared at me, and a faint flush appeared in her cheeks. "I have not thanked you both properly." Her gaze took in both Holmes and me. "You saved my life. Had you not come, I would have jumped. I would be dead now." Her face went paler still, and she bit at her lower lip.

Michelle touched her arm, startling her, and she flinched wildly. Michelle drew back. "Oh, pardon me."

Rose shook her head, her lip still between her teeth. "I'm sorry. I... I... It's only..." Her mouth contorted, moving as if it had a will of its own. Her breath came out in a shudder, and tears filled her eyes. "Forgive me–I... I don't know what's the matter."

Michelle stepped forward, carefully put her arm around Rose and grasped her shoulder. "Oh hush, my dear–it's perfectly all right to feel dreadful."

"Is it?" Rose had begun to cry.

"After all that you have endured–*yes*." She looked at Holmes and me. "Give us a few minutes, and we shall join you downstairs. I also need to change into something less fashionable and more practical."

Holmes's gray eyes showed his concern, and he nodded. Rose turned away from us, letting Michelle shelter her in her arms. Again I reflected how odd it was to see a woman who could make Michelle actually look small. Rose was some three inches taller and even more broad-shouldered. The two were a contrast: Rose with her black dress and black hair, her face so pale, while the light from the big windows made Michelle's electric-blue dress glow and shone on her light brown hair.

Holmes and I went silently down the hallway to the gallery, and traversed it to the stairs. In the great hall, our footsteps echoed faintly overhead. A shaft of sunlight slanted down from a window, a great yellow diagonal before us, the tiny dust motes dancing like gnats. Even on a sunny day, the black granite of the walls gave the vast chamber a funereal air. Constance stood up from a chair, turned and smiled at us. I suddenly realized that Michelle was the only woman I had ever seen at Grimswell Hall wearing a bit of color—Rose, Constance, Mrs. Fitzwilliams and all the maids were always in black.

"Going for a stroll? The day is very fine. Lord Frederick has already gone out. I shall gladly keep an eye on Rose while you are walking."

My hand shot out to grasp Holmes's arm, but I was too late. "She will be joining us shortly," he said.

Constance's face somehow expanded from horror. "Not Rose?"

Holmes nodded. "Yes, Rose."

She turned to me, just as I had feared. "But, doctor—you agreed she needed rest—absolute rest. You cannot—you cannot—oh, she must not go out! With her nerves, the least strain…! Oh, I forbid it!"

I forced a nervous smile. "Please, Constance, the exercise will do her good."

"When she has been up half the night?—when her nerves are at breaking point?—when she suffers from… brain fever? When she sees phantoms like the ghost of her father? Oh dear God, no!"

"She may be slightly tired, but—"

"Then she must rest, mustn't she? A nap is the very thing, not trekking about the moors. And what if it should rain? The sun is out now, but for how long? The weather can change in an instant. If she should be soaked to the skin in her frail and weakened condition, what then? Pneumonia or worse!"

"I hardly think—"

"Then you must agree with me! Please, doctor, her very life may be at stake! I have stood by quietly, but I really must insist—I am her guardian, after all. She's all I have left, the last of our poor family! I cannot..."

Holmes had a look of weary disgust. I tried twice to interrupt her, but she cut me off each time. My head had begun to ache, and I realized exactly how tired I really was.

Constance suddenly paused, raised her eyes and folded her arms resolutely. Coming down the stairs were Michelle and Rose, both wearing sturdy brown woolen jackets and skirts. Michelle had a stern expression, and she had hold of Rose's arm. The younger woman had washed her face, but her eyes were red—and wary of her aunt.

"What is going on?" Michelle asked. "What is this din?"

"Constance is concerned that walking may not be good for Rose's health," I said.

Constance nodded fiercely. "Certainly not! Absolute rest is what the poor girl needs! I will not have it."

Michelle let go of Rose and stepped forward. She and Constance were almost exactly the same height. "Have you ever studied medicine, Miss Grimswell?"

"No, but—"

"Then I suggest you leave Rose's treatment to those who have."

"But her nerves, madam, and she is so frail! Surely—"

Michelle gave a sharp laugh. "*Frail?* Look at her!"

"She is tall, yes, but weak and ill and—"

"Nonsense! She is a strong, healthy young woman who has had more than her share of fears and worries. Fresh air and activity are exactly what she needs."

"How can you say such a thing? Oh, old Doctor Herbert knew better. And how—how can a woman be a doctor, anyway? I've never heard of such a thing."

Michelle's jaw stiffened. For a second or two, I wondered if she might actually strike Constance. "By studying for years and working much harder than any man!"

"I may be an ignorant old woman, but I'm her family—her only family—and I only want what's best for her. I forbid it—I forbid it! Rose, surely you must know that you are not up to this. Don't you feel weary and agitated, poor lamb? You must go back to your room. Let me tuck you into bed and get—" She tried to touch Rose, but Michelle stepped between them.

"Miss Grimswell, my husband and I are physicians, and it is our professional opinion that the young lady would benefit from a walk."

Constance stared at me in horror. "Not you, too, Doctor Vernier—not you! I thought we had an agreement, I thought—"

"Miss Grimswell—Miss Grimswell…" Michelle was almost shouting to get a word in. "Please stand aside, and do stop bullying your niece!"

"Bullying her!" Constance's voice was a wounded bellow.

"Yes!"

Constance's eyes grew all teary. "Rose," she said softly. "Dear Rose."

Rose put her large white hand over her forehead. "Oh, auntie…"

"See—*see!* She is—"

Michelle resolutely grasped Rose's hand, then led her past her aunt toward the doorway.

"Rose, you cannot be leaving! Rose—"

"*Silence, madam!*" Holmes's voice thundered even as he struck the granite floor with the iron ferrule of his stick. The hall immediately grew silent. Holmes glared, letting it linger a while. "That is quite enough. You have had your say. If you were truly concerned about your niece's well-being, then you would not so needlessly upset her."

Constance glared back. Her jaw moved sideways in a characteristic gesture, her teeth grinding slightly. She opened her mouth, then turned and stalked away.

I let out a tremendous sigh. "Oh well done, Sherlock—well done! I thought nothing could ever quieten her."

We quickly fled the hall and went outside. A path constructed of granite slabs came up to the main entrance of the hall. We paused to savor the sunshine on our faces and the quiet of an autumn day. The wind could be heard in the muted rustling of the yew and oak leaves.

Michelle took a deep breath and smiled. "The air is divine, so different from London. And I, too, thank you, Sherlock. You quite vanquished her." She turned to Rose. "I hope you understand, my dear, that Henry and I would do nothing to risk your health."

Rose smiled; she too was clearly relieved. "Oh, I know that. I only wish… It is so hard to disagree with her."

Michelle laughed. "So I see! Well, where shall we go?"

Holmes raised his stick and set it on his shoulder. "Miss Grimswell, would a walk to the tor—to Demon Tor—be too difficult for you?"

"No, not at all. It is not far, and there are only one or two steep parts. The view is spectacular."

Holmes nodded. "Very well. You may lead the way."

We went around the house through the yews, and then some great silent oaks, their gnarled limbs nearly black, their leaves shades of bronze or russet. The half-rotted smell of fallen leaves and crushed acorns was dank and rich. From one of the trees came the hoarse caw of a rook. The trees ended abruptly, and the rising ground of brownish faded heather and green grass led to a jumble of boulders, which the locals called "clitter," and then the black granite slabs of the tor. A path of sorts, one worn into the reddish earth by centuries of footsteps, led upward.

We all savored the warmth and silence, so welcome after the long, cold night and Constance's outburst, and before long, we were all breathing too hard to speak much. After rising briefly, the path vanished, but Rose led us up through the boulders. At the top a cold wind from the north cut into our faces.

"Oh, how beautiful!" Michelle gave my hand a squeeze. "I am so happy to be here."

Rose was smiling, but her gray-blue eyes, so luminous in the light, were troubled. She was staring down at the edge of the massive rock before us. The ragged face of black granite was blotched with lichens of yellow and green, but some twenty feet away must be a precipitous drop. It struck me abruptly—that must be the very place from which Lord Grimswell had fallen to his death. I was standing well back, but it would take only seconds to run forward and hurtle off to my death. I felt cold, sick and very dizzy. I reached out and seized Michelle's arm.

"Do not go any closer."

She was smiling, but then saw the expression on my face. "Henry, are you ill?"

"I feel... dizzy." In truth, black spots had begun to dance about before my eyes.

"Sit down," she said sharply.

I did so, closing my eyes tightly. A surge of nausea made me gasp, then swallow hard, forcing down a foul burning substance. Michelle had knelt beside me, and I sagged against her, my hand grasping for hers. "It is... too high," I muttered.

"We should not have brought him up here," Michelle said. "I should have known."

"What is it?" Rose asked, obviously worried.

"He suffers from vertigo, and he is probably exhausted as well."

I took a deep breath and eased open my eyes. We were facing away from the precipice. "I only need a moment's rest. It was… the surprise. The rise was so gradual, I didn't realize how high we were climbing."

Holmes also knelt beside me. The brim of his hat cast a shadow over his eyes. "I too should have known better. I'm sorry, Henry. The site is also an unpleasant one for Miss Grimswell."

"But why?" Michelle asked. "It is so beautiful."

"Because of what happened to her father."

Michelle scowled. "Oh, I am an imbecile. Perhaps we should go back."

Rose's sigh was barely audible over the murmur of the wind. "I have not been here since his death, but it was time. This was perhaps his favorite spot in Dartmoor. We came here together many times. He would never want me to consider it out of bounds."

Holmes sat down beside me on the uneven rock, setting his walking stick alongside us, then removed his hat and raised his face to the sun. "We could all do with a breather."

Rose and Michelle also sat, so we were all in a row atop that granite, our legs before us where the rock sloped downward slightly. Michelle was to my right, still holding my arm, while Holmes and Rose were to my left. High above a large bird soared silently, probably a lone buzzard seeking prey. Grimswell Hall must have been behind us, but to the southwest and north were two companion tors, and across a long brown patch of moor was a wooded area.

After a brief silence, Holmes spoke. "Miss Grimswell, I regret having to speak of unpleasant things, but here in the bright sunlight and amid the splendor of nature might be the best place to talk about last night."

"Oh Sherlock," Michelle said, "must you?"

"I would like to talk about it," Rose said. She leaned forward and turned to me. "Doctor Vernier…?" Her voice had a questioning note.

I smiled. "Please, after all we have been through together, you must call me Henry."

She nodded. "I shall. When you came into the sitting room after dinner and... found Rickie and me together..." Her fair skin was very sensitive to her emotions, and her cheeks had colored. "I was embarrassed, terribly embarrassed, and I only wanted to run away and hide. Rickie was... Earlier I had felt almost intoxicated, but by then I only felt odd and rather sick and... afraid." She drew in her breath. "I thought I must finally be going mad."

Holmes had clasped his hands together, his arms round his knees. "Anyone who had been drugged and did not know it might make that assumption."

"I went to my room and removed my uncomfortable shoes and my stockings. I thought of putting on my nightgown, but my head was still spinning. I collapsed onto the bed and buried my face in a pillow. It was much better with my eyes closed, and I was finally starting to relax when I heard his voice. 'Rose, Rose,' he whispered. I knew at once who it was. I was... terrified."

Michelle abruptly stood, stepped around Holmes and me, and sat beside Rose. She grasped the girl's hand.

"From where exactly did the voice seem to come?" Holmes asked.

"The fireplace. He even said to come sit by the fire. He was taunting me."

"Ah, very good! I know exactly how this was done, Miss Grimswell. It must be difficult, but tell me briefly what he said and when he finally appeared."

"He... he told me I was home at last, and that I must join him. The tainted blood of the Grimswells flowed in our veins, and it was time to end the abomination of our family. I was mad and sick and must join him. Until I did, I would have no peace, neither day nor night."

"And he told you to go to the tower?"

"Yes, that was the last thing. He said it just after he appeared—he screamed, 'Go to the tower–jump–jump–or I shall be your companion ever more!'" Her voice had begun to quaver, and I saw Michelle's hand tighten about hers.

"And he was at the window by the fireplace?"

She nodded.

"Tell me exactly what you saw."

"A white face–his face–all waxen and dead with glowing lights where his eyes should have been, a kind of black cowl about him."

"Did you have a good look at him, or only a brief glance?"

She shook her head. "Brief. I could not bear–"

Holmes struck his stick on the granite. "As the villain hoped! Miss Grimswell, you have been duped. I have explained to you how you were drugged, hashish put into your coffee, and you are better today, are you not? Well, I shall explain this apparition, and you must trust me and set all thoughts of madness aside. Your bedroom is on the second floor. You share a chimney with an empty room on the third floor. I was up there last night looking about. Someone spoke to you through the chimney. Perhaps they used some tubing to amplify the voice. Another person was on the roof, dangling down a dummy complete with a white mask and a hidden lamp. The person in the chimney used a cord to communicate with the person on the roof, a simple tug probably being the signal to lower the dummy. The gravel on the roof was disturbed."

Rose stared at him, her forehead creased. "Could it have been only that, only a... mask?"

"Yes. *Yes.*" Again Holmes struck the rock with his stick, then stood, stepped forward and turned to face us three. "It is monstrously simple."

"But the voice–the face–were truly his."

"Someone studied your father's voice and has a talent for mimicry. As for the face... You said it was dead-looking. We may be dealing with an actual death mask."

Rose looked horrified. "But he would never have allowed such a thing!"

Holmes's smile was brief and dreadful. "I doubt he had any choice in the matter." My head seemed oddly empty, my thoughts sluggish, although I felt vaguely fearful. "While he lay below, dead, someone could have easily taken an impression." The buzzard was gone, and behind Holmes was only a vast blue sky.

Rose's head slumped, and she put her hand over her face. "Oh God. They... they... killed him?"

Holmes sighed softly. "Yes."

"Who are these people!" Michelle exclaimed.

Eleven

When we returned to the hall, everyone seemed to be waiting for us. Digby exclaimed how much better Rose appeared and begged to be included in our next outing. Rose smiled hesitantly while Michelle struggled to hide her disapproval. Next, a penitent Constance appeared and loudly begged pardon for "a poor, meddling old woman." Our protestations to the contrary, something in Holmes and Michelle's eyes told me all was most definitely *not* forgiven.

And finally, after Digby and the ladies had departed, George appeared out of nowhere, actually making me start. Normally the footsteps echoing through the hall announced anyone's arrival. Holmes and I had been standing before the fire, the reddish light of the sinking sun flooding the chamber and giving everything a bloody hue.

"Is the mistress quite well?" he asked softly.

Holmes stared silently at him.

"She is," I said at last. "You saved her life, you realize."

George's habitual grin was nowhere in sight. "Thank God. Well, I'd best…"

Holmes stroked his chin, then let drop his long, slender hand. "She very nearly jumped from the tower. Have you ever seen the body of someone who has fallen from a great height?"

George paled. "I... have."

"A very unpleasant sight. The contrast with the living, vibrant young woman would be most striking."

George appeared as dismayed as I, but he tried to smile. "It is..."

"I shall want to speak with you soon, George. Whenever you are ready."

"Me? But sir, why should you...?"

"Do not wait too long—for your own sake. The game may be more dangerous than you realize, the stakes far higher."

George opened his mouth, glanced about, then closed it. Above us in the gallery was the sour-faced maid, Maria.

"Think about what I have said, George. You saved Miss Grimswell's life, a fact I shall not forget."

George nodded, then backed away, turned and walked across the hallway to the stairs.

"What was that all about?" I asked.

"Have you not wondered how George knew Miss Grimswell was in danger?"

"He saw her in the hall, and doubtless she appeared dreadful."

"The lady does not recall seeing him," Holmes said.

"Surely if she were distressed she might—"

"She was disorientated and upset, not stupefied or intoxicated." Holmes gave his head a shake. "Really, Henry, can you deduce nothing on your own?"

Annoyed, I did not pursue the topic.

Dinner that evening was actually pleasant. I, of course, was in excellent humor because of Michelle's arrival. Rose was relieved at feeling better, and she and Michelle already seemed to have become bosom friends. Michelle kept a wary eye on Digby, and her presence had a moderating effect on that young man, rendering him actually bearable. Constance was still penitent and pleasantly subdued. She must have left the menu to Mrs. Fitzwilliams, for we were spared many courses and rich sauces, a delicious roast beef being the sole offering.

Holmes was rather quiet, but I sensed that a problem preoccupied him. However, after dinner, in the sitting room, he made peace with Constance.

"If I have appeared rather gruff, madam, I hope you will forgive me. You must understand that I share your concern for Miss Grimswell, representing as she does the last of your illustrious family."

Constance dabbed at her eyes with a handkerchief. "No, no, Mr. Holmes. You are too kind. I have already acknowledged that I am at fault."

"No matter. As we are in accord, there is no reason to dwell on past unpleasantries." He sipped at his cognac while Michelle gave me a puzzled look. "This is a remarkable elixir. Perhaps you could tell me something of the Grimswells, Constance. I have read the entry in *Burke's Peerage* about the viscount and had some discussion with Fitzwilliams, but I know little about the rest of the family."

Constance shook her head sadly. "There's precious little of us left, I fear. Only Jane and myself."

"Victor Grimswell's father, Robert, the prior viscount, had a younger brother. That brother was your father, Phillip. Were there other brothers or sisters?"

Constance sighed. "None living."

Holmes's eyebrows sank inward. "Were there some who died?"

"One. Uncle Jonathan was the middle brother, born in 1807. I fear he met a bad end." She glanced warily across the room at Rose. "There are two unpleasant strains in our family, impurities in our very blood—a melancholy disposition, a dark mood, and a violent temper. Madness is often the result."

Michelle's mouth formed a tight smile. "That seems more than two things."

"What happened to Jonathan?" Holmes asked.

"He quarreled with a disreputable companion in a tavern, cursed and blasphemed. The companion seized a knife and plunged it into his throat. He died almost at once." She shook her head. "A black business. He was known for his impieties, his cruelty and his drunkenness."

Holmes nodded thoughtfully. "How old was he at the time of his unfortunate death?"

"Only twenty years old."

Holmes frowned, his eyes briefly troubled. "As for your generation, the viscount had only a sister, I believe."

Constance nodded, her expression growing still more mournful. "Yes, poor dear sweet little Agnes. She died of the fevers when she was only eight, the poor sad little angel. I was five years older than her, and we had been great friends. It happened a year after Annabelle, my own dear little sister, passed on." Constance dabbed at her eyes with the handkerchief. Her grief seemed genuine, not the usual bluster, but something about her still grated at me.

Michelle sighed and set down her glass. "Nothing is worse than the death of a child."

Holmes had kept his eyes fixed on Constance. "So you also lost a sister. But your sister Jane is still living."

Constance sniffled loudly. "Jane—poor dear, mad Jane."

"There were only the three girls in your family? So now you two sisters and Rose are all that remain." He raised his glass, holding it between himself and the fire, then swished the liquid lightly; the brandy had a warm glow. "How regrettable. I take it neither you nor your sister were ever married?"

Constance gave a gruff laugh. "Heavens, no! I always knew I'd be an old maid—big, plain and dark as I was. Now Jane, on the other hand, always had gentlemen coming to court her. She was fair and beautiful, with a tiny waist and tiny hands." She held up her huge hand with its thick fingers. "Not like this paw! She favored the Spencers, our mother's family, rather than the Grimswells."

"Curious then that she never married."

Constance's laughter had a harsh quality this time. "Hardly! No money, Mr. Holmes. Beauty is all very well in a young lady, but it is not enough to make a match. Until Victor made his fortune, the Grimswells never had much beyond the hall and the land, certainly not enough for a younger son with a taste for luxury. I'm afraid, too, that my father had a genuine knack for losing money. Every enterprise he came near ended in ruin. My grandfather, then Jonathan, then my uncle Robert, and finally cousin Victor, all had to help him out more than once."

Holmes finished his brandy and set down the glass. "From what you say, I gather your mother did not come from a wealthy family."

She nodded. "That is true enough."

"Yet she managed to find a husband. Your sister was not so lucky, despite her charms. Certainly, however, there must have been some man who was dear to her."

Constance laughed again. "Oh yes, the poor sweet fool! She was smitten with an earl's son, Lord Douglas Shamwell, a handsome pup, but a bit of a bounder. He never actually promised to marry her, but she thought they had an understanding. This state of affairs lasted two or three years, but he finally married another, a banker's daughter. Jane was stricken, poor lamb. In fact..." Her face had grown mournful. "That led to her first nervous collapse. She was never the same after that."

Michelle had grown sterner and sterner looking, her smooth brow furrowing. She opened her mouth to speak, but Holmes furtively shook his head, putting his forefinger before his mouth, while Constance was not looking. Michelle turned to me, but I only gave a slight shrug. "No man will ever send me to an asylum," she said softly. Her ferocity made me smile.

Holmes shook his head. "A sad tale, but all too common, I fear. If fortune spared this Lord Shamwell, I trust that someday a Divine Judge will render justice upon him."

Constance's dark eyes blinked, and she nodded. "His marriage was a barren one, nary a child born, and he met a bad end, he did, Mr. Holmes. He died early this year of a wasting ailment. His wife is a veritable saint, a kind and generous woman, but he was not the husband he should have been. He had... a wandering eye."

Holmes's fingers drummed upon his knees. "Again, all too common. Douglas Shamwell, the name is familiar to me. I suppose he was well known in London society? And he died just this year? I hope it was in winter—an appropriate time for so cold a villain."

"So it was." Constance nodded sternly.

"No doubt in January?"

Constance nodded again, but her eyes showed a certain puzzled wariness.

"Women frequently show no judgment whatsoever in choosing the men they love. I have seen far too many such cases, often ending in tragedy. However, perhaps your sister was spared a life of misery. The earl's wife could not have been happy."

Constance smiled grimly. "Perhaps, but she was miserable in the midst of opulence. Having to beg for money and count every penny is not an agreeable way to live, but of course, I cannot really complain.

We had no real claim on Victor, but he was always so generous to us. That is another reason I feel so responsible for Rose. If not for Victor, poor Jane would be in a common madhouse instead of..." She sniffled once. "The grounds of the asylum are beautiful, the doctors and their associates so kind."

Holmes drew in his breath slowly, sat upright and glanced at the fire. "Which asylum might it be?"

"Marshall House. It is near London, and—"

Holmes nodded. "It has an excellent reputation."

Michelle and I looked at one another. We had spent a depressing morning there. The grounds were indeed beautiful, the house magnificent, the cost per patient astronomical, but the care was poor, the doctors indifferent, the staff hostile and impatient.

"Jane is as happy there as could be expected, but I do wish... One does not like committing one's own dear sister to such a place. That is why..." She gazed across the room at Rose, who was talking happily to Digby. "I worry so about Rose." She scratched at her chin, then slipped the end of her little finger into her mouth and picked at something. "Jane was only four or five years older than Rose when..." She sighed. "Oh, this wretched Grimswell blood! Sometimes I wish I had never been born into this family. There is a curse upon us—there is." Her mouth formed a weak smile, but her huge, dark eyes stared into the fire. She touched her chin, then set her big, swollen-looking hand upon her lap.

Michelle opened her mouth, hesitating. "I do not believe in curses."

Constance smiled. "That's because you're young, dear. When you've lived as long as I have, you'll believe in curses."

"No, I will not."

Constance shrugged, then turned to Holmes. "Mr. Holmes must believe in curses."

Holmes stared back at her, his eyes somber. "So I do."

I felt of flicker of dread in my chest. Michelle frowned. "Oh Sherlock, you cannot be serious."

"I am most serious. The causes may not be supernatural, but there are curses. And the accursed."

Later, as we were going upstairs to retire, Holmes pulled me aside. Michelle, Digby and Rose were ahead of us with their own candle. "Tell Michelle," he said, "that I want her to stay with Miss Grimswell at a secluded inn near the village of Grimpen tomorrow night."

"What on earth for?"

"Because you and I shall be in London tomorrow night, and I dare not leave the girl here unprotected. The four of us shall leave first thing in the morning, but no one in the house will know where we are really going."

"London—why are we going to London?"

"I have some inquiries to make, and there remains one Grimswell whom we have not yet met."

"But…" The dread I had felt earlier returned. "Jane Grimswell."

Holmes nodded, a faint smile tugging at his lips. "Exactly."

The Marshall House did have beautiful grounds, and the red brick dwelling was well over a hundred years old. (The bars over the windows were a recent addition.) Holmes and I had taken a very early train for London. Even in late afternoon, the fog still hung gray and heavy over the lawn, the yellow light of the sun feebly trying to burn through. Holmes asked the hansom driver to wait, and then we advanced to the front door, our breath forming clouds of vapor. The brawny male attendant who greeted us was dressed in white, while Holmes and I wore black overcoats, top hats, trousers and boots.

The office was splendidly furnished: heavy oak furniture with leather upholstery, cherry wood paneling, a crackling wood fire going on the grate, and a window overlooking the lawn. The doctor set down his pen, then rose, smiling widely. His hairline had receded since I had first known him, but the enormous brown mustache which hid his mouth was a form of compensation. His frock coat, striped trousers and linen were impeccable, on a par with the expensive decor.

"Ah, Henry, how good to see you again. And this must be—oh, yes—the celebrated Mr. Sherlock Holmes!"

"It is he," I said. "And this is Doctor Edward Morrissey, whom I have known for many years." And nearly always found insufferable, I thought to myself.

Morrissey extended a pale, freckled hand. "A great honor, Mr. Holmes—a great honor! Most assuredly, you have no greater admirer in all the realm than your humble servant. When Henry telegrammed this morning—gad, I was flabbergasted! I've read every one of Doctor Watson's stories."

Holmes's smile faltered at this. "It is a pleasure to meet you, Doctor Morrissey. I hope our call is not too late, but we must leave first thing in the morning."

"Not at all. I understand." He stood and glanced at the male attendant. "Higgins, I'll just show them up to Miss Grimswell's room."

Higgins nodded. He had the shoulders of a stevedore, but something in his eyes and the curl of his lip troubled me.

We started for the door. "What can you tell us about Miss Grimswell's condition?" I asked.

"Oh, she's a harmless old bird, but daft as a loon. She has been here as long as I have—for about ten years now."

"And what particular form does her insanity take?" Holmes asked.

"She is rather a mix of things—a certain paranoia, which in her case involves the Devil and his minions being after her, severe melancholy with a tendency toward catatonia, and she does see things which are not there, now and then, usually infernal agents and that type of thing. Still, a rather sweet old lady compared to some."

We had gone up a flight of stairs and started down a hallway. From one side came a low, incessant moan which triggered an odd sensation at the back of my neck. Morrissey did not seem to hear anything.

"Does her sister visit her often?" Holmes asked.

"No—thank goodness!"

"Why do you say that?"

"Her sister's visits invariably worsen Miss Grimswell's condition. Generally, as I said, she is a placid soul, but after the last visit there were attacks of screaming, dreadful hallucinations and difficulty sleeping."

"How do you account for that?" I asked.

"I cannot. The sister seems pleasant enough. She usually leaves in tears herself, and I have to console her. Frankly, I have encouraged her to stay away—discreetly, of course. Visits are often a source of disruption to our patients and needlessly upset everyone."

I thought of a cutting remark but kept it to myself. Morrissey had never had much in the way of human feeling, and his work seemed to have drained even that small amount.

"Here we are." Morrissey rapped on the door, then opened it before anyone could reply. "Ah, good morning, Miss Grimswell! And how are we this fine day?"

The room was small and austere, a brass bed, a tiny desk, a few trite pictures on the wall. Near the window sat a small woman in a rocking chair; it creaked slowly as she rocked. She gave Morrissey a cold, slow stare. "I can only speak for myself, and my rheumatism troubles me sorely today."

"A pity, that." Morrissey's broad smile contradicted his words.

"You have some visitors: Mr. Sherlock Holmes, the famous consulting detective, and his associate, Doctor Henry Vernier."

Miss Grimswell gave us a puzzled stare. "Not Doctor Watson?"

Holmes glanced at me, his eyes amused. "No, madam. You have heard of me, then?"

"Certainly I have."

"I would like to ask you some questions." He turned to Morrissey. "Preferably in private."

Morrissey nodded. "As you will. Just thrust your head out the door and call for Higgins if you need anything."

Jane Grimswell's face stiffened. "Keep Higgins away from me!"

"Now, now, Miss Grimswell. He only wants what is best for you. We all do." He closed the door behind him.

Miss Grimswell glanced at the door. "Miserable vermin, all of them," she muttered. Her hair would originally have been light brown, but had turned mostly white and hung in long, straight, dirty strands. Her face was thin and wasted, and she had dark, haunted eyes which stood out against her pale skin. She wore a thick gray woolen robe and heavy slippers, her hands hidden in the robe pockets. The chair creaked as she rocked.

Holmes and I approached her. He took the chair from the small desk, turned it about and sat. Jane stared out the window through the bars. "Too pat," she murmured, "too pat."

"What is too pat, madam?"

"Those stories. You always figure everything out, and it all fits together like the pieces of a jigsaw puzzle. Life is not like that. Nothing fits together. And the villains in the stories are silly. The Devil is missing, the dark parts, the scary parts."

Holmes smiled. "I did not write those stories, and I do not greatly care for them. Watson does often leave out the important parts, and I cannot always figure out everything. Sometimes I need help. I believe you can assist me."

"I can assist no one. I sit here in limbo waiting for death, longing for death, but afraid of death all the same. Much of my life I fought with the Devil, but now I am tired and..." Her dark eyes glittered as they filled with tears. "At least here there are only petty demons, comical ones. It... it does not seem just."

"What does not seem just?" I asked.

"*Everything.*" Her hand suddenly appeared, touched her eyes, the fingers thin and delicate. Constance had been right: her sister's hand bore little resemblance to her huge, swollen hand—or to Rose's large, strong one.

"Have you heard what happened to your cousin, Lord Grimswell?"

"Of course. He fell from the tor and smashed himself to bits."

"Do you think it was an accident?"

Her laughter affected me like the moan I had heard in the hallway. "Certainly not."

"Then what happened?"

"The Devil was pursuing him, chasing him, haunting him, and Victor could not help but jump. When the Devil chases you, you will do anything to escape. Victor was lucky."

"Lucky?" My voice was incredulous.

"He is at peace now. The Devil can torment him no longer." A smile twisted her mouth. "The Devil has lost him."

"And what of Rose Grimswell?" Holmes asked.

"Ah. The sweet creature." The monotonous creak of the rocker made me briefly consider putting my foot on a runner to stop the noise. Jane's eyes glistened again, the grayish-yellow light from the window illuminating her sad face. "The poor thing." A tear trickled down one cheek but she did not touch her face.

"Has Rose visited you?"

"Yes. Many times. She is the only one who…" She stared out the window. "It has begun, has it not? The Devil… She has seen the Devil, has she not?"

"Yes," Holmes said.

"And he speaks to her." She sighed wearily, and her tiny hand clutched at her dirty hair. "I knew it must happen, but still… He will not stop–he will hound her until… If she is lucky, he will kill her like he killed her father."

She said this with a terrifying, utter sincerity. The dread which had been my companion at Dartmoor began again. "How can you say such a thing?" I said.

"Would you wish a place like this on her? There are young girls here, poor sad wretches."

Holmes's hands clutched at the chair back as he stared at her. "I believe I can save Rose Grimswell."

Jane laughed wearily, even as the tears began. "A mere mortal cannot best the Prince of Darkness. Satan rules here on earth. Only in the next world is there hope, and even then, I wonder. If the Devil wants her, you can do nothing. You will only be destroyed."

Holmes stared directly into her eyes. "I have fought devils before and won."

"Perhaps, but you have not fought *the* Devil."

"Who is the Devil, Miss Grimswell?"

She lowered her eyes, seemed to notice her hand and quickly thrust it back into the pocket of her robe. "I… I do not know."

Holmes drew in his breath slowly, then let his hands drop to his side. He glanced briefly at me. "What can you tell me about your sister Constance?"

Morrissey's warning should have prepared me. Her lips clamped tightly shut, and her eyes opened wide even as the color faded from her face. I had never seen such obvious terror, such fear, and it upset me. Something had changed in that room that seemed to amplify our fear, something had happened, but my mind leaped about like some rabbit, incapable of rational, linear thought. Abruptly it came to me—silence filled the room, total and overwhelming silence, because the chair had stopped rocking.

Holmes reached out with his long arm and set his hand on her shoulder. "Please, you must not—I will not let anyone harm you."

"You… you cannot help me. No one can protect me here."

"I might be able to get you away from this place. My cousin here is a physician and could assist you."

I was still too caught up in my own anxiety to speak.

"He cannot help me—you cannot. This is a dreadful place, but I am safe here from the Devil and from *her*. If I am quiet, if I am still, they will not pursue me. If I leave these walls, I will be hunted down and devoured in an instant. I am trapped—I am trapped."

"No, not if—"

"Silence!" she shouted. "What do you know of it? What do you know of me? You cannot fight the Devil—they are too strong, far too strong, and they do not care how much they hurt you! They enjoy human suffering—they feed upon it—it is meat and drink to them. That is true even of the minor demons, the ones in white or frock coats. I must remain here until I die. There is no escape for me." The sudden fury had seeped away like blood from an old wound.

Holmes had lowered his hand. His gray eyes showed his dismay. "There are things I must know—things you must tell me. You… you were never married, were you, Miss Grimswell?"

The rocking chair began to creak again. "*No.*"

Holmes ran his hand through his black hair. "But you were in love with Lord Douglas Shamwell, were you not?"

Again her eyes filled with tears. "Yes."

Holmes turned to me, his eyes showing an unfamiliar desperation. "Madam, I must ask you a question which may seem impertinent—which *is* impertinent—but I must know the answer. Rose's life may be at stake, as well as other lives. Have you... have you ever had a child?"

The chair ceased moving, and her eyes widened. When it came at last, her laughter was pained and savage. "*No.*" She sobbed, then covered her face with her forearm and the sleeve of heavy wool.

Holmes's face was red. "Forgive me, I–"

"I was pure and good, but that was not what the Devil wanted—he wanted someone as foul and luxurious as himself, someone who would couple with him and give birth to his spawn. Their bodies are white—they writhe about one another like serpents. *I have seen them.*" She lowered her arm, her eyes fixed on Holmes. "He would only mate with another demon, a female, because they were really only one—only *the same*—and their... their get was the *same.*" She turned to gaze out the window. "It took me a long time to understand that. I was so hurt, so upset, I... I tried to kill myself when I found out about them. I wanted to die." She raised her fists, letting the sleeves of her robe drop and revealing the ragged red scars on her wrists just below the palms. I felt a visceral shock, as if a knife had slid into my own belly.

"Oh, God—how awful I felt. It was worse than anything. My life since has been nothing but pain, but not that dreadful agony, that gaping wound. I... It was only later—long afterward—when I saw that thing they had created, that I truly understood. It never had anything to do with hurting me or finding me wanting. The Devil is *one.* He takes different forms, but he is always the same. The Devil mates with the Devil, and the Devil is born again and again. They are all the same. They truly are." She smiled and nodded weakly.

I felt nauseated, and my hands were cold. I could think of nothing to say. She was, after all, hopelessly insane. Holmes had gone very pale, but he had not taken his eyes off her. His hands gripped the chair back again, the tendons standing out.

"I have been a fool." He swallowed, his Adam's apple bobbing. "The Devil… had a child, a son, and the child… was exactly like the father."

She smiled and nodded.

"And just like the mother. And they were all the Devil." Holmes seemed to be talking to himself.

"Yes." She nodded eagerly. "You understand it *perfectly*." Her eyes were red, her face streaked with tears, but she seemed childishly pleased.

Holmes glanced at me. "Can we go?" I asked. My voice shook slightly.

He stood abruptly. "Yes." He stared down at Jane Grimswell. She had begun to rock and was staring out the window through the bars. He hesitated, then touched her shoulder. "Thank you, Miss Grimswell. I have hopes that your cousin–that Rose–may yet be saved."

She shook her head sadly. "You cannot beat the Devil, Mr. Holmes. No man can."

"Nevertheless, I shall try." He picked up his top hat, and we started for the door.

"Mr. Holmes?"

"Yes, madam?"

She was staring at us both. "I shall pray for you all the same. I… oh, I hope you will succeed."

"Thank you, Miss Grimswell."

We stepped outside, and he closed the door. I felt almost dizzy, my hands still cold and clammy. "The poor tortured soul," I muttered. "She is totally mad. Constance did not tell us she had tried to kill herself."

Holmes said nothing. We started down the hallway. The low moan was still coming from behind the same door. "Lord, this is a dreadful place!" I wanted to run down the stairs and get outside, but I restrained myself. "We have come all the way to London for nothing."

Holmes gave a fierce, savage laugh and stared at me. "*Hardly.*"

Twelve

Holmes had some further mysterious visits to make that evening, but I went home and slept that night in my own bed. Tried to sleep, rather—the visit with Jane had been very disturbing, and Michelle was still back in Dartmoor.

The next day, we all returned to Grimswell Hall late in the afternoon. Dartmoor was a welcome sight, the air clean and bracing after the stench of London. The ride to the hall was spectacular, the terrain so varied—the sweeping, barren expanses of the moor, the streams of cold clear water, the patches of stunted woods with twisted black oaks, their leaves gone, the marshy dark mires where man or beast trod at their peril, and the black granite tors atop the hills set against the luminous sky. However, as we drew closer to our destination, my spirits sank.

Michelle took my hand. "Is something wrong?"

I shrugged, then glanced at Rose Grimswell and Holmes. "No."

Michelle frowned. She knew me well: she could read me like a book.

Soon we were following the drive through the trees, the massive edifice of dark stone ahead. We stepped down, and the heavy oaken doors of the main entry swung open. George stepped forth to greet us. The familiar grin seemed lackluster, and his eyes had an odd, strained look. "Welcome back, gentlemen and ladies." His eyes flickered about, rested on Holmes, and then he reached out to slip something into Holmes's hand. Michelle and Rose had gone by and did not see this.

"Well, it's about time." Digby's voice had a weary drawl. He wore a checked Norfolk suit of a hideous brownish-green shade. "I thought you had *all* ended up in some bog or another."

"Heavens!" Constance exclaimed. "Don't even joke about such things! And how are you, Mrs. Vernier? Are you quite recovered?"

Michelle smiled, a glint of humor showing in her eyes. "Oh yes, I feel much better. I had quite a chill."

Our excuse for not returning the night before was that Michelle had fallen into a bog during our trek. Since we wished to get her warm and dry as quickly as possible, we had gone to a nearby inn. As it was late and the weather foul, we had decided to spend the night there, and then Holmes and I had business in Grimpen during the day. This was the story we had all agreed upon, and we had a note sent to the hall late the day before.

Digby gave Rose a petulant smile. "I'm growing rather weary of being left out of all these outings. I might as well be back in London."

"An excellent idea," I murmured. Only Michelle heard me, and she stifled a laugh.

Rose took his arm and smiled. "Come now, Rickie, would you really have wanted to rise at six in the morning yesterday?"

Digby shrugged. "Perhaps not, but–"

"Tomorrow we shall all go for a walk after breakfast, and you will be included, I promise."

"Splendid. The day was not entirely wasted. I met the delightful widow at the farm down the road. Something of a mystery, what she's doing in so godforsaken a place. Well, tomorrow I'd like to hike up to Demon Tor and finally have a look at the view."

Constance opened her mouth, then closed it. She shook her head. "All this exercise—it cannot be good for a body."

We went upstairs to dress for dinner, but first I stopped by Holmes's room. "What did George give you?" I asked.

"Ah, you saw that, did you? It was a note asking me to meet him by the menhir down the road at nine."

I frowned. "That sounds dangerous."

Holmes smiled sardonically. "No one is safe with a murderer on the moors, but I shall be armed."

I hesitated, then sighed. "I shall come with you."

"Very well, Henry." He drew aside the curtains and stared outside. "The clouds are lifting. It should be a beautiful evening."

So it was. The stars were dazzling, far brighter and more numerous than in London. We could see them in a band overhead between the trees as we strolled down the drive, our boots striking the hard granite underfoot. Holmes wore a woolen overcoat, a bowler hat and gloves. His left hand held his stick, and his right was in the pocket where I had seen him place his revolver. Somewhere nearby in the trees came the wavering hoot of an owl, a disembodied voice overhead. The wind was faint, just a touch on our faces.

Soon we left the trees and followed the path onto the moors. A bright moon, almost full, was low in the eastern sky; it cast our shadows before us. The moor was a great silent presence, grass and heath reduced to a dark rolling plain, the distant hills and tors silhouetted against the bright night sky.

I shook my head. "One should not have to worry about murderers on a night like this when all of nature is so splendid."

"Man brings his own darkness wherever he goes, a darkness with none of the beauty of a Dartmoor night."

Abruptly, a strange cry rose through the night, almost human in its yearning, yet alien all the same. "Good Lord," I said, "what...?"

"A fox, Henry. That is the mating cry of a vixen, and if I am not mistaken—look there." He raised his stick and pointed to where a small dark shape with a bushy tail trotted across the moor. "A male, no doubt. To him that cry was a siren song." To our left came a series of high-pitched, staccato barks. "And that is another male replying."

The wind picked up briefly, then died down. Out from under the trees the sky was truly magnificent, a vast starry expanse dominating the dark plain. The misty belt of the Milky Way split the sky, fading where it met the moon. Some stars were blue diamonds, others yellow or red. One reddish star was particularly brilliant.

"Do you know that star?" I asked. "The bright red one there."

"That is not a star, Henry, but a planet—Mars."

"The god of war," I murmured.

"Yes, and a reminder of our combat. Curious. The planet itself is nothing more than a point of reddish light. Man gives it the connotations of blood, war and strife."

"Blood and strife," I said. The moors seemed as far from London and its teeming masses, vehicles, buildings and noise as one of the planets above us. Despite the danger which might await us, the quiet beauty of the wild landscape moved me.

"I should like to come back here when our business at the hall is finished, perhaps for a walking tour with Michelle. I hope... I hope Dartmoor is not ruined for me by..."

"It will not be. Dartmoor is older and vaster than mere man. I only hope man himself does not ruin it."

"You think we have that power?"

"I know we do. Did you not hear me discuss with Miss Grimswell how the ancient stones have been pulled down and used to build a farmer's fence and the like? Farmers try to fence off the moor. There are a few small woods in Dartmoor, but the large oaks were cut down two hundred years ago, the wolves all slaughtered about the same time."

"Frankly, I am glad this evening there are no wolves on the moor."

Holmes gave a snort of laughter. "There you are wrong. There is a creature far worse than a real wolf loose on the moor."

"Surely you cannot mean a werewolf?"

"No, something far worse. The werewolf is an interesting invention, but he is all bestial savagery with no cunning or intelligence. This creature is a man, but he is missing something essential. His heart is that of a beast—no, worse than that. He willingly kills his own kind. No animal, no wild beast, does that, so I am wrong to say he has the heart of a beast. He has the heart of a reptile or amphibian, something cold and unfeeling and primitive. Or perhaps, worse yet, he is one of those rare monstrosities who enjoys killing, who enjoys slaughtering his own kind."

"Oh, dear God," I murmured.

Holmes stopped and seized my arm. In the moonlight I could see his white face with the beaked nose under the bowler hat. "Forgive me, Henry. I had no right to ruin so beautiful an evening with my dark reflections. I should have kept them to myself."

"You think our adversary is that black?"

"I know he is."

"But no one at the hall seems capable of—"

"We are not dealing only with the people at the hall. No, our adversary, as you rightly called him, does not live at the hall, although he has his ally there."

"How can you—?"

Holmes raised his stick. "There is our destination." The menhir stood before us, a slab of blackness with the moon and stars behind it.

I took a breath and tried to regain some of the simple joy for the night's beauty, but it was futile. I was afraid again. "But he is a man—not a monster?"

Holmes sighed. "You have not been listening. He is not a supernatural being, but that does not make him less loathsome or frightening. He is something worse. If he was a different species or a supernatural creature, then his evil might be more comprehensible." He drew in his breath, then cried, "George! Are you here?"

The murmur of the wind stirring the heather and bracken was all we heard. A bird flew by, a dark shape overhead, and from its hoarse cry I recognized it as a raven.

Holmes sighed. "I feared this."

"Feared what?"

"That he would not come."

Holmes reached into his pocket, opened his coat, then struck a match. His hands and his watch showed briefly. "It is after nine."

"Perhaps he was delayed."

Holmes's laugh was bitter. "No doubt."

As we waited, I began to pace. The night grew chiller, and thin streaks of cloud began to obscure the magnificent sky. Holmes pulled off his glove, took a cigarette from his case, then smoked the cigarette slowly. I walked around the menhir, crossing its shadow periodically, but the shadow began to blur and fade as the clouds covered the moon. I could not seem to hold still, but Holmes stood without moving, a dark figure akin to the slab of granite which rose over us.

Nearly half an hour must have passed when I said, "I do not believe he is coming."

"No, Henry. He is not." Holmes sighed, then shook his head. "Damnation."

"Perhaps we should go back to the hall and simply demand to speak to him."

"We shall not find him back at the hall."

"No? Where is he, then?"

"Probably somewhere on the moor. He is in all probability quite dead and can tell us nothing."

I opened my mouth and tried to control the sudden fear clutching at my throat.

"I tried to warn him." Holmes sounded angry. "I told him it was dangerous." He took out another cigarette, lit it, and exhaled a cloud of white smoke.

"Can we go back?" I wanted very much to be in a warm bed with Michelle, even though I doubted I would sleep much that night.

"We might as well." The end of the cigarette glowed red. "If we do not, the fog will soon swallow us. Look." He raised his stick.

Ahead of us, the land fell to a grove of stunted trees, now hidden. A gray-white fog lay there like some quiet ocean, slowly advancing, or perhaps it resembled some biblical plague, an icy mist which would kill everything it touched. I told myself that such thoughts were foolish.

Holmes gazed up at the stars, his mouth grim and taut, then threw down the cigarette butt. "Let us…" He seemed to freeze in place, then his hand shot out and caught my arm, the fingers digging in deeply. "Look there—on the tor!"

My eyes swept up the dark hill, and then caught the silhouette atop the jumbled granite of Demon Tor. "Good Lord," I whispered. A man stood there, a figure all in black, his face white, and beside him was a huge black dog. My insides felt as if snakes or other slithery creatures were there, and again I struggled to master my fear.

"Should we… should we…?"

"That is him, Henry—the devil behind all this affair."

"...pursue him?"

"No, it would be useless. He doubtless knows his way about better than we do. If we start for the tor, he will simply turn and go down the other side. There is nothing we can do." Holmes's voice shook with anger.

"Let's get away from here."

"Yes."

Holmes walked rapidly. My legs seemed pleased to be moving, although they would have preferred a run. The night seemed quieter than earlier, and damper, the mists closing in on land and sky. To the side came a sound, loud and jarring, wild and cruel—laughter, a man's laughter.

Holmes stopped, then turned abruptly and started for the tor. "Wait!" I cried. "Wait!" I seized his arm. The laughter had stopped. "You said it would be futile."

Holmes drew in his breath. "And I was correct."

Clouds had covered the moon. They drifted away, and the moonlight showed the sharp, jagged edge of the tor, the shapes like horns, but no one was there now.

Holmes drew in his breath, then roared, "Coward!" at the top of his lungs, the shout shattering the night's stillness.

"For God's sake—let's get away from here."

Holmes smiled at me, his face ghastly pale in the moonlight. "Very well, Henry."

As usual, Holmes was correct. When we returned to the hall, George was nowhere to be found. No one had seen him leave, and no one had any idea when he might return.

My past attempts at deceiving Michelle had ended in abject failure. Moreover, I wanted very much to tell her what had happened. Still cold and rather fearful, I did so as we lay together in bed. The blue-white moonlight came through the mullioned window, but I could not see her face. Her hand had tightened about my arm. "I thought we had discussed this—you were not going to go off again without telling me."

"You would have wanted to come, and Sherlock would have never allowed it."

"Men can foolishly risk their lives whenever they wish, but with women it is not permitted." She sounded both hurt and angry.

"Do not be angry—not now—not tonight. I…"

She kissed me fiercely, and I pulled her as close as I could. "Please be careful, my dearest," she said. "Promise me that at least you will not take foolish risks."

"You must know I am not foolhardy. I am generally too frightened to be foolhardy."

She laughed. "Good!" My intermittent shaking had finally stopped.

Neither of us slept well that night. At one point early in the morning, Holmes and I met in the hallway, both of us wanting to check on Rose at the same time. She was sleeping peacefully, with the maid Meg also asleep in the room.

In the morning George had still not reappeared, his absence the main topic of discussion among the household. Holmes said nothing, but I knew he was certain George was dead. We went for a walk after breakfast, and as Rose had promised, Digby was included. The others hiked all the way to the top of the tor, but this time I remained below. The gradual slope did not trigger my vertigo, but I was wary of the view from higher up, spectacular though it was.

We had just returned from the walk when Fitzwilliams led Doctor Hartwood into the great hall. The young man wore his battered jacket and muddy boots, the same casual attire as the first time he had come calling. He held his cloth cap in his hand, and the top of his forehead was pale white compared to the red-brown skin of his face. He gave

Michelle a curious glance, a slight frown furrowing his brow, but his eyes restlessly swept round the vast chamber. Rose and Digby had gone upstairs to the library together.

"Mr. Holmes, I had hoped to find you here." Again his eyes seemed drawn to Michelle.

"Doctor Hartwood, this is my wife, Michelle Doudet Vernier. She is also a physician."

He nodded, a curious look in his eyes. "Are you, ma'am?"

She smiled at him. Her face was lightly freckled from the sun, her cheeks flushed from the walk on the moor, and she was quite beautiful. "I am." She held out her hand. He hesitated, then shook it. His fingers might have been shorter than hers, but the span of his knuckles was immense, his arms and shoulders worthy of a blacksmith or stevedore. For an instant only, longing showed in his eyes, the longing of a lonely young man for a woman he knew was unattainable.

"Oh." We could gauge little from his monosyllabic response.

Michelle was suddenly wary. "Do you not approve of woman doctors, Doctor Hartwood?"

"I've never known one. I've no basis on which to approve or disapprove. We'll see."

Michelle smiled again. "Fair enough."

Hartwood turned back to Holmes. "Miss Grimswell is occupied?"

"For the moment," Holmes said.

"Good." He sighed. "I hate to again be the bearer of bad news, but I have found a dead man on the moor, one I recognized—the tall servant who liked mastiffs."

Michelle's smile vanished, and my stomach lurched. Holmes nodded. "I have been expecting such news. I hope you did not bring the body with you."

Hartwood shook his head. "No."

"Good. I shall want to have a look before anything is disturbed."

"I shall come," I said, although it was the last thing I wished to do.

"And I," said Michelle.

Hartwood shrugged. "As you will. It is not far."

Hartwood's horse was tied up out front, but he started off on foot at a fearsome pace, his eyes locked straight ahead. The day was another fine one, the sky a clear, vibrant blue. A few long-lived flies droned lazily about. Once we were clear of the trees, he stopped, set down his bag, and folded his arms. "I'll not go another step until you tell me what is going on at Grimswell Hall."

Holmes smiled faintly. "What have you heard?"

"Every sort of nonsense. Just this morning, two different people in Grimpen told me they had seen the viscount's ghost on the moors last night, a giant man in black with an evil hound at his side. The town is abuzz with such talk. People are afraid to go out after dark. And..." He hesitated, his eyes worried.

Holmes nodded, his gaze intent. "Go on."

"Some say Miss Grimswell is insane. That cannot be—that isn't true." Despite his best efforts, it came out almost as a question.

Holmes stared at him, weighing his thoughts, but Michelle could not restrain herself. "It most certainly is not true!"

Hartwood eased his breath out through clenched teeth. "Thank God. She seemed troubled, but I did not think... I don't really know her. She is in danger, is she not? If there is any possible way, I should like to help."

Michelle gave him a stunning smile. "That's very kind of you."

Holmes took off his hat and smoothed back his hair. A few days in Dartmoor had put some color in his cheeks, the customary pallor gone. "It may be possible, Doctor Hartwood. But you might begin by taking us to the body."

Hartwood nodded, then began walking. "Is she really ill, or is it only nerves?"

Michelle and I glanced at one another. "She has been under a considerable strain," I said. "But…" I looked at Holmes.

"Someone has been doing their best to frighten her," he said.

Hartwood scowled. "Who?"

"That is what we are attempting to discover."

"What kind of villain would…? Do you think they actually mean to harm her?"

Holmes's smile was glacial. "They mean to murder her."

Hartwood's eyes widened, even as he stopped and seized Holmes's arm. "Good Lord—you are serious. You must get her away from here—you must—"

Holmes winced. "Doctor Hartwood, you have an impressive grip."

He released him at once. "Pardon me—I only… Would she be safer somewhere else? In London?"

"Possibly, for a while, but our opponent is cunning and ruthless. At least here… I hope to flush them out."

"But why? What can she have ever done?"

Holmes stared at him. "Have you no idea?"

"None."

"Her fortune," he said. "Someone wants her fortune."

Hartwood seemed astounded—and appalled. "*Her fortune*? She has a fortune? Oh, damn." The word slipped out, then he glanced at Michelle. "Pardon me, ma'am, I only… I did not know there was any fortune." For some reason, he seemed genuinely upset by this discovery. "I thought a daughter could not inherit the title or the land."

"The title will go extinct," Holmes said, "but because her father and grandfather broke the entail, she may inherit Grimswell Hall. Her father also had considerable personal wealth."

"Oh." He shook his head. "I suppose…" He swallowed. "It is well that she may keep her home and… that she is provided for." He strode on, his pace still rapid. We were approaching the twisted clump of woods at the foot of a hill rising to Demon Tor.

"I… There is one other thing I must know." His eyes were locked straight ahead. "Is she really engaged to be married to *that*…?" The final word was filled with contempt, and he broke off his speech.

"The situation remains unclear," Holmes said.

Michelle smiled, her nostrils flaring. "She could not be such an imbecile." Hartwood slowed down and turned to her, his eyes incredulous. Michelle was still smiling. "Well, she could not, you know." A sharp laugh slipped from Holmes's lips.

Hartwood's massive chest slowly swelled as he drew in his breath, his relief obvious. We had almost reached the woods. Several crows sat on the branches of the low trees. At our approach, one by one, they flew upward with noisy caws and bursts of chatter.

"I did turn him over," Hartwood said. "The crows had not really begun on him yet, and I did not want them picking at his face." This explanation did not seem to perturb Michelle or Holmes, but it gave me a queasy feeling. Dead people I had seen aplenty, but not after they had served as food for scavengers.

Holmes shook his head. "I doubt he was killed here. The murderer must have transported him. That in itself is not insignificant. George was lean, but tall, and weighed about one hundred and seventy pounds. Tell me, doctor, what attracted you to these woods? They do not appear inviting."

"The crows. I had never seen so many here before, and I wondered what had attracted them. If it was some poor sheep or pony which had been injured, I'd have put the beast out of its misery."

Holmes suddenly leaped before Hartwood and raised his stick.

"Stop!" he cried. Hartwood stumbled and stepped back. Holmes was down on his knees at once, staring at the grassy turf. "Remarkable—quite remarkable."

Hartwood gave us a baffled look, but Michelle and I had no explanation. However, the source of Holmes's excitement soon became obvious. We had reached a damper patch of ground, and there before us was a footprint—a very large footprint.

Holmes shook his head. "No shoddy manufactured boots for our friend here. With a footprint like this, he must have his boots custom-made. He must be at least a size fifteen. The tread is quite distinctive. Were we in London, I could find his bootmaker. Would you all be so kind as to remain exactly where you are a while longer?" He rose, then began to walk slowly away from the footprint. He was bent over, his head almost at the level of his waist.

"Ah." He fell again to his knees.

I leaned forward, but a heather hid the spot. "What is it?"

"The footprint of a gigantic hound."

Hartwood stepped forward. "Let me see."

"Do not move!" roared Holmes. "You may look soon enough."

Holmes walked outward in overlapping circles, each larger than the last, the center being the first footprint. He stopped next to one of the granite rocks where the woods began. "Here is another." He pointed with his stick. "The impression is shallower, although the ground is softer. The footprint is pointed in the opposite direction. The first one was made while he was carrying George here, the other as he departed. Please swing around this area and join me in the woods. The ground further on is too rocky for any prints."

We did so, but by the time we joined him, he was on his knees again. "Look here." Several brown spots stained the white granite and its luminous coating of yellow and green lichens. He rose. "I do not think I shall need you to lead me to the body, Doctor Hartwood." He pointed with the ferrule of his stick at the trail of dried blood across the rocks.

Although the leaves of the dwarfish oaks were gone, it felt colder in the woods, and the wind was a low murmur through the gnarled, barren branches. Ferns sprouted between the rocks, their saw-toothed leaves huge and green, and the trunks of the oaks seemed to have grown out of the rock itself. Their bark was spotted with lichens, and whitish-green moss clung to the twigs at the end of the branches.

George lay face down in a hollow between two trees, his head and back covered with a heavy tweed jacket. It had a few rents in the fabric where the crows must have picked at it, and his trousers were torn. Holmes pulled off the jacket, and we could see his yellow hair, one whitish ear and his white shirt.

Holmes knelt, then slowly pulled him over. "Oh Lord," I whispered, turning away. His lifeless eyes were still open, his jaw slack, but his throat was a bloody, mangled mess, his shirt front all stained reddish brown.

"Poor man," Michelle whispered. "What could have done that to him?"

"The cause of death is obvious," Holmes said. "The jugular was severed, but this... It is supposed to resemble the work of a wild beast, our giant dog, but... Notice how sharp this edge is here, and... I wonder, Doctor Hartwood, do you have a scalpel or probe in your bag?"

"Both. Which would you like?"

"A probe."

Hartwood handed him the long, slender silver instrument. Holmes explored the wounds with the tip slowly and meticulously. I tried to assume my stiff-upper-lip medical manner, but I noticed the dried blood all over George's face and his lifeless eyes staring up at the sky. I felt cold and queasy. "Do close his eyes, Sherlock." He did so. Michelle glanced at me, then took my hand and squeezed it tightly. "I never much cared for corpses," I said.

Hartwood had knelt beside Holmes. "He must have died last night. Rigor has come and gone."

"Around eight in the evening," Holmes said. "Ah—as I expected. Look at this." He was holding the probe at the end, and the shaft sank into George's throat some three or four inches. By way of sympathy, I felt a cold twisting sensation in my own belly. "Someone thrust a knife into his throat, something with a long, narrow blade. That is what killed him. Then that person used some other instrument to rip at the throat and simulate the work of a wild beast. However, no animal could have produced a wound this deep."

"Why would they have carried him here?" Hartwood asked.

"Are there any tales told about these woods?"

Hartwood smiled faintly. "Many. All sorts of ghouls and fiends lurk here."

Holmes stood up. "An excellent spot for a werewolf or vampire."

"But you have just demonstrated—"

Holmes smiled. "I was being ironic, doctor. Our ghoul has his reputation to live up to. Perhaps we should frustrate his plans and not tell anyone we found the body here."

From somewhere deeper in the woods came several caws. I raised my eyes and through the branches saw some small hawk soaring overhead.

Holmes bent over, wiped the probe on George's shirt, then handed it to Hartwood. "Thank you. We had better take the body back to the hall. Perhaps we had better fetch a horse."

Hartwood shrugged. "No need. I'll carry him."

I raised an eyebrow. "It must be at least a mile."

"Exactly," Hartwood said. "No use bothering with a horse." He put the jacket over George's face, then took an arm and leg and hoisted him up over his back. A small branch cracked and broke. Holmes adjusted the jacket so it would not fall off, and then we left the woods.

The day was still a fine one, but I had only to glance at Hartwood and his grotesque burden to recall that a murderer was loose on the moor. Before, the knowledge had been hypothetical, abstract. I had not known Lord Grimswell, but yesterday at this time George had been alive and well. I wondered again what he had wanted to tell us.

"Burden" was perhaps the wrong word to use for George's corpse: Hartwood showed no signs of discomfort or strain whatsoever. He might as well have been carrying a sack of feathers. When we had almost reached the house, he stopped. "I cannot just lug him in like this. I'd best set him down and get someone to help me fetch him later."

Holmes raised his eyes; they had been far away. "Quite so, doctor, quite so."

Hartwood slipped George off his back, then leaned him against the trunk of a yew. We got the tweed jacket about his shoulders. At least his eyes were still closed. Hartwood touched the dead man's face with his big hand, the gesture curiously tender for so big and powerful a man. "Poor devil." He pulled a handkerchief from his pocket and covered the face and throat with it. "I wonder if he even knew what was coming."

"He knew," Holmes said. "He knew."

We continued down the path, then went up the two granite steps to the massive oaken doors. Holmes used the knocker. The door soon swung open, revealing Fitzwilliams. The old man looked terrible, his eyes haunted, his mouth almost bluish. Holmes stepped past him, but Michelle took his arm. "What is the matter? You had better sit down."

A great wail echoed through the vast hall, and then Constance swept toward us. She wore the usual black dress, and her outstretched hands clutched a white handkerchief. "Can it be? Is George dead?"

"Yes," Holmes said.

She gasped, then sobbed loudly, her hands tightening about the handkerchief. "Catastrophe follows catastrophe! Disaster follows disaster! Truly we Grimswells are accursed."

Holmes took half a step back, his eyes sweeping the hall. "Where is Miss Grimswell?"

"Disaster," sobbed Constance, "black disaster."

Hartwood stepped forward and seized her arm. "Where is she?"

Constance drew in her breath. "Let go of my arm, young man!"

He did so, his face grim. "Where is she?"

"In the conservatory."

Holmes let his breath out through his teeth. "She is well?"

"Certainly."

"Then what has happened?"

Constance bit at her lip, her red-rimmed eyes opening wide. "Victor has disappeared!"

"Victor," I mumbled. "Who is Victor?"

"Lord Grimswell," Holmes said.

"But he is dead!" I exclaimed.

Michelle had helped Fitzwilliams to a chair, but he still appeared dreadful. "His body has vanished," he said. "From the vault—the family vault in the Grimpen Cemetery."

Holmes gave a single piercing laugh, then bared his teeth and shook his head. "Oh, marvelous! Better and better—what will this devil think of next?"

Something in his eyes made me seize his arm. "Sherlock, are you quite well?"

He drew in his breath slowly. "Forgive me, I... One could almost admire so perversely devious a mind if it were not..." He turned to Fitzwilliams. "Sir, I must speak with you. Perhaps in the library." And then to Constance: "Is Miss Grimswell alone in the conservatory?"

"Yes, Lord Frederick went out to try to find you." She sniffled. "Oh, whatever will become of us all?"

Holmes turned to Michelle. "Could you see to her? She should not be alone."

Michelle nodded. "Of course. Henry, perhaps you could get Mr. Fitzwilliams a brandy. He is not well." She grasped my wrist. "Watch him." She started to leave, then turned to Doctor Hartwood. "Would you like to come with me?"

His eyes showed brief amazement, then he slapped at his trousers with his cap. "*Yes.*"

Michelle smiled. "Come, then."

I went to Fitzwilliams and put my hand on his shoulder. He felt so frail and bony, so little left of him.

Constance sobbed loudly again. "I wish I had never been born into this terrible family! Will our troubles never end? Oh, what can happen next?"

Holmes's mouth formed another brief, ghastly smile. "That I think I know."

Thirteen

Fitzwilliams sat in one of the library's massive oak chairs; it made him appear even smaller, diminished. He slowly sipped at the glass of brandy. Some color had returned to his wasted cheeks, yet he still appeared ill.

Holmes stood with his back to us, one hand grasping his other wrist as he stared out the windows. "Your loyalty is commendable, but I assure you that I shall not allow any scandal to blacken Lord Grimswell's reputation. Remember, too, that he is dead now and his daughter's very life is at stake. The time for delicacy is past." He turned. "He was seeing Mrs. Neal, was he not?"

Fitzwilliams sighed, then nodded. "Yes."

"How long had this been going on?"

"A few months." Fitzwilliams stared down at the glass of brandy; only his dark brown eyes did not reflect his age. "He... he wanted to marry her."

"What?" I exclaimed.

The old man continued to stare at the brandy. "It was very nearly arranged, I believe." He lifted his head. "It made him happy, happier than..."

Holmes set one hand on the table. "And did they meet mainly on the moors?"

Fitzwilliams nodded. "Yes. He went for walks, once or twice a day. He... often winked at me before he went out."

Holmes's eyes were fixed on the old man. "And did they often go up to the tor? Demon Tor?"

"Yes, I believe so."

A peculiar dizziness suddenly swept over me, a milder form of my vertigo, and I sat down in one of the other chairs.

"So he had probably gone to see her the evening he was... he died?"

Fitzwilliams raised his head, his face again losing color. "Yes."

"She could not have pushed him," I said, almost to myself. "He was a big man, while she is so small and slight."

Holmes glanced at me. "If someone is slightly off balance or if they are not expecting it, a very slight shove will suffice."

"Oh, dear God," Fitzwilliams groaned. He took a big swallow of brandy.

"Most likely another person was involved. I shall discover the truth. So you kept Lord Grimswell's involvement with Mrs. Neal a secret?"

"Certainly—certainly. How could I have ever suspected she...? His heart was not good, and Doctor Hartwood said it was heart failure. Why cause a scandal when...?" He licked his thin, pale lips. "Lord Grimswell was a gentleman. He wrote those strange books and was very intelligent, but he was a gentleman. He would never have... His behavior toward Mrs. Neal must have been proper. Perhaps he should not have seen her alone, but he would have never... dishonored her. I could not allow people to spread ridiculous stories, and then too, the lady begged me not to tell."

Holmes rose up briefly on the balls of his feet. "Did she?"

"She was very upset. She said they had agreed to be married later that summer, but now that he was gone, she did not want anyone to know about it."

Holmes tapped nervously at the table. "Now, think very carefully before you answer this question. Did Lord Grimswell ever actually tell you himself that he wished to marry Mrs. Neal?"

Fitzwilliams frowned momentarily, then nodded. "Yes. A month before he died. He said it would be good to have a young mistress in the hall again after so many years, but... he wondered how my wife and Miss Rose would take to her."

Holmes nodded, then rubbed at his chin. "What did you think of Mrs. Neal?"

"Think of her? I did not know her."

"But she did come to see you, you said."

He shrugged. "She is very pretty. She seemed sweet enough, and she did weep for the master."

"Did she?" Holmes's voice had a certain sarcastic edge.

"Yes, sir."

Holmes nodded. "Thank you, Mr. Fitzwilliams." He turned to me. "Henry, would you accompany me to Merriweather Farm?"

"Now?"

"Yes–*now.*"

"Of course."

Holmes started for the door. I poured more brandy from the decanter into the old man's glass. "Sit here until you feel quite recovered."

"Thank you, sir." He looked up at me, his face anguished. "Did I do the wrong thing?"

"Certainly not. Your behavior was exemplary, but it was good of you to tell us the truth."

I hurried down the stairs and found Holmes waiting impatiently by the front door. We walked through the trees and headed out onto the moor. The landscape had become familiar to me, the desolate but beautiful expanse stretching to the horizon and the vast blue sky with banks of clouds, but I hardly saw anything, my thoughts in turmoil.

At last I said, "Do you think she killed him?"

"Probably not."

"Who then?"

"Our man in black, the fellow we saw atop the tor last night."

"That was not—it was not Lord Grimswell?"

"Of course not!"

My head ached. I felt the pain about my eyes, as if it had poured into the sockets, and my thoughts were wild and scattered. One won out over the others. "You told Constance you knew what might happen next. What did you mean?"

"That is the reason we are on our way to Merriweather Farm."

My mind was sluggish, but with the realization I felt a sudden visceral fear. "Mrs. Neal—you think—something may happen to her."

"Exactly, Henry. She may be the next victim. I only hope she is still alive to answer my questions."

I felt faintly dizzy. "Oh." I stared up at a patch of clear blue sky. It seemed so far removed from the moors and the horror lurking there. Momentarily I felt as if I were falling into the sky, somehow falling upward into its depths. I stumbled.

Holmes's hand shot out and seized my arm. "Are you ill?"

"No. I only…"

"Perhaps you should sit down for a moment."

"No, I would prefer to walk."

Holmes watched me closely, then drew in his breath deeply and exhaled. "Forgive me, Henry, if I seem curt or ill-tempered. It is not you with whom I am angry. I dislike being bested, especially when the result is murder. I should have dragged George away the minute I knew he was willing to talk, but then..."

I sighed. "And you must forgive me. My behavior has been... unmanly."

"Oh, nonsense!"

"It is true, but I... We have had our adventures together, but I have never faced a cold-blooded murderer before, one so eager to kill."

"Murder is the ultimate crime, the ultimate sin. As I have said, a person who will murder his own kind is worse than a beast. You are right to be afraid."

I smiled wanly. "Michelle does not seem to be afraid."

"She should be—if not, she lacks your good sense."

I laughed.

"I am serious. I would not want a fearless companion—I know you will not take stupid risks. That is why Michelle should not even be here—you should send her back to London."

I could not help but laugh. "I would like to see you try to send her back to London."

Holmes glared and shook his head, then a smile broke through. "I too am lacking in courage. Besides, Miss Grimswell needs her companionship."

Ahead we saw Merriweather Farm, the rectangular dwelling built of solid granite with its shale roof, a structure which appeared almost as ancient and unassailable as a menhir or tor. The giant oak before the house had lost most of its leaves, and the branches formed an elaborate twisted pattern of black before the sky. We walked down the stone path, and Holmes seized the weathered green knocker over the door, then hesitated.

"If she does not come..." He rapped loudly three times, then stepped back and folded his arms.

The moan of the wind was quieter down there where the farm sat than up on the hillside near the hall; all the same, we could hear its soft, ceaseless murmur.

"Who's there?" A woman's timid voice came faintly through the massive timbers.

"Mr. Sherlock Holmes from Grimswell Hall. I must speak with Mrs. Neal."

"Just a minute, sir." The door swung slowly inward, and there in the shadow stood a plump, small young woman in the rough-spun garments of a villager. "She's in, sirs. This way."

We stepped inside, and Holmes seized my arm. "Leave all the talking to me. Reveal nothing–nothing at all."

I nodded. The woman led us into the kitchen. Mrs. Neal sat in a rocking chair before the stove, her needlework on her lap. She set it aside and rose to greet us. Overhead, two enormous hams hung from hooks in the dark, aged beams of the rafters. Various pots, kettles and dishes were stacked on open shelves, and the large black iron stove gave off a welcome glow of heat.

"Mr. Holmes, Doctor Vernier–how good of you to stop by. I hope you will pardon me for receiving you in the kitchen, but it is the warmest room in the house–quite cozy as you can see. I am glad you have come for tea at last. Susan, put on the water. But where is Miss Grimswell today? I hope she is not ill."

"We do not need tea," Holmes said. "I fear this is not a social call."

"No? You may leave us, Susan." With a nod, the maid departed. Mrs. Neal had stunning clear blue eyes, and they gazed innocently at Holmes. "What then?"

"There has been an accident involving someone at the hall."

"Oh dear. I hope Miss Grimswell–"

"Miss Grimswell is perfectly all right."

A frown briefly wrinkled her clear, smooth brow. "That is a relief." Her eyes shifted to the right, then the left. "Who, then?"

"It is certainly no one you could have known."

The polite smile on her lips seemed rigid.

"One of the servants, George, has been killed."

Her mouth opened, and we heard the sound of her breath being sucked in. Her face twitched, and one hand suddenly reached back to grasp the top of the rocking chair. She closed her mouth and swallowed hard, sending a ripple along her slender throat. Her face had had a pleasant flush, but now began to lose color.

"You are correct. I did not know him."

"Someone cut his throat and bled him to death like an animal."

She gasped and covered her mouth with her tiny hand.

"Sherlock," I said, dismayed.

"It does not matter, Henry. She did not know the fellow, but she must have a kind heart all the same. She appears rather ill. Perhaps you had better sit down, madam."

"Yes—thank you." She stepped round and nearly fell into the chair. "I... Forgive me, but..." Her eyes shifted about, glancing every which way. She drew in her breath. "Such violence, such brutality, does make me ill, even though this person was not known to me."

Holmes's smile was ruthless. "As I said, Henry, a kind heart."

"I have always... I am not strong, it is true, and stories of cruelty and violence always upset me. Perhaps... I had hoped to escape such black deeds in the wilds of Dartmoor."

Holmes was still smiling. "Did you?"

"Yes, of course. Here there are no robbers or villains, not like in London, and..." She withdrew a lacy white handkerchief and dabbed at her eyes.

Holmes laughed sharply.

"Sherlock," I said.

His smile vanished. "Further pretense is unnecessary, madam. You need not play the bereaved widow with me."

Again she turned the full force of her blue eyes upon him. "Whatever do you mean?"

"I mean that I know all about you, George and a certain tall man with big feet and a large dog."

All the color left her face, and her eyes were fixed on her hands. They were shapely and delicate, but minute compared to those of Michelle or Rose. "I... I have no idea what on earth you mean, Mr. Holmes."

"I also know about your part in Lord Grimswell's murder."

She raised her head, her eyes fearful. "*What?*"

"You lured him onto the tor, and then your friend pushed him over the edge."

"I..." She drew in her breath, and her hands formed fists. "I was not there—I was not! I did love Lord Grimswell, it is true..."

"You never loved him!" Holmes was vehement.

"I did. Perhaps it was not right, but I did."

"Then why did you lure him to his death?"

"I... I did no such thing."

"You cannot fool *me*, madam. I am not susceptible to your female charms. I see you for what you are."

"And what is that?"

"Something beautiful but deadly—a poisonous snake perhaps, an adder."

"How dare you, sir!" Her voice lacked any real indignation.

"You are a pathetic and contemptible creature."

"Please, Sherlock." I knew he would not say such things if they were not true, but I could not bear to see a woman ill-treated.

"I have seen your kind before. God has given you the gift of great

beauty, yet you use that gift only for evil—you are like some spider..."
The image triggered a sudden recollection, which made him cover his
forehead with his hand. "No, no, not like a spider," he whispered to
himself, "not a spider." He lowered his hand, and much of the rage had
left his face. "No matter what you are, you are in grave danger. I suggest
you tell me everything, and then I shall get you away—I shall find a safe
place for you."

Again her throat rippled as she swallowed. "I have no idea what you
are talking about."

Holmes began to pace about the kitchen. "Perhaps you did not know
what he intended, but no, you must have known. He has killed Lord
Grimswell, George and probably one of Lady Rupert's maids. He will
not hesitate to kill again. George was going to tell me what he knew. He
may have been willing to see Lord Grimswell murdered, but perhaps
that changed things. He felt sorry for Rose Grimswell. He was willing
to frighten her, but not to help murder her. His knowledge was a threat.
That is why he was killed."

Mrs. Neal said nothing, but her eyes had a fearful intensity.

"You are next, madam. You know too much to live."

She shook her head, and managed a smile. "This is some dreadful
mistake, Mr. Holmes. I have no idea what you are talking about. I...
I did love Lord Grimswell, it is true, but all this other business... You
mistake me for... someone else."

Holmes stood before her rocker. "Do I? He will kill you, I swear he
will. Surely you must know that."

Somehow she managed to keep smiling. "Who on earth are you
talking about?"

"I am talking about the monster loose on the moor. He is not a
vampire or werewolf, but he is their equal in evil—something worse,
even. You are expendable, madam. Perhaps you think... He certainly

cannot love you, no more than you loved Lord Grimswell. There is only one woman he truly loves—the one who bore him."

She struck at her legs with her small fists, her face reddening. "*No.*" She twisted her head to the side and clenched her teeth. "You are wrong—you are wrong. I mean… I… I do not know what you are talking about." She straightened her neck and assumed an insipid look. "This is all madness. How dare you speak to me as you have? How dare you? You have insulted me deeply. Where is your breeding, sirs? You are no gentlemen, that is certain. I must ask you to leave."

Holmes stared at her and shook his head. "He will kill you."

"Go away—now. *Please.*" Her voice had faltered.

Holmes sighed wearily. "I was wrong to mock you, but I was angry. You did not see Miss Grimswell nearly frightened out of her mind or George with his throat ripped open. Whatever your crimes, you do not deserve what will happen if you remain here. Let us take you to Grimpen. You can—you can escape. I know nearly everything now, madam, and… I do not want to see you dead."

The brief flush of anger had left her. She looked drained, already lifeless. "Please go, Mr. Holmes. Please leave me."

Holmes stared at her, but she lowered her eyes. He seized his stick and put on his hat. "Come, Henry."

"But if—"

"*Come.*" He stopped at the doorway. "Justice is a strange and terrible thing, madam. Sometimes justice is not desirable at all. If you change your mind—and I pray you will—come to the hall or flee to Grimpen, whichever you will. But do not remain here."

Mrs. Neal had nothing to say. Her face seemed waxen, her beauty illusory, and she appeared frozen in the chair, unable to move.

"Sherlock—"

"Let us go, Henry."

I caught one last glimpse of her blue eyes. They were curiously empty, vague and distant. Something in her mouth and eyes made me realize I was seeing the real woman now, a person very different from the blond vapid widow of her sentimental tale.

We went through a barren sitting room. "We cannot leave her," I said.

"You heard what I told her, Henry. I tried—I honestly tried. We cannot force her—she must choose. She must choose to save herself."

The plump maid opened the door for us. "Good day, sirs."

Holmes hesitated. "It would be better if your mistress were not left alone tonight."

The girl's smile faltered. "I can't... I can't be here after dark. My father will pick me up soon, so we'll be back home by sunset."

Holmes scowled. "Whatever am I thinking? By all means, do not stay here after dark! See if... Ask your mistress to return with you to Grimpen when your father comes. Will you promise me that? Try to persuade her. It is no longer safe here."

"Surely, sir."

"Good afternoon."

Holmes set off at a desperate pace, his eyes locked ahead. With a heavy heart, I followed, pausing once to glance back at the lonely farmhouse, the ancient granite dwelling set against the desolate moor and the bleak sky of Dartmoor, a sky which had lost its vibrant blue and begun to fade.

When we reached the hall the light had diminished even more. Holmes said hardly a word and, once inside, went silently up the stairs. I hesitated, then crossed the hall and went to the conservatory.

I opened the heavy doors, and it was like being outdoors again, the glass overhead filling the room with an abundance of soft light. Laughter floated through the air, a gentle sound, and then another laugh which I recognized–Michelle's. The ferns thrust their broad, jagged leaves toward the sky, and the potted palms rose higher still. The gravel crunched lightly under my feet.

Michelle and Rose sat together on the teak bench. They had not seen me, and I stopped walking so they would not. Rose was smiling. Michelle had leaned forward and seized her wrist with her big white hand. She wore a brilliant reddish-purple dress, a favorite of mine, and as usual, the dazzling color contrasted with Rose's somber black. Michelle's face was flushed slightly, and Rose stared at her, a smile on her lips. Her hair was black, while Michelle's was a light reddish brown. Their faces were different, but both were lovely women. Something about them made my eyes fill with tears.

At last Michelle turned and saw me. "Henry, what are you doing there?"

I forced a smile and stepped forward. "The two of you looked so happy together, I did not want to intrude."

Michelle's brow furrowed. "What has happened?"

"Uh, nothing important." I tried to control the pitch of my voice. "I shall tell you later." My eyes were fixed on her, and she understood.

She smiled, but all the playfulness had gone out of her eyes. "Rose and I have been talking about men. I have warned her not to take them too seriously." Something made a plop in the pond, and Michelle turned. "Goodness, look at them."

The koi hovered over the blue tiles on the side of the pond near me, torpedo shapes in agitated motion–white, gold, black and orange, singularly or in various mixtures of colors. The white scaly monster opened his mouth in a greedy O, the two whiskery points again reminding me of flexible fangs. Startled, I took a step back. Several others raised their heads out of the water, their mouths greedily opening.

"Ugly things," I murmured.

Rose smiled at me. "They will not eat you. It is nearly feeding time, and they are ravenous. Fish are very greedy creatures."

Michelle stood. "I am rather ravenous myself. Dinner time must be approaching."

Rose lowered her head, her smile fading away. In the gray, diminished light, her eyes appeared gray as well. Michelle smiled at me, then put her hand on the girl's shoulder. "Come, my dear. This is a lovely place, but I am sure you would like a quiet moment before you dress for dinner."

"I forgot—I actually forgot for several minutes…" She reached up and put her hand over Michelle's. "You are very kind—and very amusing—but now… I still cannot believe George is really dead, and my father—"

"Your father is dead, too," Michelle said sharply, "not wandering on the moors, and when Sherlock finds these grave robbers, they will pay for their crimes—all of their crimes."

"Somehow it almost seems wrong to have been happy."

"It is never wrong to be happy. Life has sadness enough for us all, but come, let us go prepare for dinner."

Rose stood, and again I was struck by her height. I had never known a woman three inches taller than Michelle. The three of us started for the doors. Behind us the fish made agitated splashing noises. Michelle glanced at me, her eyes worried and inquisitive. She could tell I was upset.

"Did Digby find you?" I asked.

"He did, but then he was banished." Michelle's voice grew stern. "Luckily for him. Doctor Hartwood showed remarkable restraint, but I think he would have hit him at last."

Rose shook her head. "I do not understand why Rickie behaves so abominably."

"I told you why," Michelle said. "He is jealous of Doctor Hartwood, as well he should be, since the doctor is hopelessly in love with you."

I stopped abruptly and glanced at both women. Rose had lowered her eyes, her face reddening. "That's silly. He hardly knows me. He could not..."

"Many men—especially those in the better circles—are obtuse, but someone like the doctor sees your true beauty."

"Oh, Michelle—I am not beautiful."

"Yes, you are, and it is time you realized it. Digby is too foolish to see it, but a normal man, one who is free of certain prejudices about female stature, waist size and hair color, could not fail to recognize it. Sherlock and Henry both have an appreciative eye for women. Tell her she is beautiful, Henry."

I laughed, although such talk made me faintly uncomfortable. "Michelle is quite right."

Rose would not look at me, but her flush deepened. "You cannot... you do not mean it."

"I certainly do mean it." My voice was resolute.

"Oh... Thank you, Henry, thank you very much—but let us talk about something else."

We had reached the foot of the stairs in the great hall. A man appeared above us, then came bounding down, two or three steps at a time. Holmes's eyes were wild, his mouth open in a snarl of exertion. "For God's sake, Henry!" He seized my arm, wrenching me away from Michelle. "Come with me! Hurry!"

"What is it?" Michelle asked.

Somehow I knew, and the ever-present dread seemed to materialize from out of the shadows of the hall and seize my heart in an icy fist. I turned and strode after Holmes.

"Henry—what is it? Where are you going?" I heard her run after us.

Holmes turned, his eyes furious, his face pale and frightful. "By God, Michelle—you stay here! Rose needs you—I shall take care of

Henry." He seized my arm and pulled me forward.

"But—"

"Stay here!" Holmes roared, even as he wrenched open the door, and then we were practically running down the pathway. The sky through the branches had a reddish hue.

"What is it?" I managed to say. "Did you see something?"

"I was in the tower. At the telescope. Watching the farm." His words came in brief bursts; he was breathing hard as we nearly ran. "I saw him coming. The man. The dog."

"Oh no! So soon?"

"We… we shall never be in time." He pushed open a gate marking the entry to the Grimswell estate and did not bother closing it. "Why wouldn't she…"—he gasped—"…listen to me?"

The sun had sunk minutes ago, and the wind had turned cold. Something black flew by in an erratic path overhead—probably a bat. Before, we had not covered the distance between the hall and the farm in less than three-quarters of an hour, but we must have done it in half that time. When we were nearly there, Holmes stumbled, then fell to his knees, coughing wildly. Somehow he managed to get to his feet and stagger on. I shook my head in dismay, convinced years of tobacco smoke had ruined his lungs.

He stopped again when the house and tree stood before us. Still panting, nearly wheezing, he withdrew a revolver from his jacket pocket and handed it to me. "Here."

I shook my head. I was breathing hard, but I was not so overwhelmed as he. "I cannot hit anything."

He took another revolver from the opposite pocket. "We may have to shoot both the man and the dog. Do not hesitate in the least if… Come."

"Should we just rush in?"

"Yes."

The first stars were coming out overhead, and all about us the heather, grass and stones were blending into a dark shapeless mass. The door was open. Somehow the sight of that black narrow gap of shadow running its length terrified me. Holmes went in first.

"Mrs. Neal!" he shouted. "Grace!"

The house was dark and silent, not a sound to be heard.

Holmes gave a great sigh. "Oh, we are too late."

I tried to speak, but nothing came out. "Perhaps... perhaps she fled."

Holmes gave his head a single shake. "No."

He glanced about, then noticed a candle on the table near the door. He struck a match and lit it. His face was gaunt and drawn; he appeared both exhausted and ill from our near-run. Neither of us had even bothered to put on our hats or overcoats. "Unless I am greatly mistaken, Henry, this will be hideous."

"Then let's get it over with."

The sitting room was deserted, but a small table and chair had been knocked over. We found her in the kitchen, a heap of black silk, white flesh, yellow hair and blood. Holmes pulled her over, and her head fell at a peculiar angle, revealing the dark pool of blood staining the granite floor. Her throat was a bloody, mangled mess, and I turned away, afraid I might somehow vomit even though my stomach was empty.

"This is what a real victim of a wild beast looks like. The hound tore out her throat at last, but she put up an incredible struggle for one so small. Look at her hands and arms."

I turned slowly. Holmes held the candle over her. The black silken sleeves had been shredded, and her white arms and hands were covered with wounds and blood.

"She tried to fight it off, but the hound was far too strong for her. It may have outweighed her." He hesitated, then bent over and closed her eyes. Dimly I realized that broken crockery, pots and pans littered the room. I turned and quickly walked back outside.

I held the revolver in my hand and stared up at the splendid night sky. The stars would again be marvelous. I was still warm from our exertion, but my hands had begun to tremble, and soon my jaw as well. Holmes was so long in coming that I thought I should go and look for him, but I could not. I was too frightened—I could hardly think.

When he came out at last, I was relieved but still afraid. "He is gone, long gone," Holmes said. He stared up at the sky. Mars was a bloody orb low in the east. "This did not need to happen. I begged her to leave—you heard me. I begged her repeatedly. It is her own fault."

"No." I shook my head. "No one chooses such a death—not that way."

He was silent a long while. "You are correct, Henry. She managed to convince herself that he would not kill her. She thought… she thought he loved her." His laugh was anguished. I turned to him, but his face was hidden in the growing darkness. "Poor silly little fool, poor fool."

He took a step forward, then another. A broom leaned against the wall near the doorway. Suddenly he seized it by the bottom, the straw, and began to whack savagely at the granite wall. On about the third blow, I heard a splintering noise. "Stop it." I tried to seize his arm. "You will hurt yourself—stop that!"

He threw aside the broken shaft, then leaned against the wall. "This damned beast!—not the hound, *the man*—I shall slaughter him myself, Henry, I swear it!"

"No, no." I shook my head.

"Yes, I shall… I shall drive a stake through his heart!" His laugh was nearly a sob. "I shall fill him with silver bullets. I shall smother him with garlic. I…"

A strange sound slipped from between my lips, a noise which I realized must be laughter. Holmes gripped my arm fiercely. "Let us get away from here, Henry. For once I do not feel like examining the scene of the crime. The cause of death is obvious—and horrible. I know who did it, and that he and his dog are out wandering the moor even now. Let us leave this dreadful place."

"Yes," I said. "Yes." I could not stop shivering. "Are you cold?"

"Yes, Henry. I am."

Fourteen

ᴄ⟩

Late that evening, the four of us met in Holmes's room for a sort of war council. The day's events had left me shaken and exhausted. I had never encountered two murdered corpses in a single day, nor did I wish to ever repeat the experience. Michelle and Rose were somber, but they had not had as much physical exertion as Holmes and I.

Holmes sat before the fire smoking one of Lord Grimswell's magnificent pipes and staring at the coal glowing on the grate. He did appear tired, but his gray eyes were alert and agitated. "I fear," he said at last, "that it might be best to return to London."

"What?" Michelle exclaimed. I felt only relief. "You would just give up?"

Holmes exhaled a cloud of smoke. "I have little choice. I know a great deal about these villains, but the only way I can flush the man out is by using Miss Grimswell as bait. That I will not do."

Michelle frowned thoughtfully. "What exactly do you know? Is it not time you told us?"

I realized Holmes must be keeping much from us, and I gave an emphatic nod. "Yes, you must tell us."

Holmes stared at the coal, pipe stem between his lips, and shook his head.

"Why not?" Michelle asked. "Don't you trust us?"

"Trust has nothing to do with it. I know you could keep it secret, but it would change your feelings and your behavior. Something in your manner would show when you are before certain people."

"What people?"

Holmes smiled but said nothing.

"Now you are being smug!" Michelle said.

Holmes gave a long sigh. "If so, I regret the impression. I wish I could tell you everything, but I dare not at this time."

Some thought struggled to solidify in my mind. "The man on the moor is not acting alone. He must have an ally in the hall. You do not want that person to suspect anything."

Holmes nodded, smiling. "Very good, Henry. You are learning. Our association has taught you something after all."

"It is Digby, is it not?" Michelle asked eagerly.

Rose raised one hand, her eyes pained. "Oh, no—it cannot be."

Holmes withdrew the pipe stem again. "I did not gather you together for idle speculation. We must decide whether to remain here in Dartmoor or return to London. I hesitated somewhat in discussing this with Miss Grimswell, but—"

Michelle sat bolt upright. "How could you not discuss it with her? Her life is at stake!"

"I did not wish to frighten her, if possible, but I eventually reached that conclusion." Holmes's eyes had grown cold and faintly angry as he spoke to Michelle. "By now you should all realize exactly how dangerous our opponent is. In the last twenty-four hours, he has murdered two people in cold blood. Both were former friends and accomplices whom he feared might assist me. The woman at the farm was most likely his paramour."

"How do you know that?" I asked.

"Because of her stubborn refusal to flee. Given what I had told her, any reasonable person would have left at once. She stayed because she loved him and could not believe that he would hurt her."

Michelle shook her head. "Oh, how... stupid women can be."

"Many of the worst villains are quite charming. I believe there was a third victim, one of Lady Rupert's maids." He turned to Rose. "I spoke with Lady Rupert briefly in London late Sunday evening. One of the maids had disappeared right after you departed. They found her body at a nearby inn a day later. She must have let him into the house and helped him arrange for the voice which you heard in your rooms."

Rose's big white hands closed about the ends of the chair arm. "Oh dear God—who was it? Which one?"

Holmes sighed. "I do not recall a name. Also..." He stared at the fire, his mouth tightening.

Rose swallowed, the motion rippling across her long white throat. "Also?"

Holmes took a draw on the pipe, then let out the smoke. "As you realized on Demon Tor, this same person was responsible for your father's death."

Rose's lips parted. She too had gained some color under the Dartmoor sun, but now she went pale. "God help me," she said softly. Her eyes began to tear up. "But why...?" Michelle leaned over and gave her hand a squeeze.

"For the same reason he wants you out of the way—your family fortune. With your father gone, you are the only remaining obstacle."

Rose gave a savage laugh. "Can we not...? Oh, they can have the blasted money, if only they will leave me in peace!"

"That would never be possible, and even if it were, such creatures should not remain in human society. There is also the matter of the many crimes they have committed."

Rose sighed. "Oh, I know that. I only..."

Holmes held the pipe in his left hand, but the long fingers of his right tapped restlessly on the dark woolen tweed over his knee. "We have reached a stalemate. Our adversary is leery of making another move in the hall because he knows I am fully on guard. If Miss Grimswell were to venture out on the moors alone, either during the day—or especially at night—her life would be forfeit at once. As I indicated, we might try to set a trap using her as bait, but the risk would be far too great. I could not live with myself, should this villain be taken at the cost of your life." He stared at Rose as he said this.

Michelle's forehead briefly crunched in thought. "Why not use me as bait?"

"What!" I exclaimed.

Holmes gazed at Michelle with a certain weary amazement.

"You could put me in a black-haired wig. I am nearly the same height and build as Rose. Did you not say she sleepwalks? I could wander out on the moor with my arms outstretched, my eyes half closed, but beneath my gown would be a revolver. I do know how to use one, and—"

"Michelle, this is madness!" I shook my head repeatedly. "Absolutely not! Have you gone completely insane?"

"You need not lose your temper at my even suggesting it, Henry—you need not take that tone of voice. It is a plan which should be considered."

Holmes shook his head. "No."

"And why not? You cannot simply—"

Rose grabbed Michelle's arm and shook her head wildly. "No, never—do you think I could allow another—a—a friend to take such a terrible risk for me? No, Michelle. *No.*"

Holmes's lips formed a brief, grim smile. "You are outvoted, Michelle. Such a plan would be far too dangerous, especially at night."

Michelle kept her lips clamped tightly shut and inhaled through her nostrils.

"However, your courage is admirable, all the same."

Rose stared at him, her eyes confused. "Have I been sleepwalking again?"

"Yes," Holmes said.

"How odd. I have not done so since my first year away at school."

Michelle bit at the tip of one finger as she frowned in thought, then she lowered her hand. "Perhaps if Rose and I went out alone together, we might draw this monster out. We could depart by ourselves during the day, and you men could follow. I would have a revolver."

"Michelle, stop it!" I cried. "Please leave yourself out of these ridiculous schemes!"

"Don't you shout at me!" she exclaimed.

"I'm sorry, but you did not see… you did not see…" My voice caught in my throat, my eyes filling with tears, and my face twisted in an odd, uncontrollable way. I was remembering again Mrs. Neal's lifeless body in a heap, Holmes turning her over, all that ripped flesh and red blood… I staggered to my feet and turned away from them before I completely broke down.

I would have fled, but Michelle had grasped my wrist. "Oh, Henry. Please…"

"If anything were to happen to you…" I could barely get the words out.

"All right, I'm sorry. Come on now." She drew my arm round and looked at me, then reached up and touched my face with her hand. I could not speak, but a laugh slipped out. "I did not mean to upset you."

"It has been… such a terrible day."

"Please sit down." I let her guide me back to my chair. She sat as well.

Holmes shook his head. "We are getting nowhere. I am beginning to regret calling us together. Perhaps some time alone before the fire with a pipe would have been more productive. Henry was right, Michelle. I could no more accept using you as bait, than I could Miss Grimswell."

Michelle's jaw stiffened. She glanced at me, then at Holmes. "Yet if you could use yourself as bait and trap this monster, you would do so in an instant."

Holmes smiled, genuinely amused. "Indeed I would."

"Sherlock, you can be absolutely infuriating at times!"

"Michelle, will you acknowledge no difference in the treatment of the sexes? Women are not to be used as bait. Besides, you are married and a physician. You have a husband, friends and patients who would suffer greatly from your loss. I am a solitary sort, as you know. My absence would not be much missed."

Michelle's cheeks were still flushed. "That is more infuriating still. You are Sherlock Holmes! England could never bear your loss—you are a great force for good and a foe of evil. You are unique and irreplaceable, while I am—"

My head was throbbing. "Oh please, that is quite enough. Every human life has value, and no one is to be offered as bait. If it is any consolation to you, Michelle, I would not volunteer myself as bait—I am too cowardly. Now let us drop the damned subject."

Holmes gave an emphatic nod. "Yes."

Michelle sighed. "Very well. Perhaps I was…" She seized my arm again. "I am glad you do not want to be rid of me. I only wish…" She sank back into the chair and shook her head. "It is so hard to just sit by and let these monsters… I only wish I could do something!"

Rose's eyes had gone back and forth, watching us all during our debate. Now she stared incredulously at Michelle, and it was difficult to know what she was feeling—puzzlement, awe, fear?

Holmes set down his pipe. "If we remain here, Miss Grimswell, you are in grave danger, but our adversary may possibly show himself in desperation and be apprehended. He may try something again in the house. If we return to London, I shall see you established safely, your whereabouts known only to us. Perhaps that might be best. Retreat does seem cowardly and goes against my nature, but… You have said little, but you will have the final say in the matter. Which would you prefer?"

Rose stared at the fire, her chin raised high. Her long white fingers clutched again at the ends of the chair arms. The huge pupils of her eyes turned to us from under her black thick eyebrows. A single strand of hair had come loose and fallen across her forehead.

"Let us stay one more day. Let us go back the day after tomorrow, Thursday."

Holmes smiled. "A compromise of sorts. Very well, that is what we shall announce tomorrow."

Michelle glanced at me, troubled. Rose smiled faintly, but I thought I saw the fear in her eyes and in the stiffness of her mouth. Michelle stood, yawned, then extended her hand to me. I took it and rose wearily. My legs still ached from the mad dash to the farm.

"Wait." Rose raised one hand, palm up, her fingers curving slightly. "Before you go, I must… I must thank you all. You have all been so good to me. You have willingly entered into this dreadful business and tried to help me—and you have saved my life. I would be dead by now if not for you. And if all that were not enough…" She swallowed once. "You have… you have offered me something so very precious—your friendship."

"Oh, my dear." Michelle took her hand, drew her up out of the chair and embraced her. "You are quite welcome."

"Yes." My voice shook.

Holmes did not speak, but when Rose looked at him, he gave a brusque nod. He picked up the pipe, noticed it was empty, and reached for the container of tobacco. His thoughts seemed to be elsewhere. "Tell no one anything except that we are leaving on Thursday morning. If anyone asks, the decision was mine. I shall handle Digby, Constance and the Fitzwilliamses." A quicksilver smile pulled at his lips. "And do not pay attention to any nonsense I concoct for them."

That night, despite my fatigue, I could not sleep. Michelle tried to stay awake and keep me company, but she was tired too and fell asleep around midnight. I went down the hallway and looked in Holmes's room. Through the slight fog of smoke, I saw him seated before the fire, obviously lost in thought, the pipe stem clamped between his lips. I went back to our room and stared out of the wavery, ancient glass panes. The moon was nearly full, dazzling, and lit up the rolling expanse of the moors. As always, the wind moaned incessantly.

I realized our opponent might well be out there staring at the hall. I felt suddenly cold and went back to bed. Visions of George's or Grace Neal's corpse came to me again and again, and when I slept my dreams were so terrible that wakefulness was preferable. I sat up and tried to remain awake, but slumped over instead and sank into the mire of dreams. They were indistinct, but filled with dead-white faces, torn flesh and blood. Lurking nearby was the man in black. At one point I realized he was in the room with Michelle and me. My efforts to scream or run were futile, and he slowly advanced toward us. His jaw had an odd shape, his teeth long and sharp.

Michelle woke me at last, but the terror would not leave me. I clung to her, felt the familiar curves of her body and slipped one hand under her nightshirt and onto her bare thigh. "Poor darling." Her hand closed about mine. I slept then, but when I woke shortly after eight, I felt almost wearier than the night before. Michelle, an inveterate early riser, was gone, but when I went down to the breakfast room, I found only Holmes there.

The day had begun gray and cold, a heavy mist enshrouding the dark trunks and leaves of the trees. The yellow wallpaper with its tiny flowers and the lace curtains were still cheerful, but the room seemed muted and despondent in the dim light. Holmes was drinking coffee from a blue and white china cup. His thin face was clean, his cheeks freshly shaven (I had not dared touch a razor yet), and his shirt and collar were dazzling white. He had dressed formally in a black frock coat and waistcoat. He gave me a brief, pained smile.

"Do I look so bad?" I asked.

"Yes."

My laughter was feeble. "I shall not be sorry to leave Dartmoor."

"I regret you had to visit Dartmoor under such unpleasant circumstances."

I went to the sideboard and began raising silver lids. Something about the kippers, their color or smell, reminded me of dead flesh. Nausea rose in my throat, and I slammed down the lid. In the end only some scrambled eggs and a dry piece of toast were on my plate, but I hardly had an appetite for even so little. I ate silently while Holmes sipped his coffee and stared out at the misty woods.

"If we were to stay much longer," he said at last, "we would risk being snowed in. Blizzards are not uncommon in late November, although likelier in December. The cold and the wind on the moors are hard to imagine. The temperature can fall well below freezing."

I shuddered. "I can imagine it all too well."

The door swung open and Constance approached us, her pink face under the lacy cap obscenely and impossibly cheerful. She was the last person I wanted to see.

"Good morning, Doctor Vernier, Mr. Holmes," she boomed. "Is it true what I hear? That you are leaving tomorrow?"

Holmes sipped his coffee, then dabbed at his lips with the napkin. "Yes, I believe so."

Constance shook her head, her smile gone. "No wonder, with all these terrible goings-on. I don't mind telling you, Mr. Holmes, that I am frightened."

"Justifiably so."

"I am not by nature superstitious, but after all that has happened—especially to Victor–I... I do not truly think this man on the moor is him, but I am sure he cannot be... well, quite normal. Oh yes, I too am ready to leave."

Holmes nodded. "Again, that is quite understandable."

"Besides, Rose does need someone to look after her."

My fork slipped from my hand and clattered on the plate, even as I grimaced. Constance turned to me, but by then I had recovered.

"If she is leaving, there is no reason for me to stay behind, and of course, a young lady must be chaperoned. She cannot live alone in London."

It was because I had come to know and like Rose so well that I was so utterly dismayed. I managed to hold my tongue and glanced down at my plate to hide my face. The thought of that lovely young woman saddled in London with this suffocating old woman...

The door swung open again, and another person of a cheerful countenance entered. I had thought Constance was the last person I wanted to see, but here was serious competition. Lord Frederick had resurrected the green frock coat, although no carnation had been found for the lapel. He was actually whistling, some tune from *Pinafore* or *Pirates of Penzance*.

"Good morning, old chaps, madam." Still whistling, he began lifting lids and piling food onto his plate.

Constance's brown eyes focused on him, her glance sullen. "As I was just saying, Rose cannot be alone in London. She must have someone to look after her, and after all, she is the only family I have."

Holmes gave a slight nod. "Your claim cannot be denied."

Digby pulled out the chair next to me. "Thinkin' of departin' the old pile, are we? Back to the seat of the empire, jolly old London, Big Ben and Westminster? It's about time. I still don't believe in ghosts and spooks, but whatever is going on, there's too many bodies lyin' about. I'm ready to leave. Besides, all this fresh air and desolate landscape get tiresome. I'm ready for a good dinner at Simpson's and a night at the club. One misses male companionship after a while."

"We plan on leaving tomorrow morning," Holmes said.

"Oh, excellent!" Digby's smile was enthusiastic. He paused his fork midway between plate and mouth, a piece of kipper impaled with silver. His plate was loaded—bacon, sausages, fried tomatoes, beans, eggs and potatoes, stewed prunes and more—something of everything.

"And I, of course, shall go along to look after Rose." Constance gave a nod of emphasis.

"Nonsense," Digby said, even while chewing and swallowing.

"Nonsense? What do you mean?" Constance's brow furrowed ominously.

"No need for that if she's going to marry me, and I've nearly brought her round. You needn't worry, Constance. I shall look after her."

This was a fate worse than being chaperoned, and I could not restrain myself. "Rose has said nothing..." Holmes's eyes narrowed, he gave his head an almost imperceptible shake, and I let my words trail away.

Constance sat up in her seat. "Lord Frederick, isn't it about time you discussed your intentions with me? After all, I am her only living relation."

Digby paused, fork poised before his mouth, then laughed. "Oh, really now, Constance—you're hardly related at all. You're not an auntie, just some very distant cousin. I'd think, too, that you'd be happy to see the girl married off to an upright scion of one of England's oldest families. Pardon the blowing the old horn, but after all, they aren't exactly knocking down the door to get in line, are they? Unless... Surely you wouldn't want Hartwood in the family? Besides, it's not really your business after all, is it, old dear?"

Constance seemed to swell before our eyes. "How dare you speak to me that way, young man? My family is as old and distinguished as yours—and my father was Lord Grimswell's brother—just as you will be a marquess's brother someday. Both situations are equally worthless. You have no title, no lands, no money, nothing to offer Rose—you will only be taking from her, and I have always suspected... You only want her money, don't you? You have never loved her."

Digby kept smiling and eating, but his cheeks reddened. "Of course I love her."

"It's her money, isn't it? Can you deny you want the money?"

"No, but I want Rose most of all. The money is like... frosting on the cake."

Oh Lord, I thought, he is hopeless.

Constance had also grown quite red. She was so large and formidable a woman that she gave the impression she could easily devour the slight, thin Digby. "So you say, young man, but I have my doubts about you."

"You are welcome to them, but they won't matter to Rose."

She set her big, swollen-looking hand on the linen tablecloth. "Rose did not have all these troubles before she met you. She did not hear dead men talking to her and see ghosts. It makes a body wonder."

Digby slammed his hand onto the table. "Don't be an utter idiot,

Constance—you are talking nonsense, silly nonsense!"

"Am I? You said you wanted her money. What would you do to get it?"

"*Nothing dishonorable*—is that clear enough for you? No one likes an old meddler, especially when they are being particularly foolish. If I marry Rose—as I trust I shall—I shall not forget this conversation. Besides, I have my own suspicions about who the man on the moor is."

Constance was scowling but looked puzzled. Holmes put his knuckles under his chin. "Do you now?"

Digby had picked up his fork and resumed eating. "Yes."

"Pray tell us whom you suspect."

"Who has a bad habit of stumbling upon corpses and then appearing here?"

I frowned, unable to think whom he meant, but Holmes smiled. "Ah. Doctor Hartwood."

"Doctor Hartwood!" I exclaimed. "But he—"

Digby nodded. "First the dog, then George. And he was Lord Grimswell's doctor. For all we know he gave him some medicine that killed him, made him so dizzy he fell off the tor. And now he's after Rose."

"Now that really is nonsense," I said.

Holmes was still smiling. "What he claims has a certain logic."

"Oh, he feigns well enough." Digby's smile grew smug. "He acts as if old cupid has cleft his heart in twain, but I'll wager all those pounds sterling are in the back of his mind. There are men who will kill for that kind of money—I am not one of them—but they do exist."

"That is certainly true," Holmes said.

Constance appeared both wary and puzzled. "I am not so sure."

Digby cut up a strip of bacon into neat pieces. "I've heard you say enough bad things about Hartwood, Constance."

"Oh, he's not old Doctor Herbert's equal, but I never said he was a murderer." Her forehead was creased. "I shall have to think about this. A murderer. There is so much evil in the world. Maybe…" Her mouth formed a brief, grotesque smile. "My sister is always talking about the Devil being at work. Perhaps, after all, there is truth in what she says. So much wickedness." She slowly stood up, then turned to leave.

She had almost reached the door when Digby spoke. "We must ask Rose whom she wishes to accompany her back to London—you or me. I'm sure the decision will be a difficult one for her."

Constance gave him a venomous look, her pink face contorting with rage. Something about the white lace cap and black dress suddenly seemed ludicrous—they did not fit so large and powerful a person—and she appeared curiously sexless. It was a swinging door, or she would have slammed it shut behind her.

Digby's pale blue eyes glared triumphantly at the door. "Pathetic old cow. She is ultimately rather laughable."

Holmes stood. "Would either of you care for coffee?"

I shook my head, but Digby nodded. "Please."

Holmes returned with two cups of coffee. "So you still have hopes that Miss Grimswell will marry you?"

His mouth full, Digby nodded. "I do, Mr. Holmes, I do. And I shall protect her, rest assured of that. And if you find this monster—especially if you expose him as Hartwood—you will be well paid."

Holmes's smile was cold. "My payment is of little concern to me, not in this case."

"No?" Digby's plate was clean at last, and he set down his napkin. "Why not? If I marry Rose, I shall see that you are well paid."

"I shall keep that in mind."

"Do so. Especially now, given all that has happened… Rose must understand that marrying me is the only thing that makes sense. I can get her away from Grimswell Hall and Constance, and I can protect her from that murdering fiend. I may not... I may not be good for much—I know you both think me a pretentious fool—but I am capable of that, and I do love her, in my own way. Wild, passionate abandon is not my style, howlin' at the moon and goin' down on the knees and all that, but my feelings for her are genuine, all the same." He took a sip of coffee. "And even if... Certainly I can offer her more than some country-bumpkin doctor. She is a woman of intelligence and education, and what would she talk about with him? Farmer Brown's gout? Sheep herding? She'd be bored to death in a month."

I had shown incredible restraint, but I spoke at last. "Do you truly feel you know Doctor Hartwood well enough to speak with such certainty about his character?"

He shrugged. "Oh, I know the type well enough. The species is a common one."

"And exactly how would you know his type?" I asked. "You do not associate with any men who have to work for a living, men who actually do some active good in the world."

My anger caught him off guard. "I mean no criticism of physicians, Doctor Vernier. Your calling is a noble one—if a man has the stomach for it."

This was too close to my own reflections. My head had begun to ache, and I could bear Digby's presence no longer. I mumbled my excuses, stood up and departed. Holmes soon joined me in the great hall. I was again staring out of the mullioned glass at the trees; an icy-looking drizzle had begun to fall, something between mist and rain.

"Not very inviting," Holmes said. "Unfortunately I must be going out. Keep an eye on the ladies, Henry."

"Where are you going?"

"To Grimpen and then to Merriweather Farm. Someone needs to alert the local police of Mrs. Neal's death. I shall go on horseback."

I could not repress a shudder. "Wild horses could not drag me back to Merriweather Farm."

"I do not look forward to it myself. The ladies, I believe, are in the conservatory." My eyes were still fixed on the dark green leaves of the yews amid the white mists, but I heard him sigh. He set his hand on my shoulder. "Thank you, Henry, for your help. Murder never fails to shock—never."

I soon joined Michelle and Rose by the fish pond. Michelle was relentlessly cheerful, but Rose seemed as despondent as I, and rather preoccupied. The huge koi swam about in the clear blue water, their colors striking against the blue tiles, but even they seemed faintly monstrous to me with their grotesque, hungry mouths.

Later, after lunch, I sat near the fire and tried to read a medical journal. That was a mistake, as I was far too restless. After reading the same paragraph several times, I let my head fall back against the chair. It would be good to get back to London and some semblance of normality. Suddenly sleepy, I closed my eyes.

I had nearly dozed when soft, languid music filled the hall, the notes played beautifully. The piano—someone was playing the piano, the grand piano which had sat in a corner silent and unused during our entire stay thus far at Grimswell Hall. I opened my eyes and leaned forward. The top was up, and Rose stared down at the keys, the tension of her concentration showing in her forehead and her tight lips and jaw. The piano was black, as was her dress and her hair, but her face stood out in the shadow.

The music sounded like Chopin, probably one of the *Preludes*, the left hand carrying the urgent melody. Her playing was quite remarkable, very clean and lucid, but with a passion one would not expect from a twenty-year-old woman. I listened in awe for the next several minutes as she went through what must be the whole set of *Preludes*. She played it with a simple sincerity that was impossible to resist.

At some point Michelle joined me, setting her hand on my shoulder and standing quietly beside me. When Rose finished one particularly beautiful piece, Michelle stared down at me, her eyes all liquid, and said, "She must play well."

I smiled. Because Michelle had little musical knowledge or experience, she usually deferred to my judgment, although I was hardly an expert, especially compared to Holmes, an excellent violinist and an avid concert- and opera-goer.

"She plays magnificently."

"The music is lovely, but so sad."

"It was written by a tubercular Polish romantic who died very young."

"I hope…" Her fingertips caressed my cheek lightly. "I hope that is not why she chose it."

When Rose had finished the Chopin, she started on a lengthy sonata which was either Beethoven or Mozart. The music sounded more difficult with many more notes, but she gave it the same ardent intensity. She then went backward in time and played something by Bach, more difficult still, with three or four contrapuntal voices. The finale was a piece by Chopin which I recognized, a thundering polonaise filled with dramatic chords played with both hands. She used the pedal and filled the entire hall with sound.

In awe, I stood up and stepped around where I could see better. Her hands had been hidden from me, but now I saw them leap about, those long white fingers totally mastering the keys, the pale skin of her wrists almost glowing next to the black silk of her cuffs. Her eyes showed both wild exultation and tremendous concentration. The final chord was deafening, all the strength of her strong arms and shoulders going into her fingers.

"Oh, bravo!" Michelle began to clap.

"Bravo indeed," I said, joining her. "Bravo."

Rose drew in her breath, her bosom swelling, blinked twice, then glanced at us and smiled. "Thank you."

Digby came walking out of the shadow where he had stood near a gigantic potted palm. "That was remarkable, Rose. I knew you played, but... I guess I'd never heard you, not in years and years, and I thought..." His smile was almost awkward, his eyes evasive. "That was so damned authoritative, nothing of the amateur at all. And you played for so long, nearly two hours. I kept waiting for it to end—not that I really wanted it to—but... Are you finished, by the way?"

She smiled up at him. Her brow glistened faintly with sweat. "Yes, I think so. I had not played in a long time. I wanted to do something which would... distract me. My fingers felt awkward. I must get back to a regular practice schedule again."

Digby's eyes were fixed on her. "I didn't know," he said, almost to himself.

"Are you ready for tea, my dear?" Michelle asked. "You must have worked up an appetite playing that way."

"Tea would be nice." She stood up and wiped her brow with her fingertips. She glanced at me.

"It was very good, Rose," I said. "You play beautifully."

She smiled at me. "Thank you, doctor... Henry." Her eyes still seemed somehow weary and troubled, despite her obvious pleasure in our admiration.

Michelle took her arm. "The tea should be in the sitting room by now."

I glanced down at the music on the piano. The thick book of Beethoven sonatas made one of the pieces obvious. Their footsteps echoed through the hall, but I lingered at the piano. The clouds had broken at last, and a shaft of tentative yellow light slanted down through the vast hall.

My eyes rose. Constance stood clutching the oaken railing running along the gallery above us. All in black, she and Rose were dressed almost identically, except for Constance's lace cap, but while Rose had a majestic beauty, Constance appeared almost monstrous, and as I had remarked before, curiously sexless. She smiled reflexively at me, then started along the gallery.

I sighed, then looked about and saw another silent spectator–Sherlock Holmes standing near the entranceway. I strode across the hall, my own footsteps echoing now.

"You are back. Did you just arrive or did you...?"

He smiled, then pulled off his gloves and put them into his hat. "I heard the end of the Beethoven, the Bach and the polonaise. Classical, baroque and romantic, the entire gamut. Her playing is extraordinary, quite sublime for one so young. She has a phenomenal talent. Those remarkable hands of hers will surely not go to waste."

"Even Digby seemed impressed. Perhaps he finally realizes she has something more to offer than a mere fortune. And how was your unpleasant business?"

Holmes's mouth stretched into a grim line. "As ugly as might be expected. The local representatives of the police came with me, and Doctor Hartwood."

"Hartwood?"

"He is the only physician in the area, and the police rely upon his assistance. In this case, cause of death was obvious. Hartwood has a strong stomach, but he said he had never seen evidence of so horrific a death. The young constable who accompanied us became quite ill. And, of course, the entire village is abuzz with gossip. Neither money nor threats will get anyone in Grimpen to venture onto the moor near

Grimswell Hall after dark. There is probably an even division between the proponents of a vengeful ghost and those of a werewolf."

I tried to smile but could not. "Back in London, before all this had happened, it was much easier to ridicule such talk."

"And as I have said repeatedly, a mortal man can be as frightening as any fictional monster." He turned to gaze out the window. "Now that my journey is done, the rain has ended. The sun is out, but it has turned dreadfully cold."

A feeble yellow light showed amid the dark trunks of the trees, but a remnant of the mists, that almost tangible air, still softened their silhouettes. The sun seemed very far away.

Dinner was a gloomy, formal affair, we men all in our black tail coats with white shirts and bow ties. Digby was the only one who appeared in good spirits. Even Michelle had grown somber. Digby chattered on, while Constance glowered at him and Rose intermittently attended to his words. Constance had insisted on supervising our "last meal," and Mrs. Fitzwilliams had apparently felt too weary to object. The meat was badly overcooked and barely edible. Digby would not touch it, and the rest of us ate a little to be polite.

After the main course had been cleared, Maria wheeled in a cart and began setting bowls with large baked apples before us. They smelled wonderfully of apple and cinnamon, and their hollowed centers had some dark pungent filling.

"The meat may have been a trifle overdone," Constance said, "but the apples are perfect. I made the mincemeat myself, Rose."

Rose smiled and stared down at her apple. Brown cinnamon could be seen sprinkled along the top, the mincemeat with its abundance of raisins piled exceptionally high. A notch had been cut in the apple, a very slight line going from the center to the wrinkly skin. "I am not very hungry tonight."

Constance grew mournful. "But I made the mincemeat especially for you—I know it is your favorite."

Rose plunged her spoon into the center and took a big scoop of the mincemeat. "It is very good."

The rest of us also began. The mincemeat had nuts and spices besides the raisins. "This is delicious," I said.

Constance glowed at our praise. "Thank you. It is an old family recipe." She enjoyed her own cooking, for she devoured her apple quicker than anyone else, all save Holmes, who had not touched his.

"Don't you care for baked apples, Mr. Holmes?" Constance asked.

"It appears quite delicious, but my stomach feels somewhat unsettled. I must regretfully pass. Perhaps tomorrow morning, before we depart."

Rose had eaten about half the apple and set down her spoon. Constance watched her. The light from the tall white candles in the silver holders cast a flickering golden glow across the white linen tablecloth, the silver settings and the crystal glassware. Rose's hand toyed with the spoon, which seemed tiny alongside her large white hand. Her blue-gray eyes stared into space, her thoughts obviously elsewhere.

"Is it cooked through?" Constance asked.

Rose frowned, her thick black eyebrows coming together. "What?"

"Your apple. Is it cooked enough?"

"Oh, yes." Rose began to eat, her eyes watching her aunt.

Constance reached forward and took a piece of hard candy from a bowl, then her lips puckered slightly as she sucked upon it. Rose finished the apple and set down her spoon. She and Constance stared at one another. The frown reappeared on Rose's brow, a troubled look in her eyes, while Constance continued smiling, the smile odd because her mouth was full.

Constance swallowed, then opened her mouth in a gasp. "Uh," was all that came out. "*Uhh.*" She stood up, her massive hands pawing wildly at her throat, even as her face darkened. I stood, but Michelle was faster. She threw down her napkin, stood, took two steps nearer, then her arm swung round and her hand struck Constance squarely between the shoulder blades. The piece of candy burst from Constance's mouth and made a piercing ping against a glass. She drew in her breath, coughed once, and breathed loudly.

Michelle handed her a glass of water. "Drink this."

Constance's face began to return to its normal color. "Thank you, doctor."

Michelle frowned. She was wearing a beautiful blue gown, one which left her shoulders and long neck bare. "Hard candies should be banned. People can choke to death on them."

"You saved my life," Constance said. "I'd have choked to death for sure. I'm very grateful."

Michelle nodded. We all sat back down. Rose still had a troubled look. Holmes was staring at her, his mouth and eyes grim. The fingers of his hand drummed upon the tablecloth, a half-inch of white cuff showing below the black woolen sleeve of his tail coat. I thought he was staring at Rose, but perhaps it was only at the empty china bowl before her.

Fifteen

We sat together sipping brandy or port, the room heavy with the odor of burning wood, on what I hoped would be our last evening in Dartmoor. It was clearly a man's room: the massive furniture was made of dark oak and red leather, paneling of a similar dark wood rose to the wainscoting, and the carpet was another crimson hue. Everything seemed suffused with a faint tobacco smell.

Digby and Rose were on the sofa, both in black, he with the white front of his shirt and tie, the thick cigar which he had demanded dangling between his slender fingers, a glass of cognac in the other hand. He talked incessantly while she stared down at the arm of the sofa, her white hands moving restlessly about on her lap. Fitzwilliams, also in black, stood in a corner watching like some aged, weary hawk to see that nothing was amiss. Constance held a tiny glass of port in her immense hand and spoke to Holmes, whose eyes restlessly wandered the room like caged beasts.

Michelle set her hand on mine. "What is wrong, Henry?"

I shrugged. "I still feel shaken. Pardon me, I must make dreadful company. You look so ravishing in that dress. The light gives your bare arms and shoulders a rosy glow. How I wish…"

"Hush." She stroked my hand. "Soon, I trust, we will be home together in our own bed."

I felt a familiar longing, and I put my arm about her. "We have certainly had little time for one another of late."

Rose sat up abruptly, her lips parting, eyes widening, as she put her hand over her bosom. Although the firelight made it harder to see, her face paled. Digby did not notice, but Holmes leaned forward in his chair.

Michelle's petticoats rustled under the silk as she stood. "Rose, are you ill?"

Rose closed her eyes and swallowed once. "I… I am only tired." Her eyes opened and gazed into the fire. "Perhaps… I shall retire for the evening."

Digby set down his brandy, then withdrew his gold watch with a great flourish. "But it's barely eight, Rose."

Rose drew in her breath slowly. "All the same, I think I shall retire. My… my head aches."

Holmes was watching her very closely. "Do you feel… peculiar?"

"No. Only tired." She was still staring at the burning wood. "I shall go upstairs." She stood.

"Let me come with you," Michelle said. "I shall see you settled for the night."

"Thank you, but you needn't trouble yourself."

Constance finished her glass of port. "Oh, I can tuck the girl in. It will be like old times." She also stood.

"I would just like to be alone for a while."

Michelle's eyes were troubled. "If that is what you wish."

"I'll just see you up, dear, then leave you." Constance took one of the small candles burning near the door.

Rose brushed a strand of hair off her forehead. Digby smiled at her. "Pity you don't feel better, Rosie. See you first thing in the morning."

We all said polite goodnights, but Rose did not speak. The two ladies departed, Constance holding Rose lightly by the arm. Constance was the only woman who did not appear small alongside Rose. Although Constance was two or three inches shorter, she no doubt outweighed Rose considerably and appeared larger. In their plain, somber black dresses the two looked like votaries of some funereal cult, but Constance was clearly high priestess.

Holmes withdrew his cigarette case. As he smoked, he paced. The black tail coat and trousers accentuated his tall, slender frame. Digby continued to chat amiably, although no one paid him much attention. At last Holmes threw his cigarette butt into the fire and said he, too, was retiring for the evening.

Michelle and I followed him into the great hall. In that vast dark chamber, the brilliant blue of her dress was muted, but if anything, her beauty was even more striking.

"Michelle," Holmes said, "would you check on Miss Grimswell after Constance has left? I want to be sure—"

I seized Holmes's arm. "Hush—here she comes." Despite the shadowy darkness, I recognized Constance walking along the gallery above us.

We passed Constance on the stairs. She smiled broadly. "The poor little lamb is all settled for the night. I'm sure a good night's sleep will do her a world of good."

We walked silently along the gallery, the framed former Grimswells all hidden in darkness, and then down the hallway. Holmes and I waited a few feet away while Michelle rapped gently at Rose's door. She murmured something, and a few seconds later, it opened. Michelle stepped inside.

Light from the doorway to Holmes's room spilled into the hallway.

We waited briefly and then went to his room. As usual, a coal fire had been started, and it was comfortably warm after the chill of the hallway. I had sat in a chair and Holmes had again begun to pace when Michelle appeared.

"Well?" Holmes asked.

Michelle appeared puzzled. "She says she feels perfectly well, and yet her behavior seems odd. She has not been so distant with me before. She would not seem to meet my gaze. And…"

"And?" Holmes asked.

"She had a piece of paper in her hand when I entered. Perhaps… She put it under a book quickly, as if she wanted to hide it."

"Blast it." Holmes shook his head, then went directly to a chest of drawers and withdrew his revolver and a dark lantern. A sense of dread, never far distant at Grimswell Hall, settled about my heart. He took off his tail coat and white bow tie and put on a tweed jacket. "Henry, would you accompany me?" He opened the lantern to light it.

"Certainly."

Michelle folded her bare arms resolutely. "I am coming too."

A sudden fury flared in Holmes's eyes, but he struggled to restrain it. "You shall do no such thing. You will remain here. If Miss Grimswell should call, someone must be close by."

"But–"

"There is no time for foolish arguments. The moment of crisis may be at hand, and I cannot have you constantly disputing my authority. Will you do as you are told, or must I ignore you entirely?"

Michelle's jaw tightened, the anger showing in her eyes. Although I sympathized, I sided with Holmes. She was all too eager to throw herself into danger. "I shall stay," she said at last.

"Good. I doubt you will miss much. Our search may well turn out to be a boring waste of time." He rummaged in another drawer and withdrew a second revolver. "Henry insists you know more about revolvers than he. Keep this with you. We shall leave the door open so you can hear better should Miss Grimswell call."

Holmes started for the door, but I paused to kiss Michelle's bare shoulder. "Thank you," I murmured.

Holmes took the ancient stairs at the end of the hall up to the next floor. The only light came from the lantern, its beam dancing on the wooden floor.

"What are we looking for?" I asked.

"Ghosts," was his brusque reply.

We spent the next hour or two walking about the many halls and rooms of that wing of the ancient edifice. Most chambers were obviously long out of use. The damp air smelled musty, and ghostly white fabric covered the furniture. The ever-present wind rattled the window panes, and more than once, panic clawed up my throat as I fancied some figure lurking in a dark corner or beneath a thin sheet. We also went up onto the roof. The wind hurled stinging bits of icy rain into our faces, and dark swollen clouds rolled across the vast sky, the moon a veiled presence behind the swirling mists. However, we saw no sign of anyone.

When we returned at last to Holmes's room, Michelle rose. Holmes gave his head a fierce shake. "*Nothing.*"

She took my hand. "Oh, you are freezing."

"Did you hear any word from Rose?" Holmes asked.

"No."

He frowned. "I must be certain she is well. It would be best if you spoke to her again, Michelle."

Michelle sighed. "Is it...? I hate to wake her if she is sleeping."

"There is no helping it."

We went the few feet down the hallway to Rose's door. Michelle hesitated, then knocked gently. "Rose?" In the hallway, sheltered from the wind, was a heavy, all-encompassing silence which permeated the massive walls about us. I was afraid again. Michelle knocked more loudly. "Rose? *Rose.*"

"Blast it," Holmes muttered, as he tried the knob. "The door is locked, as I advised, but I have the key. If she does not—"

"Yes?" The voice from behind the door was faint.

"I wanted to be certain you were not ill," Michelle said. "May I come in?"

"I am just resting," Rose said. "I am well. Give me a little while longer, and you can have Meg come in for the night."

Holmes pointed at the doorknob and whispered, "Have her open it."

"Can you let me in for a moment, my dear? I shall not pester you for long."

"Oh, I am so tired." Rose sounded near tears.

Michelle turned to Holmes. "Can we not…?"

"I must get in there!" he whispered fiercely.

"I'm sorry, Rose—please, we must…"

"One minute."

"Rose?"

The silence grew like a great wall all around us. Holmes clenched his fist and struck it lightly against the wall. "I like this not. I—"

The door swung open, revealing Rose's pale face. "Oh," she said, when she saw Holmes and me. She had removed her black dress and put on her night clothes, a white nightshirt and long white robe. Her long black hair was down, spilled onto the white fabric.

"Forgive me," Holmes said. He strode past her into the room, and we followed. Holmes was peering under the bed. Next he went to the wardrobe and looked inside. Rose appeared pale and ill, her eyes feverish. Holmes paused by a small table, stared at a large book, then lifted it. Nothing was underneath.

"I am sorry to disturb you," Michelle said.

Holmes had examined every place where someone might be hiding. He also pulled aside the curtains and looked out the windows. At last he gave a harsh sigh and came back to us. "Again, forgive me, Miss Grimswell. I had to be certain. Is there anything you need to tell me?"

Her eyes were curiously unfocused, as if she were asleep. "No."

Holmes's brow was furrowed. "Are you absolutely certain of that?"

Michelle touched her gently on the arm. "My dear, you must know that—"

Rose's eyes filled with tears. "Oh, must you all make it so difficult! How often must I say 'no'? Excuse me—I am tired—only very tired. Please leave me alone. *Please.*" She slowly drew in her breath, steadying herself. "Send Meg in now. I want to go to sleep."

Holmes nodded. "Very well. Be sure to lock your door for the night before you go to bed."

We went into the hall, and Rose closed the door behind us. Holmes stalked away, muttering something savagely. He turned to us. "Michelle, would you be so kind as to find Meg so they can be settled for the night?"

A savage yawn contorted my face. "Lord, I am tired myself."

Michelle took my arm. "You need to get to bed."

"Not yet." Holmes started back toward his room. "We must have another look about."

"But it is after ten, and I thought you searched everywhere," Michelle said.

Holmes turned again. "I do not plan to sleep tonight. However, I shall only need Henry for another hour or so. We must check the rooms again, especially those above Miss Grimswell."

The back of my neck felt cold. "You suspect the same trick as last time, an apparition at the window?"

"I suspect *something*. She is behaving…" He shook his head angrily. "Something is wrong."

The house seemed colder and darker than ever, and again, fear hovered always nearby. We were gone a long time, but we found nothing. Afterward, the three of us sat in Holmes's room staring silently at the fire. The clock on the mantel showed quarter to twelve, but neither Michelle nor I made any move to leave. My cousin's agitation had proven contagious, and I doubted I would sleep much that night either.

All the same, when I closed my eyes, I found myself in another dark silent room. Moonlight shone through the mullioned panes of glass, and then a face was there, a face split into quarters by the lead. I recognized Victor Grimswell from his portrait: black hair and a huge mustache, thick eyebrows, but his skin was a deathly blue-white color. He smiled at me, his lips parting slightly, and I saw the tips of the canines resting on his blood-red lips. My heart seemed to stop beating, and then his face swelled, grew—which was impossible—I did not want to move—but I must be going to the window. He drew his upper lip back, and then something touched my arm. I started wildly.

Michelle's face was a welcome sight. "What is it?" she asked.

"A bad dream."

"Perhaps we should go to bed."

"Sherlock may need us."

Holmes was staring at the fire, so lost in thought he had not even heard a word. He had a pipe in his hand, and a cloud of rich-smelling smoke surrounded him. Abruptly he stood up and turned to us. "Of course—of course! The answer is staring me in the face. It is obvious when you think about it." He glanced at us, then his eyes settled on Michelle even as an odd smile pulled at his mouth. "You must have given her the idea. Certainly you gave her the idea, and I… My own prejudices, my own assumptions, have completely blinded me! But it is not too late, I trust. We must–"

A voice rose over the wind sound: *Mr. Holmes, Mr. Holmes.* Holmes frowned. "Did...?" he began, but this time there could be no mistake.

"Mr. Holmes! *Mr. Holmes.*" Fitzwilliams staggered through the door and leaned on the table, ready to collapse. Holmes went to him in an instant and seized his arm, holding him up. The old man's face was pale, his lips nearly gray. "Mr. Holmes... Ah, thank God, thank God, you are..."

"What is it, sir?"

"Miss Rose–you must stop her."

Holmes clenched his teeth. "Oh Lord, what has she done?"

"She went outside. She was in a daze, sleepwalking again, like when she was a wee girl. I tried to stop her, but she said she had to see her father, see him at midnight by the front gate. I tried again to stop her, but she was too strong–too strong for me. I tried..."

"Oh God," I whispered.

"Damnation." Holmes pulled the old man toward a chair and sat him down. "Henry, get yourself a heavy coat." He put on his own overcoat, a bowler hat, and seized the revolver. "We have not a moment to lose. Rose's life is at stake. Michelle, look after Mr. Fitzwilliams. Meet me at the front door, Henry–*quickly.*" He rushed out.

I grabbed a candle and started down the hall, muttering a few nervous curses as I went. I threw aside my formal tail coat, put on a tweed jacket, then searched the wardrobe for my heaviest coat. I turned to discover Michelle seated and lacing up a leather walking boot. It looked quite ludicrous alongside her blue silk gown.

"What are you doing?" I asked.

"Changing my shoes. I suggest you do the same, but hurry."

"You are not–"

Her mouth formed a familiar, resolute expression, her jaw stiffening.

"I am going, by God, unless you and Sherlock wish to waste time trying to restrain me. It will not be easy, even for two of you."

I had wrenched off my patent leather pumps and was pulling on a boot. "I wish you would stay here."

"I shall not."

We rushed downstairs and found Holmes standing before the big doors. Digby stood beside him, his hands hidden in the pocket of his overcoat. He smiled at us. "Ah, the more the merrier." Holmes's brow furrowed ominously as he stared at Michelle.

"What is he doing here?" I asked Holmes, indicating Lord Frederick.

"I heard all the commotion," Digby said, "and came a-running."

Holmes's eyes were still fixed on Michelle. "Please go back upstairs, Michelle."

"No."

"If you will not—"

"You said there was no time to waste, Sherlock."

Holmes muttered something darkly under his breath, turned and opened the door. The rain had ceased, but the wind was louder than ever; above us the branches of the great oaks and the tall evergreen yews swayed. Clouds covered the moon, but its hazy orb still breached the darkness. We started down the granite pathway toward the gate, our breath forming smoky white mists. I found myself nearly running to keep up with Holmes. All around us, tree limbs groaned and shook from the wind.

"Bit of a chill in the air," Digby said amiably.

"Michelle," Holmes said, "do you still have the revolver I gave you?"

"Certainly."

I glanced at her, surprised. I had forgotten about the revolver.

"I say," Digby said, "why not let me have it? I'm a pretty good shot, you know."

Holmes shook his head. "We shall see."

Digby raised his arm. "Someone has opened the gate. No sign of Rose, though."

As if on cue, a figure all in white stepped out from behind the trees and walked between the two granite pillars out onto the moor. Holmes broke into a run, and I did the same. We reached the gateway in time to see Rose walking toward the hillside and the clitter scattered below Demon Tor. Another person came out of the trees.

"Miss Grimswell!" he shouted.

The voice was familiar. "Hartwood!" I exclaimed.

"I knew it!" Digby was triumphant.

"Miss Grimswell! For God's sake, beware—run!" Hartwood raised an arm; then the huge full moon broke free of the clouds, flooding the moor, its grass and heath, with cold blue-white light; and we all saw the black shape loping toward Rose, so large that I mistook it for an instant for a horse or pony, rather than what it was—a hound. Rose turned and saw it coming straight for her, but she seemed unable to move.

"Shoot it!" I cried.

"Not at this range!" Holmes ran, and we followed.

Hartwood was faster. Even as he bounded forward and leaped over clumps of stones, he managed to slip out of his coat. He passed Rose, then whirled the coat about his forearm and stood his ground. The dog veered toward him, then leaped and seized his arm in its huge jaws. Hartwood staggered, but remained standing. Rose seemed to come to her senses; she hesitated, her arms rising even as she backed away. Hartwood swayed awkwardly, then fell. He and the dog rolled about furiously on the grassy turf, the animal growling and snarling, now Hartwood on top, now the beast.

Holmes reached them, revolver in hand, the barrel raised toward the sky, but he did nothing, no doubt fearing he might hit the man, not his foe. Hartwood had his arms before him as he struggled desperately to keep the dog from tearing at his throat. The moon gave its sleek black coat a white sheen. At last Holmes bent over, seized the dog firmly by the collar, and yanked the beast away even as he lowered the barrel. The crack of each shot was deafening so near. The mastiff made a pathetic noise between a bark and a howl, twisted about and fell dead on its side, two bullets having passed through its brain.

Hartwood sat up, clutching at his left arm and the remnants of his coat all in tatters. "Oh, thank God—and thank you, sir."

"Well," Digby said, "we have our man on the moor at last."

"What are you talking about?" Hartwood's face was white and shaken under the moonlight.

"Do not be an utter ass," Holmes said to Digby. "Hartwood is not the man we seek."

"Then what was he doing here?"

"Watching out for the woman he loves, and a good thing, too. He was close enough to distract the hound. We would have been too late to save Rose."

"But…" Digby's voice had a plaintive note.

"*There!*" Holmes's arm swung around. "There is your man in black!"

He had appeared out of nowhere, his arms folded. His face struck me with fear—I had seen him in my dream and hanging amid a frame on the wall of Grimswell Hall. He had the same large black mustache and eyebrows. His skin was an eerie luminescent white, glowing, dark circles under his malevolent eyes. A cowl surrounded his face, part of a black cloak.

"Dear Lord," Hartwood moaned, "it *is* Victor. It cannot be. He is dead—I saw…"

Holmes ran forward, but I was too horrified to move. The man rushed toward Rose. She stood as if frozen, a ghostly figure in her white gown, the wind blowing her long black hair about her. The man seized her arm, and I realized he must indeed be a giant, for he towered over even Rose. He jerked her about and pulled her uphill toward the tor.

Hartwood groaned as he stood up, swaying slightly. I touched his arm—the shredded sleeve was wet and sticky with blood. "You are hurt," I said.

"It is nothing, a few minor lacerations."

"They will need stitching," Michelle said.

"Later." Hartwood stumbled forward. "We can't let that monster have Rose."

Digby's lips were tightly set, and for the first time I saw something like embarrassment in his face.

Holmes had a head start, but the man moved quickly, dragging Rose along. The moon was still out; under its brilliant light the huge fragments of black granite scattered about the hillside cast shadows. The man's cape swept behind him while Rose stood out because of her white gown. Our adversary's goal was obvious—the summit of Demon Tor.

Holmes was closing on them, but when he had nearly reached the top, the man stopped abruptly and turned again, one spidery black arm grasping Rose about the waist, his other hand below her chin. His white hands were on the same grand scale as the rest of him, and he wore no gloves. "Stop where you are!" he shouted. "One step more, and I'll open her throat from ear to ear!" Moonlight flashed off a blade.

We all halted at once. Holmes was about twenty feet below them, while we were twice that distance.

Behind me I heard Hartwood's labored breathing. "He... he sounds something like Victor, yet..."

"Go back," the man cried. "Go back or I'll cut her throat." His voice was deep, yet strangely muffled, a rolling, ominous bass.

Michelle glanced at me, anguished. We could not see Holmes's face, but he did not move. The hand with the revolver hung at his side.

"You heard me—get away!"

"No," Holmes said. "I am afraid I cannot oblige you."

"I'll kill her—in God's name, I'll kill her!"

"I believe you, but if we depart, you will kill her all the same. However, in that case, you might go unpunished. I intend to remain here, and I promise you, I give you my solemn word, that if you harm her, I shall shoot you dead."

The man laughed. "How clever of you to reason that all out. Your reputation for brains appears deserved, Mr. Holmes."

"You might as well take off your mask. You will be more comfortable."

Again the man laughed. Something about his uncaring nonchalance sent a chill up my spine. "Thank you, but I prefer to leave it on."

"Why? You will not escape us. Besides, your great size makes you a marked man. Would you not prefer to be comfortable while we are speaking?"

More laughter. "You are a clever dog, Mr. Holmes."

The right hand kept the knife at Rose's throat, but the left rose, tore away the mask and pulled back the cowl. The mask struck a rock, and then the wind hurled it away. The face revealed did not have the artificial luminescence of the mask, but there was a curious resemblance: a younger visage with the same black mustache, sharp nose and high cheekbones. The angry dark eyes had, of course, remained the same.

"Who *is* he?" Hartwood mumbled.

"That is better." The deep voice rang out clearly now.

"The mask made no difference to me," Holmes said. "Fluorescent white paint does not frighten me, and I know exactly who you are, who your parents were."

"Do you really?" He sounded sarcastic.

"Your father was an earl who unfortunately neglected to marry your mother."

His smile vanished. "You bastard." The irony of this insult did not escape me.

"I know why you killed Victor and why you wish to kill Miss Grimswell. Unfortunately for you, a murderer cannot inherit."

The man had his left arm wrapped about Rose. He held the short, deadly blade up, then touched it lightly to her neck just below her jaw. Her face was white under the moonlight, her eyes curiously unfocused, her lips clamped tightly shut.

"What is wrong with her?" Michelle moaned. "Why does she not…?"

"She has been drugged," I whispered.

"I want you to throw me your revolver, Mr. Holmes."

Holmes laughed. "You know I cannot do that. You would kill her anyway and us as well. We have a stalemate, but I can offer… If you will release her, I shall let you escape."

"No," Michelle exclaimed.

The man laughed. "Now it is you who take me for a fool. Do you expect me to fall for such nonsense?"

"I would give you my word of honor."

The man's smile was ugly. "The word of an English gentleman. I fear I cannot accept it."

Holmes was silent for a moment. The wind rose, sweeping downhill, its icy touch on our faces. "I can offer you an alternate hostage. I shall trade places with her."

"No, Sherlock," I said. "Dear God, no!"

The man stared at him, still smiling. "You would put down your weapon and trade places with her?"

"Yes. I would give the revolver to my friends and then remain while she leaves with them."

Rose blinked, and her lips clearly formed the word "no."

"How chivalrous, how gallant. Unfortunately, your life is of no value to me. Granted there would be a certain satisfaction and a notoriety in eliminating a man of your reputation, but it would not earn me a penny. Miss Grimswell, on the other hand..."

"I have told you that a murderer cannot inherit. There is also the circumstance of your birth. Your scheme is finished—failed utterly. I promise you that. We have a stalemate."

"Not exactly, Mr. Holmes. Not if I give up my scheme and accept my fate. Not if I willingly choose death—for us both."

Michelle's hand reached out and gripped mine. Holmes did not speak for a long while. Rose's eyes had opened wide. The wind swept her long black tresses over the white gown.

"Why would you make such a choice?" Holmes asked.

The giant was still smiling. "Perhaps because I would like to put an end to the wretched Grimswells once and for all. Her blood may not be polluted, but mine is—twice polluted, you might say—on both sides of the family. My father was every bit as vile as I, but he lacked the spine to act. Of course, he had nothing like the Grimswell Curse to live up to. Not that villainy matters much among peers. Plenty of lords—earls, marquesses, viscounts, even dukes—are as degenerate as I, their very blood tainted and rotten, yet no one has the bad taste to hold it against them. They did not have the misfortune to be born out of wedlock and then to lose all in one final wager. And perhaps I would like to take this poor, pitiable creature with me. Really, I'd be doing her a favor."

"You lying cur!" Hartwood shouted. "You heap of filth!"

The man laughed. "Oh, really, doctor. I have heard it said that love is blind, but I never believed it until now. She is dark, plain, and much taller than you. What a comical pair you would make."

Hartwood stepped forward, his face very pale. I seized his arm. He grimaced, then fell to his knees. Michelle and I knelt beside him. What remained of his left sleeve was soaked with blood, his fingers wet with it. He struggled to rise.

"No," Michelle said. "You are hurt, and he will not let you near him."

"Quite right, doctor." The man glanced over his shoulder, then backed uphill, pulling Rose along. "You would only force me to cut her throat. If we go off the tor together, she might have something of a chance. She could conceivably survive the fall. She is a pitiable creature. I know all about her. The Grimswells are either evil monsters like me or feeble contemplatives like her father. I would have invigorated the strain, but no matter. She was almost too easy to manipulate, so very predictable, and the drug makes her even more docile. Oh yes, and the Grimswells do have more than their share of insanity. Look at poor Jane."

"We know about Jane." Holmes advanced a furtive step or two. "She might have done well enough if she had not been tormented, if someone had not pushed her over the edge."

The man laughed. "That particular strategy has worked quite well for us. It's odd, but I do feel something of a father to Rose. I have been told that I bear a striking resemblance to Victor by someone who knew him intimately."

"By the woman at Merriweather Farm." Holmes's voice shook. "You need not have killed her. George's loyalty might have been suspect, but never hers."

The man's smile vanished. "I had to be sure. I could not risk it."

"She loved you, did she not?"

"What of it?" Somehow this casual remark, revealing such an abyss, such a lack of any human feeling, was more chilling than anything he had yet said. "That is close enough, Mr. Holmes." He raised the knife again, pressing the tip against Rose's neck. I felt Hartwood's arm muscles tighten. "You are sure you would not like to leave?"

"No, I shall not."

"It might be amusing to cut her throat, or I could merely stab once, just here. Once the artery is pierced there would be no saving her. How amusing with three doctors standing by, utterly helpless." He gave a chuckle. "That would be amusing to watch. Nothing any of you could do."

He showed his teeth as he smiled, and a trickle of blood appeared on Rose's throat, black in the moonlight, a tiny rivulet. Her eyes opened wide, her lips drawing back to reveal her clenched teeth. Hartwood moaned softly.

"Yes, either way I shall be doing her a service, but somehow the fall seems more appropriate, killing her and myself just as I killed her father." He laughed, and the hand with the knife drew back, even as his other hand rose to grip her arm.

Rose opened her mouth wide and lunged for the knife hand, biting down hard. His fingers jerked open, the knife falling; she had him just below the thumb. He screamed loudly, a jagged, irregular sound, and grabbed her black hair with his free hand. Holmes raised the revolver, but hesitated.

"Let go—damn you! *Ahhh.*" He yanked at her hair, then gave her a great clap on the side of the head with his left fist. She closed her eyes and fell, and Holmes's revolver flamed. The man in black staggered, his gigantic white hands all a-fumble. In the end he clutched at his right hand with his left, rather than trying to hold the wound in his shoulder. "Oh, you bitch," he moaned, "you treacherous bitch." He lashed out with his boot and caught Rose in the side.

Holmes fired again and started for him. He did not seem to feel the second bullet, but only turned, his long legs taking a few quick last steps to the top. For an instant he showed against the gray-white sky, a black shape with the cape swirling about him, and then he was gone. He had not hesitated, and we heard no scream, no sound but the wind.

Holmes knelt beside Rose and helped her to her feet. Michelle and I rushed to them. Rose was crying now, sobbing loudly. She swayed, then reached out and seized Holmes, her strong white hands clutching at his back, drawing him to her. She was trying to talk, but we could not understand her. Holmes was startled, but then his right hand rose and patted her gently on the back.

"Oh, thank you," Rose cried, "thank you!"

Holmes smiled. "You did most of my work for me this evening, Miss Grimswell. Later I shall lecture you, but not just now. Are you hurt?"

"My head hurts so, and I still feel so very strange. The moon is… the moon is so bright."

Michelle gently drew her away and touched her cheek. "You are going to have quite a bruise on that side of your face. It's lucky he did not strike your ear. Where did his boot catch you? Here, I believe." Rose winced. "Most likely it is only bruised, but he may have actually cracked a rib or two."

I put my hand on Rose's shoulder. Her whole body was trembling, and the tears ran from her eyes, her mouth open wide in a smile even as she wept. "It is over, Rose—you are safe now—you are safe." She slipped her left arm about me and pulled me nearer, catching both Michelle and me in her strong embrace.

Holmes's smile faded, something grim and dark showing in his eyes. He turned and started for the summit. I wanted to follow, but I dared not. Merely thinking about the fearful drop and the broken body lying on the granite far below made me anxious.

Digby and Hartwood stood by awkwardly, a look of envy on their faces. I slipped free and turned to Hartwood. "We must see to that arm of yours."

"It is nothing," he said, but he was clearly near the point of collapse.

Digby took off his overcoat. "This won't fit you, but at least you can put it over your shoulders, and it will keep your teeth from knockin' together so."

Hartwood shook his head.

"Come on, old boy—you're the hero of the hour, one of them, and I look the fatuous dolt, all my fine theories in a shambles. Show a bit of magnanimity and take the fallen foe's coat. I still have my Norfolk jacket, and it's quite heavy."

Hartwood gave him an odd look. It had been quite a speech. "Thank you, but Rose has more need of it than I."

Digby sighed and shook his head. "Curses, upstaged again." He handed his overcoat to Rose. "Here, Rosie—take it."

Michelle had let her go. She looked first at Digby, then at Doctor Hartwood. "No, guh... give it to Doctor Hartwood." Her teeth were chattering.

"Come now, Rosie. You can't refuse chivalry, after all."

She let him put the coat over her shoulders, then her hands drew it about her even as she shuddered. "Thank you, Doctor Hartwood—oh, thank you. You saved me, too. When I saw the dog... Oh, I could not move."

"We need to get you both inside," Michelle said. "It really is freezing out here." She turned to look uphill.

Holmes appeared at the very summit of Demon Tor, a black figure atop the black granite, the vast moonlit sky behind him. The clouds scudded like great restless behemoths, the moon illuminating their slow movement as they swallowed up clear sky and stars. Holmes started down.

"Did you see him?" I asked. The others were quiet. Rose seemed to hold her breath.

"Yes. He could not have survived the fall." He looked at Rose. "He will haunt you no more. You are free of him."

She began to cry again, softly at first, but then in sobs which shook her shoulders and made Digby's coat slip to the ground. It was too small. Michelle held her.

"Thank God it is all over," I said.

Holmes's brief smile was joyless. "It is nearly over."

Sixteen

When we entered Grimswell Hall, several lamps were ablaze and most of the maids up. Fitzwilliams staggered forward, took one look at Rose, then went to a chair and collapsed. "Thank God," he said. "Thank God. If anything had happened…"

His wife also teetered forward, then steadied herself with one hand on the back of the chair and extended her other small, gnarled and trembling hand. "Rose—oh, my dear child."

Rose went to them and grasped one each of their hands. Because she was so tall, in an odd inversion, she recalled a mother with two small children. She stared down at Fitzwilliams. "If you had not told them…"

Holmes smiled. "As you knew he would."

Rose had some of the color back in her cheeks, and she gave Holmes a brief, conspiratorial smile.

Constance stepped out of the shadows, a tiny lace handkerchief clutched in her huge hand. "Yes, God be praised that all is well. We have been so worried. And the man…?"

"Dead," Holmes said, "fallen from the tor."

Constance clapped her hand over her mouth, and her dark eyes seemed to shimmer, some strange passion briefly overwhelming her, and she turned away, for once, all too briefly, at a loss for words. "How horrible," she muttered at last.

"I cannot believe it," murmured Mrs. Fitzwilliams. "I cannot believe we are free at last. The Devil is not so easily beaten. But at least... the master is not damned—oh, I know it now! His soul is in Heaven, after all." Her voice broke.

"Hush, Prudence," Fitzwilliams whispered softly, caressing her tiny hand.

Michelle had led Doctor Hartwood to a chair near the fire. He was pale and shivering, and his entire arm and the shredded white sleeve were red with blood. "I shall just get my bag," she said, "then clean and dress the wounds." She turned to one of the horrified maids. "Could you please get me a large pot of hot water and some towels?"

"Why don't the rest of you warm up with me in the kitchen?" Constance's smile was rather fierce. "I have made some hot chocolate. I knew you would be needing something hot." She stepped forward and took Rose's arm. "Poor Rose, you are freezing."

Michelle started for the stairs. "I shall be along later."

"We'll save you some, dear."

"Hot chocolate does sound wonderful," I said.

"Bit bland for me." Digby shook his head. "I could use something a good deal stronger. I'll wager Hartwood could, too, especially if he's to be stitched. Undiluted scotch whisky is the best medicine. I'll pour us both a good jolt." He pulled off his yellow gloves and went to the sideboard where the whisky and the gasogene for making soda water were kept.

"You may have your strong spirits. Chocolate is the very thing." Constance led Rose toward the kitchen, and Holmes and I followed.

Rose turned, her eyes anxiously seeking out my cousin. "You're still trembling, poor lamb. You must tell me all about this dreadful business."

The huge cast-iron stove almost glowed with heat, and the kitchen was warm and cozy, unlike the great hall with its endless chill. The dishes from the evening meal had been washed, dried and stacked, the pots scrubbed and hung up. A small table and chairs were on one side of the room. Constance drew out a chair for Rose. I took another. I was exhausted, my legs weary, and it felt wonderful to sit. I pulled off my gloves and unbuttoned my overcoat. Holmes remained standing, his slender white hands hanging at his sides against the black wool of his overcoat.

Constance set down thick china mugs, then went to the stove for a big iron kettle. She poured the steaming brown liquid into the mugs. The sweet, pungent smell filled the kitchen.

"I do not want any." Rose's voice was soft and very tired.

"Oh, nonsense, dear—you must drink some. It will warm you up and get your blood flowing." She picked up a cup and sipped it. "Just right—not too hot, not too cold—not too bitter, not too sweet."

"It smells heavenly." I lifted my cup. Holmes moved remarkably fast, lashing out with his hand and knocking the cup sideways so it smashed onto the stone floor. He had done it so skillfully that none of the hot liquid touched me, but I was surprised—and angry. "What are you doing!"

"Watching out for you, Henry. Curious substances have a way of making themselves into food and drink here at Grimswell Hall. Coffee and baked apples. And hot chocolate." He was staring at Constance.

Rose said nothing, but her mouth stiffened, her black eyebrows coming together. Constance reddened, covering her mouth with her big, swollen-looking hand. "Whatever are you saying, Mr. Holmes? There is nothing wrong with the chocolate. I tasted it myself." She raised her mug. Holmes watched her, tension appearing about his mouth and eyes. His hand twitched once, but then he was still as she drank deeply from the mug. "It is very good." She turned to Rose. "Won't you drink yours, dear?"

Rose shook her head. "No. I am still recovering from the apple. I feel so bizarre. It was even worse than the last time. You must have put in more."

"*Rose*–what are you saying? Why would I want to harm you? Or Doctor Vernier or Mr. Holmes?"

Rose's blue-gray eyes were angry. "I do not know."

My head had begun to ache, the fatigue numbing my senses. It was nearly two in the morning. "Why would she want to harm us?" I asked dully.

"Because she blames us for her son's death," Holmes replied. "He was an evil creature like his mother, a vicious murderer, and I would have had few qualms about shooting him dead. However, he took his own life–he jumped from the tor rather than being taken prisoner and facing the hangman for his crimes."

A look of utter dismay showed on Rose's face, both horror and anger evident. "Oh, Lord," I murmured, "not Jane–but *Constance*. He was a Grimswell. He would have been the heir, the last male, but only if he were... legitimate."

"Which he was not," Holmes said, "but she arranged something with the earl, the father, before his death. The man was as contemptible, as lacking in morals or decency, as she and her son. He also disliked his wife. What better trick to play on her than rendering their marriage null as bigamy? Constance must have some document purporting to show that she was indeed married to the earl. As you say, that would make her son the last male in the line: he would become the viscount, the new Lord Grimswell. More important, with Rose dead, he could also pursue her father's great wealth, all the property and the money left to her. However, they had to act before she married–they could not allow that, for her husband would then inherit everything."

Constance had clenched her fists. "Preposterous lies–slander–you have... no proof."

"While Henry and I were in London, I spoke with the earl's steward. He told me you had visited his master a few months ago, shortly before he died. There cannot be two women who fit your description."

Constance laughed harshly. "Not two women so ugly, you mean."

Holmes shook his head. "I did not say that."

"But you thought it! Men are all the same... Vile. Disgusting. They think you are ugly, but if you give them what they want, they will end up groveling at your feet. Jane could have had her earl, but she did not understand that. She could have had him in a second if she'd forgotten her precious virtue."

Holmes stared at her. "You took him from her coldly and deliberately, knowing full well what it would do to her."

"I did her a service! He was a beast, a pig. She would have been miserable married to him. Any woman would have been."

"You have always tormented her, have you not? You must have hated her."

Constance's smile was answer enough. The familiar mask of the amiable old auntie was gone, the real woman revealed. "Yes, I did hate her. She was the fair, tiny, beautiful one, while I was always *poor* Constance. Her sympathy was what infuriated me most." She reached out a hand toward Rose, who drew back instinctively. "You see, Rose, I do understand how you feel. I have never felt any animosity toward you or Victor. If there had been a way to make Geoffrey a wealthy viscount without harming either of you, I would have gladly done so. I sympathize with you, dear–honestly I do. Life is a hard business for women like us, and I would have actually been doing you a favor if–"

"Do not do me any favors." Rose's voice shook. I had never seen her so angry. "I am not like you—not like you at all."

Constance laughed. "No?"

"*No.*" Rose shuddered. "No!"

"She is absolutely correct," Holmes said. "She is nothing like you."

"The blood of the Grimswells flows in her veins."

"What of it?" Holmes exclaimed. "She has her mother's blood as well. She is only distantly related to you. Her father was an honorable and brilliant man. Every family has its share of drunkards, lunatics and criminals; it has nothing to do with blood or curses. You chose to be the monster you are—just as your son chose—and now you must suffer the consequences of your evil deeds and cowardly choices."

"You—*you*—you dare call me a coward?"

Holmes's nostrils flared, and he leaned forward, setting both hands on the table. "A coward of the worst kind—you used tricks and subterfuge, poisons and deceit—you tried to drive a fine young woman, your own relation, mad. You helped kill your cousin, who always looked out for you and your sister. You are beneath contempt and beyond comprehension. I should have left you for the hangman as well, but I allowed you and that cowardly bully of a son to take your craven way out. Now have the decency to keep quiet and spare my ears and Rose's any more of your drivel." His hands began to quiver, and he stood up.

Constance glared at him. Her complexion had lost its pinkish cast, and a few drops of sweat showed on her forehead. Her dark eyes were monstrous, pained and raging, and neither she nor Holmes would look away. Rose appeared ill, and I felt sick myself.

Constance suddenly clenched her teeth, then groaned, grinding her teeth briefly. "With Rose, it would not have been personal, but with you..." She tried to smile even as her face went nearly green. "I would have liked to kill you, Sherlock Holmes—how I wish I could have..."

Again she clenched her teeth, her hands clutching at her belly just below her bosom.

"What was in the chocolate?" My voice quavered.

"No doubt something very quick and deadly. Painful, too. Possibly aconite or cyanide."

Rose's eyelids fluttered. "Oh, God." She was ashen. "I feel sick."

Holmes inhaled through his nose. "Get her away from here, Henry. This will not be pleasant."

"Gladly." I stood, my own legs swaying briefly. I took Rose's arm and helped her up. We started for the door.

"Goodbye, Rose." Constance's voice was a croak, her face ghastly, her eyes bulging from their sockets.

Rose looked at her but said nothing. We walked quickly down the dim hallway. She was trembling again. I held her big hand loosely in mine. It felt cold yet sweaty. I could think of nothing to say and squeezed her hand tightly.

"There you are at last." Michelle smiled at us. She looked absolutely beautiful. "I was just coming. How… What has happened? What is wrong?"

"I shall tell you, but first we need something to drink. Where are Hartwood and Digby?"

"Digby and Fitzwilliams are putting the doctor to bed. I forbad him to try to walk back home tonight."

I poured Rose and myself each a glass half full of whisky. She sat on the sofa between Michelle and me. Michelle put her arm around her. The first swallow set her coughing. I told Michelle all that had happened. As I was finishing we heard Holmes's footsteps echoing softly through the hall. Something about the sound made the back of my neck feel cold; my shoulders rose involuntarily, my teeth clenching.

"I cannot believe it," Michelle said. "I cannot believe it."

Holmes's forehead was furrowed, his mouth taut. "She will trouble you no more, Rose. Now it truly is over."

Rose began to cry, and Michelle drew her closer. "Hush." I leaned over and gripped Rose's forearm tightly.

Holmes's eyes glanced about the shadowy hall, the granite walls a great silent presence all around us. "Few people of any age are tested so severely, Miss Grimswell. You have undergone the worst of trials and not merely survived, but... you have demonstrated a quite remarkable courage. I would never have imagined... It is said that adversity can bring out hidden strengths. In my experience, the reverse is usually the case—hidden weaknesses pour forth—but not with you. I shall have to alter my estimation of the female sex. I should give you a scolding for what you have done, but your bravery has so overwhelmed me that I cannot. I can only offer you... my deepest and most sincere admiration." His face had flushed, and Rose stared up at him in disbelief.

Michelle frowned. "Sherlock, whatever are you talking about?" That was the question I also wanted to ask. I had never seen my cousin so overcome, especially before a young woman half his age.

"Actually, Michelle, you are partly to blame." The mocking smile showed affection.

"Sherlock!"

"Your speech last night made her resolve to take matters in hand, all that talk of decoys and bait. When she realized that she had been drugged again, she decided to try to take advantage of it. She resolved to—as you put it, Michelle—do something. She used herself as bait to trap the man on the moor. She was not sleepwalking at all. She deliberately left the house knowing full well the deadly peril she faced. However, since she wanted to catch our killer, not become his next victim, she had to figure out a way to alert us. Quite cleverly she pretended to be sleepwalking and told Fitzwilliams exactly what she was about to do. She knew he would come to me and that she would be followed. However, she was still taking a frightful risk."

Michelle's eyes widened. She turned to Rose. "Is this true?"

Rose nodded.

"How could you do such a thing?" Michelle exclaimed. "Are you mad?"

Rose stared at her, her mouth opening. Holmes frowned. A laugh burst from my lips—a very odd sound. I tried to restrain myself, but I could not hold back my laughter. Holmes glanced at me, his dark eyebrows briefly diving inward, then he too laughed. Rose smiled warily.

"Henry! What is so amusing?" asked Michelle.

"You are," I managed to say. "You who wished to go out at night in your nightgown with a revolver and a black wig."

"I never thought... Rose, you should not have kept it a secret. I never talked about doing anything completely on my own. Why did you not tell us?"

"Because I knew Mr. Holmes would never allow it."

Holmes nodded. "You were correct. You had me quite puzzled this evening. I could not imagine what you were up to, although I did finally figure it out—too late. I was almost certain you had been drugged, but why would you not admit it? I feared..." His expression grew somber. "You had endured so much, I thought something might have finally snapped, your reason... Did you receive some communication from your supposed father? I thought he might try to speak to you through the chimney again. That was why Henry and I patrolled the house."

Rose's hands formed fists. "There was a note on my bed. He wrote that I was to meet him by the gate at midnight, that we must speak, and he threatened the most terrible things should I not appear or should I tell anyone. He signed it as my father, but I no longer believed it might be him."

"Constance must have left the note as she was saying goodnight, and she probably returned and destroyed it while we were all out on the moor. Still, they were taking a chance. Thus far they had never left any tangible evidence that anything existed beyond the deluded mind of a young girl. The note would have proven once and for all that you were not imagining anything. They were desperate because they knew we were leaving the next day, and you might marry Digby in London. That would vastly complicate things."

"But even if she were not married," I said, "how could they possibly claim her fortune? Her will left most everything to medical charities. We sent that letter to her solicitor."

"Ah, but when the long-lost Grimswell appeared from America or Australia to reclaim the title, he would have argued that his dear cousin would have left everything to him if she had only known of his existence. A good solicitor would have had little trouble getting Grimswell Hall and the land—they generally go with the title—and most of the rest of her fortune as well, I suspect. However, were she married, retrieving the money from Digby or his family would have been far more difficult. They decided to hazard all on a final effort. Of course, the murders had shown to all but the most superstitious that something was terribly amiss. What did they threaten in the note?"

"That you… that you would all be killed. Torn to pieces, one by one." Her voice caught in her throat.

Holmes smiled grimly. "Constance would have liked to kill us all."

Michelle was staring at Rose, her eyes pained. "I wish… I wish you had told me."

Rose sighed. "I dared not, but do you not see?" She gripped Michelle's hand in hers. "I could never have done it if not for you."

Michelle stared closely at her. "Oh, my dear—I do not know—"

"I have never met anyone like you. Being around you has made me see that... And when you talked that way last night, I... I realized that perhaps I might actually do something. I was so tired of being buffeted about—of being toyed with and... tortured. You made me understand that I could fight them, that I..." She put her hand alongside her cheek. "Oh, my head is spinning, and I am so tired of all this."

Michelle put her arm around her. "Well, I am glad it has ended and that you were not badly hurt. When I saw that dog running at you... Thank God Hartwood was there."

I glanced at Holmes. "So he was hoping to protect Rose?"

"Exactly. He knew her life had been threatened, and he feared the worst. He may have been the only inhabitant in all of Dartmoor who would have willingly chosen to spend the night near Grimswell Hall. The locals are terrified of the place. He determined to watch the house and see if he could apprehend the mysterious man on the moor." Holmes looked at Rose. "He admires you greatly."

"He is very... kind. I must admit that when I saw that dog coming at me I completely froze. I was expecting a man, not a great beast."

"I wonder how many nights Hartwood spent out there," I said.

Michelle smiled. "Two. I asked him about it while I was stitching him up. Also, 'admire' does not do justice to his feelings for you, Rose."

She sighed wearily, then raised her eyes and stared at Holmes. His smile faded away, a puzzled look appearing in his eyes. "Mr. Holmes, who... whom do you think I should marry?"

His brow furrowed, his lips parting. Rose continued to stare at him, color appearing in her cheeks. Holmes ran his long fingers back through his black oily hair. "My dear young lady, I could not presume... to tell you such a thing."

Her eyes with the swollen black pupils had a hot intensity. "No?" she murmured.

"No."

Michelle glanced at me; we both understood. Rose lowered her gaze at last, then wiped at her eye with her fingers. "Forgive me. I... I should not have..." We had seen her dressed in black for so long that the white gown was still a surprise. She pushed her black hair back over her shoulders, and her long throat rippled as she swallowed. Her cheek had begun to swell and change color. Holmes gazed across the hall at the fireplace, where coal smoldered on the grate.

"I could not presume..." His voice was almost a whisper. "I know very little about such matters, or about women. They remain one of life's mysteries. My own heart belongs to another, one of the few whose life has been as dark and strange as my own, one who may never..." He stopped abruptly, then stared again at Rose. "I can tell you this. You are young, quite beautiful, intelligent and remarkably talented. You have more to offer most men than they could ever give you in return, and any man who is not an absolute imbecile would be honored to have you as his wife."

Rose stared at him, her eyes going all liquid. At last she said, "Thank you, Mr. Holmes."

I felt as if something were caught in my throat. "Every word he said is true."

Rose turned to me. Michelle smiled. The silence of the great, empty hall was overwhelming, and we all let the quiet sink into our weary bones. I closed my eyes, savoring the moment, feeling the link between us four and my sense of relief. For once at Grimswell Hall, I could not hear the moan of the wind.

Next morning, a Thursday, we awoke to discover that several inches of snow had fallen, and a blizzard had begun. We could not leave Dartmoor for another four days. It was a peaceful time, everyone relieved that the danger which had hung over Rose was gone at last. She played the piano often, and we spent several pleasant hours in the conservatory. The gray-white light of the desolate sky shone through the glass upon a jungle of green ferns and palms and lit up the koi, their colorful, scaly forms contrasting with the blue tiles. It felt odd to look up from the fish and see huge fuzzy snowflakes drifting about beyond the glass.

Constance was laid to rest in the frozen ground the day before we left, the funeral the strangest I have ever attended. Her son was still below Demon Tor on a slab of granite, covered by more than a foot of snow. Rose was good-hearted enough to ask about recovering the body, but Holmes told her the effort would be far too dangerous. Spring might come before the body could be found. The mother and son deserved their fate, but not so Rose's father. The dying Constance had told Holmes that Victor lay at the bottom of Grimpen Mire, deep in oozing mud. A sheet of ice now sealed his tomb. Three Grimswells were dead, while Jane remained at the asylum in London, but at least with Rose safe, there was hope for the future of the family, if not for the Grimswell name. And in the end, what did a name—a mere jumble of letters—matter?

We left the following Monday morning. The ride to the village revealed a different Dartmoor than I remembered. Gone was the dark, somber moor; the snowy plain was vast and white, only a few black or brown leaves or shoots showing, and the streams had frozen solid, blue ice gripping the lichen-stained boulders. The wind on our faces was glacial. The sun came out, blinding on the snow. Overhead buzzards still soared, and once we saw a fox break into a trot and hide behind a slab of granite.

In Grimpen we waited silently for the train, pacing about to keep warm. Rose looked grave. Even Digby appeared uncharacteristically thoughtful. We three men all wore heavy black overcoats and gloves. Holmes had on his silk top hat, a sign he was ready to return to proper London society. Rose also wore black, but Michelle had on her mauve coat with the sable collar and cuffs.

We heard the train before we saw it, the plume of smoke appearing in the distance, and soon the locomotive pulled into the station, the ancient engine clanging and banging. The porter stepped down, and Holmes and I handed him our suitcases.

Michelle smiled at Rose. "It is time to say goodbye, but we shall see you soon."

Rose managed a smile. Her face looked pale in the bright sunlight, the blue in her eyes overpowering the gray. Her black hair was bound up and hidden under a hat. She seemed ready to cry. She sighed, white vapor appearing before her mouth. "I do want to stay here by myself for a while, but even so... We have been through so much together. I shall miss you all very much."

Michelle kissed her on the cheek. "You will always be welcome in our home. Remember that. I expect you quite soon—no more than a month."

"Thank you, Michelle—for everything."

I set my hand on Rose's shoulder, then embraced her. "We truly have been through a great deal together, Rose."

"Oh, Henry—we have." She stared at me, her eyes hesitant, then her mouth stiffened, and she leaned forward to kiss me, a little awkwardly, her lips only half touching mine. She drew back and stared at me. "You are the kindest man I have ever known." She swallowed once, let go of me and stepped back. She turned to Michelle. "You are a very fortunate woman."

Michelle smiled at her, then her eyes shifted to mine. "I know."

Digby's smile was weary. "Goodbye, Rosie."

"Goodbye, Rickie." She kissed him on the cheek, the kind of kiss a sister would bestow upon her brother.

Holmes drew in his breath, turned and looked at Rose. She extended her hand, the big white fingers hidden in the black leather of her glove. Holmes took her hand with both of his. "Goodbye," he said. They stared at one another.

"Thank you again. For… for giving me back my life."

The corner of Holmes's mouth moved upward briefly. "I am certain you will do something remarkable with it." He let one of his hands fall, but she kept hold of the other and looked at him with her large, serious eyes under the thick black eyebrows.

"Wait!" someone cried.

There, the picturesque village of Grimpen with its stone buildings and church spire behind him, was Doctor Hartwood, his right hand raised high, his face flushed, and something under his left arm–a dog, a puppy–the mastiff which he had brought to the hall. The dog began to squirm, and Hartwood had to hold him with both hands.

"I had to say goodbye, but I was delayed by a patient. Glad to catch you in time." Hartwood's face was all red, and his mustache had ice on it. He wore an oiled canvas jacket and tall leather boots. He shook our hands, his grip crushingly strong, the puppy pinned to his chest and staring up at us. "How is the arm?" Michelle asked.

"Nearly healed. My surgery professor at Edinburgh was no better at stitching. I must admit… most male doctors could not do half so well."

Michelle beamed, delighted with the compliment.

"Miss Grimswell, I hope you bear mastiffs no grudge." His smile was suddenly wary. "That beast on the moor was no relation to this wee fellow, and…"

Rose smiled. "Of course not." She took the dog with both hands and held him up. "He's as beautiful as ever." The puppy wiggled its paws, its head lolling as it tried to lick her face. She laughed.

"You'll take him, then?"

She nodded. "Yes."

"He'll make a good guard dog."

"I don't think I shall need a guard dog, but I would like a pet."

Michelle stroked the puppy. "When he is fully grown, you can put him on a leash and walk through Hyde Park. I shall help you select the right dress—definitely not black. You will need to fight off the men with a stick."

Rose smiled while Hartwood looked dismayed. "I shall not need a stick—the mastiff will do," she said.

Hartwood and Digby had shaken hands without a word. We stepped aboard the train. Rose was still smiling at us, the puppy in her arms, but her eyes had an odd sheen. They glistened and shined in the brilliant sunlight as she stared at Holmes and me. I could see that she did not trust herself to speak.

Soon we were seated in our first-class compartment, the barren, snowy moor rushing past us, even the distant tor all covered with white. Digby shook his head. "So Hartwood triumphs with a mutt while noble Digby, vanquished utterly, departs in ignominious defeat. Ah, well…" He sighed, then smiled a tight, deprecatory smile. "I suppose it is fitting, although…"

"Although…?" I asked.

"Well, Rosie and I had a chat, and we are to be just friends. That was how she put it—she wants to be my friend. Nothing is more infuriating, I tell you, no fate sorrier, than to be reduced to a mere friend. For God's sake—what young red-blooded man wishes to be *friends* with a woman?" He said this with such comical loathing that both Michelle and I laughed, and even Holmes smiled.

"Can't blame her, though. I behaved like… Curious how I could have missed what she was worth until it was too late. I suppose I saw her as the ugly duckling for so long, that I didn't notice when she finally became a swan. I say, that's rather clever, isn't it? Oh well, you all saw it at once, while I… No character, I suppose. I think I've learned a lesson or two. Maybe I can still reform, turn over a new leaf, rise from the ashes, that sort of thing." He looked at Michelle. "Tell me, Doctor Doudet Vernier, you do not find me totally repelling, do you? Perhaps you could give me a candid, impartial opinion."

Michelle smiled wickedly. "Not totally."

Digby shook his head. "I asked for that."

"If it is any consolation to you," Michelle said, "I did tell her that I thought she should marry no one for a few more years. I know many do not share my opinion, but twenty is much too young to be married. I told her to write, play the piano and toy with the affections of many eligible, handsome young men. Besides, it is always good to make a man sweat a bit before yielding."

She was smiling at me. "Oh, so that explains it," I said.

"Perhaps all is not lost." Digby nodded. "Yes, hope springs eternal in the breast and all that rot. Still, the dog worries me. Every time she looks at the slobbering canine, there's another reminder of old Hartwood. No, I am bested. She will marry him, bear a dozen enormous children, male and female, six of each, with hands and shoulders worthy of the village smithy."

Michelle's eyes grew stern. "What is wrong with large hands and shoulders?"

Digby grinned. "Why, nothing at all. I find 'em charmin' in a woman, quite irresistible."

Michelle laughed. "No, you are not totally repellant after all."

Holmes took out a pipe and began to pack it with tobacco. His eyes stared out the window at the snowy moor.

"I say," Digby said, "that's a beauty of a pipe–isn't it from the hall?"

Holmes glanced down. "Yes. It was a gift from Rose."

Digby looked mournful. "Well, you have more to show than... I hope she paid you a goodly sum as well. I'm afraid I haven't a penny, but she can afford to be generous."

Holmes only shrugged.

"She did pay you, didn't she?"

Holmes sighed, then gave Digby a withering glance. "She did offer to pay me an extravagant sum of money, but I declined."

Digby was truly amazed. "You did? *Why?*"

"Because I did not feel I could take her money."

Digby stroked the end of his reddish-brown mustache. "Imagine that? But I still don't understand..."

"I do not take money from friends, and she did reward me. She rewarded me..." His eyes came back into focus, and he smiled at Digby. "She rewarded me with a pipe."

Digby gave Michelle and me a quick glance. "Uh, quite so."

Digby was quiet after that, and while Michelle leaned against me, the compartment filled with the odor of a very expensive tobacco, one which would be forever linked in my mind with the bleak landscape of Dartmoor, a lurking sense of dread, and a beautiful young woman in a white gown standing in the shadowy darkness of Grimswell Hall.

ACKNOWLEDGEMENTS

The websites on the Regency period or the peerage set up by Laura Wallace, Allison Lane and C. Allyn Pierson were very helpful to me in resolving issues with peers, titles, proper forms of address, marriage, inheritance—and especially the entail! Buried in Jane Austen's *Pride and Prejudice* are also many useful facts about the entail. Ms. Pierson was also kind enough to engage in a lengthy e-mail exchange on the entail. As usual, these women must get credit for what is right in the novel, while any errors must go to the author.